TIES THAT BIND

AN ORDINARY IMMIGRANT

CORINNE AARSEN

978-1-9993810-9-7 (mobi)
978-1-9995353-1-5 (e-pub)
978-1-9995353-0-8 (paperback)

This novel is dedicated to my loving,
wonderful, funny, strong mother.

Jennie (Jantje) Brouwer Aarsen
1926 - 2016

Kees & Anneke de Haas family

- Greta
  b Mar 1918
- Harri
  b May 1919
- Jakob
  b Sep 1920
- Sijmon
  b Dec 1921
  d Oct 1927
- Hendrik
  b Jul 1923
- Wiekje
  b Dec 1925
  d May 1938
- Roelena
  b Jan 1928
- Sijmon
  b Mar 1929
- Ebeltje
  b Aug 1931
  d Sep 1932
- Willem
  b Nov 1933
- Pieter
  b Nov 1935

GLOSSARY OF DUTCH WORDS

Alstublieft - please
Bedankt – thanks
Boer – farmer; also can be used as a derogatory term to indicate lack of manners
Boerin – farm wife
Broers – brothers
Bruine bonen – dried kidney beans (usually referred to as a meal served with boiled raisins and syrup)
Dag – bye
Dank je – thank you
Dat is goed – that is good
Den Haag – The Hague, Netherlands
Doekje – dish cloth
Dominee – minister of the church
Een hapje – a small bite/a snack
Eet smakelijk – enjoy your food
Eieren - eggs
Friesland – a Province in the Netherlands

(pronounced Freece-lund); the dialect is "Fries" (pronounced Freece) and the inhabitant is "Frisian.

Gaat het wel goed – are you alright?

Gebeden – prayers

Gebruik niet zo veel – don't use so much

Gereformeerde kerk – the denomination of the de Haas family in the Netherlands; stricter and more conservative than the Hervormde faith. The sister church in North America is 'Christian Reformed'

Gekke jongens – crazy boys

Gezellig – cozy, warm, comfortable, welcoming

Goedenacht – good night

Gordijn – curtain

Got zegen je – May God go with you

Grauwe erwten – dried brown peas

Heel knap – very handsome

Heel mooi – very nice; very good; lovely

Hervormde kerk – the state Reformed church that is more liberal than the Gereformeerde kerk

Hongerwinter – the hunger winter

Hou op – stop

Huisbezoek – house visit (from the church minister and/or elders)

Huisvrouw – house wife

Ik ben bedroefd – I am saddened; I am filled with sorrow

I kook – me too

Ik zal het aan hen vertellen – I will tell them

Jezus' naam – Jesus name (to end a prayer)

Ja – yes

Jongens – boys
Jij klootzak – you piece of shit (very rude)
Juffrouw – Miss (address for unmarried woman; used in this novel for the school teacher)
Kerk – church
Kerkhof – graveyard
Kerstfeest – Christmas program
Kind – child
Kinderen – children
Klein – little or small
Kleine aap – little monkey, often a term of endearment to a child
Klompen – wooden shoes
Klootzak – VERY rude swear word meaning asshole
Knap – handsome
Koek – cake (referring to a spiced loaf cake)
Kom dan – come then
Kroket – breaded, fried meatballs
Lepeltje – miniature spoon
Liefje – dear one/sweetheart (used for children)
Lievelingskind – darling child
Man – husband
Meisjes – girls
Mevrouw – married woman (Mrs.)
Mijn vrouw is geweldig – my wife is wonderful
Mijnheer – Mr.
Moe – mom (pronounced "moo")
Moeder – mother
Mooi – nice/beautiful
Nee – no
Onderbroekje - underwear

Oom – Uncle
Op zondag – on Sunday
Ouders - parents
Pak voor je broek geven – give you a spanking
Pannenkoek – pancakes
Pepermuntjes – peppermints
Peultjes – sugar peas
Potverdrie – a mild exclamation of annoyance, exasperation, or frustration
Praat Hollands – speak Dutch
Prachtig – wonderful
Rotjongen – an irritating ("rotten") boy
Schatje – darling/beloved one; used as term of endearment for a baby/child
Sinterklaas – St Nicholas
Speculaas—a Dutch shortbread cookie
Stamppot – mashed potatoes and vegetables (often turnips) all mixed together
Stroop – syrup
Suikerbeest—animal shaped sugared candies
Tante - Aunty
Theelepeltje – miniature teaspoon
Tot ziens – goodbye, farewell, until later
Vader – father
Van – from
Van harte gefeliciteerd – happy birthday
Wat nu – what now?
Welsprekend - eloquent
Welkom – welcome (to my home, for example)
Welterusten – sleep well
Zakdoek – handkerchief
Zeven – seven
Zich gedragen - behave

Zitten – sit down

Zuiderzee – a shallow bay of the North Sea separating Noord-Holland from Friesland

Zwarte Pieten – Black Peters (helpers of St. Nicholas)

PART I

1949

1

LETTER TO ROELENA FROM HENDRIK

Dear Roelena,

Thank you for your letter dated December 28. Let me start by wishing you a very happy birthday. I pray your twenty-first year is filled with health and happiness. And I hope your Clarence does his best to make you feel special. Thanks to your descriptive letters, I feel I know and like him despite not having yet met him. In their letters, the rest of the family seems to like him very much. I look forward to meeting him one day.

Things here are very sobering still on account of last year's flood. We're all very thankful that the community banded together to help farmers save livestock. Sheep were trussed and brought in canoes to high ground and milk cows and cattle were herded onto trucks and brought to hilltops out of harm's way. I helped milk the cows for two weeks until the farmers could bring them back to the barns. But orchard and berry farmers are really suffering. If only they could have marched their trees up to the hilltops, but that obviously wasn't possible. It will take years for these agricultural lands to recover. And so many homes still need to be repaired after being immersed in river water. Many walls, inside and out, are still covered in black sludge. It's a rather dismal sight, truth be told.

But I have much to be grateful for given that our orchard, and our houses and outbuildings, are on the hillside above Mission. We have not lost what so many others have. But I pray this valley never again has to bear witness to such devastation. The good news is that the municipalities are investing in flood prevention to ensure our communities never have to face such a disaster again. I joined a community group that intends to present solutions about where to build more dikes and such like. It's a bit of a laugh, actually, because some of them think because I'm Dutch I personally know how to build a dike. Although when it comes to holding back the sea, there is something to be said about learning from the Dutch.

I have been in the Fraser Valley now for just over two years. Despite last year's flood, I never doubt that I made the right decision. In fact, the flood actually inspired a heightened appreciation within me for this beautiful valley. Before when I looked at the spectacular, snow-topped mountains above us, I was touched by their beauty. But I now see the potential for the disaster they can bring in spring if all that snow melts too fast and the river overflows its banks. I want to make this place better, and not just improve how crops are grown and harvested, but I want to do whatever is necessary to keep it safe from future disaster. God has indeed created a magnificent world for us to inhabit, but we must steward it appropriately.

Our orchard is looking very promising for this coming season, especially in comparison to so many others. I feel guilty about that sometimes. I volunteer my time in the community to help recover and regenerate the soil in the flood plains where the damage was the worst. I am also helping to clean or even rebuild those houses that are now beyond repair.

Every day I am still learning something new from the Radstaaks and others about the business of nurturing and cultivating our orchard. And I've met a fascinating old man who lives down the road, a Mr. Hunt, whose father came here as a teenager during the Gold Rush somewhere around 1860. He's quite the story-teller and it's enthralling to listen to his tales. But he also is a wealth of information about trees and knows everything there is to know about every kind of fruit that can be grown here. He's a real icon in this area, and I've taken to visiting with him one evening a week. It's a real highlight for me.

Gladys is doing well. She and I see eye-to-eye on many things, and I find her company very restful. I hope you are able to come for a visit this summer with Pa and Moe if Moe's health permits. It would be so nice for you to meet her, and I know she is looking very much forward to meeting everyone in the family, but especially you. I know I said I would try to visit Alberta once a year, but I only made it back that first fall after I moved. Perhaps I'll be able to come this fall, with another car full of fruit, of course. We shall see what God has in store for me.

How are the rest of the family? Is Willem getting decent grades in school? Pieter tells me about his grades, of course, but Willem's letters are short and give only a tantalizing glimpse of his days, although he does report the exact number of weasels he trapped and his exact earnings from selling the pelts, as well as a full description of the rifle he's saving up to buy. I continue to offer my sincere thanks to God each time I receive a letter reporting that Moe is well. I am thankful you are there to relieve her of the burden of household tasks. I now realize I should have appreciated all that you do while I lived at home. I hope this belated expression of gratitude means something to you, even if it comes rather later than it should have.

Have you heard from Harri lately? His letters are so rare that I must resort to asking others in the family for news of him. Please continue writing as often as you can. I enjoy your newsy letters more than I can say.

Your loving brother,
Hendrik

2

SATURDAY, JANUARY 22

The long kitchen table in the de Haas farmhouse was roomy that morning with only six occupants lingering over their breakfast of porridge and bread. When the family had gathered the month before for a meal on Christmas Day, the table had accommodated eleven adults and five children sitting elbow-to-elbow, with the youngest baby in a highchair at the corner.

The family didn't often linger at the table after they'd finished eating, not when there were so many chores still to be done in the house and on the farm. But this was a special day—it was Roelena's twenty-first birthday.

Birthdays in the de Haas family were always acknowledged; they were an opportunity to give a special, personalized gift and an important occasion to celebrate a loved one. But Kees and Anneke had created a tradition of making their *kinderen's* twenty-first birthdays special.

"Van harte gefeliciteerd, kind," Anneke said, wishing Roelena a happy birthday and handing her a wrapped gift.

Roelena's eyes were sparkling. In the past, Roelena's

birthday gifts had been practical items—lengths of fabric to sew new dresses and coats, or a pair of new shoes or boots. But this was her twenty-first birthday, which for her older siblings had been acknowledged with a special keepsake item from their *ouders*—gold cufflinks for the boys and a necklace for Greta. Roelena felt certain the contents of this small rectangular box, wrapped in thin blue paper and which fit easily into the palm of her hand, could not possibly be practical, unless it was a box of hairpins. But that seemed unlikely.

Roelena gently shook the box, but it made no sound.

"Just open it," her fifteen-year-old brother Willem instructed in an impatient tone.

"I'm savoring the moment," Roelena stated, giving Willem a good-natured smile.

Willem had by no means grown into a charming, well-mannered young man—at least not yet, Roelena thought—but he had been behaving rather well these last months despite the fact that the virtue of patience still eluded him. Pieter, she saw, was as excited by the mysterious gift as if it had been handed to him instead of his sister. He'd turned thirteen two months before, but hadn't yet lost the sweetness of his childhood. Roelena hoped he never would. Her brother Sijmon, only fourteen months her junior and who was usually calm and unruffled, was also showing eager interest in the contents of Roelena's special gift.

Roelena untied the ribbon and then removed the wrapping paper, revealing a box covered in plush dark green velvet with the words *York Jewellers* stamped in gold across the top. She bit her lip and looked up briefly at her *moeder*, sharing a smile of anticipation. Her *ouders* had never given her jewelry before.

"Open it, Roelena!" Pieter insisted, practically bouncing in his seat.

When Roelena lifted the lid, she let out a gasp. The box

was lined with ivory satin and had more gold lettering on the inside of the lid. Nestled in the bed of the box was a bracelet that had four strings of tiny, dark red stones, with matching miniature stones decorating the gold clasps on each end of the bracelet. It was the prettiest jewelry Roelena had ever seen. She could never have guessed her *ouders* would choose something so beautiful to mark her twenty-first birthday. And it was clearly expensive. Her throat closed and she had to blink away tears as she stared down at the magnificent bracelet.

"It's so pretty," Pieter gushed from where he sat at her elbow.

"I can't see," Willem complained. "Hold it up, Roelena."

Roelena tilted the box so that Willem and Sijmon, who sat across from her, could see the contents. The bracelet was in no danger of tumbling out as a narrow strip of elastic held each end attached to the bed of the box.

Sijmon whistled and looked impressed.

Willem's eyes widened and he said, "Wow wee! That's pretty nice."

"Pretty nice?" Roelena repeated, her voice thick with emotion. She briefly looked over at her *moeder*. "Oh Moe, *dank je*. It's *heel mooi*. I've never seen anything so beautiful." Roelena felt mesmerized by the bracelet, hardly able to tear her eyes away from it and hardly daring to believe this lovely bracelet was hers.

Anneke smiled indulgently at her daughter. She was feeling well, and was glad for it. She hadn't suffered an angina attack since before Christmas. And on this special day, she intended to lighten a little of Roelena's workload. "You work so hard, my dear," Anneke stated. "We wanted to give you something extra special. The stones are red garnet. The jeweler said they're the birthstone for January."

"Do you like it then, *kind?*" Kees asked.

"Yes, Pa. Very much!" Roelena rose, her face shining as she gave first her mother and then her father an affectionate hug. *"Dank je,* Moe. *Dank je,* Pa."

"Can I see?" Sijmon asked.

Roelena moved to stand beside Sijmon and set the open box on the table at his elbow. She leaned over it and carefully freed the bracelet from its bed, draping it across her bare wrist. "Isn't it beautiful?"

Sijmon nodded. "Very nice."

Roelena moved to stand beside Anneke's chair. "Will you fasten it for me, *alstublieft?"* She handed the bracelet to her mother, then turned up the sleeve of her cardigan.

After Anneke fastened the clasp, they all took a moment to admire Roelena's wrist.

"All right, come sit down, Roelena. Pieter, go get the Bible," Kees instructed. The de Haas family began each meal with a prayer of blessing, and ended the meal with a Bible reading and a prayer of thanks.

"But Pa, what about *my* gift for Roelena?" Willem asked in a conspiring tone.

"What?" Roelena had been about to sit but paused beside her chair, startled.

Willem gave her a playful grin as he held out the book-sized parcel wrapped in brown paper he'd hidden under his chair while Roelena had dished up the porridge. "You only turn twenty-one once," he announced.

Often for birthdays the siblings made small items or did something special, but they didn't usually give a wrapped gift. Roelena certainly hadn't been expecting this additional present, and especially not from Willem. Maybe he was on his way to growing up to be a nice young man, she thought.

"You shouldn't spend your pocket money on me," she protested, taking the package from Willem and feeling a thrill of pleasure at seeing the magnificent bracelet dangling on her wrist. She sat down and turned the parcel over in her hand, feeling the contours of it, certain it was a large book. Maybe one of those picture books of the Canadian Rockies. "And it's so carefully wrapped. I hardly dare open it."

"Just open it, Roelena," Willem urged impatiently.

She took care not to rip the paper so she could use it again. When she pulled back the paper wrapping, she saw that the gift wasn't a book but a picture album. The green leather cover had the word *Photographs* embossed in gold across the centre and the binding was tied with a twisted black and gold cord.

"Oh, Willem, it's perfect. *Dank je*," Roelena declared, pleased with the gift. She'd been taking photographs on her used Voigtlander Brillant box for the last ten years, and enjoyed pasting the small, black-and-white photos into albums for the whole family to enjoy. She or her parents also regularly included a photo or two in their letters to their relatives in the Netherlands, Indonesia, and Iowa. "I can't wait to paste photos in it. And I'll take a few snaps later today, to mark my birthday."

Willem snorted. "You just want an excuse to have another photograph of Clarence so you can moon over it," he teased.

Roelena rolled her eyes in disgust and thought, so much for Willem turning into a nice, young man.

Willem gave his sister an impish grin. "Open the cover. Look what I wrote inside."

Roelena opened the album and read the English inscription written on the inside cover. *"To my sister Roelena on her 21st birthday. May God bless you today and always. Love Willem."*

She looked across the table at the brother who'd tried her patience over the years more times than she could count. Would he or wouldn't he grow up to be a nice young man? She wished she knew the answer. "Willem. *Dank je.*"

Willem shrugged, but he was clearly pleased with his sister's reception of his surprise.

Pieter rose then and retrieved the Bible, handing it to Kees. But when he resumed his seat beside Roelena, he offered her a gift the same size and shape as the bracelet box.

"What's this?" Roelena regarded this third wrapped package in surprise, then looked up at the rest of her family. Her *ouders* and all three of her brothers were grinning at her, clearly reveling in their ability to surprise and delight her on this special day.

"This one is from Sijmon and me," Pieter said. "I hope you like it."

Roelena took the gift, her smile wide as she addressed her brothers. "What a surprise! I can hardly believe this." And she really couldn't. I'm so blessed, she thought, swallowing hard against the sudden lump that clogged her throat. *So blessed and so loved.*

Inside the gift from Pieter and Sijmon was another narrow, rectangular box with hinges on one side. But the gold cursive writing on the bottom right hand corner of this one said, *Schaeffer*. Roelena smiled in delight, knowing what the box would reveal. When she opened the lid, the tiny hinges creaked stiffly.

"A new fountain pen," she gushed in pleasure. "That's exactly what I need. Thank you, Pieter. Thank you, Sijmon."

"And it's got special ink." With eager hands, Pieter slipped out the pen from the strip of cloth that kept it nestled in its velvet bed. "It's silver, so you can write on the black pages of your new photograph album." Pieter slipped off the cover the pen, then demonstrated by making a small mark on the edge of the brown paper. "See? Do you like it?"

Roelena took the pen Pieter held out to her, then put an arm around him and gave him a one-armed hug. "It's such a thoughtful gift and exactly what I would've picked out myself.." She met the gazes of her other two brothers and her parents. "Really, everyone, thank you."

Kees cleared his throat and picked up the book Pieter had set at his elbow. "Now then, shall we read the Bible?"

3

SATURDAY, JANUARY 22

"Sijmon, you don't have to come with me, you know," Roelena informed her brother.

Sijmon had just come into the porch from outside after starting the car so that it would warm up before Roelena left to pick up her boyfriend. For over a year now, Roelena had been collecting Clarence every Saturday afternoon and bringing him to the farm to spend the evening and all day Sunday with Roelena and her family. The young couple had begun courting soon after Clarence's arrival in the community eighteen months before, and Roelena's family had welcomed the outgoing, cheerful young man into their midst. Kees and Anneke approved of him, not only on account of their shared faith, but also because he was hard-working, industrious, and kind, and seemed to genuinely care for their daughter.

Clarence also got along well with Roelena's brothers—although he'd yet to meet either Harri or Hendrik. Roelena's three younger brothers who still lived at home each had a special relationship with her boyfriend, including the reticent Sijmon who chatted even more with Clarence than he had with their cousin Conrad. Often during the long summer evenings when it stayed light until well past ten o'clock, the three youngest de Haas boys took Clarence fishing or shooting. Clarence had also become good friends with her married brother Jakob, as well as Roelena's brother-in-law, Frank, and all of Roelena's nieces and nephews adored him. And why wouldn't they?

Clarence was friendly and good-natured and funny. He was also well read, and could speak knowledgeably on a wide range of subjects. Clarence, Frank, and Jakob—all good talkers—frequently debated issues, from the pros and cons of the immigration laws the government imposed to whether the prices of livestock and grain were increasing at a healthy rate. It was only when they discussed church issues that their debates became a little heated. Clarence was a traditionalist, while Frank and Jakob were progressive and open to change. An issue they were currently debating was their church's songbook, which consisted of over two hundred hymns inspired from the Book of Psalms. Some of the more liberal Christian Reformed Churches had begun using new hymnals that included, in addition to the favourite Psalms, hymns written and composed by a range of Protestant Christians over the last couple centuries. Currently, a heated debate was going on in the Pine Glade church community about whether their *kerk* should embrace this modern new song-book. Clarence agreed with the conservatives, who saw no reason to replace the hymnals in their country *kerk*, whereas Frank and Jakob wanted their *kerk* to adopt the new song-book. The issue was still being debated and hadn't yet been resolved.

Roelena didn't mind that Clarence tended to be conservative and traditional, admiring instead how he could argue his point without getting angry or causing a rift in a relationship. For the most part, he was everything she'd always wanted in a man who one day might be her future husband. He was steadfast in his faith; he was clever, funny, and easygoing in nature; and he was tall, strong, and good-looking.

The only downside of courting such a well-liked man was that his popularity in her large family meant Roelena had to compete for his time and attention. She was rarely alone with him for more than two minutes. And on those occasions when they did happen to be alone, it didn't last. One of her siblings would no doubt come along and spoil it, just like Sijmon was doing now. And on Roelena's birthday of all days.

Roelena tucked her arms into the heavy wool coat she'd sewn with her sister Greta's help and began buttoning it up. She'd taken her bracelet off, but would put it on again when she returned to the house. The thermometer showed a temperature of eleven degrees Fahrenheit, a relief from the week before when it had dipped to minus thirty. "Sijmon, it hasn't snowed for over a week. The roads are in good condition. I can go by myself."

Sijmon lifted one shoulder in a dismissive shrug. "I know. But I want to come."

Roelena didn't hide her exasperation as she slipped on her winter boots, then wound a scarf around her neck. "Weren't you the one complaining you hadn't had time to look at the latest *Family Herald?* Besides, I'm picking up Marliese on the way back. She's staying overnight, too. You really don't have to come, Sijmon," she added in a firm tone as she pulled on her floppy crocheted toque.

"Roelena?" Anneke called from the kitchen. "Take Sijmon with you. You'll be glad of his company if the car breaks down before you get to Clarence's farm."

Roelena pulled a face at her brother, but called out in a polite tone. "Yes, Moe."

"And close the door, *meisje*. I can feel the draft."

Roelena did as her *moeder* asked, realizing that if she'd closed the door between the kitchen and the porch like she was supposed to, Anneke wouldn't have overheard their conversation and vetoed her desire to pick up Clarence on her own.

"Well, *I'm* driving," Roelena stated, slipping on her mittens. She pointed her index finger at her brother, but the gesture was ineffective given that her hand was engulfed in wool. "And that's not open for negotiation."

Sijmon shrugged again in easy-going compliance.

Outside, Roelena and Sijmon's breath formed clouds of vapor around their faces as they navigated the snow-covered sidewalk towards the car, their footsteps squeaking on the pristine packed snow. Roelena had to squint against the glare of sun. There hadn't been a breath of wind all morning, and the bare branches of the trees, covered in hoar frost, looked magical against the brilliant blue of the Alberta sky. She'd taken photographs of the hoar frost in previous winters, attempting to capture the stunning contrast of white, diamond-studded trees against the indescribable blue of the sky, but the black and white images hadn't done nature's resplendent display justice. One day, she promised herself, she would have a camera that took colour photographs. Then she could capture on film these marvelous contrasts and send the images to her friends and family in the Netherlands.

Twenty minutes after leaving the farm, Roelena turned into the long driveway of the Boutilier farm, carefully navigating the narrow track between high banks of snow as she drove the car towards the rather dilapidated house. Pierre Boutilier, although a decent farmer, was a lousy handyman.

Clarence lived in the house with his employer's family, including their four young children. As he'd taken carpentry in trade school before emigrating from the Netherlands, Clarence had been fixing things around the Boutilier house during the winter months when there were fewer outside chores to do. Given he was only halfway through his three-year contract to work for his Canadian sponsor, Clarence knew he would be able to make a significant improvement to the neglected home.

"Clarence must be working on the shutters," Sijmon observed as Roelena pulled up in front of the house.

"Yes, he said he was going to take them down this week."

Clarence had told her he intended to remove the decorative, paint-peeled shutters from where they framed the double-paned storm windows. In the evenings after his chores on the farm were done, he would first repair them and later paint them before re-hanging them in the spring.

As soon as Roelena pulled into the drive, Clarence appeared on the sagging verandah and jogged down the steps carrying his overnight bag.

"Sijmon, let Clarence sit in the middle," Roelena instructed. Sijmon could have sat in the back seat, but the sparse heat from the Ford's meagre heater barely warmed the front. Besides, Roelena liked having an excuse to sit shoulder to shoulder with Clarence.

"I know that, Roelena," Sijmon chided in a disgruntled tone.

"Hi ya, Sijmon," Clarence said, grinning and thumping Sijmon on the back with a gloved hand.

"Clarence," Sijmon responded with a nod and a matching grin.

Sijmon remained standing at the open passenger door as Clarence slid along the front bench seat. Clarence gave Roelena an exuberant hug and a long, affectionate kiss. "Happy birthday, sweetheart." He kissed her again for good measure before turning to Sijmon. "Okay, you can get in now. No more kissing."

Clarence often teased Sijmon about his obvious discomfort at their display of affection, telling him that things would change soon enough when Sijmon started courting. As far as Roelena knew, Sijmon had yet to show any interest in finding a girl. Roelena, much as she loved Sijmon, couldn't imagine any woman falling for her quiet, taciturn brother. It wasn't that he was shy, but he had so little to say, at least to girls. And he never made any special effort to be charming or flattering to any of them. Roelena didn't like the thought of Sijmon being a life-long bachelor, but she also despaired at the thought of him ever meeting the right girl.

Roelena loved that her boyfriend was affectionate and tactile. When they weren't around Roelena's parents, Clarence often had his arm around her and frequently planted light kisses on her lips, her cheeks, or her forehead. Now, sitting next to her on the bench seat, she felt him drape his arm around her shoulders. She enjoyed the feel of it there, despite the multiple layers of their winter wear.

As soon as Sijmon slipped into the car and slammed the door, Roelena put the car into reverse. When she twisted her head to look behind her as she backed up, Clarence took that as an opportunity to kiss her again.

She giggled, then said for Sijmon's benefit. "Sijmon noticed you've started fixing the shutters."

Clarence removed his arm from behind her and instead rested his hand in its big leather glove on her knee. With the two men chatting comfortably in English, Roelena turned onto the road and headed back the way they'd come. Unlike Ingrid, Jakob's war bride from the Netherlands, it hadn't taken long for Clarence to become fluent in English. And he preferred to use his second language as much as possible, arguing that, since he'd made the effort to become Canadian, the least he could do was learn the language.

Half an hour later, Roelena pulled into the van Laar's driveway. When Marliese didn't appear right away, Roelena put the car into park and pulled on the brake. "I'll go see where she is," she said as she stepped out of the car, leaving it running.

At the door of the van Laar farmhouse, she knocked to announce her arrival but then let herself into the porch. No one would have expected her to wait outside in the cold.

"There you are," she said as Marliese entered the room. She eyed her friend as Marliese turned to shut the door that separated the porch from the narrow hallway, the straps of her quilted overnight bag over her shoulder. "I didn't think you heard us drive up," Roelena added.

"I heard you." Marliese's voice was uncharacteristically quiet.

Roelena frowned. Normally her friend would've been bubbling with excitement about this chance to have a break from her family. Had Marliese had another rousing argument with her sister? Or her father? Marliese got along fine with her mother, who was rather meek, but she argued regularly with her spinster sister Alieda and clashed as often with her conservative, domineering father. "What's the matter?"

Marliese had her back to Roelena as she retrieved her winter things from the row of hooks on the wall and suddenly sank against the wall of coats, dropping her head and sobbing. Alarmed, Roelena went to her friend's side, removing her mittens and tucking them into her pockets before laying a hand on Marliese's heaving shoulder, tugging gently until Marliese turned.

"Marliese? What's wrong? Why are you crying?"

Marliese looked up at Roelena. Her eyes were red and puffy, yet it did nothing to mar her beauty.

"I got a letter from Conrad yesterday," Marliese said. "Oh, Roelena," she wagged her head in denial. "You'll never believe what he wrote."

"He can't come this summer either?"

It had been two-and-a-half years since Conrad and his family had visited Alberta. Despite his promises, Conrad hadn't yet managed to visit.

Marliese took a deep, shuddering breath, then spoke in a dull, flat tone. "He's getting engaged," she said. As soon as she said the words, fresh tears appeared and she dropped her face into her hands as a new wave of sobs engulfed her.

Roelena stared at her friend, momentarily at a loss for words. "What?" she finally managed. "Engaged? To be married?" At Marliese's nod, Roelena added, "But, Marliese, that can't be."

Marliese and Conrad had never stopped writing each other. A month or two before Christmas, Roelena remembered Marliese sharing her concern that the frequency of his letters had declined and that his tone, at least according to Marliese, had been less intimate. Roelena, happy and in love herself, assured her friend that Conrad must be busy with their new store, and that if the letters were still coming, then Marliese had no reason to fear his feelings might have diminished. Roelena now realized Marliese had indeed been right to worry.

Marliese continued to sob, her words muffled against her hands. "He says he...he values our friendship...but he's going to propose...to a girl in his church *named Louise*," Marliese wailed.

"Oh, Marliese. I can hardly believe it." Roelena embraced her friend, rocking her slightly like she would a child. Damn her cousin for letting Marliese down! And she wouldn't feel one little bit guilty about cursing. If Conrad had truly done what Marliese claimed, he deserved to be lambasted with a string of curses.

"Listen," Roelena said, pulling Marliese's wrists down so she could see her friend's face. "Do you want to skip coming over? Stay here instead?"

"Good gracious, no! Alieda and Moe know something is up, but I can't tell them. I just can't. Not yet."

"Then don't," Roelena assured, rubbing her hands up and down Marliese's arms. "Clarence and Sijmon are waiting in the car. I'll sit in the back with you and, once we get home, we'll go straight up to my room. I'll say we're going to work on the new photograph album I got for my birthday."

"Shit!" Marliese screwed up her face. "I'm a terrible friend, aren't I? Happy Birthday, Roelena." Marliese leaned forward and gave Roelena a hug, then retrieved a lace-trimmed *zakdoek* from the pocket of her dress and dried her face. "I didn't forget. It's just, I can hardly think of anything aside from Conrad's letter."

As Marliese looked like she was going to start crying again, Roelena reached behind her and retrieved her friend's coat. "No more tears until we get to my room where we can talk freely."

After Marliese buttoned up her coat, Roelena handed over her hat, scarf, and mittens, then picked up the quilted bag Marliese had brought into the porch. "Is this everything?" Roelena asked. Marliese nodded.

The girls left the house, their footsteps squeaking on the packed snow. At their approach, Sijmon got out to move into the back seat.

"Sijmon, you drive," Roelena called. "We'll sit in the back."

Sijmon looked surprised, but quickly made his way around to the driver's side of the car.

As she got into the back seat, Marliese said hi to the boys but kept her gaze downcast.

After Clarence shuffled over to the passenger side of the front seat, he turned to grin at Roelena. "You like her company better than mine now?" he teased.

Her boyfriend and her best friend had never bonded, a circumstance that disappointed and concerned Roelena.

They each had outgoing, gregarious personalities and should have become friends, but Clarence interpreted Marliese's sharp wit and unrestrained playfulness as thoughtless, selfish, and unkind, while Marliese thought Clarence too conservative, going so far as to claim he was a younger version of her pig-headed and dictatorial father. Roelena didn't agree with Clarence, arguing that her clever and witty friend was simply bored and restless; neither did she agree with Marliese's unkind portrayal of Clarence, claiming his conservative outlook was appealing for its undeniable clarity. Despite Roelena's efforts over the last year-and-a-half, her boyfriend and her best friend only tolerated each other. Regardless of their lack of friendship, Roelena remained both in love with Clarence and loyal to her oldest and dearest friend.

When Clarence make the jibe about her preferring Marliese's company, Roelena knew he was only half joking. Regardless, she kissed him, unable to resist his laughing face so close to hers. "That surprises you?" she teased.

Clarence thumped his hand dramatically against his chest. "I'm wounded."

Roelena playfully pushed at his shoulder. "Hardly. But it's cold back here, so get us home quick, Sijmon."

Roelena settled into the seat beside Marliese, losing her grin when she saw her friend was on the verge of tears. She knew better than to say anything, so she took her friend's mitten-covered hand in hers and held it for the duration of the ride home.

4
SATURDAY, JANUARY 22

When built in the spring of 1939, the de Haas farmhouse had no indoor plumbing, central heating, or electricity, but it was no different from the dozens of farmhouses on the quarter sections of land radiating out from the church the Dutch immigrants had built on a country lane. Like their counterparts, the de Haas homestead was heated from the cast-iron, wood-fired range in the kitchen. Keeping the wood-box full was an essential chore, especially in winter.

In 1946, the same year the County of Bellecourt brought electricity and phone lines to a block of countryside south of Sandpiper Lake, Kees de Haas hired a carpenter and handyman to build a second house on the farm for his son Jakob and Jakob's war-bride wife. The carpenter/handy-man installed indoor plumbing in both the new house and the homestead kitchen, pantry, and porch—where Roelena did the wash once a week—as well as in a new bathroom carved out of what had been Kees and Anneke's bedroom closet.

Two years later, Kees hired the same man to install ducts in each house and install an oil-fired, forced air furnace in each of the two basements. Although Roelena still used the wood-fired range in the farmhouse kitchen for cooking, it was no longer the only source of heat. Instead, electric fans pumped hot air from the basement furnace through the ducts to warm the whole house, including the upstairs bedrooms. The winters with their short hours of daylight were still cold, but when the occupants in the house needed heat, they simply adjusted the thermostat.

Prior to the installation of the furnace, Roelena had no reason to linger in her bedroom. When her chores were done on any given evening and she was free to entertain herself, she would sit at the kitchen table near the heat of the range and insert photographs into her album or paste special items into her scrapbook. Other times she would sit on the couch in the living room with her parents and brothers and listen to a comedy show or music program on their battery operated radio while she did her handwork—darning socks; knitting sweaters, vests, socks, mittens, and scarves; crocheting baby clothes, slippers, pillow covers, hotplates, and afghans; and making hook rugs out of rags. If she didn't feel like doing handwork, Roelena would catch up on her correspondence, writing letters to her family and friends in The Netherlands, Indonesia, and Iowa, or to pen pals she'd made in response to ads in *The Banner*, the North American Christian Reformed Church's monthly publication. By the fall of 1948, with electricity and central heating in the house, Roelena had the option to seek solitude in her bedroom to read or write letters by the light of an electric lamp mounted on the top bar of her iron headboard.

On the winter afternoon of Roelena's twenty-first birthday, she and Marliese went directly to Roelena's small bedroom. The day had grown overcast and the double-panes of glass at the dormer window, thick with frost, barely let in any light. The single overhead light was on, illuminating the room with its pink and yellow floral wallpaper, yellow chintz curtains, and colourful hooked rugs dotting the linoleum floor.

Marliese sat atop the white lace coverlet—the handmade crocheted spread matched the lace *gordijn* at the window—on Roelena's double bed, watching her friend read Conrad's letter. Both girls wore wool-blend stockings, slippers on their feet, and knitted cardigans. Despite the furnace in the basement, the cardigans and slippers were necessary in the middle of winter, unless they were near the range in the kitchen.

Roelena stood by the dormer window, a frown on her face as she read her cousin's letter.

Dear Marliese,

This is the hardest letter I've ever had to write, and likely the hardest thing I'll ever have to do. First, despite what you might think once you read my news, I want you to know that I've cherished every letter you've written. I treasured the words on the pages, which always made the sound of your voice echo both in my head and in my heart, so much so that it sometimes felt like you were right here with me.

If only you had been, standing beside me I mean, for I blame the distance that separates us. It's been so long since we've seen each other and so much has happened since that long ago visit to Alberta. Please don't hate me, Marliese. I cannot bear the thought of you cursing me, yet I know you will because you are spirited and you do nothing halfway, which is exactly why I fell in love with you in the first place. But between your curses, remember to love me just a little for what we once were and what we could have been.

But I procrastinate. This is about the fiftieth letter I've begun with the intention of sharing my news, but every time I start I can't seem to finish. I am a coward, Marliese, that I will freely admit. An appalling coward. And I fear my procrastination will have made things that much worse for you. But I know I must be honest with you now as you deserve nothing less. In fact, you deserve more, so much more. I'm only sorry it's not in me to give.

I've wanted to tell you about Louise for months now, but I found I just couldn't. I knew if I did, I would be putting an end to the special joy of coming home and finding a letter from my dear friend Marliese, or the joy of hearing your laughter echo in my head as I read and re-read every word, or the joy of reliving the feeling of our shared touches. Meeting you lit something within me, and because of that, a part of me selfishly doesn't want my friendship with you to end. But I fear it must.

Marliese, there's no easy way to say this, no way to prepare you, and for that, too, I am at fault. If only I had mentioned something about Louise months ago when her family moved here, then you might have been prepared. But I didn't because I knew if I shared something of my growing feelings for her, you would think I no longer loved you, and you would have stopped writing me. And I desperately wanted to prevent that unwelcome outcome. Because I do love you, Marliese. I always will. It's just that you're so far away and Louise is here, and I love her, too.

I intend to ask Louise to marry me, but I knew I needed to write this letter to you first. I know we had an understanding, of sorts, even though we never addressed it specifically in words. I also know that, if we could have seen each other again, things would now be different.

But it hasn't worked out that way, has it? And I shoulder the blame for that. Perhaps I wasn't sufficiently courageous when my parents vetoed my desire to revisit Alberta. Perhaps I should have defied them and snuck away in the middle of the night, taking my car and leaving a note. But I didn't. As I said, perhaps I truly am a coward.

A part of me wishes you and Louise could meet for I feel certain the two of you would be friends. She's a warm, loving person, and although she is not as spirited as you or as strikingly beautiful—and that's no slur on my intended wife for she is as pretty as a spring flower—it's simply a statement of your rare beauty. Nevertheless, she is very much like you in spirit, Marliese. She laughs easily, enjoys playing sports, and loves to be surrounded by her loved ones.

So now you know, and now you're likely cursing me. Someday when you've found a better man than me to love, please find it in your heart to forgive me. My affection for you hasn't diminished. It never will. I've always been true to you in my heart, if not in my actions. Beautiful Marliese, is it selfish of me to ask that you not hate me over much?

Regardless, if you do despise me, it doesn't change the fact that I will never cease to cherish your memory. Marliese, I wish nothing but the best for you. I pray daily that God will bless you now, and in the future, whatever it holds.

You have my enduring friendship, always and forever,

Conrad

When Roelena finished re-reading the unwelcome and heart-breaking news in Conrad's letter, she lifted her head and regarded her friend with unveiled disgust. Marliese was leaning against the thin bars of the iron headboard, her back cushioned with pillows. Her hands lay on her lap, fiddling with a wadded handkerchief.

Roelena shook her head as she addressed her friend. "I don't know what to say, Marliese. Except I'm just so appalled. And bewildered."

Marliese leaned forward and adjusted the pillows behind her so they cushioned her more comfortably before settling back into the pillows. "Me too. I feel, I don't know...empty." She frowned, fighting tears, then added, "That's not right, though. I feel too heavy inside to be empty."

Roelena glanced down at the letter. She was struggling to process Conrad's shocking and unexpected news. She lifted her head and regarded her friend. "I just can't believe it. And I can't believe he sent me a birthday card and made no mention of..." Roelena gestured at the letter in her hand, "...this...?"

Marliese lifted one of her perfectly arched brows. "Well, he could hardly tell you before telling me."

"Of course. But still. He shouldn't have sent me a card, then." Roelena shook her head. Her words were coming out all wrong. "I don't mean it like that."

Roelena was angrier than she'd been in a very long time. She glared back down at the letter. Her insides were churning like a blustery winter storm. She was *so mad* at Conrad, madder than she'd ever been at Willem during one of their childish fights. What Conrad had done to Marliese was cruel. And unexpected. And so very, very wrong. He'd betrayed her. He'd betrayed them all.

In the beginning of Conrad and Marliese's long-distance correspondence, Roelena had actually expected the letter writing to fizzle out, anticipating that Marliese would lose interest, perhaps even break Conrad's heart a little. She certainly never expected to see her friend this heart-broken, and all because of Roelena's cousin. "Oh, Marliese, you must hate him. I know I do." Roelena knew it was unchristian to feel this way, but she couldn't help it.

Instead of railing against Conrad, Marliese shook her head, looking down at her fingers and fretting with the handkerchief. "I wish I could. Hate him, I mean." She looked up and met Roelena's shocked gaze and shrugged without apology. "But I love him, Roelena. And he loves me. You can see that, can't you? It's obvious from his letter."

"Marliese? He's not…" Roelena searched for the right word. "He's not *allowed* to say he loves you. Not when he's going to ask this other girl to marry him. It's not right."

"But the fact that he still loves me is my only comfort right now."

"Comfort?" Roelena was confused. She stared at her friend without comprehension. Roelena would've expected Marliese to string every swear word she knew together and curse him to hell and back. Why wasn't Marliese storming about and railing against what Conrad had done? Why wasn't she condemning him for the unfaithful rat he was? Instead, the spirited effervescence that had formerly characterized Marliese had completely disappeared. Roelena supposed that was to be expected given her friend's broken heart. She assumed the feisty element of Marliese's personality was laying dormant, temporarily flattened by the boulder of emptiness Marliese had described. Her true nature would re-emerge, given time. Regardless, it angered Roelena that Marliese was soothing herself with Conrad's meaningless declaration of abiding love. It was somehow wrong to witness Marliese clinging to his words as if she'd won some kind of consolation prize. Marliese's acquiescent response was almost more unexpected than Conrad's unwelcome news.

Roelena moved to sit on the end of the bed, leaning lightly against the thin rails of the foot board so that she was facing Marliese. When she addressed her friend, she spoke in the same tone she used when chiding one of her young brothers. "Marliese, you can't let him get away with this," she stated, tossing the letter onto the bed in disgust.

Marliese immediately snatched it up, smoothing out the crinkles from Roelena's clenched fist.

Roelena stared at her friend, incomprehension furrowing her brow. "Marliese? You can't take comfort in telling yourself he loves you. *You can't.* What he's done is *wrong*. He's misled you now for months, by the sounds of it. I know he's my cousin, but he's a dirty, rotten scoundrel for doing this to you."

Roelena's strongly worded criticism didn't alter her friend's placid composure. She stared at her friend, utterly perplexed. "Why aren't you spitting mad?"

Marliese gazed toward the window, although there was little to see through the frost other than a patch of colourless sky. She spoke in a spiritless tone, "I don't care if I live or die."

Horrified, Roelena crawled up the bed until she could turn and sit beside Marliese. She took one of her friend's listless hands in hers and spoke with earnest zeal. "Marliese, don't ever say that again. You can't want to die."

"I didn't say I *wanted* to die," Marliese responded, turning her deadened eyes to meet Roelena's concerned gaze. "I said I don't care if I die. It's not the same thing."

Roelena searched her friend's brown eyes for a spark of life. Even during Marliese's bluest moments, something had always been brewing in their dark depths. But now Roelena saw only an unfamiliar flat dullness. She felt as if she were looking into the eyes of a stranger. Roelena's voice was quiet when she spoke. "Marliese, you're scaring me."

Marliese looked away. "I don't mean to." She sighed heavily, and then sat up, carefully tucking the letter into the pocket of her dress before swinging her feet off the bed. She rose and moved to the chair where Roelena had placed Marliese's cloth bag. The button flap was open, as she'd already retrieved her slippers.

"I have a birthday present for you," Marliese stated, retrieving two parcels the size of books wrapped in foil paper, one gold, the other red. She returned to the bed and stood in front of Roelena, holding out the parcels without ceremony. "Open the gold one first."

Roelena stared at Marliese, then spoke with the same impatient tone she sometimes used with Willem. "Marliese, I don't care about my birthday, or the presents." She tugged on Marliese's wrist, forcing her friend to plop down beside her, peering into her friend's face with deep concern.

Marliese hung her head, her gaze on the parcels in her lap. When she spoke, she sounded as tired as Anneke during one of her bad spells. "Roelena, I can't talk about it anymore." She placed the presents on Roelena's lap. "Please, just open them."

"But…Marliese?"

Marliese met Roelena's gaze. "I need to not think about Conrad for a little while."

Roelena stared at Marliese for a few more seconds, then sighed and nodded reluctantly. They could stop talking about Conrad, she supposed, but she knew Marliese wouldn't stop thinking about him. Not for one second. And neither would Roelena. But tomorrow night when she had time to herself? Roelena would write a scathing letter to her cousin and tell him exactly what she thought.

"Open the gold one first," Marliese repeated as if her repertoire of words had become limited.

Roelena reluctantly picked up the square foil-wrapped parcel. By the feel of the uneven ridges along their edges, Roelena knew it wasn't a book. She took the same care with the pretty paper as she'd taken with her earlier gifts. When she pushed aside the foil to reveal the contents, and despite her concern for Marliese, she smiled in unveiled delight. The gift was a framed print of a Victorian woman in a ruffled lilac gown with matching bonnet and sitting on a bench in a flower garden. In one hand she held an open parasol above her head; in the other, a painted fan trimmed with lace. She was looking up as if talking to the fat winged cupid who hovered in the air above her.

Roelena chuckled, then looked at Marliese. "Moe won't like this."

Roelena knew her *ouders* would not be impressed with the image of Cupid, which was a secular, or possibly even Catholic, depiction of a saint with heavenly power, a power that belonged solely to the Holy Trinity—God the father, Jesus his son, and the Holy Spirit. Regardless, Roelena found the whimsical image delightful.

"My Moe didn't approve either. But it's not for your *moeder*, or mine. It's for you."

"Well, I love it. Thanks, Marliese." The two women hugged briefly.

"Now open the red one."

When she revealed the contents of the next gift, Roelena chuckled outright. The same woman sat on the same bench in the same beautiful garden in the same ruffled dress. She held her open parasol in one hand but her fan lay forgotten on the bench beside her. Instead of talking to a cupid, the beautifully dressed young woman was smiling at the handsome, top-hatted gentleman sitting beside her, the woman's free hand tucked into the crook of the elegant man's elbow.

"Marliese, they're charming. Where did you get them?"

"I went with Siebren and Gertie to Calgary a few weeks ago. I found them in a gift shop there."

Siebren was Marliese's married brother, and the only one of her four siblings Marliese got along with. He and his wife Gertie had been married for eighteen months and, only two weeks before, announced they would have a baby in July.

Roelena held the framed pictures side-by-side, delighting in the fanciful theme. "I hope you didn't spend too much."

"I didn't. The gift shop was having an after-Christmas sale."

Roelena rose and walked to the wall opposite her bed where a framed picture of a bouquet of roses hung above her tall chest of drawers. She held the new pictures, took down the old one, then held up the two new ones over the patch of faded wallpaper, glancing over her shoulder at Marliese. "If I put them here, I'll be able to see them from my bed."

Marliese smiled politely.

Roelena's shoulders slumped as she lay the pictures down atop the dresser. She turned and regarded her friend. "Do you want us to stay here?" Roelena asked. "I'll say you're sick and bring us up some tea. We can look at the new *Ladies Home Journal* that Mrs. Dickson brought this week."

Marliese shook her head, then rose and moved towards the door. "I will not be the reason you don't spend your birthday with your boyfriend," she said in a determined tone.

For a moment, Roelena thought her friend's characteristic spirit was beginning to resurface. But when Marliese opened the door and turned expectantly towards her friend, Roelena saw her eyes. The lifelessness in them made Roelena want to weep.

Conrad was in for a nasty letter.

5
SATURDAY, JANUARY 22

A Saturday afternoon on a relatively mild winter's day in January would not usually have found Clarence and the de Haas boys lingering inside. They would normally have been doing any number of outside activities, either chores on the farm—mending fences, cleaning the barn of manure-laden straw, chopping wood; or more manly outdoor activities—ice-fishing, setting snares and traps, hunting for game birds in the reeds by Sandpiper Lake; or possibly even pursuing some form of entertainment, which in the winter would either be skating or sledding. But today was Roelena's birthday. Later the boys would go outside to do the usual chores—milking and caring for the pigs and chickens—but for now the youngest de Haas boys were in the kitchen with Clarence.

Clarence's expression showed his delight when Roelena finally emerged through the door at the bottom of the enclosed staircase with Marliese on her heels. He was sitting at the kitchen table between Willem and Pieter, the latest edition of the *Family Herald* lying open on a page advertising a Winchester bolt action, single shot, .22 rifle that claimed to be *for every purse and purpose*.

"You've decided to join us," he announced with a pleased grin. "And just in time for tea," he added as Sijmon placed a freshly brewed pot on the table.

The surface of the table, Roelena saw, also had mugs, the everyday milk and sugar pots, a tumbler of *theelepeltjes* for those who took sugar, and a plate of buttered, sliced *koek*, the Dutch spiced loaf that was a staple in their home. As Marliese quietly made her way around the long table and took a seat beside Sijmon, Roelena saw Clarence raise his eyebrows, surprised by Marliese's atypical subdued silence. Roelena quickly moved to stand behind him, resting a hand on his shoulder and causing him to look up at her. In response to the question in his eyes, Roelena shook her head, silently pleading with him to make no comment about Marliese's uncharacteristic behaviour.

Roelena was relieved to see Clarence take her cue and refrain from uttering whatever comment he'd been about to make. She was also relieved Clarence was the only one of the boys who noticed Marliese's reticence. Sijmon was never particularly observant—and even if he was, he wouldn't be inclined to comment; Pieter was still too young to notice such things; and although Willem might have commented, he was too engrossed in the rifle advertisement.

"Roelena, can we show Clarence the photo albums?" Pieter asked, looking up at his sister. Even as a young boy, Pieter had loved to pour over the family pictures, examining every detail. As a teenager, his sweet sentimentality hadn't yet faded.

"He's already seen them, but sure, go get them. You know where they are." The bottom two drawers of Roelena's dresser was filled with items for her hope chest—lace doilies, embroidered pillowcases, and even a large crocheted bedspread Anneke had made the winter before. But the middle drawer held her scrapbooks, camera, and the family photo albums.

"Oh wait," she said, stopping Pieter who looked over his shoulder at her. "My new jewelry is on my bedside table. Can you bring it down with you?"

"New jewelry?" Clarence asked.

Roelena was pleased to also see a glimmer of interest in Marliese's gaze. "Wait until you see what Pa and Moe gave me," was all she said, taking a seat beside Marliese. She would've preferred to sit in the chair Pieter had vacated next to Clarence, but she wanted to show her support for Marliese.

Having lost Clarence's interest in the ad for the rifle, Willem pulled the magazine over until it was directly in front of him, then bent his head to ogle the ad, which depicted a father sitting in an arm chair dressed in a suit with his son on the floor at his feet. The boy looked to be about twelve and was holding the new rifle with a look of delight, the open cardboard box on the floor beside him. Roelena knew Willem was picturing himself on the floor at Kees's feet with that new rifle in his hands.

"Did Roelena tell you, Clarence?" Pieter announced when he returned thirty seconds later. He set three full albums on the table in front of Clarence, then handed the rectangular jewelry box across the table to Roelena. "She got a new album today from Willem. And Sijmon and I gave her a pen with silver ink for writing on the black paper."

"I'm glad to hear my girl is being appropriately spoiled," Clarence said.

Even Willem set his magazine aside when Roelena revealed the contents of the jewelry box. She removed the bracelet and asked Marliese to put it on her wrist, and they all took a few moments to admire it.

"I haven't given Roelena her birthday present, yet." Clarence smiled across the table at Roelena. "Should I give it to you now?"

"That's *four* presents in one day," Pieter stated, impressed.

"Actually Marliese brought me a present, too."

"*Five* presents," Pieter gushed, his eyes wide.

"Six actually. Marliese gave me a pair of framed pictures." Roelena smiled at Marliese, but her friend barely noticed. "She had them wrapped separately, so it counts as two gifts, don't you think?"

Roelena could see Clarence bristling at Marliese's seemingly aloof response. She reached across the table and gripped his hand, giving him a look that indicated her desire for him to bite his tongue. She was relieved when he smiled and enveloped her hand in both of his.

"I want to see them," Pieter said.

"I'll show you later, *liefje,*" Roelena said.

The women in their family—Roelena, her sister Greta, her *moeder*, and even her sister-in-law Ingrid—still addressed Pieter using this childhood endearment. The boy sometimes complained that he was too old for it, but Roelena found the habit too difficult to break.

"Actually, *seven* presents," Willem corrected. "Ingrid's bringing something when they come for dinner tonight. I saw her wrapping it."

"She is?" Roelena said, a pleased smile on her face.

"Seven presents?" Pieter's tone dripped with envy.

Clarence addressed Pieter. "Could you go to my room and get Roelena's present from my bag?" When he stayed overnight on Saturdays, Clarence shared a room with Sijmon.

Pieter dashed back up the stairs, his footsteps thumping loudly on the bare wooden floorboards.

"Why is Pieter running up and down the stairs?" Anneke

asked, coming into the kitchen and standing at the foot of the table. "Is the tea still hot?" she added, setting her mug down.

"Yes, it's fresh," Sijmon said. He lifted the pot and strainer and began pouring tea into everyone's mugs, including his *moeder's*.

Roelena answered Anneke's other question. "Pieter first went to get the photo albums—we're going to show Clarence—and now he's gone to get the birthday present Clarence has for me."

Anneke nodded, then turned to Marliese. "How are your *ouders,* Marliese? Are they well?" Roelena and Marliese had been friends since the first week the de Haas family arrived in the Pine Glade community. Anneke was used to seeing Marliese in their home.

"They're both fine," Marliese responded in an over bright tone. "They're happy the cold snap has passed. Pa couldn't get our car started last week."

"Yes, neither could we."

"Roelena's bracelet is lovely, *Mevrow* de Haas," Marliese stated, acknowledging Roelena's beautiful jewelry.

"Dank je, Marliese."

Anneke regarded her daughter's friend for a long moment, but was almost immediately distracted when Pieter burst through the door at the bottom of the staircase holding a rectangular red box tied with twine.

"Roelena has another present to open, Moe," Pieter announced, handing the package to his sister with a flourish.

Smiling shyly at Clarence, Roelena took the box the size of Clarence's fist and pulled off the twine before removing the lid. She lifted out a tissue-wrapped object, and pealed back first one layer of tissue and then another and another. Everyone except Marliese chuckled as they watched.

"Oh, this is the last one," Roelena announced after peeling

away five layers of tissue. She brushed aside the final layer to reveal a glass keepsake box. Colourful flowers were painted on the sides and top and the edges soldered in gold filigree. She glowed with delight as she unlatched the miniature lid, then proudly displayed it on the palm of her hand for all to see.

Anneke was standing on Roelena's left and lifted the box from her daughter's hand. "You can keep your silver necklace from Holland inside, Roelena. Or your new bracelet. What a lovely gift, Clarence," Anneke added before handing it back to Roelena. Anneke retrieved her full mug of tea and returned to the front room.

"It *is* lovely," Roelena gushed, handing it to Marliese to admire. She stood and walked around the table to Clarence, bending to give him an affectionate hug and a quick, chaste kiss. "Thank you, Clarence." Then she rested a hand on Pieter's shoulder, giving him a gentle nudge. *"Liefje,* let me sit here. You go sit beside Marliese." Marliese would be fine, Roelena thought, feeling a little guilty for abandoning her friend. But she wanted to sit beside her boyfriend. After all, it was her birthday.

"It's a beautiful gift, Clarence," Marliese stated quietly, handing the box across the table to Roelena.

"I thought Roelena, being beautiful herself, would like a gift of something beautiful as well."

Willem immediately feigned gagging in response to Clarence's compliment.

"Oh, Willem, stop." Roelena scolded, leaning forward slightly to look past Clarence at her exasperating brother. "Just you wait. A few years from now we'll all be laughing at *you* fawning over *your* girlfriend."

"Not a chance. You'll *never* hear me say," and here he changed his voice to a mocking falsetto, *"a beautiful gift for my beautiful girl."*

"Are you making fun of me?" Clarence demanded in mock anger.

Willem snorted in disdain. "*Ja!* Of course I'm making fun of you. Listen to yourself."

"Can we look at the albums now?" Pieter suggested impatiently. "Let's start with the oldest one first."

Pieter reached for the book that had been full when the family emigrated from the Netherlands, turning it so it faced Clarence and opening it to the first page. He took a piece of *koek* from the plate at the end of the table, then sprawled on his belly across the tabletop so he could get a better view of the upside-down pictures. When Sijmon leaned his forearms on the table to see better, Marliese reluctantly shifted to do the same.

As six heads poured over the photographs in the album, sipping their tea and nibbling on *koek,* the four siblings commented on each photo, recalling a memory or explaining who the people in the pictures were, or interrupting each other when they suddenly recalled a forgotten detail. Some of the photographs were of their *Tante* Hennie—their father's sister—who'd mailed photographs to them all the way from what had once been the Dutch colony of Indonesia. Before the war, she'd worked as a nurse, but later died in a Japanese prison camp. Other photos were from one of their mother's sisters, their *Tante* Aaltina, who'd also lived in Indonesia with her husband, *Oom* Jaap. Aaltina had been in the same prison camp as Hennie, but she'd survived, as had her five children. Her husband had died on the Burma Road, though. Roelena relayed to Clarence how their *Tante* Aaltina had written them a letter after the war, explaining how she'd prayed for Jaap every day until the day came when she knew he no longer needed her prayers. Much later, she'd learned he had indeed died on that very day. After the war ended, Aaltina and her five children—Roelena pointed at a picture of them—moved back to The Netherlands. None of Roelena's brothers and sisters had ever met these relatives, and likely never would.

They continued to page through the album, showing Clarence and Marliese pictures of their steep-roofed home in the village of Andijk in Noord Holland with the grass-covered dike rising above it in the background. The album also included photographs of their siblings who'd passed away. Little Sijmon had died at the age of seven after having his tonsils removed, and baby Ebeltje had died at eleven months from a fever. Their other sister, Wiekje, who closely resembled Roelena in looks, died from a burst appendix at the age of twelve. These children were gone, but they hadn't been forgotten, even by the siblings who'd never met them or were too young to have memories of them.

Midway through looking at the prized family albums, Clarence looked up and was struck by the sight of the five bent heads around him. He felt a sudden rush of belonging to this family. It was so strong, it almost knocked the breath out of him. He had no relatives in this country, but these people had welcomed him, taken him in, treated him like a son, an uncle, and a brother. Except Roelena, of course. He didn't want her to look upon him as a brother. He studied her profile, noticing for the first time the minute freckles at her hairline. He'd known for a long time that he would one day marry this woman and become a true member of this family, but now he knew it without a shadow of a doubt. He envisioned a time in the future when his and Roelena's children would be engaging in the same activity as this group; he and Roelena would be in the front room enjoying a companionable silence while their children and their friends would be in the kitchen paging through family photo albums—possibly even these—and sharing stories.

In that moment of clarity, he realized this powerful feeling was the answer to every question, asked or unasked;

this was why God gave human beings breath; this was why humans had the ability—no, the gift—to love. This was why people got up in the morning hopeful, and went to bed at night content. A wife, children, loved ones—these blessings begot companionship, belonging, and purpose. In that moment, in the warm and cozy kitchen of the de Haas family farmhouse, Clarence felt like he was standing in front of the very door that led to the rest of his life. Never before had he felt such utter peace and clarity. Goosebumps rippled up his arms. Impulsively, he leaned over and gently laid a hand on Roelena's bent head.

She startled and turned to him, and he took her face in both of his hands and kissed her tenderly. When he pulled back and dropped his hands, he saw the questioning look in her eyes.

"What was that for?" she whispered.

He shook his head and smiled mysteriously, then forced himself to look down at the album. "Where was that taken?" he asked, pointing randomly at one of the photos.

Marliese was the only one at the table to witness this tender exchange. She'd noticed Clarence staring at Roelena with a strange, wondering look in his eye before he'd kissed her. Marliese knew she should be happy for her friend, but in that moment, it took all her energy and focus not to sob. Not that anyone was paying her any attention. She blinked away her tears and dropped her gaze to stare unseeingly at the photographs.

"That's on the steamship *Veendam*," Sijmon was explaining. "The ship that brought us to Canada in 1936. It was exciting. I was only seven, and asked Pa if we could see the engine. But the crew wouldn't let us."

"I was only two-and-a half," stated Willem in a mournful tone. "I can't remember it at all. But Roelena got in trouble for throwing her teacup over the railing," he added enthusiastically, happy to recall a time when someone other than himself had gotten into trouble.

"I didn't get into trouble."

"No," agreed Sijmon. "But Jakob did on account of boat jail."

Clarence laughed. "Firstly, why would you throw your teacup over the railing, sweetheart? And secondly, what on earth is boat jail?"

Roelena chuckled, glancing at Marliese, glad to see she was listening or, at least, feigning attention. "We were outside on the deck, and the stewards came out with trays of what I thought was tea."

"You were nine, right?" Clarence asked.

"Yes. It was April, and I remember it being brisk and cold out on deck. Not cold enough to go inside but cold enough to make a hot cup of sweet tea very welcome. Moe was sitting on a bench sheltered from the wind. She had Willem beside her and Pieter on her lap."

Pieter nodded happily. "I remember."

"No you don't," Willem ridiculed. "You were just a baby."

"I do so remember."

"No you don't," Willem argued.

"Yes, I *do*."

"Don't be an idiot," Willem scoffed.

"Willem! Leave it," Roelena warned.

"Ja," added Clarence, hoping his intervention would prevent the brothers' silly disagreement from escalating into something unpleasant. "I want to hear what happened."

Roelena gave him a grateful smile as she continued. "I was with Pa, Jakob, and Wiekje by the railing. I took a cup from one of the stewards, but when I took my first sip I discovered it was some kind of broth. I didn't like it and told Moe I didn't want it. Moe had her own hands full—holding Pieter and trying not to spill her drink. She said for me to throw it overboard. I remember going to the railing, which was about as high as my armpits, and tossing the mug over. And then everyone was shouting at me, or it seemed like everyone was, but it was just Moe and Pa and the older kids. I hadn't realized Moe only meant for me to throw the *contents* overboard, not the cup."

"But what was boat jail?" Clarence asked with an amused frown.

Roelena rolled her eyes. *"Jakob.* When everyone shouted at me, I started crying. Moe told Jakob, who would have been about fifteen then, to take Wiekje and me for a walk around the deck. The minute we got out of earshot of Pa and Moe, he told me that if any of the people who worked on the boat found out what I'd done, they'd report it to the captain and the captain would put me in boat jail. And boat jail was worse than land jail, because in boat jail, no visitors were allowed, not even your parents. And I would have to stay there until we reached Halifax. And even then, the captain might not let me out. Then Jakob said one of the stewards had likely seen me throw the cup overboard and was probably informing the captain that very minute. I started wailing then, terrified out of my wits. Jakob couldn't shush me, and finally had to bring me back to Pa and Moe. I don't remember how he was punished, but I do recall Pa being really, really angry with him."

"I never tease you bad enough to make you cry, Roelena."

It was hard to tell if Willem's tone held pride or disappointment.

"That's not true," Roelena scoffed. "But I will admit, I've always been thankful you're not older than me. Contending with Jakob and Harri's teasing was bad enough."

"Not Hendrik?" Clarence asked. He knew Roelena, in addition to her three younger brothers, had three older brothers, although he'd only met Jakob.

Roelena shook her head. "His teasing was mild compared to Jakob and Harri's."

Clarence had an arm slung loosely on the back of Roelena's chair. "But sweetheart, don't you think it's rather wonderful?"

"What do you mean?" she asked.

"Your fingerprints are on the bottom of the Atlantic Ocean. That's kind of neat. It makes me wish I'd tossed something overboard."

6
LETTER TO CONRAD FROM ROELENA

Cousin Conrad,

I will not apologize for the tone of this letter or the words I am about to write. Whether you expected me to or not, I've read the letter you wrote to Marliese, and I am appalled by your deception these past months. You should have told Marliese about your altered feelings when you first met this Louise. The fact that you did not makes you a cad of the worst possible sort.

I cannot believe you continued to write to Marliese these past months as if you loved her in the manner of a man who might one day propose marriage. And don't excuse yourself by claiming that future outcome was not what you both anticipated. When you and Marliese first started corresponding, I did not expect it to last, but over these past three years, Marliese indicated that your letters were both frequent and ardent, which created an expectation of a certain outcome, at least for Marliese. Do not dare refute this, Conrad! Mayhap I cannot speak for you, but we both know Marliese envisioned a future where the two of you would be together as husband and wife. It confounds me that, at the same time your feelings for this other woman were growing, you continued to write to Marliese, giving no hint that your feelings of love for her were lessening.

You should have been truthful, Conrad! You should have written honestly to Marliese months ago. And you should certainly not have professed your love and admiration for Marliese in your last letter! You no longer have the right to proclaim such feelings, not after what you've done. In my eyes, by proposing to this other woman, you are betraying Marliese in the worst possible way. I truly cannot believe you of all people had the capacity to behave so badly. But you did, Conrad, and your behaviour is dishonourable and disgraceful.

I have urged Marliese not to write you ever again, and I implore you not to write to her. But if you do, you must refrain from professing your love for her, as doing so serves no purpose given your intentions towards this other woman.

This is my last letter to you as I feel I cannot continue our correspondence. I once thought of you as more than my cousin. I thought we had become good friends, and that respect and caring had been permanently cemented between us on account of our frequent correspondence and during your visit. But now your deplorable actions have greatly disappointed me.

I do not expect you or even want you to respond to this letter. Given the heartache you have caused in my dearest friend, I cannot find it in my heart to wish you either health or happiness.

I remain your cousin, but no longer your friend,

Roelena.

7

FEBRUARY

In winter, the rural landscape west of Bellecourt remained blanketed in snow for months on end. Leafless trees and evergreens stood like patient sentinels awaiting the first warming, life-giving breath of spring, their buried roots locking them in the frozen ground while, beneath thick layers of ice in the deepest streams, rivers, and lakes, water trickled slowly and sluggishly.

On those days when the overcast skies hid the magnificent blue of the Alberta sky, the red-roofed barns dotting the quilted fabric of fenced pastures, fields, and farmsteads brought a splash of welcome colour to the dull winter greys and whites. Smoke puffed from chimneys, promising warmth within homes. Double-paned windows remained permanently frosted at the edges, and roof edges dripped with pristine tentacles of ice. On the coldest days, livestock gravitated from the snow-covered pastures to the barns and lean-tos, huddling together for warmth in the straw.

In early February, the temperatures on this frozen Alberta prairie dipped to well below minus twenty degrees

Fahrenheit, bringing with it harsh, icy winds from the north. Farmers bundled in thick layers and ventured outside three or four times every day to check on their animals, bringing straw for their bedding, hay and grain to the cows and horses for their feed, kitchen scraps to the pigs, and pellets of compressed grain to the laying hens. With the water in the drinking troughs frozen solid, the de Haas boys made repeated and multiple trips from the well-house to the animals. Each time they ventured out, the dog—who was allowed to stay in the porch when the temperatures got this low—trotted after them as if to ensure their safe return. At dawn and dusk when they did the milking, they crouched on their milk stools and leaned close against the warm, docile creatures, stealing what warmth they could. The barn cats huddled nearby, mewling plaintively for their share of the warm milk from pails that steamed in the cold.

The families who lived more than a few miles away from the Pine Glade church didn't make it to *kerk* those first two Sundays in February. Those who did manage to attend arrived in horse-drawn sleds huddled under blankets with hot bricks at their feet, as not a single car or truck would start. The caretaker who lived across the road from the church lit fires in the two pot-bellied stoves early in the morning on both Sundays, one in the basement kitchen and one in the sanctuary, but these barely provided sufficient warmth in the cavernous building that had not yet been fitted with an oil-fired furnace. They cancelled the afternoon church services on each of the two Sundays so that families could quickly and safely return home after the morning service, their horses seeming as eager as they to return to their familiar, warm shelters.

During those chilling weeks in February 1949, Roelena was grateful her chores kept her inside the house near the wood-fired cooking range, and grateful, too, for the relatively new creature comforts in their farmhouse—central heat, electricity, and running water. Unlike their Langelaar neighbours who were without running water for more than a week, their water pipes didn't freeze and no one had to venture outside in the Arctic wind to use the outdoor privy.

After seventeen gruelling days of bone chilling cold, the blessed relief of a chinook blew in from the south. This welcome phenomenon occurred once or twice each winter thanks to the massive mountain range guarding the southwestern Alberta prairie. Warm, moist air flowed east from the Pacific Ocean, dropping its moisture on the peaks of the Rockies four hundred miles inland. The air mass, now warm and growing warmer as it moved further east, slipped down the side of the mountains towards Calgary where temperatures rose to above freezing in less than a day, melting more than a foot of snow and causing havoc on roads now clogged with water and slush. At the de Haas farm, which was conveniently located on the northernmost edge of these favourable chinook winds, the thermometer mounted on the back porch showed twenty degrees Fahrenheit where barely more than a day before it had registered minus twenty. The warm chinook winds not only raised the temperature, they chased the clouds away. When the sun came out, the brilliant blue of the sky against the white of fresh snow was so intense it practically burned the eye.

With this welcome warmth, everyone, including the animals, seemed eager to venture outside once again. Horses and cattle meandered out to their pastures, pawing at the snow to uncover the frozen grass beneath. Pigs wandered into the fenced woods, burying their snouts in the snow searching for frozen pinecones and fallen leaves and berries. Even the hens dared to venture out of their straw nests in the chicken house to scratch at the shallow snow on the side of their coop where Ingrid scattered their pellets.

On the afternoon of the second day of the chinook, all seven of the Langelaar children walked the half mile to the de Haas farm, with the oldest, a fourteen-year old girl named Margaret, pulling a sled holding her three-year old brother Teddy. The purpose of their visit was to pass on an invitation from their parents, Gerrit and Cornelia, to join the Langelaar's at a skating party at Sandpiper Lake the following Saturday, weather permitting., Despite their trek, the Langelaar children were full of energy after their enforced confinement. They'd missed multiple days of school due to the bitter cold. Most of the de Haas family, including Tomas who would soon turn three years old, were also suffering from cabin fever. Everyone except Anneke bundled up and played in the snow, transforming the de Haas front yard into a family of snowmen in front of a duo-entrance snow fort. When Kees and Roelena returned from doing the shopping in town, Roelena joined the adults and kids in the front yard for a riotous snowball fight, with Kees and Anneke enjoying the game as a spectator sport from the comfort of their front room.

After their mid-day meal the next Saturday and since the weather cooperated for their skating party, nine people piled into Kees's 1941 four-door Ford Sedan for the short journey to the lake—Jakob behind the wheel with Ingrid and Pieter wedged between him and Kees. Roelena, Clarence, Willem, and Sijmon, with Tomas on Sijmon's lap, sat in the back. Although Anneke hadn't had an episode that confined her to bed since before Christmas, she wasn't well enough to skate, and would remain at home with her six-month old grandson, Kees, named after his paternal grandfather. In the trunk they'd packed their skates, a crate with a large cloth bag stuffed with straw and three, two-quart mason jars of hot chocolate, a handful of chipped mugs, a couple of old hook rugs, two hockey sticks, enough firewood to build a fire, and a bag of fat marshmallows—a newly discovered campfire treat.

The mood of the group was as festive as on Sinterklass Eve. The car was noisy with conversation and then laughter as the group in the back shifted, accidentally bumping elbows, knees, and heads. When they arrived at the lake, they piled out of the car. The Langelaar family was already on the ice, as were at least a dozen people Roelena didn't recognize. Little Teddy, almost a year older than Tomas was half-trotting, half-skimming across the ice wearing his strapped-on blades over his winter boots, pushing a wooden chair in front of him for balance and looking as happy as Roelena had ever seen him.

Roelena and Ingrid retrieved the rugs from the trunk and laid them on the lake edge while the boys brought the wood, skates, and snacks. Roelena claimed her skates from the pile and sat on a rug beside Clarence, her plaid wool skirt as warm as a blanket across her lap. They'd all learned to skate in the Netherlands as children using the same strap-on blades that Teddy was wearing. Roelena now had a pair of white skates that were slightly too large for her feet. She removed her mittens and winter boots, then tugged on a pair of thick wool socks over her wool-lined cotton stockings before slipping her feet into her skates.

"Here, sweetheart, let me lace them up for you," Clarence volunteered.

He'd already laced his skates—they'd been a present to him from Roelena's parents that first Sinterklaas after he and Roelena began dating. He shifted so he knelt in front of Roelena, wedging her foot between his knees before pulling the laces of the boot tight, wrapping the extra length around her ankle before tying a knot.

"Clar-ence?" Willem called in a mocking sing-song voice from where he sat a dozen feet away, his head bent over his own laces. *"Could you help me lace up my skates? I'm too helpless to do it by myself."*

Roelena had slipped her mittens back on once Clarence started helping her. In response to Willem's teasing, she gathered a handful of snow from beside her hip and threw the ball at Willem. She would've been content if her snowball hit her brother at all, but she was especially delighted when it splattered against the side of his face, startling him and evoking a roar of displeasure.

"Clarence, you realize what you've done?" Jakob asked from where he sat tying his own skates near Willem. Tomas, who sat on Jakob's left with his legs in his wool one-piece snowsuit stretched straight out in front of him, was intently watching his mother buckle on the straps of his two-bladed skates. "If I don't lace Ingrid's skates for her, I'll look bad thanks to you."

Roelena knew Jakob would have laced Ingrid's skates regardless of what Clarence had done, but Jakob always leveraged any opportunity to tease.

"You can't help but look bad, Jakob, what with that mug you call a face," Clarence jibbed.

Everyone within hearing howled at Clarence's amusing retort.

Roelena grinned in contentment as she listened to Jakob and Willem trade friendly insults with her boyfriend.

While Clarence started lacing her second skate, she looked over his shoulder at the skaters on the lake. Pieter and Sijmon were already on the ice, each with a hockey stick. They'd joined Gerrit and four of the Langelaar children, including Margaret, the oldest child and their only other son,

Wouter. Gerrit had cleared a small rectangle of ice and made a makeshift hockey rink by placing a variety of scarves, mittens, and toques to mark the goal posts on each end. The remainder of the frozen surface of the lake had only an inch or two of snow as the relatively warm winds they'd had that week kept the flat surface relatively clear. Roelena saw that Teddy Langelaar had now abandoned his chair and was teetering with focused determination around the outer edge of the cleared area, falling often but immediately picking himself up and starting again. Cornelia was skating near her two youngest daughters, who were slightly more accomplished than their brother Teddy. Cornelia, though, was as graceful as a swan. Roelena had always marvelled at how the large, rather lumbering woman became so graceful on ice. But it was Roelena's father who was the most accomplished skater of them all. Kees was already distant, his powerful strides making him practically fly across the frozen surface. She knew that, as a teenager, Kees had competed in canal races and had frequently won. Even now, at sixty years of age, he could still outskate his grown sons.

"There, sweetheart. All done."

Clarence's announcement interrupted Roelena's thoughts. He rose, then reached out a bare hand. She put her mitten-clad hand in his and let him tug her up. Then the young couple were on the ice and gliding hand-in-hand across the lake. Roelena had left her toque in the car, thinking she didn't need it, but the wind was colder than she'd expected. She let go of Clarence's hand and unwrapped the scarf from her neck, setting it on her head and tying it under her chin so that her ears were covered. Clarence, meanwhile, retrieved his mittens from his pockets and slipped them on. Instead of re-clasping hands, Clarence stretched his right arm behind Roelena's waist, grasping her right hand in his at her right hip, and taking her outstretched left hand in his where it crossed in front of him on his left. They resumed skating, matching their strides and swaying in rhythmic perfection as they made a big arc around the other skaters. They were soon joined by Jakob and Ingrid, little Tomas left happily in possession of Teddy's abandoned chair. The two young couples chatted and laughed as they skated, the activity all the more pleasurable from having been cooped up inside for so long.

Roelena wished she'd thought to detour to collect Marliese on the way to the lake. Her friend was still melancholy and low-spirited after receiving Conrad's unwelcome news the month before. The skating and the fresh air would have done Marliese a world of good, Roelena thought, but it was too late to get her now. And besides, their car had been bursting at the seams. There would not have been room for another adult.

The younger children approached the two couples and begged them to play crack-the-whip, needing the superior strength of the adults to increase the speed of the slingshot skater. They took turns being at the end of the line of ten, squealing in glee when it was their turn to be flung away like a stone from a sling-shot, whizzing along the bumpy surface of the lake ice. They followed that with a game of fox-and-goose, using Gerrit's shovel to create a giant wheel of pathways in the snow-covered ice and making a hub that allowed only three people at a time to claim sanctuary. The children squealed in glee when they managed to tag one of the adults, then shrieked in feigned alarm as they were chased down the shoveled paths of the giant spoke.

Finally, tiring of the games, they all retreated to the lakeshore, joining Kees and Gerrit at the fire they'd built. When Roelena removed her skates, her feet ached from the unforgiving stiff boots and she reveled in relief at slipping on her wool-lined winter boots. Then Margaret helped her pass around mugs of cocoa. The drink was no longer hot, but it was warm, sweet, and tasty. The older boys took out their pocket knives and made roasting sticks, then took turns roasting the sugary treat, sending up a collective exclamation of dismay when a morsel caught fire or dropped off the stick and into the embers. With the bag empty, the cocoa drunk, and dusk threatening, they covered the remaining embers with snow, then piled back into their respective cars.

During the drive home with the Langelaar car already out of sight somewhere ahead of them, Kees suddenly spotted a snowy owl swooping near the fence line on the side of the road, pointing it out to the occupants of the car. Unlike other owls that are active at night, snowy owls hunted during the day. This particular owl seemed to have spied a mouse, or some other tasty morsel, just as they were driving by. The occupants of the car jostled each other to catch a glimpse of the magnificent creature, hoping to witness it catching its prey. But they forgot the owl and shrieked in a collective gasp when the car plowed into the soft snow on the side of the road and abruptly stopped. Sijmon had one arm around his nephew, which prevented him from flying off his lap when the car hit the ditch while the adults were wedged in so tight they barely shifted.

Laughing, they piled out of the car on the driver's side, as the passenger side doors were buried in the deep snow of the ditch. They hadn't thought to pack shovels for their short journey to the lake, but the boys took turns digging out the snow from behind the tires using the hockey sticks, their hands, and their feet. Ingrid, Roelena, and Tomas stayed on the road, shouting encouragement and trying their best to answer Tomas's repeated questions about why his dad had steered them into the ditch. The women temporarily considered walking home. They were less than two miles from their farm, but decided that four grown men and two good-sized boys would soon free the car from the ditch.

They were wrong though. In the end it took close to an hour to get the car back on the road. It hadn't actually taken long to shovel aside the snow, but pushing the car backwards up the incline on tires that couldn't get a grip proved impossible. In the end, they had to clear a path of snow in the ditch for the car to drive forward and up. This would have taken even longer but for the help of a man and his two teenage sons who drove by and stopped to help. Not only did the stranger have a shovel in the back of his truck, he also had bags of sand, which they dumped onto the snow for traction. By the time the car was back on the road, it was almost dark, and Roelena, Ingrid, and Tomas had begun walking home simply to keep moving and stay warm. Once in the car and a mile down the road, Jakob stopped the Ford to pick up Roelena, Ingrid, and Tomas.

Back at the de Haas farm, the skaters, their cheeks rosy and their clothes damp, tumbled into the warm kitchen filled with the aroma of chicken soup and freshly baked bread. Roelena had formed the loaves, buns, and cinnamon buns before leaving for the lake, and Anneke had put them in the oven after they'd risen. Tomas was the first to greet his *Oma*, excitedly sharing the news of how they'd driven into the ditch to see a snowy owl.

They'd returned home much later than planned, giving Ingrid no time to make supper for her family, so it was decided that Jakob, Ingrid, and Tomas would stay at the farmhouse for supper. Clarence trooped outside with Roelena's brothers to milk the cows and do the chores, while Anneke and Roelena put an extra leaf in the table before setting it for supper. Kees retreated to the front room to read in his usual chair wearing the glasses he'd reluctantly purchased a few months before. Tomas contentedly played at his *Opa's* feet with the blocks and miniature animal figurines kept in *Opa* and *Oma's* toy box, giving his usual running commentary of conversation on behalf of each animal. Ingrid remained in the kitchen nursing the baby and contentedly chatting with her sister- and mother-in-law while they waited for the boys' return.

8

SATURDAY, FEBRUARY 26

After supper, Jakob and Ingrid took Tomas and the baby home while Kees and Anneke relaxed in the front room where Kees read his book and Anneke crocheted. In the kitchen, Roelena washed the dishes, Clarence dried, and Pieter put them away. Willem made multiple trips outside to get wood until the crate by the stove was filled to overflowing while Sijmon swept the kitchen floor and then made another pot of tea, setting out mugs and the sugar pot.

When they were done these small chores, Willem went to his room to get his prized arrowhead collection, which Clarence had asked to see again. The five of them were now gathered around the foot of the table where Willem's collection was spread out on a clean, linen cloth. The three dozen arrowheads were made from an assortment of stones in a variety of colours, sizes, and shapes. Almost all of them had been found by the de Haas boys while clearing and plowing their or their neighbours' fields. The smallest was barely longer than a thumbnail, and most certainly had been an arrow point, while the largest, easily as big as Clarence's thumb, had likely been the projectile point of a spear. The colours varied from the palest grey to a dark grey-blue.

Willem's collection was not entirely uncommon amongst these early European settlers in the west, given the lands they inhabited had once been home to Alberta's Indigenous peoples. Farmers, and even gardeners in the small towns, often found Indian artifacts, including arrowheads, spear points, axes, and hammer-stones. Clarence shared Willem's fascination with these captivating objects that gave a glimpse of what life had been like for the region's original inhabitants. Clarence was fully aware that similar artifacts could be found in the Netherlands, only in Europe they were from civilizations hundreds, perhaps even thousands, of years removed from Clarence's generation. The artifacts in Willem's collection were fascinating to him because the people who made and used them had inhabited these lands less than one hundred years before.

"Do you want to sit beside Clarence, Roelena?" Pieter asked.

Clarence sat at the foot of the table with Pieter in the prized spot on his right and Willem on his left, with Sijmon beside Willem.

"That's all right, *liefje*. I'll sit beside you," Roelena said, pulling out the empty chair and taking a seat. She always preferred to sit next to her boyfriend, but she knew how much Pieter and Willem each enjoyed his undivided attention.

Clarence, too, would've preferred his girl next to him, but he was too good-natured to make a fuss. He picked up one of the stone arrowheads. "Where did you find this one, Willem?"

Willem knew every detail of each object in his collection. "I found that one four years ago when I was helping pick rocks in de Graaf's potato field."

Clarence was examining each arrowhead one-by-one. "Every time I see these I'm struck by how exceptional they are. And unique." Clarence held up two that were similar in size and shape, but different in the type of stone and the details of the design. "Look, that one has a notch on the bottom, whereas this one has notches on both the bottom *and* the sides."

"Yes, and see?" Pieter eagerly reached for an arrowhead made from a speckled white stone, holding it beside the two Clarence held. "This one has notches in a triangular shape but the notches on the ones you're holding are straight, like a stem."

"Then there's this one," Willem asserted, not to be outdone by his brother. "Feel how sharp the edges still are."

Clarence put down the two arrowheads he'd been holding and took the opaque brown object from Willem. "I wonder how many attempts were made before ending up with something as perfect as this? It's so small and thin."

"*Ja*, and look at how it's made," Willem enthused. "See the flaking? Whoever made it would have had to be very skilled in order to chip the stone so precisely."

As the boys debated the complexity of how each object was made, Roelena lifted the oversize teapot with its crocheted cozy. Using the strainer with the Delft-blue handle, she began filling the mugs of tea. "Sijmon, did you tell Pa and Moe you made a pot?"

"Yup," Sijmon responded in his usual succinct manner.

"Thanks sweetheart," Clarence said as Roelena put a mug of sweetened tea at his elbow. Then he turned to Willem. "Which one of these is your favourite?" he asked.

"This one." Willem picked up a large, greenish-coloured arrowhead with streaks of ivory, holding it up for Clarence to examine. "See? It's not made from any of these other stones. It's completely different. I think it came from a warring Indian nation, maybe from as far away as Montana."

"Would they really have traveled from that far away?" Clarence asked.

Sijmon had been studiously examining each of the arrowheads even though he'd seen them all numerous times. He responded before Willem had the chance.

"When we first got here, an Indian man and his wife lived on our yard in a tent. His name was Louis, and he helped us clear the trees. Harri was the only one with enough English to talk to him. He told Harri that Indian tribes had battled against distant tribes from what's now the northern U.S. Harri actually found a spear head, three times bigger than this."

Sijmon laid the largest object on his flattened palm so they could all imagine the size of the object Harri had found.

As Sijmon continued to speak, Roelena arched her eyebrows, astounded yet again at how talkative her reticent brother became when he was with Clarence.

"He could see that Louis really wanted it," Sijmon continued. "So he gave it to him. Harri told me later he regretted giving it away. He always thought we'd find another one that size, but none of us ever did."

"Louis isn't an Indian name, surely?" Clarence frowned. "I always thought they had names like, I don't know, 'Running Fox', or 'Walking Thunder' or something."

Roelena nodded. "He told Harri he was Metis and told us they're descended from the early European French inhabitants in Quebec who intermarried with the Indian tribes. His family name was French, too, not only his first name. Chapette, or Chateau, something like that. Moe would remember."

"What was he like?" Clarence asked Roelena.

"I barely remember him. I can easier recall his wife."

Roelena answered. "Her name was Marie. She came to the house once. That's when we lived in the old house, the one that's our chicken coop now. She asked for *eieren,* or so we thought. We were impressed she knew the Dutch word for eggs, so we gave her a basket, but she shook her head and said *eieren* again and made a sweeping, flat gesture with her arm. We finally realized she was asking to borrow our *iron.* I remember because Moe was so impressed that she wanted to iron her washing even though they lived in a tent."

"I don't remember that," Pieter said.

"Pieter, use at least half your brain." Willem scoffed. "You were a baby. Of course you don't remember."

That first summer, when the Metis man and his wife lived on their property, Pieter had been less than a year old.

"But I do remember. They had a little boy, and I remember him."

"Pieter, you can't possibly remember them," Roelena insisted gently. "You only think you do because you've heard us talking about them over the years."

"No," Pieter shook his head emphatically. "I remember. Their little boy had no shoes. That stood out for me because I never saw anyone go outside without shoes before. I *do* remember," he asserted in response to their sea of doubtful looks.

"All right, Pieter. I believe you," Roelena said soothingly.

"No you don't, Roelena." Willem spat. "You're just saying that to make him feel better."

"And that makes her kind," Clarence intervened, hoping to defuse the siblings' bickering. "That's why I fell in love with her," he added, resting his warm gaze on Roelena, who smiled back at him. Clarence turned his attention back to Willem. "You'll appreciate that trait in your future sweetheart."

Willem pretended to choke, then had to stop himself

from actually falling off his chair on account of his exaggerated theatrics, which made everyone laugh.

"I remember lots of things from when I was a baby," Pieter unwisely insisted. "I remember crossing the Atlantic and Roelena throwing her tea cup overboard and then crying because she thought she was going to boat jail."

"No, you don't. You were six months old," Willem argued.

"But I *do* remember. Roelena, I was sitting on Moe's lap, wasn't I? And I saw you throw it over the railing."

"You did not, Pieter. You're being stupid."

"I am *not.*" Pieter insisted, raising his voice and leaning forward to glare at Willem. "You're just jealous because your memory is shit."

Roelena's mouth dropped open. Had Willem spoken in such a manner, she wouldn't have been shocked. But Pieter? "Pieter, what if Moe were to hear you talk like that?"

Pieter glanced warily towards the front room.

"She will hear because I'm gonna tell her," Willem threatened, half-rising from his chair.

"Don't you dare," Roelena warned. "Sit down, Willem."

"Why?" Willem demanded, reluctantly sinking back into his chair. "You're always taking his side. If I swear, I get in trouble. He swears and nothing happens."

"That is not true, Willem. You swear *all* the time, but you only get in trouble the few times you're caught."

Willem had the wherewithal to look mildly abashed. "*Ja,* maybe. But now Pieter's been caught, hasn't he?"

Clarence cleared his throat loudly. "I didn't hear any swearing." He looked innocently at Willem, then turned to wink at Pieter, who beamed up at him.

Willem groaned. "Great. You're taking his side, too?"

"I'm not taking any sides," Clarence stated, shaking his head. "I'm just saying that since my girl didn't hear any swearing, then neither did I. So, if your Moe were to come in and ask if any of us heard any swearing, I would have to answer the same as my girl."

When Clarence directed his humorous gaze to Roelena, she felt the warm glow that always ignited in her chest when Clarence looked at her that way. He'd just professed that he loved her for being kind, but Roelena knew that Clarence's well of kindness was ten times deeper than her own. One day, after Clarence was free of his commitment to his Canadian sponsor and free of the debt he was slowly repaying for his passage to Canada, they would marry. But when Clarence looked at her the way he was looking at her now? She wished for only one thing—that they marry tomorrow.

9

LETTER TO ROELENA FROM CONRAD

Dear Roelena,

Thank you for your letter of January 23. I do hope you enjoyed a wonderful birthday celebration and, as I stated in my card to you, I sincerely wish you a year of blessings.

I know you told me not to respond to your letter, but I feel I must say just a few things. First of all, I accept that your loyalty to Marliese and your corresponding anger following my letter dictates you withdraw your friendship from me. I simply want to say that it is my sincere hope that, with time, you find it in your heart to forgive me. I sorely miss your letters and would like nothing better than to resume our correspondence. At the same time, I entirely accept that you feel unable to continue our friendship. Perhaps this sounds strange, but I also admire you for your unwavering loyalty to Marliese, who most certainly deserves to be loved and treasured.

I want to also say that you are right on every count—I should have behaved in all the ways you outlined in your letter. A better man than me would have done so. The man I wish I was would have done so. I doubt that this short missive will change your low opinion of me, but please know that I shall spend the remainder of my lifetime striving to become that better man.

If there ever comes a time when you can find a small space in your heart to welcome back your remorseful cousin, please know I shall be overjoyed. I will always be your friend. That I promise.

I remain your loving cousin,

Conrad

10

THURSDAY, JULY 7

When the de Haas family emigrated to their farm near Sandpiper Lake in 1936, the Province of Alberta boasted two bustling cities, each with a population topping 80,000. Edmonton, located in the centre of the Province, and Calgary, nestled two hundred miles south in the foothills of the Canadian Rockies. The older of the two settlements, Fort Edmonton was home to rival fur trading companies as early as 1795. Eighty years later when the North West Mounted Police built Fort Calgary on the banks of the Bow River, they carved out a wagon trail from Fort Calgary to Fort Edmonton. This track came to be known as the Calgary and Edmonton Trail, or more simply, the C&E Trail. It linked Montana, the head of navigation on the Missouri River, with settlements in Alberta, including Fort Whoop-Up, which later became Lethbridge. By 1888, vehicles on the trail included freighter wagons—which took two weeks to transport their goods and passengers—and closed light stagecoaches—which were much faster and took only five days. In 1891 when a railway was constructed following the overall route of the C&E Trail, the stagecoach service ended and travel time between the two Forts was reduced to a mere twelve hours. In that same decade, a gravel road was built alongside the railway. This new road was first paved in the 1930s, then re-paved and renamed Highway 2 in 1945.

The de Haas homestead, ten miles west of the old C&E Trail, was equally distant from both Edmonton and Calgary. But if the family needed to visit a city, they always chose Edmonton because Anneke's brother Jan and his wife Stina had a farm a few miles east of the northern city.

On an early morning in July, Roelena, Clarence, Jakob, and Ingrid were on their way to link up with the C&E Trail for their trip to Edmonton driving Kees's 1941 four-door Ford sedan, with Ingrid upfront in the passenger seat and Roelena in the back with Clarence. They hadn't considered taking Jakob's 1932 Ford Model AA truck as it was notorious for breaking down; Sijmon spent as much time tinkering under the hood as Jakob spent driving it.

The two couples left the de Haas farm early before Sijmon, Willem, and Pieter had even finished the milking. They wanted to reach Edmonton by mid-morning to make the most of their two-day getaway. They would have supper and stay overnight at their *Oom* Jan and *Tante* Stina's, then complete a few tasks the next day—including indulging in a movie matinee—before returning to the farm late the next evening.

The main purpose of their outing, at least for Roelena and Clarence, was to purchase an affordable engagement ring.

Roelena had been surprised when Clarence showed up after supper a week ago Wednesday. Although they often saw each other on a week night in the summers when the evenings were long and the *kerk's* Young Peoples' Society met at the lake to play ball or have wiener roasts, they hadn't planned to meet that night. When Clarence showed up on their doorstep in Pierre Boutilier's old truck, Roelena was surprised, but she noticed that her *ouders* weren't. Anneke even seemed to be bursting with suppressed excitement. When Clarence somewhat formally asked Roelena to accompany him on a walk, Roelena finally realized what was about to happen and her heart seemed to give a joyous leap in her chest. They left the house and walked hand-in-hand, mostly in silence, across the north field to the knoll where one could see a twenty-mile stretch of undulating countryside to the north and west, including a slice of Sandpiper Lake. When they stopped on that hillock, Clarence dropped to one knee and looked up at Roelena, a hint of tears making the blue of his eyes glimmer. He spoke in a determined tone, although his voice had a distinct catch as he informed Roelena that she'd make him the happiest man alive if she agreed to marry him.

Of course Roelena said yes. She'd known Clarence would one day propose, but also knew he didn't feel free to officially ask for her hand in marriage until he was free and clear of his debt for his passage to Canada. What Roelena hadn't realized was that Clarence had strived to repay this loan by early June so he could propose to his girl on the exact date they'd met two years before. Initially, Roelena was surprised when Clarence didn't produce a ring, but then was pleased to learn he wanted to take her shopping in Red Deer so she could choose it herself.

Back at the house after they announced their welcome news to Roelena's parents and brothers, Anneke advised they shop for the ring in Edmonton instead of Red Deer, and then suggested they take Jakob and Ingrid along as chaperones for an overnight getaway. She shared that Jakob had been wanting to make a short trip away without the kids, and this news was the ideal opportunity.

They'd chosen a date when Jakob could be away from the de Haas farm for a couple days and Clarence could be excused from his duties on his sponsor's farm, where he had one more year to work before his contract was complete. During their two-day absence, fifteen-year old Margaret Langelaar would stay with Anneke in the big house, while Frank Steenbergen's two sisters—Lucy, who was twelve, and Hettie, who'd just turned sixteen—would babysit three-year-old Tomas and little Kees, who would have his first birthday in August.

Both couples were dressed in their Sunday best, the men in their suits and fedoras, and the women in dresses. The aquamarine trim on Roelena's cotton dress matched the buttons on the white summer cardigan she'd knit the winter before. As soon as they turned out of their driveway, Roelena leaned forward in her seat to address her sister-in-law, her tone filled with excitement.

"Ingrid, this is going to be so fun, isn't it? But won't it feel strange for you to be away from your *kinderen* overnight?" Roelena spoke in Dutch, the language her sister-in-law still preferred.

Jakob quickly answered Roelena's question before his wife had the chance, his tone a mix of serious intent and exaggerated playfulness. "Yes, it feels strange for Ingrid. But she is over-the-moon happy to have two days to devote entirely to her poor, neglected husband."

Jakob had been pleading with Ingrid for months to embark on an overnight outing away from their children. It wasn't until Roelena added her pleas—after all, Clarence and Roelena couldn't travel to the city alone—that Ingrid finally agreed.

Ingrid smiled indulgently at her husband's silly antics before turning to address Roelena. "To tell you the honest truth, it feels wretched. I know it's only been five minutes, but I'm already missing them." She had to raise her voice to drown out Jakob's protests. "However, I know my husband will be treating me like a queen for the next two days, which will make me forget all about how much I miss my *kinderen*."

"Indeed, your majesty," Jakob quipped in a grave, obedient tone. "But the real question is, will the *kinderen* even know we're away? Tomas thinks Hettie's purpose in life is to listen to everything he has to say. With undivided attention."

Tomas was a natural chatterbox. If there was no one available—or willing—to listen to him, he still talked—to his toys and books if he was inside the house, and to the bugs, spiders, and caterpillars he spied if he was amusing himself outside. He was a precocious child and had learned to form sentences early. He'd just turned three, but could communicate as well as a five-year-old.

Clarence was nodding his head in emphatic agreement. "That boy could chatter your ear off if you let him."

"I wonder where he gets *that* from?" Roelena stated dryly with a telling look at the back of her brother's head. She was reclined comfortably against the back seat, pleased to feel Clarence's arm settle around her shoulders. She gave her fiancée—she loved the sound of that word—an amused grin. "Wasn't it funny what Tomas said when we left?"

Clarence snorted in amused agreement, then addressed the occupants of the front seat. "I can't believe your three-year old son would instruct his parents to *zich gedragen*. He's a little *dominee,* instructing you to behave like that."

"That just shows how often we tell *him* to *zich gedragen,"* Ingrid interjected with a chuckle.

"Well, your kid makes me laugh every time I see him," Clarence stated.

"They're both adorable," Roelena stated with an indulgent aunt's pride, not wanting the baby to be left out of the admiration.

"They are, aren't they?" Ingrid agreed, her voice wavering as she blinked away tears.

Jakob glared at Roelena's reflection in the rear-view mirror. "If my wife cries, I will blame it on you, Roelena. And then I'll stop the car and make you get out. Clarence, don't think you can stop me."

"Jakob," Roelena leaned forward and slapped the back of her hand against her brother's shoulder. "You make it sound like I have made Ingrid cry. I would never."

"Hey, don't hit the driver. And that's a big, fat lie. How many times have I come into my kitchen to find you there, and Ingrid weeping?"

"Oh for goodness sake, Jakob," Ingrid protested. "You can't blame Roelena every time I shed a tear. You know I cry at the drop of a hat."

"Ingrid, your husband has a brain the size of a pea. He should spend less time joking and more time being a compassionate listener. Don't you agree?"

"Making someone laugh *is* a form of compassion," Jakob argued.

"Stop it, you two," Ingrid interrupted. She shifted so that she could regard Clarence who remained comfortably reclined behind her in the back seat. "Does it make you crazy, Clarence, when they natter at each other like that?"

"Nah. I figure Roelena is doing me a favour. She bickers with Jakob and gets it out of her system. And then she doesn't need to bicker with me."

"What?" Roelena briefly feigned dismay, before snuggling against Clarence's side.

"See?" Clarence said with a grin as he pulled her close. "With me, she's all sweetness."

"And why shouldn't I be? You treat me with respect. Unlike some people I won't bother to name."

"Jakob, don't." Ingrid interjected, holding up a finger. "I'm making the first rule of this outing. Jakob and Roelena, you are not allowed to bicker." Ingrid spoke over Jakob's protestations. "If you dare to argue with your sister, I swear Jakob, I will start talking about how much I miss the *kinderen*. And I won't stop."

They were approaching the junction that, once heading east, would intersect with Highway 2, the old C&E Trail. As Jakob slowed the car, he gave his sister a stern look in the rear-view mirror. "Roelena, you be nice to me and I'll be nice to you. Okay?"

"But Ingrid," Roelena protested. "He's making it sound like *I'm* the one who's not being nice to him. You can't expect me to let a statement like that go by, can you?"

Ingrid turned to Roelena with pleading puppy eyes.

Roelena laughed at her sister-in-law. "All right. But Jakob has to buy me a banana split," she quickly added.

Jakob waited until a truck passed, then turned east onto the wide, graveled road.

"He would be happy to buy you a banana split. Wouldn't you, dear?"

Jakob feigned a sickly sweet smile. "It would be my pleasure to buy my sister a banana split upon my royal-highness wife's command."

"What's a banana split?" Clarence asked.

"What's a banana split?" Jakob demanded. "Are you telling me your girlfriend—"

"Fiancée," Roelena interrupted.

"Fiancée…hasn't introduced you to the ultimate divine supreme-ness of a banana split?"

"Jakob," Ingrid practically choked. "Don't be so blasphemous!"

"Ja," Roelena declared. "If Pa heard you describe anything other than God as divine, he would be very disappointed."

"As if I'd say such things around Pa."

"Well, Jakob's not half as blasphemous as Marliese," Roelena pointed out with a laugh.

At her comment, Roelena felt Clarence stiffen, and she mentally kicked herself. She shouldn't have mentioned Marliese, but her friend's name had popped up naturally.

Roelena's friendship with her childhood friend was the only major sore spot between her and Clarence. Lately, Marliese's behaviour had changed, and not for the better. Marliese had become brittle over the past six months since receiving Conrad's letter. Where before she'd made outrageous statements for the sake of a good laugh, now she tended towards insensitivity, sometimes even cruelty, something Clarence couldn't abide. Marliese also smoked openly on the steps of the *kerk* after Sunday service, shocking the community, embarrassing her *Moeder,* and infuriating her rather terrifying *vader*. Even Anneke was concerned Marliese might become a bad influence, not because Roelena's behaviour had altered, but because Roelena defended Marliese and refused to change anything about their friendship. Roelena couldn't tell her *moeder* about Conrad, but she had told Anneke that Marliese's recent abrasiveness had to do with a disappointment over a man, assuring her *moeder* that this phase would pass. Roelena had also repeatedly tried talking to Marliese about her unwholesome behaviour and how it was negatively impacting their families and their community, but Marliese had begged Roelena not to turn into a self-righteous busybody and humourless prig like everyone else. Knowing the extent of Marliese's disappointment over Conrad, and also feeling somewhat responsible given that Conrad was Roelena's cousin, Roelena didn't have the heart to lecture her further.

But that didn't change the fact that Roelena was deeply concerned about Marliese, especially now that she'd begun dating one of the recent immigrants in their community. Wilfred Kampenaar had arrived the year before along with three other young men. From the start, Roelena hadn't liked

Wilfred, and neither, at least initially, had Marliese despite Wilfred being as handsome as a film star. But the arrogant and self-important man had pursued Marliese from the start. It had been a wasted effort then as Marliese was still corresponding with Conrad. But after getting her heart broken, Marliese stopped resisting the bumptious man's advances. Spending time with Wilfred seemed to bring out the worst in Marliese. Roelena didn't believe Marliese would have given him the time of day had she not been so vulnerable in those months following the receipt of Conrad's letter. The old Marliese had found Wilfred attractive, yes, but she hadn't tolerated his egotistical superiority. Now, she was as carelessly unkind as Wilfred.

Roelena had earlier made the mistake of sharing her concern about Marliese with Clarence, but their conversation only made Clarence reinforce his belief that Marliese was not a suitable friend for his girl. This discussion had resulted in their first serious argument. Regardless, Roelena refused to abandon Marliese, believing that her fun-loving, warm-hearted friend would re-surface, given time.

Roelena regretted mentioning Marliese, and quickly changed the subject back to food, a topic she knew was a favourite of Ingrid's who loved to cook and bake. It seemed all those years of starving during the war had inspired a fascination with food. The gaunt-looking young mother who'd arrived on their doorstep three years before had blossomed into a pleasingly plump woman. And Jakob encouraged her to cook and eat whatever she wanted, pleased that his wife would never again be so heartbreakingly skinny.

Roelena addressed her brother. "Jakob, we should go to that coffee shop that serves that amazing pecan pie. Do you remember where it is? I think I can find it. It's close to the University." Roelena was rarely in Edmonton more than once every one or two years, but she knew how to find that café.

"Good idea," Jakob said. He'd stopped the car at the intersection where the graveled road met Highway 2, and was waiting for a break in the traffic so he could turn north.

"Pecan pie," enthused Ingrid, her eyes lighting up. She turned to regard the passengers in the back seat, bracing her hand on the top of the bench as Jakob accelerated onto the paved road. "Have you tried pecan pie, Clarence?" she asked, knowing it wasn't something any Dutch housewife ever served in the Netherlands. She added in English. "It's delicious."

Roelena felt Clarence relax as the topic of conversation moved to sharing their favourite traditional Dutch foods, some of which they could replicate or purchase in Canada, but others only a distant memory. She sighed in contentment, leaning further into the hollow of Clarence's arm, but then sat up suddenly when she felt something change in the car's rhythmic motion.

"Whoa," Jakob said, signalling and slowing down. "I think we've got a flat."

"What? You can't be serious," Ingrid protested. She was used to having to pull off the road while in their old truck, which regularly broke down. But they'd taken Kees's car for this trip to the city because it was reliable. Yet now here they were, pulling to the side of the road the same as they did when traveling in their truck.

Jakob stopped on the wide shoulder and they all climbed out of the car, standing in a half circle near the ditch regarding the back, passenger-side flat tire. Vehicles on the highway continued to whiz by them.

Jakob stared moodily at the flat, tilting his hat back and scratching his forehead. "I don't believe it. This isn't supposed to happen in Pa's car."

"But it's not so bad," Ingrid said. "Nothing's wrong with the engine. This can be easily fixed, right?"

"Of course it can," answered Clarence in a cheerful tone. He moved to the back of the car and opened the trunk. "The sooner we change the tire the sooner we get moving." He lifted his head and looked over at Roelena, offering her a warm grin. "And the sooner we get a ring on that finger."

"How can I help?" Roelena asked, skipping over to Clarence's side, her eyes sparkling. Nothing would get her down. Not today.

Two minutes later they were once again standing in a semi-circle, only this time they were staring into the back of the car. Their faces bore a range of disgruntled expressions.

"I blame bloody Sijmon," Jakob muttered.

Clarence had removed the spare from where it perched against the back seat. It was propped on the pavement against the back bumper. Clarence had also revealed the compartment where the tools were kept. But the space for the jack was empty. And the tire couldn't be changed without the jack. They all knew Sijmon was likely to blame. He was the only mechanic in the family. He must have borrowed the jack to work on Jakob's truck and had forgotten to return it.

"Well, this is a pickle," Clarence observed.

"It's worse than a darn pickle," Jakob grumbled.

"We'll just have to wave down a car," Ingrid suggested, intent on defusing Jakob's growing annoyance. "A good Samaritan will lend us a jack."

"You mean all those good Samaritans in the cars whizzing past?" Jakob demanded in a testy tone.

"Would you stop to help if you saw a broken-down car with two capable-looking grown men standing beside it?" Ingrid shook her head. "I think not. You'd be thinking, *oh, those ladies don't need help. They have men with them.*"

Jakob made an irritated noise deep in his throat, obviously annoyed that his wife was right.

Ingrid turned and strode a few steps away from the back of the car, facing the oncoming cars. She raised an arm in an obvious request for help. The next two cars went by without slowing, but the third one, a shiny green Packard, turned its indicator light on and slowed, pulling onto the shoulder and stopping behind them.

When the well-dressed young couple emerged from the car and approached them, Roelena immediately recognized the woman. It was their neighbour, Patricia Talbot. She looked as modern and stylish as the women in the advertisements in the *Ladies Home Journal*. She was wearing pleated red trousers with a black and white striped sleeveless shell, a red stretchy hairband holding back her blond curls. Her lipstick matched her hairband, and the black-and-white kitten-heeled sandals matched her shell. Roelena felt her cheeks flush as Patricia approached, seeing in her mind's eye Patricia in the woods with her blouse open and that tall, dark-haired man bending his head towards her exposed breasts. That scene no longer haunted Roelena the way it had in those first months, but she'd certainly never forgotten it. In the years since then on those rare occasions when she saw Patricia in town, that scene in the woods would always replay in her mind. Perhaps because of that, she'd never said more than hello. And now Roelena would have to converse with Patricia while at the same time trying to banish the disturbing images of that amorous scene she'd witnessed all those years ago.

Roelena's gaze went to the man who accompanied Patricia. He was tall with wavy brown hair, but he wasn't the man who'd been with Patricia in the woods that day; Roelena had never seen him before or since. This man was offering them a friendly smile, shaking first Jakob's then Clarence's hands, and nodding politely to Ingrid and Roelena before asking how they could help. When he learned they had a flat tire but were missing a jack, he immediately turned to retrieve the jack from his own car.

Roelena could no longer ignore Patricia. She wished her cheeks weren't flaming, and could only hope her companions didn't notice.

"Hello," Patricia said. "I don't believe we've ever formally met, but I know who you are. My father has the farm west of you. John Talbot? I'm his daughter, Patricia. Patty."

"Yes, of course," Jakob said. "That explains why you look familiar. This is my wife, Ingrid. And my sister Roelena and her fiancée, Clarence."

After introductions had been made, Clarence turned to wheel the spare tire closer to the flat while Jakob claimed the tire wrench from the back of the Ford and went to loosen the lug nuts.

Patricia's eyes briefly flickered to Roelena's bare left hand. "How long have you been engaged?" she asked, her tone friendly.

Roelena lifted her left hand as if in apology, and said, "Oh, just since last week. We're heading to Edmonton to buy a ring." She felt gauche beside this stylish woman, and wondered if her discomfort would have been less had she not witnessed Patricia being made love to by a strange man in the woods.

"How wonderful," Patricia enthused, stepping to the side when the man she was with went past her carrying the jack. "We bought my ring in Edmonton at the Woodward's department store." She held out her hand where a flashy diamond solitaire sat. "I would highly recommend going there," she added as both Ingrid and Roelena admired her ring. "They had lots of selection and good prices."

"Thank you," Roelena said, knowing she wouldn't go

anywhere near a store that sold diamonds that expensive looking. She didn't know the cost of Patricia's ring, but whatever it was, it would be well beyond what Clarence could afford.

"When are you getting married?" Patricia asked.

"Next year. Either before harvest or after. And you?"

Roelena had seen that Patricia only wore an engagement ring, not a wedding band.

"This year, after harvest. October 22," Patricia gushed. "Will you marry in your Pine Glade church?"

"Yes. And you?" Roelena wished her vocabulary hadn't suddenly become so limited.

"In town at St. Andrew's United," Patricia answered.

"Oh, is that the church of red brick?" Ingrid asked in halting English. "With the coloured windows? Very beautiful?"

Ingrid's English had improved over the last few years, but she still wasn't fluent so it was mostly Roelena who conversed with Patricia, although their pretty blond neighbour did most of the talking. They learned that Patricia's husband-to-be was named Roland Green and he worked in Calgary as a petroleum engineer, an occupation Roelena had to translate as best she could for Ingrid. Once married, the couple would live in Calgary, and Patricia couldn't wait to leave her parents' farm.

Twenty minutes later, with the spare mounted and the flat stowed in the Ford's trunk, they shook hands once again before climbing back into their respective cars.

When they were once again motoring down the highway, Ingrid turned in her seat and regarded Roelena. "Why did you seem so out of sorts when we were talking to Patricia?"

"Oh." Roelena felt herself blush again as she stammered a response. "Only...well...it's just that she was congratulating me about being engaged, and I don't have a ring yet." Roelena couldn't look at Ingrid or Clarence, knowing her words sounded falsely shallow.

But Clarence didn't notice. Instead, he lifted his arm and wrapped it around her shoulders, pulling her close. "Well, we'll be remedying that before the day is out, won't we sweetheart?"

11
FRIDAY, JULY 8

"Do you love it?" Roelena asked Clarence.

It was Friday afternoon and they were sitting in a small café in downtown Edmonton. They had just come out of the matinee showing of *The Broken Arrow,* a film about a soldier in the American west in the days before the pioneers had built their towns and cities. The man had fallen in love with a young Indian woman, but their relationship had been fraught with barriers and hurdles. In the end, as the woman lay dying from an arrow wound, both Ingrid and Roelena were sobbing uncontrollably, along with every other woman in the theatre.

Now, tears forgotten, they were indulging in the promised banana split before making the two-hour return journey to the farm.

"It's delicious, sweetheart," Clarence responded with enthusiasm.

"It *is* delicious," Ingrid agreed in English. She was savoring every mouthful, and also regularly stealing chocolate sauce from Jakob's dish to augment her dwindling supply.

"Hey. *My* banana split, *my* chocolate sauce," Jakob insisted in English as he moved his dessert out of her reach.

"But I love the chocolate sauce best," Ingrid pleaded, switching to Dutch.

"So do I."

"As much as I love it?"

Jakob made the mistake of looking at Ingrid. From the first moment he'd seen her that day in Friesland, he'd been helpless to resist her. Jakob sighed, then grumbled in feigned annoyance as he let Ingrid scoop most of his chocolate sauce into her dish. "But if you get my chocolate sauce, then I get your pineapple sauce."

"Fine by me," Ingrid promptly agreed, scooping her pineapple sauce into his dish.

Clarence eyed Roelena suspiciously. "I don't have to give you *my* chocolate sauce, do I?"

Roelena chuckled. "Not after buying me this ring," she practically sang, holding out her left hand so that the ray of sunshine coming through the window made the tiny diamond sparkle.

Roelena had been very deliberate about her choice. They'd been in a crowded little jewelry store on Jasper Avenue where she'd pointed to the rings with the smallest diamonds, requesting the price from the obliging jeweler before agreeing to try them on. She'd finally decided on one that fit her finger perfectly and was priced at only forty-two dollars. It was neither the prettiest nor the flashiest ring in the showcase, but it was the one she knew Clarence could afford; therefore, it was the one she wanted and the one she intended to always treasure.

"But Clarence," Roelena teased, a note of feigned concern in her voice. "You may have to give your chocolate sauce to Ingrid."

Ingrid laughed at Clarence's look of exaggerated dismay.

"Don't worry. I'll commandeer my husband's chocolate sauce, but I couldn't possibly take yours…unless you freely offered, of course."

But Clarence was nothing if not generous. "Uh…you can have my chocolate sauce if you like, Ingrid," he said, sliding his dish towards his future sister-in-law.

"I'm kidding, Clarence."

"No, I insist. I won't be accused of being less of a gentleman than that *boer* husband of yours."

"Well…if you insist." Ingrid dipped the tip of her spoon into Clarence's chocolate sauce, but when she tasted it, she wrinkled her nose in aversion. "No thanks. Your sauce doesn't taste as good as Jakob's."

Ingrid noticed Roelena dreamily eyeing her ring again, angling her hand so the ring caught the sunlight. "Roelena, do you love it?"

Roelena smiled widely, unable to lift her gaze from the ring. "I do. It's absolutely perfect," she stated in utter contentment.

During the return journey, the two couples began sharing stories of their journeys across the Atlantic.

"We hit a terrific storm and most of the passengers were ill," Clarence was saying. "I didn't know I had natural sea legs, but I sure was glad to discover them."

Ingrid was sitting sideways in the front seat, her left arm draped across the back of the bench. "I definitely don't have sea legs. Our Atlantic crossing was calm. But the North Sea? That was awful." She wagged her head. "The sea was vicious, and I got so sick. I don't know how I would've cared for Tomas if I hadn't met Sophie." She addressed Roelena. "I told you about her, right?" At Roelena's nod, Ingrid continued. "Sophie didn't get sick, and neither did Tomas. You know, Roelena, I just realized, Sophie reminds me of your friend, Marliese."

Roelena froze, wishing Ingrid hadn't mentioned Marliese, but Ingrid followed this statement with a question for Clarence.

"Did they have a band playing when you docked? When we docked, they were playing, *Here Comes the Bride*."

From behind the wheel, Jakob glanced briefly at Ingrid. "I don't remember you telling me that."

She nodded at Jakob, then turned her attention back to Clarence.

"There was a band playing, but I don't recall the song. Did you depart from Rotterdam?"

"No. From Antwerp, in Belgium."

"What was the name of your ship?" Clarence asked.

"Well, from Antwerp to Southampton we were on the *Lady Rodney*. From there to Halifax, we were on the RMS *Aquitania*, which thankfully was much bigger. And there were no storms on the Atlantic."

"We docked in Halifax, too," Roelena said. "Then spent the day walking around. I remember Moe commenting on the lovely houseplants in the windows but then shaking her head in disapproval at how badly the curtains needed a wash."

Ingrid laughed. "I can hear your Moe saying exactly that. Most Dutch *huisvrouws* keep a clean, tidy house, don't they?"

"Did you have time to look around Halifax?" Roelena asked.

"No. I only saw the docks and the train station. There was this huge crowd of people waving at us from the dock, cheering as if we were the heroes of war returning home instead of a ship full of war brides."

"One of the first ships, I think," Jakob stated. "That's why there was fanfare."

"That makes sense," Clarence stated. "We were one of the first immigrant ships since before the war, and there was a lot of fanfare when we arrived in Montreal. But we were cheering louder than anyone on the docks. Ingrid, you can count your blessings you didn't leave Rotterdam on June 14, 1947 on *The* Waterman." A note of disgust crept into Clarence's tone. "And not because of the storm, but because there were not enough toilets. And the ones they had, backed up. Ugh, disgusting! I stayed out on deck as much as I could. I witnessed many a head hanging over a railing. I even saw one man loose his false teeth. Hey!" Clarence turned to Roelena. "Just like your tea cup. His teeth are on the bottom of the Atlantic."

Ingrid looked horrified. "Oh, no. How did that poor man get his teeth replaced?"

"I'm guessing he sought the help of the Red Cross volunteers when we docked in Montreal."

"I remember some people being seasick on our voyage, but not a lot," Jakob said.

"Well, on the *Waterman,* there were only about two hundred of us who weren't sick, which meant more than six hundred were confined to bed. Us healthy ones volunteered to carry messages between the women and children's quarters and the men's."

Roelena wasn't at all surprised her kind and outgoing fiancée had volunteered to help his fellow passengers on what must've been a trying journey, but she was puzzled about his reference to separate quarters. "But why would families be separated?" she asked.

"Ja," Jakob said with a frown, keeping his eyes on the busy highway. "We were able to room together as a family."

"Because the *Waterman* served as a troop ship during the

war. It still had huge open areas filled with bunks and hammocks. There wasn't any privacy, so they put the women and children in one section and the men in another."

"So what messages did you deliver?" Ingrid asked.

Clarence snorted. "Oh, my! Some I wouldn't dare repeat verbatim, like the one *huisvrouw* who told me to tell her *man* to jump overboard. Except she sprinkled that with words that scorched even my ears. I'm not joking," he insisted when the others hooted with laughter.

"I spent two days on a barge," Ingrid argued with a smile. "I doubt there's any swear words you could say that I haven't heard."

"Well, that may be true, but Roelena here is an innocent. And I want to keep her that way." Clarence wrapped both arms around Roelena and planted a kiss on the tip of her nose.

Roelena wished they were alone so she could kiss him back properly. Instead, she asked, "How was the food on your crossing? Ours wasn't very good."

"Fantastic. Although that's only because I hadn't had white bread since before the war. Later, when everyone got their sea legs, the food lines were long, but I remember it always being worth the wait."

"And the worst thing would've been the toilets," Ingrid stated. "It sounds awful."

Clarence pulled a face. "Worse than awful. When we finally got to Montreal, the senseless powers-that-be had a welcoming ceremony. There were lots of boats in the harbour, all different sizes, tooting their horns. Real festive. Crowds on the dock were waving and cheering. They even had reporters there from newspapers. The Dutch Ambassador to Canada came on board and gave a speech from the bridge. And another man, from the Immigration Department

I think, gave a speech in English. But all we wanted was to get off that stinking ship."

"We didn't have speeches, did we Jakob?"

"Not that I can remember."

"What were the speeches about?" Ingrid asked.

"Oh, just how Canada welcomes the Dutch because we're industrious and hard-working. And how important it is for us now to become loyal Canadians. And there were men and women from the Dutch Christian Reformed Church on the dock, handing out mimeographed sheets as we got off the boat. I kept mine; it's in my Bible at home. It says: *Be sure to use patience and diligence as you move into the occupation we have arranged for you. And if you meet with difficulties, don't forget the Dutch proverb: The persistent one wins.* I took that to heart, see? I persistently pursued Roelena, and now I have her."

Roelena turned her face to kiss Clarence again, happiness bubbling in her veins. She loved being engaged to this man. And she couldn't wait to marry him.

"We're just grateful you're willing to take her off our hands," Jakob teased.

"Hey!" Roelena protested, sitting forward. "You promised to be nice. Didn't he, Ingrid?"

"Oops, I forgot. But Clarence, you said you docked in Montreal? Not Halifax. That's at least five hundred miles west of Halifax, isn't it?"

"I think so. Why?"

Jakob harrumphed. "We should've docked in Montreal. It would've shortened our train ride by at least a couple days."

"But you arrived in April." Clarence stated.

"*Ja.* So?"

"The Saint Lawrence Seaway would've still been frozen in April. Well, parts of it, anyway."

"Good point," Jakob conceded with a nod.

"I wonder why my ship went to Halifax then," Ingrid said.

"We docked in September. And then spent five days on the train. Even though I knew it would be that long, the distance is incomprehensible when you come from the Netherlands, isn't it? Mind you, if we hadn't had to stop every five minutes to let off a bride, the trip might have been shorter."

"I recall getting really bored on the train." Roelena distinctly remembered the endlessness of that train trip even though she'd only been nine-years old. "Moe was cranky, probably on account of trying to make Willem behave. He was just a toddler, but he was a handful. But it's a long time for a child to be cooped up inside. It's probably good, Ingrid, that Tomas was a baby during your trip."

"Yes. Some of the children on the train did get a little wild. And noisy. But that wasn't the worst part of my journey." Ingrid shook her head emphatically.

Clarence pulled a sympathetic face. "Backed-up toilets on the train?"

Ingrid chuckled. "No, the toilets worked fine. It was the awful husbands."

"But I thought your traveling companions were all war brides," Clarence said.

Roelena realized she'd never shared Ingrid's account of her sister-in-law's journey to Canada with her fiancée. She knew what Ingrid was about to say, but was nevertheless interested.

"Some of these women hadn't seen their husbands for over two years, or longer," Ingrid explained. "Some claimed they could barely remember the sound of his voice. A few of the women even admitted they were dreading getting off the train. They were terrified of the life they had to face with a man they'd married so recklessly in the craziness of the war. Most, me included," Ingrid said proudly, reaching out a hand and briefly touching her fingertips to Jakob's neck above his shirt collar, "were eager to reunite with their husbands."

Jakob smiled and lifted one hand from the steering wheel to press his wife's palm against his cheek, planting a kiss on Ingrid's fingers before releasing her hand.

"Unlike some of those brides, I was eager to start my life here. And the way Jakob greeted me at the station in Edmonton was exactly how I imagined all the brides would be greeted. With delight, and affection, and hugs, and kisses. Even tears."

"And flowers," Jakob stated.

Ingrid laughed. "Yes, and flowers." She turned to Clarence. "But I say it was awful because some of those men only shook their wife's hand instead of hugging or even kissing them. Can you imagine? And a handful of the husbands didn't touch their wife at all. Not even their hands. It was heart-breaking. I've often wondered about those girls, especially the ones who were greeted without a drop of emotion. Young women embarking on a new life in a vast, strange country without even a hug. Can you imagine? And if there was no affection on the station platform, did it come later? I mean, there had to have been affection at some point, or why had they married?" Ingrid shook her head. "I hadn't expected to see that lack of love. I'd assumed all war brides were happy, like me. And my friend Sophie."

Roelena glanced out the window at the passing scenery, noticing the sign for Ponoka. She remembered her Pa telling her that the odd-sounding name was an Indian word that meant elk. She also recalled him saying that a Dutch Christian Reformed family had recently settled there, but they were too far away from Pine Glade to come to *kerk*, and that he'd promised to visit them once a month for Christian fellowship.

"Did you see any icebergs?" Jakob was asking Clarence, then immediately added, "Oh, you wouldn't have. You crossed in June, right?"

"Yes, but we did see icebergs. The deckhands told us it was unusual in June, but it had been an unseasonably cold spring. That was a fascinating sight, but also pretty daunting considering what happened to the Titanic."

"I crossed in September, and didn't see any icebergs," Ingrid stated.

"You know what has always puzzled me?" Clarence asked, after a moment of silence. "The seagulls. They stayed with us from The Netherlands all the way to Canada. It was as if they were immigrating, too. I've often wondered, though, were they Dutch seagulls? Or Canadian seagulls?"

The rest of the drive flew by. It seemed only a short while later they were turning into their drive, Ingrid impatient to reunite with her children and Roelena eager to show her *moeder* the beautiful engagement ring she'd chosen.

12

FRIDAY, AUGUST 26

The chokecherry tree is one of the most widespread in North America. It flowers in June and by late August provides a feast of berries that grow in drooping clusters up to six inches long, with each cluster containing eight to twenty miniature cherries. Although a riverside shrub, the trees thrive in fields, on roadsides, and at fencerows and forest edges, and produces their best fruit when exposed to long-term sunlight. Perhaps best of all, these small trees—some would argue they're merely bushes—are devoid of thorns, making the berries easy for harvesters to access.

A staple for Indigenous tribes, this fruit was pounded flat and dried in the sun. European settlers harvested them as well, making jam, jelly, syrup, wine, and juice. Although the berries were easy to harvest, pickers had to contend with the unpleasantness of mosquitoes pestering them, as well as competing with a multitude of animals—deer, bears, chipmunks, raccoons, deer mice, and a wide variety of birds—who also feasted on the ripe berries.

Roelena picked a wide variety of wild berries throughout

the summer—wild raspberries, blueberries, strawberries, Saskatoon berries, and chokecherries—and often rode to a berry patch on one of the farm horses. She especially loved chokecherries not only because they were tasty, abundant, and easy to harvest, but because their hardy outer skins meant they'd keep for days after collection, giving her lots of time to preserve them. At their juiciest when over ripe, the ideal time to harvest the abundant chokecherries was late August and early September when their skin was dark purple, almost black.

Roelena was limited not by how many berries were available for picking, but by how many berries she could carry home again. On this particular afternoon, her chore of harvesting the almost over-ripe chokecherries was lightened on account of Marliese being available to help. The young women would ride two of the horses down to the creek that ran through the north field of the Trunkett farm, two miles due east of the de Haas homestead. Mr. Trunkett was an old bachelor farmer who, years ago, had given the de Haas children permission to swim in his creek, pick berries from the bushes on his lands, search for arrowheads in his plowed fields, and set snares and shoot magpies in the small woodland area near an abandoned beaver pond.

Because Anneke was confined to bed after a bad angina attack more than three weeks before, Marliese had volunteered to stay with Roelena, although her underlying motivation was to get away from her nagging spinster sister and irascible father. Marliese had been helping Roelena with the household chores, including canning and bread-baking, even the dreaded washing on Tuesday. That morning, they'd canned six jars of green beans and another six jars of applesauce. Now, with the dinner dishes done after the mid-day meal and Kees in the house to help Anneke if needed, Roelena and Marliese had the afternoon to themselves.

After changing into light-weight cotton trousers and short-sleeved blouses, the girls left the house with a two-gallon aluminum pail in each hand, pleased that their afternoon's work took them out of the stuffy farmhouse and into the summer sunshine. Roelena intended to use the chokecherries to make a huge batch of pancake syrup. After washing the berries thoroughly, removing any twigs, leaves, and bugs, Roelena would add some of the boiled apple juice she'd put aside to improve the flavour of the wild berry and let them simmer on the stove for a few hours. Once cooled, she'd fill cheesecloth bags and get one of the boys to squeeze out the juice, later boiling the liquid with sugar to make the pancake syrup and feeding the pulp left in the bag to the pigs.

Pieter was waiting for them on the drive, holding the horses he'd caught and bridled, Smokey for Marliese and the more temperamental Ginger for Roelena. The girls didn't bother with saddles but rode bareback. Pieter gave them a leg up, then handed up the pails, their handles tied with a length of twine which they draped over the horses' withers, letting the buckets hang by their knees. They chatted happily as they kicked their mounts into a steady walk down the drive and onto the dirt road. Each time a vehicle approached, they steered their mounts into the ditch and waited for the vehicle to pass, waving away the dust cloud before guiding the horses back onto the road.

Thirty minutes later they were at the creek on Bachelor Trunkett's farm. They tied their mounts to nearby saplings, letting the horses graze. Before approaching the chokecherry bushes, they kicked off their shoes and rolled up their trouser legs, wading into the cold, pebble-bottomed creek and scooping up handfuls of the clear water to quench their thirst.

Soon after, their canvas shoes back on their damp feet, they each tied an empty pail around their waist with a second length of twine Roelena had brought. Then, with both hands free, they began stripping the miniature cherries from the bushes, quickly and proficiently, pausing every now and then to swat at a pesky mosquito. When needed, one of the girls would hold aside a branch so the other could reach a particularly full cluster hidden within. It wasn't long before they'd each filled a pail, depositing their full pails in the shade before tying their second bucket around their waists.

Away from the farmhouse and at no risk of being overhead, the friends chatted freely, their talk shifting to the recent Young Peoples' Society rally that had taken place during the August long weekend at the Sandpiper Lake Bible Camp. Roelena had only been able to attend for one day and night, sleeping head-to-head with Marliese in bunks in the girls' cabin. Anneke hadn't been well, and Roelena couldn't be spared for more than a day, but Roelena had made the most of her short get-a-way, making new friends and catching up with old acquaintances from their sister churches. The numbers of young people who attended the rally had grown considerably over the last few years thanks to new immigrants, most of whom were young men. While picking the berries, the girls passed the time dissecting the personalities and characteristics of their fellow singles.

But when Marliese proclaimed how much she missed her boyfriend Wilfred, who was away on a month-long trades course, Roelena frowned, absently encouraging a stem to release its cluster of berries before plopping them into her pail. "I can't see what there is to miss," she grumbled. It was an unkind comment, she knew, but it was also honest.

"Don't you miss Clarence when you don't see him?" Marliese challenged.

Roelena's hands paused as she looked over at Marliese. "That's hardly the same thing," she commented, resuming her task.

"It *is* the same."

"No. Clarence and I are engaged. You and Wilfred have been dating for only a few months."

"Fine then, it's not the same." Marliese said in a snappy tone, then added. "Wilfred adores me. And I miss being adored. I *like* being adored. As do you."

It was obvious to anyone who saw Marliese and Wilfred together that Wilfred was over the moon in love with her, but it wasn't until Conrad had broken Marliese's heart that Marliese allowed Wilfred to woo her. Early in their courtship, Roelena had cautioned Marliese, saying that just because things hadn't worked out with Conrad, that was no reason to take up with a man as unpleasant as Wilfred. She hoped the courtship would be short-lived given Wilfred's obnoxious personality. But Marliese had simply shrugged and indicated that the sooner she was proposed to—by a non-farmer—the sooner she could leave her parents' house.

Roelena made an effort to keep her tone neutral. "The difference is I adore Clarence as much as he adores me. You can't say the same about Wilfred."

"So?"

"If you don't adore him, why do you miss him? Why are you dating him?" When Marliese didn't immediately respond, Roelena looked over and saw her friend frowning. In annoyance? Or was Marliese simply pensive and thoughtful as she considered her answer?

Marliese finally responded. "If the fact that a man is madly in love with me isn't sufficient reason to date him, then factor in that Wilfred isn't a farmer. And he's ambitious. And he's a dreamboat."

He *was* handsome, Roelena had to admit, plopping a handful of berries into her pail. And he wasn't a farmer, which was important to Marliese. Wilfred had a good job as a maintenance man at the federally run Agricultural

Research Station, and lodged in town. But he was not ambitious, at least not how Roelena defined ambition. He was competitive and a sore loser, as evidenced by the recent ball game they'd played at the Young Peoples' Society Rally. He was also thoroughly opinionated and obnoxious, and Roelena didn't understand why Marliese dated him.

When she spoke, Roelena didn't bother to hide her dislike. "I'd call him overly competitive, not ambitious."

Marliese pushed against a branch to reach a thick cluster of berries. When she responded, her tone held a defensive edge. "He *is* ambitious. He may only be a carpenter right now, but his supervisor sees his potential. That's why he's been sent on this course. He'll be a manager one day. You'll see. And that's because he's ambitious—intent on rising above the competition. And he will be successful in the long run because he's persistent and knows how to get what he wants." Marliese paused, then added in a lighter tone. "Besides, he's not a farmer."

"I wish you wouldn't make it seem like farmers are beneath you."

Marliese scoffed. "You know I don't think that. But you also know I'm not cut out to be a farmer's wife. And anyway, I like that Wilfred has goals. And he doesn't care what other people think. That's admirable." She paused, then added almost cautiously, "He's also a *really* good kisser."

Roelena laughed aloud at that comment, it was so typical Marliese. She'd frequently heard her friend make these same types of comments in the past, but not in reference to Wilfred. Marliese had kissed more than her fair share of the young men in their circle. And after kissing them, she slotted them into categories of bad, sloppy, good, and really good kissers. Roelena had much less experience with kissing than Marliese; she'd only kissed two men, Geert and Clarence. But even with her limited experience, she understood why kissing was different from one man to the next. She would never say it aloud—she found the topic far too personal—but to herself she admitted Geert had fallen into the sloppy kisser category while Clarence exceeded—by leaps and bounds—the really good kisser category.

"I wish you'd categorize men by how they make you feel and how well they treat you instead of how good or bad they are at kissing."

"I tried that. It didn't end well," Marliese stated in a neutral tone.

Roelena stopped picking and stared over at her friend, who didn't stop what she was doing. "Marliese, I know Conrad ended up being the worst kind of cad, but that's—"

"He's not a cad," Marliese insisted, keeping her eyes on her busy hands.

Roelena huffed impatiently, turning her attention to the berries within her reach. "It makes me so angry when you insist on defending him." Roelena hadn't told Marliese about the letter she'd recently received from her cousin. Nor would she.

"Be angry then, if you choose," Marliese said, her tone sharp. "I'll never believe he's a cad. He's wonderful." Then she added in a whisper, "He's perfect."

Roelena wasn't sure if Marliese had meant for her to hear that last comment, but she wanted to shout, *he's nowhere near perfect!* Instead she said, "Obviously you're still in love with Conrad. But then it makes no sense whatsoever for you and Wilfred to be courting."

"Of course it does."

"What do you mean?" When the juice from a handful of burst berries stained her palm, Roelena realized she was crushing the hardy cherries in her annoyance. She lightened her touch and continued picking.

"Isn't it obvious?"

Roelena suddenly felt as annoyed as if she was arguing with Willem. "No, Marliese. It's not obvious. That's why I'm asking."

"I saw the wedding announcement," Marliese confessed in a soft tone.

Roelena's hands stilled. They'd received the announcement card from her Aunty Wilma in July for the September wedding. She hadn't intended for Marliese to see it.

"How did you find it?"

"When you went down to the cellar after supper on Tuesday, I asked Sijmon if he'd received a wedding announcement from Conrad. He showed it to me."

"Marliese." Roelena starred at her friend who seemed overly intent on the berry bushes despite her sluggish fingers. "I didn't want you to see it because I thought it would make you sad." Roelena frowned, recollecting something from earlier that week. "Wait. Is that why you insisted on taking the clothes off the line by yourself after I came up from the cellar?" It had puzzled Roelena why Marliese had been a little snappy about not needing Roelena's help to retrieve the clean laundry. Now she understood.

"I just needed to shed a few tears without anyone seeing," Marliese said. She must have felt the intensity of Roelena's stare as she finally turned, dropping her hands and meeting Roelena's gaze. "He's getting married in *eight days,* Roelena."

Roelena ticked her tongue, but spoke in a gentle tone. "Marliese, you'll never get over him with that kind of talk."

Marliese looked away for a moment, shaking her head and crossing her arms before refocusing on Roelena. "But you don't understand, Roelena. You think a day will come when I'll be able to say I'm over him."

"I know it seems impossible now, but that day *will* come."

"Why? Because you got over Geert?" Marliese snapped. "You can't compare what I went through with Conrad to what you had with Geert. It's ridiculous. It's like comparing apples and...I don't know. The moon! Honestly, Roelena. You're such an innocent."

It was easy for Roelena to dismiss anything hurtful Marliese said because she saw the gaping, raw wound in her friend's heart. Although, Marliese was right; Roelena was an innocent. And she had indeed been comparing her ridiculous disappointment all those years ago following the end of her and Geert's non-courtship with Marliese's disappointment following Conrad's devastating news. Apples and moons were not in the same category.

Both girls remained silent as they resumed picking. For a time, the only sound was that of the berries dropping into the pails.

Eventually Roelena asked, "What did you mean when you said *of course* it made sense that you should be dating Wilfred while you're still in love with Conrad?"

Marliese answered in a flat tone. "Just that Wilfred's nothing like Conrad."

"Exactly. That's my point."

"No, Roelena," Marliese said softly. "That's *my* point."

Roelena dropped her hands, lightly resting them on the edges of her pail as she frowned pensively at the branches, but then her face cleared when she finally realized what Marliese was saying. If Marliese couldn't have Conrad, then she didn't want to be with a man who reminded her of Conrad. She wanted to be with someone who was opposite to Conrad. Well, Roelena thought, Wilfred was definitely nothing like Conrad, although they were both scoundrels in their own way.

Roelena stepped to the side and distractedly began harvesting a fresh cluster of cherries. "But Wilfred isn't..." She let her words trail off.

"Nice?" Marliese said, then shrugged. "I actually know

that. But at least he's not a farmer."

"And that's enough?"

"No. He's a good kisser, and..." Marliese hesitated before adding, "He also knows what he's doing in bed. Not that we've ever done it in a bed." Marliese began jerking the berries from the clusters in rhythm with her clipped words. "The car, yes. The woods, yes. The beach, yes. The river bank, yes. Behind the—"

Roelena had been standing motionless, staring at her friend, but now finally found her voice. *"Marliese!* Are you saying that you're ...?" Roelena couldn't say the words. She briefly pictured Patricia Talbot on that long ago day in the woods, but banished the image before she could replace the woodland lovers with an image of Marliese and Wilfred.

Marliese stopped what she was doing and turned to regard her friend with a look of defiance. "Yes, Roelena. I am. We are having sex. There. I said it. We've been having sex for two months now. And, frankly, it's amazing. And not just because it feels good, but when he's got his hands all over me, I'm not thinking about Conrad. And that, *just that,"* she made a sharp, pointing gesture with her finger, "is a relief and makes it all worth it."

"But Marliese! What if you get pregnant? You'll have to marry him."

"Would that be so bad? It would get me out of the house." Marliese delivered this information with indifference.

"But... you don't love him." Roelena was still staring at her friend in bewildered dismay.

Marliese's tone was accepting. "So? Why does it matter that I don't love him? I'm never going to love a man like I love Conrad. It's just not possible. And Wilfred makes me forget about all those disappointments, even if only for a short time. Besides, I've discovered that I like sex." Marliese seemed to be contemplating the berry bushes, then said.

"Maybe that's the real reason why I'm missing him," she mused.

"I'm just so..." Roelena shook her head and turned back to face the berry bushes, but she couldn't seem to remember what she was supposed to be doing. Marliese's shocking news had left her suddenly incapable of performing even the simple task of choosing which berries to pick.

Roelena startled when she felt a hand on her arm and realized Marliese had come to stand beside her.

When she spoke, Marliese's tone was uncharacteristically apologetic. "Roelena, I'm sorry. I didn't mean to shock you. Although I am relieved you know. I've been wanting to tell you."

"Well, don't expect *me* to be glad you told me." Roelena shook her head, still bewildered by what she'd learned.

"Do you hate me?"

Roelena snorted, looked unseeingly towards the creek, then back to Marliese. "I should."

"But you don't?"

Roelena sighed, then patted the hand Marliese kept on her forearm. "No. But I am worried about you. What if you get pregnant?"

Marliese lifted her hand from Roelena's arm and waved it dismissively. She kept her focus on Roelena though, regarding her with a troubled gaze. "You're disappointed."

Roelena could see the deep well of sadness in her friend's eyes and hated Conrad for putting it there. No matter how unchristian it was to hate someone, she really hated her cousin. And she hated Wilfred, too, for showing up at a time when Marliese was at her most vulnerable. She heaved a sigh. "No, Marliese," she lied. "Not disappointed. Sad, though. Really sad."

Marliese lifted a shoulder in a listless shrug. *"Ik ook,"* she said, then repeated in English, "Me too."

13

LETTER TO ROELENA FROM HENDRIK

Dear Roelena,

Thank you for your letter of December 7 describing the Sinterklaas celebrations at the farm. I can picture the excitement of Tomas, with kleine *Kees trotting after him, searching for the note from Sinterklaas to find out where Zwarte Piet hid the presents, and of course eating too many* pepernoten*. I joined the Radstaak's for their Sinterklass Eve celebration. Clarence and Gertrude have only Davy, who's a little older than* kleine *Kees, but his sister was there with her five children. They reminded me of the Langelaar's with their noise and ruckus, but it was very enjoyable to witness their excitement.*

You must've heard by now of my telephone call to Pa and Moe sharing the good news about my engagement to Gladys. I feel so blessed by God that I will have such a faithful and hard-working woman as my wife who also has the ability to laugh easily and the steadfast faith and innate wisdom to guide our future family in the ways of the Lord. No doubt Moe told you that we planned to marry next fall after the harvest, but I'm sad to report that her family has been given some terrible news. Cornelius, her father, has been having respiratory issues, but we've just learned he is in the advanced stages of lung cancer and does not have long to live. Gladys is devastated, as can be expected. She's the youngest and he's always doted on her. We've thus decided to marry right away so that her father can be there, if not to walk her down the aisle, at least to give her away. Our wedding date is January 15, which is less than four weeks away. I pray to God that Cornelius is able to attend because, if not, Gladys will be distraught rather than happy on what would otherwise be our very special day, and I would worry that Gladys will always have an element of deep sadness about what should otherwise be such a happy memory. But now I am being glum, which I hadn't intended. My job now is to bolster Gladys during this difficult time, not make things worse. So pray for us, Roelena, that God allows us to keep Cor for a few more weeks in his earthly form so that he can see his youngest child wed and Gladys can be given her father's blessing on her wedding day. I know it's not possible for my family in Alberta to make it to the wedding now that we've changed the date, but that saddens me much less than thinking of Gladys not having her father there. Regardless, we are all in God's hands, are we not?

Have you heard from Harri lately? I got a letter from him last week, a rare treat. He sounds surprisingly happy. He mentions a girl he met, Therese, from a Catholic family, and it seems she's very special to him. By reading between the lines, I would not be surprised if he soon announces his intention to marry. I know Pa and Moe always prayed their children would marry within the faith, but I can't help but be pleased for Harri even if it means being on the other side of the country and marrying into the Catholic faith.

I want to close this letter with a heartfelt wish for a joyous Christmas for you and the family. I pray that God will bestow blessings of health and happiness upon you in the new year. Got zegen je, sister. *And please write again soon.*

Your loving brother,

Hendrik

PART II

1952

14

LETTER TO ROELENA FROM HENDRIK

Dear Roelena,

Thank you for your letter dated January 6. Let me start by wishing you a very happy birthday. It's hard to believe that the little sister I left in Alberta more than five years ago is already twenty-four. I pray your year is filled with health and happiness. If I know Clarence, he will do all in his power to make you feel loved and appreciated on your special day. You really couldn't have married a nicer man. Gladys always says the very same thing. And by the way, she says for me to say hello and happy birthday; she's sitting here in the front room with me stitching on a baby quilt she made for her sister's fourth child. She says she will write again soon.

Thanks again for your long and descriptive letters. I am always happy to come home and see a letter from you as I know I will have much news of the family and all that fills your days. I will admit, I am as astonished as you that Willem's grades in his last year of high school are so consistently high and that he has already been accepted to the University of Alberta for this fall to study science. I know you, and Pa and Moe too, at times despaired that the boy would ever leave his mischievous ways behind. Greta's letters claim she always believed the lad would turn into a decent young man, and now that he's eighteen it seems he has, but I'm certain she was the only one to have been so sure. And, of course, not a one of us has ever had to worry about Pieter, but I'm also glad to hear he's getting good grades in high school. It's quite something that we have two brothers who will attend university. I do not believe that path would have been open for Willem and Pieter had we stayed in Andijk, especially given how our homeland has yet to recover from the devastation of war.

I'm very glad to hear that all is well with you and Clarence and baby Karl. It was a pleasure to see you last fall and witness first-hand what a proud and capable mother you have become. It's a pleasure to read about his little accomplishments in your letters—being able to sit up on his own is a feat that will serve him well in life! I'm assuming Jakob and Ingrid's little Alida is making the same great leaps as she is only three days older, but Jakob's letters are filled with news of the farm and Ingrid's letters, though lovely, are rather short. I am glad to hear you report that Alida and Karl's older cousins dote on the two babies. I do pray that God will one day bless Gladys and me with the joy of children and thus also provide more cousins for Karl to play with. I know Pa and Moe enjoy every one of their eight grandchildren and would like nothing better than to add to that number, and Moe especially would likely double or even triple that number.

Things here are very well. The orchard is thriving and I am pleased that by this time next year I will have invested sufficiently in our expanding operation that I will be an equal partner with Clarence and his father Henk. I continue to enjoy the work and although I feel I have learned much over these last five years, I learn something new about trees and orchards and fruit every week in large part thanks to my ongoing visits with old Mr. Hunt. Although he's less mobile now, his mind is sharper than mine. And of course, farming practices are always improving and I like to keep up with the latest advancements. On the new land we purchased last year to expand the orchard, we intend to build a large barn this spring that will help us sort and prepare the fruit for market with greater ease and efficiency, and there are some options for automation that we are also considering. Our best seller are our freestone peaches of which we now have close to a dozen varieties.

Gladys and I often reminisce about the wonderful time we had last fall with all of you. We wish we could take the farm truck to Alberta every September and bring enough fruit for all the women in the family to preserve, but perhaps we can plan something for next year. And of course we would always welcome a visit from you.. Thank you again for your kind words about all the tips Gladys gave you on which fruit to can, which to use for jams and jellies, and which to use for pies and cobblers. She's become quite the expert in preparing fruit, actually in cooking and baking anything really, and I benefit from her excellent baking and cooking, so much so that I've noticed my waistline increasing, but as long as I am active during the day I have no reason not to indulge in my wife's excellent food.

Roelena, I will close now and again wish you all God's blessings in the year to come. Please continue writing your lovely, newsy letters as both Gladys and I greatly enjoy them.

Your loving brother,

Hendrik.

15

WEDNESDAY, FEBRUARY 6

The manufacturing economy of the 1950s, no longer producing war-related items, heralded a new era of modern machinery and conveniences. In the household, many luxury items from the previous decades were now accessible to housewives of more moderate means. Advertisements for these kitchen and laundry appliances promised many benefits, including granting housewives something they'd never before had—free time. Electric mixers would make higher and lighter cakes; refrigerators had the convenience of automatic butter conditioners as well as convenient shelves in the door; while nickel-and-chrome-plated toasters and kettles, in addition to adding sparkle to a discerning housewife's kitchen, promised to make work easier and more efficient.

The 1950s also introduced modern and improved automobiles, which soon became an extension of one's status and identity. By the end of the decade, innovative new designs both in the look of the vehicle and in the engine, and improved approaches to manufacturing, standardized such aspects as power brakes and power steering. On the farms, the number of tractors quickly exceeded the number of horses. New and improved implements—plows with specialized discs and harvesters—and new machinery—combines and bailers—were introduced allowing farmers to cultivate and harvest more land more efficiently.

When Roelena and Clarence van Haarmelen married in August 1950, these modern and often expensive conveniences were financially well out of their reach; yet they felt blessed. On behalf of the young couple, Roelena's father had purchased Trunkett's farm with its quarter section of land when the old bachelor had finally moved to Hay Lakes to live with his sister, and they were repaying Kees in small monthly installments. It would take years to repay him in full, but both Roelena and Clarence felt fortunate that Kees and Anneke had been in a position to make this purchase. They also inherited the "old" 1946 Ford tractor from the home farm after Kees purchased a newer John Deere Model R diesel tractor. At a farm sale, Sijmon found a used 1935 Ford sedan for the new couple. It needed special encouragement to start, but if they manipulated the choke valve just right, the rather cantankerous engine generally came to life. The automobile wasn't reliable for long journeys, but it would get them to town and church and home again.

The autumn Trunkett vacated the farm, Clarence and Roelena's brothers plowed the fields, readying them for spring planting. They returned in May to seed those same fields with oats and barley. All the buildings on Trunkett's farm—the hen house, barn, garden shed, and granary, as well as the compact farmhouse—were in a sad state, as aged and wizened as their former owner and needed a great deal of attention. Before they began repairs though, the entire de Haas clan spent a Saturday on the property loading pick-up trucks and wagons with junk that the bachelor had accumulated in his house and on his property, bringing half a dozen truck loads to the dump and repurposing or distributing another half dozen. Roelena, Greta, and Ingrid returned the next week with Marliese and spent a day scrubbing the interior of the house from top to bottom, a cleaning they felt certain bachelor Trunkett had never done, or at least not in the last twenty years. The plain, square house had a small lean-to porch, a compact kitchen with a peculiarly large pantry, a decent-sized front room, two bedrooms on the main floor, and an attic accessed by a ladder that Clarence would eventually convert into two bedrooms. Despite the electrical lines on the country lane, the house had no electricity and Kees hired a handyman to wire the house and barn and install indoor plumbing, including building a bathroom in one half of the pantry. They could not install a telephone as the County of Bellecourt hadn't yet brought lines to that country lane.

Six weeks before their wedding, and after fulfilling his three-year obligation to work for his sponsor, Clarence moved into the neglected house. In the long summer evenings, he slowly began to fix it up, starting with the kitchen. Greta's husband Frank, who worked at the lumber yard in town, helped as often as he could, as did Roelena's brothers. When Roelena moved in with Clarence following their August wedding and after spending two days on a honeymoon in Banff National Park, the house was in much better shape than when Bachelor Trunkett had lived in it.

Roelena's little kitchen had few of the modern appliances advertised in the *Ladies Home Journal*, yet she loved it. They'd painted the kitchen a cheerful yellow, and the two windows were framed with bright flowered curtains Greta had sewn, with a lace *gordign* hanging from the middle sashes. The cast-iron range the former owner had left behind was wood-fired and hardly different from the one in the de Haas farmhouse. After electricity and plumbing had been installed, Clarence purchased an old General Electric refrigerator and a ceramic sink and drain-board stand at a farm sale. The refrigerator sat in place of Bachelor Trunkett's icebox, and the sink had been positioned under the east-facing window. A second, south-facing window next to the lean-to porch bathed the room in sunlight. A trap door in the porch led to a root cellar big enough to store sufficient produce and preserves for the young couple.

Although there was no furnace in the small house, it was toasty warm that February morning thanks to the wood-fired range and the room was lit by a single electric bulb in the ceiling and a softly glowing wall sconce on the wall opposite the sink. From where Roelena sat at the kitchen table she could see a hint of dawn lighting the eastern sky. Once Clarence was done milking their three cows, they would have a breakfast of porridge, bread, and boiled eggs.

Roelena was trying to feed her six-month old baby his usual breakfast, which was a bowl of Pablum, a specialized baby cereal that had the added benefit of nutrients and minerals to make his bones and teeth strong. She held him on her lap, his body snuggled against her side with his right arm tucked behind her and his left hand gripped in hers so that he couldn't grab any items off the table. In Roelena's right hand she held a baby-sized spoon and was trying to entice the fussing child to eat the warm cereal. Usually he loved his breakfast, but the baby had been feverish and out of sorts for days on account of teething, and wasn't interested in the Pablum.

Karl Benjamin had been a fussy newborn until Roelena realized that her milk didn't satisfy him. Since she'd switched to bottle feeding him cow's milk, his fussing had stopped and he'd been content, growing fat and happy despite his patches of eczema, which wasn't particularly unusual in babies. Since then, he'd been a good baby, sleeping through the night already at ten weeks, but for the past few days he'd been out of sorts from teething, and the night before had woken her with his fractious cries. She'd slipped out of bed hoping Clarence wouldn't wake and picked up Karl from his crib in the small second bedroom. He didn't stop crying so she'd taken him into the kitchen, turning on only the wall sconce. She soothed him as best she could, first rubbing his gums with her fingers—he didn't have any teeth yet so his gnawing, although strong, didn't hurt—then opening a sachet of teething powder. She sprinkled half of the packet onto a spoon and then put it in his mouth, letting him chew on the spoon until the powder dissolved on his tongue. Then she gave him one of the teething rings she kept in the refrigerator, the chilled rubber soothing on his painful gums. For whatever reason, he always seemed more soothed when she was standing, so she remained on her feet, swaying and crooning almost soundlessly until his cries softened. Ten minutes later, he'd fallen back asleep. She was glad she hadn't needed to heat a bottle of milk and could crawl back into bed herself. But in the morning he'd woken cranky and his fat cheeks were flushed again with a mild fever.

Roelena gave up trying to feed him the Pablum and, with an expert flick of her wrist, untied the bib and wiped his sticky face in a single motion. "Here you go, *schatje,*" she cooed, repositioning him in her arms and offering him the bottle of warm milk. He eagerly began to suckle, but then turned his head away and began to cry in earnest, waving his arms in protest and pushing with his hands against his ears. Roelena's *moeder* had previously told her that when babies are teething, the suckling on a nipple can cause pain in their ears, so she sat him up again, using the discarded bib to wipe away the trickle of milk that had dribbled onto his face and neck. She stood up, murmuring softly in Dutch and rocking him in one arm as she turned to the range and gave the oatmeal she'd mixed a stir, re-balancing the sticky wooden spoon across the edges of the thick-rimmed aluminum pot.

Roelena gazed out the east-facing window as she rocked the crying baby, admiring the dark pink on the horizon and seeing that the clear sky held the promise of another sun-filled day. They were enjoying unusually balmy temperatures for February thanks to a recent chinook, and their yard was an unsightly mix of mud and snow. Roelena kept her breathing calm and even as she crooned to her baby, reminding herself of her *moeder's* advice to remain relaxed so that her own tension wasn't transferred to the child. A few minutes later, his cries diminishing, Roelena reached for the bottle. When she touched the tip of the nipple to his lips a second time, he began to suckle contentedly. She sank back into her chair, sighing with relief.

She looked down at her baby, enjoyed the sound of his little grunts of contentment as he drank the milk. She loved every minute of her life as a wife and mother. Being married to Clarence was as wonderful as she'd imagined. And every day, Karl introduced delight and laugher into their perfect little home. An overabundance of pride might be a sin, but she took special and private delight in the compliments she received about her baby, from admiring his fat, chunky legs and the keen, brightness of his eyes to his lovely disposition and toothless smiles. Roelena had known about the deep, strong bond between mother and child, but what she felt for Karl was so far beyond that, it was indescribable. If it were a tangible thing, it would be so vast she wouldn't know where it started or ended. She'd likened this newfound discovery of the depths of her love for this new life with how God must feel for his children; a bond that was indefinable and eternal, life-giving, and somehow so full of purpose. Being Karl's mother gave her a sense of rightness and contentment about her and Clarence's path.

Karl was almost asleep by the time he'd drained the bottle. He didn't usually go down for his morning nap until close to coffee time, but she gently tugged the nipple out of his mouth and set the bottle on the table, then gently repositioned him to lay against her shoulder. She stood, rocking him a little as she patted his back, encouraging the burp she knew was there. Perhaps when next he woke, he'd be more himself. As soon as he burped, she moved down the hall to his bedroom, gently depositing him on his back in his crib. He remained asleep, thankfully, and she covered him with the soft blanket topped with the white knitted afghan her mother had made.

Back in the kitchen, Roelena gave the oatmeal a stir, frowning when she realized she'd let it get lumpy. She put two eggs in a small pot to boil, and then set the rest of the breakfast things on the table.

With the porridge simmering on the stove, two fresh eggs boiled, and a loaf of bread sliced, Roelena took her usual seat at the table then sat surveying the tiny room with a renewed sense of contentment. She loved the improvements Clarence had made—extra shelves for storage, a rack for her kitchen towels, and another folding rack near the range to dry Karl's flannelette diapers. Clarence had also sanded down the cupboard drawers to stop them from sticking as she slid them in or out. She thanked God every day for her loving and devoted husband, a home of her own, and a baby to love, and all just two miles down the road from her parents. She'd once thought Jakob and Ingrid had it perfect with their little house on the home farm, but she and Clarence were only two miles away, which was just as good.

She heard Clarence's soft footfalls on the stoop, and then the sound of the outer door of the porch being opened and closed quietly. Clarence knew from the experience of these last few days not to make any noise that might startle awake their fussing baby.

From the lean-to porch, which barely had room for two adults and whose doorway opened directly into the kitchen, Clarence stood on the newspaper-lined floor and poked his head in, giving his wife a smile and a quiet hello. He eased off his rubber boots, hung his coat and cap on a hook, and then entered the kitchen. Coming up behind his seated wife, he stooped, wrapping his arm around her and resting his palms on her flat belly, then planted a kiss on the top of her head. "He drank all his milk and fell asleep?" he asked softly, nodding at the empty baby bottle on the table.

"Yes, and hopefully he'll wake up a little happier," Roelena answered in a low voice, her hands resting on his.

"And how's the other doing?" he asked, making a circular motion with his hand on her stomach even though she hadn't yet started to show. "Were you sick again this morning?"

Roelena had been in the peak of health during her first pregnancy, but for most of the five weeks or so that she'd been pregnant with her second, she'd had bouts of nausea, a sore back, and lethargy. "Just the one time so far. But I'm feeling fine, now." She lifted her head and saw her answer hadn't removed the worry lines on her husband's forehead, so she gave him a kiss and a reassuring smile. "Moe says this one, because it's so different than being pregnant with Karl, will be a girl."

Clarence brightened and grinned. "She said that?"

"She did." Roelena knew Clarence put just as much store as she did in what her *moeder* said. Although they couldn't know for certain until their second baby was born, Roelena hoped Anneke was right.

When Clarence went to the sink to wash his hands, Roelena stood and went to the range, padding her hand with a tea towel before lifting the porridge pot and bringing it to the table.

"Sorry about the lumps," Roelena said quietly as she dished the lumpy porridge into their bowl. "I was daydreaming while I was feeding Karl, and forgot to stir it."

"As long as it's hot, that's all that matters," Clarence said good-naturedly, waiting for Roelena to join him at the table before engulfing her free hand in his. "Let's pray."

Roelena bowed her head as Clarence began to pray.

"Dear Lord Jesus, bless this food we are about to receive. Thank you for the bounty set before us. Let us never forget that it is You, Lord, who blesses us with your gracious love. And Lord, I thank you that Roelena is such a good and loving mother. Keep her healthy as she progresses in this new pregnancy. Thank you also for the calf that was delivered safely during the night. Amen."

"What? Bessie's had her calf?" A delighted smile spread across Roelena's face, erasing the tears that had threatened to fall in response to Clarence's heartfelt prayer.

"She did," Clarence answered. He poured milk into his bowl, then added a healthy sprinkle of brown sugar. "It's a heifer."

Roelena was glad it was a heifer rather than a bull calf. The heifer would eventually provide milk and also more calves to grow their small herd. Roelena was still smiling as she stirred milk and sugar into her porridge. "And Bessie's accepted her?"

This was Bessie's first calf. Sometimes a first-time mother cow didn't know what to do with the new life it had just birthed and wouldn't lick it clean or let it suckle.

"The calf was already dry when I went in this morning, and had been feeding too. Bessie must have birthed her early in the night. When I checked on her before going to bed she hadn't seemed restless. I thought it would be a few days yet before she birthed, but I was wrong."

"I'm so glad all is well."

Clarence nodded, his eyes dropping briefly to his wife's belly. "You have your first doctor's appointment today?"

"Yes, at 9:30. It's just as well Karl is down early for his morning nap. I won't have to wake him up."

"Can you stop at the hardware store and get a roll of wire mesh? I need to fix the chicken run. I don't need much, so buy the smallest roll they have."

Clarence set his empty porridge bowl aside and then sliced the top off his egg, letting the runny yolk dribble onto a slice of bread he'd put on his plate before scraping out the remainder.

At sight of the unappetizing soft boiled egg, Roelena got up from the table, feeling queasy. "Let me add that to my list before I forget," she said, glad of a reason to leave the table.

She'd never liked eating runny yolks and always boiled her own egg a minute longer than she boiled Clarence's. Her *moeder* had laughed when Roelena mentioned how she prepared Clarence's eggs different than hers, telling her that Kees had once liked soft-boiled eggs too, but once the children came and, with them, more chores, he'd learned to make do with hard-boiled eggs. Individual preferences could not be accommodated once the family began to grow, Anneke advised. But Roelena had made a silent promise to herself that, despite her mother's advice, she'd always pamper her husband in this way. If he liked his eggs soft-boiled or his bacon crispy or his potatoes fried in bacon fat, then she would take the time to do this for him. But now she considered not making her husband a boiled egg for the remainder of her pregnancy; or, at least until this stage of nausea passed.

At the cupboard where she kept the notepaper and pencils, she added 'chicken wire' to her grocery list.

"Will you visit Greta?"

"Yes, I'm seeing her for coffee before I get groceries," Roelena answered, resuming her seat and making a concerted effort not to look at her husband's plate. Her lumpy porridge was suddenly unappetizing and she set the bowl aside. It wouldn't be wasted but would be fed to the pigs. She reached for a slice of bread and buttered it.

"Shall I put a couple of empty crates in the car for the groceries?"

"Yes, please."

"What time will you be back?"

Roelena had hoped Clarence wouldn't ask her that. She didn't want to tell him that she'd made plans to have dinner with Marliese at noon, but neither did she want to lie. "I'm having dinner with Marliese," she admitted, then added in a rush. "But I'll leave a sandwich for you in the refrigerator. I'll be home early this afternoon. Karl will need his nap by then. And I'll make pork chops for supper with fried potatoes and the last of the carrots from the cellar. I'll buy a tin of cherry filling, if it's on sale, and make a pie for dessert."

Roelena deliberately buried her reference to Marliese and made a promise of favourite cherry pie to distract him from his disapproval of her continued friendship with Marliese.

But Clarence simply said, "Sounds delicious, sweetheart."

Their conversation moved to what Clarence would be doing on the farm that day. The weather had been uncharacteristically spring-like the last two weeks and the whole yard was a shallow mud pit. Earlier that year, he'd done some work on Pierre Boutelier's house and, in return, Pierre had promised Clarence a small portion of the gravel he'd ordered for his own yard. The gravel would be delivered later that morning and Clarence was going to use it to create a walkway for Roelena from the house to the car. It would replace the timber lengths of two-by-eights across the least muddy stretches that currently served as their sidewalk.

Before eating her bread and egg, Roelena stood and made a pot of tea from the kettle that had boiled. She put the crocheted cozy on the pot—a wedding-shower gift from Gertie van Laar—and then set it on the table and resumed her seat.

There were two china mugs on the table, a wedding gift from her brother Pieter. The boy had spent his own pocket money on the china and had insisted Roelena use the expensive mugs every day instead of saving them for guests. She'd taken his advice, and now preferred the taste of tea when sipped from thin-lipped china than from a thick crockery mug.

Pieter was in his second year at the high school and lived in town with Greta and Frank and their four children during the week, leaving only Sijmon in the house with their *ouders*. Margaret Langelaar, the oldest of the Langelaar children had chosen not to attend high school, and went to the home farm every weekday morning to do the cooking and cleaning, with Kees helping when needed. Roelena also went to the home farm as often as she could to help her *moeder*, as did Ingrid, despite now having three children underfoot and her own house to run. Tomas would turn five in May, and little Kees would be four in August. Their baby, named Alida after Ingrid's mother, was only a few days older than Karl Benjamin.

"Will you ask the doctor if there's anything else you should be doing for Karl to help him with his teething?"

"I'll ask, but I'm sure he'd just advise me to keep using the teething powders for as long as needed. I do want him to look at Karl's eczema, though. It's not bad, and doesn't seem to bother him, but it's not going away."

"Good idea," Clarence said, reaching for a second slice of bread.

16

WEDNESDAY, FEBRUARY 6

They were only halfway through their breakfast when they heard their dog barking. They both turned to look out the south-facing window. It spoke to the smallness of the room that neither of them had to rise from their chairs but only needed to crane their necks to see into their yard. When Clarence had left the house earlier to milk their three cows—less Bessie now that she had a new calf to feed—it had still been dark. But now the sun was just over the horizon; regardless, it was still much too early for a visitor.

"It's Pa," Roelena said, recognizing her father's car. A frown creased her brow. "Something must've happened to Moe!" she stated, her voice suddenly shrill.

"Not necessarily, sweetheart," Clarence answered in a reassuring tone as he rose. "I hope he's wearing rubber boots," he muttered as he moved into the porch and then out onto the stoop.

Roelena joined him there. She was only wearing crocheted slippers on her feet and a cardigan over her everyday dress, yet she wasn't overly cold. She watched her

Pa get out of his car, a frown creasing her brow. She was surprised to see him dressed in his town clothes, with rubber over-soles protecting his Sunday shoes and his careful attire only increased her alarm. She watched in worried silence as he patted their exuberant collie-like dog aside before navigating the zig-zag line of boards Clarence had lain out to avoid the worst of the mud.

Roelena stood to the side as her father climbed the stairs of the stoop. "Hi, Pa. What are you doing here this early? Is Moe okay?"

Kees laid a hand on her arm and pecked her on the cheek before moving past her into the porch.

Kees's greeting surprised her, not only for his silence but also for his uncharacteristic gesture of affection. She shared a concerned glance with Clarence as Kees stepped onto a clean area of the newspaper she'd lain out the day before. If she didn't take the effort to do that task, she'd be mopping the porch floor twice every day. After he removed his shoes, she and Clarence trailed behind Kees into the kitchen.

"Is there tea left in that pot?" Kees asked.

"Of course, Pa. We were just finishing breakfast."

Roelena retrieved a plain mug from the cupboard and placed it on the table across from where she'd been sitting, trying not to show her frustration when the men started commenting on the unusually warm weather. She picked up the strainer, then poured tea for all three of them.

"We could use more moisture, though," Clarence was saying, resuming his seat. "If we're not going to get more snow this winter, then we'll need a good deal of rain before seeding begins."

"It's too soon to worry," Kees responded, sighing heavily as he wrapped his hands around the steaming mug. "We often get lots of snowfall in March and April, more than all the rest of the winter months combined."

"Pa." Roelena interrupted, sitting down across from Kees and eying her father with concern. "Why are you here so early? And why are you wearing your town clothes? Is Moe all right?"

Kees sighed and shook his head slowly as he gazed unseeingly into the mug of tea. They'd been speaking in English, but now he switched to Dutch. "She's in need of your *gebeden* now more than ever, *kinderen*."

Roelena wasn't sure if she should panic. Her Pa always claimed her mother needed their prayers. Roelena deliberately kept her voice low so as not to wake Karl, but inside she was shrieking. "Pa? Is she in bed again? Should I come over?"

When Kees met Roelena's gaze, the look in his eyes filled her with dread.

"Moeder had a massive heart attack last night," Kees stated, his tone grave. "She's in the hospital in Bellecourt. I'm on my way there now."

Roelena felt Clarence take her hand. She was grateful for his steadying presence, but she kept her gaze on her father, looking for a telltale spark of hope in his eyes. The only emotions she could see, though, was heart-breaking pain and resignation.

Although Anneke had been ill on and off for more than ten years and had suffered multiple angina attacks as well as two mild heart attacks, it still came as a shock to Roelena to be told that her Moe, who would celebrate her fifty-eighth birthday in March, was in the hospital following a major heart attack. There had always been a possibility that her mother might have a bad heart attack one day, but Roelena assumed this wouldn't happen for many years yet. She'd also assumed that the heart pills her mother took would keep a serious attack at bay for many years yet.

"Why didn't you come by last night and tell us?" Roelena demanded, hearing the hurt in her tone.

"It was midnight by the time we came home, *kind.* I didn't want to wake you with this worrying news."

Kees sipped his tea intermittently as he described the events of the previous evening. After suffering a major heart attack shortly before bedtime, Kees phoned the doctor who advised him to bring Anneke to the hospital straightaway. After Sijmon and Kees bundled Anneke in blankets and carried the unconscious woman to the car, Sijmon drove them to the hospital where she was immediately admitted to the Intensive Care Unit.

"How is she now?" Roelena heard Clarence ask.

"I phoned the hospital before coming here and was told she is still unconscious."

"What does that mean?" Roelena demanded, but then immediately regretted her harsh tone when she saw her father's bewildered expression. It could only mean one thing. Anneke was gravely ill. *But she has to recover,* Roelena thought. *She has to!*

"Does Greta know?" she asked, making a deliberate effort to soften her tone. Her oldest sister and their *moeder* had an especially close relationship. Roelena couldn't imagine how Greta would receive this news.

"It's not news for sharing over the telephone," Kees answered in a sombre tone. "I'll stop there on the way to town, and catch Pieter too before he goes to school. That's why I'm so early."

"And the others? Hendrik? And Willem?"

"I'll telephone them later today, but I did talk to Harri early this morning."

"Harri?" Roelena breathed.

"Yes. I asked if he could come home."

Roelena was shocked at her father's unexpected response. She hadn't even thought of her oldest brother Harri, who lived in Quebec. She sat motionless as terror seeped into her heart. If her Pa had called Harri, a long-distance call that would be outrageously expensive, and told him to come home that could only mean her *moeder* was… she hesitated, hating to even think that her *moeder* might soon die.

"I'll sit with her this morning," Kees was saying. "I don't want her to be alone during visiting hours, even if she isn't aware I'm there."

"Of course. Pa, I'm going into town this morning. I'll come, too."

Kees shook his head. "Best not. Moeder needs quiet, and a hospital is no place for a baby."

"I'll leave Karl with Greta. I want to see Moe. And I'll babysit Greta's kids, so she can visit too."

Her father nodded absently. *"Ja, kom dan, kind,"* he said, granting his permission for her to visit.

She looked away, silently crying, *Moe! Don't go yet. I'm not ready!* Her *moeder* was an irreplaceable presence in Roelena's life. They saw each other almost every day and Roelena looked to her for advice on any number of things. And her Moe never scolded her for boasting about her baby's achievements. Roelena could not picture the farmhouse without her *moeder* in it. She couldn't picture her Pa without his wife at his side.

"Roelena," Kees repeated, startling her out of her reverie.

She looked up and met her father's troubled gaze.

Kees nodded his head at her breakfast plate. "You haven't eaten your egg, or finished your tea. You need to eat, for the sake of the baby."

Roelena and Clarence had recently shared the news of her second pregnancy with her *ouders*; they'd wait a few weeks yet before telling anyone else. Her dazed gaze drifted to the dried up, runny egg yolk on Clarence's plate, and she almost gagged. An unfamiliar surge of irritation made her suddenly stand. She didn't want food, not now that her *moeder* was in the hospital.

"I can't eat," she snapped. Her father's unwelcome news had robbed her of her appetite. Or maybe the baby had. Or both. She knew it wasn't fair to lash out at either her father or her husband, but she didn't want either of them telling her what to do when all she wanted was to get in the car and go be with her mother.

"Lena, sweetheart." Clarence rested a gentle hand on her hip, staying her escape. "Your Moe is being taken care of by doctors. If anyone can make her better, they can. You'll see. Sit down, sweetheart. Finish your breakfast."

Roelena resisted momentarily before sinking back into her seat. "I can't eat that egg. It will make me sick."

"Bread then," Clarence said, eying his wife. It concerned him that her usual appetite had evaporated with this second pregnancy.

Clarence slathered a slice of homemade bread with a generous layer of butter, then with an equally generous helping of the rhubarb and saskatoon jam Roelena had made the previous fall. By habit, Roelena glanced at her father, expecting him to say, *'Gebruik niet zo veel'*, cautioning Clarence to not be so liberal and wasteful with the butter and jam. But her Pa didn't seem to notice.

Clarence cut the bread into four squares, then set the plate in front of his wife. "You only ate half your porridge, so you must eat this. Please," he added.

Roelena lifted a piece of the bread and took a small bite to appease her husband.

"I must be off now," Kees said, setting down his half-drunk tea. "Visiting hours don't start until eight-thirty, but I want to catch Pieter before he leaves for school. Shall we pray together before I go?" Kees didn't wait for a response, but folded his hands and bowed his head.

"Father in Heaven, I ask that you hear my prayer. Watch over my good wife, oh Lord. Restore her health and allow her to come home again to be with her family, who need and love her." Kees's voice shook. He paused for a moment before continuing his prayer. *"I know you have a place reserved for us in your Heavenly Home, oh Lord, but I plead with you to look into my heart and recognize that my life here on Earth is a life shared with Moeder. Please, Lord, restore her to me and to her children. Your ways are mysterious to us, oh Lord, but I pray that this be your will. Please do not deprive us of the love of this remarkable woman. Oh, Lord, hear my prayer. Have pity on us in our time of need. In Jesus name...Amen."*

At the conclusion of his prayer, Kees immediately rose from the table. He walked to Roelena's side and briefly rested his hand on her shoulder before turning and stepping into the porch, Clarence on his heels.

Roelena remained seated and silent, fighting to hold back her tears. She wished her father hadn't prayed as he had. Usually he prayed for guidance to do God's will. But this time he'd subjected the Lord to Kees's will. Quiet tears streamed down her cheeks. She rested her elbows on the table and dropped her face into her hands.

When Clarence returned to the kitchen, he stopped and eyed his weeping wife. He'd rarely seen his wife cry. She was a strong person, not prone to tears. In the yard, before his father-in-law got into the car, Clarence had asked Kees outright if he thought Anneke would recover. Kees hadn't responded with a yes or a no, but simply said, *we must ask God to deliver on our prayers.* That's when Clarence realized how worried Kees was, an unusual state for the kind man who epitomized steadfast faith and quiet wisdom.

Words usually came easy to Clarence, but as he stared at his practical, capable wife, he realized he didn't know how to comfort her. Regardless, he moved forward and crouched beside her, one hand across her shoulders and the other around her waist.

"Roelena?" He stated. When she didn't respond, Clarence shifted, forcing her to lean into his embrace.

Roelena turned her face into his neck and put her arms around him. "I don't have a hanky," she sobbed, her voice thick and muffled.

Clarence was relieved he could provide this small bit of comfort. "I do," he said, keeping one arm around her as he retrieved a clean handkerchief from his pocket. "Hush now, sweetheart. She may recover, you know."

Roelena lifted her tear-stained face to gaze at Clarence, wiping her face as she stared accusingly at him. "But didn't you hear Pa's prayer?"

Clarence looked at her, puzzled. "Of course I did."

"But Pa always prays humbly, submitting to God's will. Today he prayed for *God* to submit to *Pa's* will," she wailed. "He knows Moe is going to die in that hospital."

He didn't believe Kees could know if Anneke would live or die. Only God knew that. "He can't know that, sweetheart. And neither can you," he stated in a gentle but firm tone.

Roelena blew her nose, then said, "The doctor has always said her heart is too weak to withstand the shock of a major heart attack. I'm afraid, Clarence. I don't want Moe to die. *Not yet,*" she added, resting a hand on her flat belly within which rested a tiny life. Her voice rose in despair. "My children need their Oma."

"Hush, sweetheart. You'll wake Karl."

Roelena, her rain of tears at an end—at least for now—

stood and went to the sink, splashing cold water on her face and drying her hands and face on a kitchen towel.

Clarence resumed his seat, but turned so he could regard his wife. "Sit down and have a cup of tea with me."

Roelena resumed her seat, then rested her hand on the tea cozy. "It's not hot anymore."

"Warm tea is fine. And you promised to eat your bread. Your Moe wouldn't like it if you let it go to waste."

Roelena watched as Clarence filled each of their mugs with lukewarm tea. "It doesn't go to waste if we feed it to the pigs," she grumbled. "And I'm not hungry."

"I know you're not, but the baby inside you is. Eat your bread."

Roelena reluctantly took a small bite.

Clarence eyed his wife approvingly. "Your Pa doesn't want to lose his wife, sweetheart. That's why he prayed as he did. His prayer is an indication of his worry, not knowledge. He can't claim to know that your Moe will die, and neither can you. But given that he's not a man prone to worry, now he's made you worry too."

"I hope you're right." Roelena stated unconvincingly.

"I am right. Trust in the doctors, sweetheart. And trust in God. You'll see, she'll be fine."

Clarence believed what he said. He also realized, if the worst happened, that he didn't need to find the right words to say to comfort his wife. He simply needed to love and care for her. No matter what happened, he would be there for Roelena. He would help her through her sadness, whether Anneke died that day or lived another twenty years. He would always be there for her.

17

FRIDAY, FEBRUARY 15

It is natural that religion—or any belief system—concern itself with both the living and the dead. Traditionally in Christianity, and even though the Bible does not prohibit cremation, Christians agreed with their Jewish ancestors that a body must be buried, not burned. Pagans practiced cremation; Christians did not.

When it came to funeral practices, the Dutch Christian Reformed Church was guided by John Calvin, the mid-16th century reformer who denounced prayers for the departed as mistaken and useless. John Calvin posited instead that one's eternal destiny became fixed at death; thus, believers who have died were already with God in Heaven and did not require intercession from loved ones left behind.

At Anneke's funeral in the Pine Glade Christian Reformed Church, the *dominee* did not pray for Anneke's soul to rest in peace. As a devout believer, peace after death was her given. The liturgy of the Christian Reformed Church funeral honoured Anneke's earthly body by exhibiting her coffin at the front of the sanctuary during the service. During his sermon, the *dominee* reminded his listeners that death is a part of God's never-ending story of redemption, and beseeched them to take comfort from knowing that every Christian's story was eternal; no death was strong enough to separate them from God's love. He venerated Anneke's Christian contribution to her family and their community, acknowledging the gift of life she'd given her children and the gift of love and dedication she'd given to their community, touching the lives of so many. The liturgy, prayers, and hymns during Anneke's funeral were reminders for all the mourners of the story of salvation brought about by Christ's death on the cross. They were saddened by Anneke's death, but also knew to take comfort in the words of the Scriptures, including those of Paul the Apostle where he reminds Thessalonians they need not grieve like the rest of mankind who have no hope.

"I'm so sorry, Roelena dear," stated Margaret Dickson, the mailman's wife. She held one of Roelena's hands in both of her own as she looked up at the tall young woman. She had to raise her naturally soft voice to be heard above the murmur of conversation in the basement of the church where the mourners had gathered following the family's short service of dedication in the cemetery. Her Scottish burr heightened the sincerity of her words. "Mr. Dickson and I have been praying that God will bring strength and comfort to help you cope with the loss of your dear mother. She was a wonderful woman, and I'll always remember her as a treasured friend."

The entire de Haas family were in the basement of the church accepting condolences from friends and neighbours. Moments before, the family had stood shivering in the biting wind as they gathered by the open grave listening to the *dominee* read from the scripture and pray, commending Anneke's earthly body to God's care.

Standing in the cold, Roelena had been overwhelmed by the sudden image of her mother lying in that thin, wooden box wearing only her best Sunday dress and shoes, without her winter coat, gloves, hat, or wool-lined boots. Roelena was relieved when that short service concluded, eager to re-enter the warmth of the church and gladder still to take her fussing baby from Marliese, thankful for his pleasing warmth. But then Clarence took Karl from her so that she could accept the condolences of the room full of mourners.

"Thank you, Mrs. Dickson. I know your kindness meant a lot to her, especially when we first arrived. And you were so patient with her, with all of us, when we were learning English."

Mrs. Dickson waved one of her hands in dismissal. "Your mother picked up English so quick. I was always astounded by that."

"Yes, she had a natural talent for languages, I think."

"And how's your beautiful son? Still teething?" asked Mrs. Dickson in a kind tone, looking behind Roelena at Clarence who held the fussing baby in his arms.

Mrs. Dickson released Roelena's hands and stepped past her to Clarence. She tried to entice a smile from the baby, but Karl was having none of it.

"Hello, Mrs. Dickson," said Clarence with a smile. "I'll hope you'll excuse my son's poor manners."

"He'll have good manners in spades once he's past this difficult stage. Don't you worry," Mrs. Dickson assured, turning to address Roelena. "Listen, dear, if you need anything, anything at all, ring me. You have my telephone number?" She frowned. "Ach, silly me. I forgot you don't have a telephone yet. Well, maybe I'll stop in next week, yes?

I would hate to see you sad with no one to talk to. Anneke wouldn't like that either."

"Thank you, Mrs. Dickson," Roelena said, distractedly eyeing Clarence as he tried to distract Karl with a teething ring. She appreciated Mrs. Dickson's offer, but she hoped Mrs. Dickson wouldn't visit, at least not soon. Right now she found the idea of visiting with anyone outside of family and Marliese exhausting.

Mrs. Dickson made to move away, but then rested a hand on Roelena's forearm and leaned in close, saying under her breath, "He's a lovely man, that husband of yours. I have no doubt he's taking good care of you."

For the first time in days, Roelena didn't offer a fake smile. Clarence had charmed Mrs. Dickson years before when he first arrived on Pierre Boutilier's farm, only a mile and a half from where Mr. and Mrs. Dickson lived in Shoalville. Mrs. Dickson had been under his spell ever since and she gushed about him every chance she could.

Clarence must have heard her, though. He leaned in and said, "I keep telling her the same thing, but it helps my cause when you tell her too," Clarence teased. Then he added, "I know Roelena holds you in high esteem."

Mrs. Dickson just stopped herself from beaming up at Clarence. Anneke's funeral was not the time for bright smiles and bantering, but it was clear she was pleased with Clarence's teasing. She wagged her gloved index finger at him. "You come and fetch me if she needs a friend to talk to. You know I would be happy to visit."

"Thank you, Mrs. Dickson," Clarence said. "I'll be sure to let you know if we need you."

Mrs. Dickson squeezed Roelena's hand one last time before moving on to offer her condolences to other members of the de Haas family.

Roelena turned her back on the room so she was facing

Clarence. She pretended to fuss with Karl, deliberately keeping other well-wishers at bay. "I don't want to be here anymore, Clarence," she said in an undertone. "It seems wrong for people to be sipping tea and nibbling cookies while Moe is out there in the cold." Roelena knew that later, after the guests left the *kerk*, the cemetery custodians would lower the coffin into the ground and cover it with dirt, a thought that made her feel even worse.

When Clarence put his free arm around Roelena's shoulder, she pressed her face against him. "Can we please go?" she pleaded, her voice muffled.

Karl began to cry in earnest, and Roelena stepped back, lifting her arms to take her son. But Clarence didn't relinquish him.

"Lena, sweetheart," he said softly, meeting the sympathetic glances of a handful of well-wishers over the top of her head. "Others here still want to offer you their condolences. You need to stay, if not for your sake then for your moeder's."

Roelena felt unreasonably angry at her husband. "But Karl is fussing. It's better if we leave. We're supposed to all meet at Pa and—"

Roelena stopped herself from saying *Pa and Moe's house.* How would she get used to thinking of the farmhouse as *Pa's* instead of *Pa and Moe's?*

Clarence hugged her close but said again that Roelena needed to stay and accept the well wishes of the remaining members of the congregation. "You'll regret it if we leave," he added.

"But Karl needs a bottle and a nap."

"I'll take him to the home farm and give him a bottle and he's used to napping there, so he'll be fine. I'll tell Jakob to take you home with them."

Roelena felt a hand on her arm and turned, pasting on a

smile as she forced herself to accept the condolences of Widow Roorda. Over her shoulder she saw Clarence leave the room with their crying baby.

Thirty minutes later Roelena was finding it difficult to hide her impatience with the repetitive and meaningless phrases. She knew the sentiment behind the words were sincere, but they provided no comfort.

"Roelena."

Roelena whirled, pleased to hear Marliese's voice.

The Sunday before, after hearing that Anneke had died in the hospital four days after being admitted, Marliese had immediately driven from town to the de Haas homestead. The farmhouse had been overflowing with visitors that afternoon. Roelena had left Karl in Ingrid and Jakob's house with two of the Langelaar girls to babysit, but all the adults, including Willem and Pieter, were gathered in the main house. Hendrik and his wife Gladys had arrived the day before, in time to sit with Anneke in the hospital before she died, although Anneke hadn't been aware of their presence. Even Harri had come home, surprising everyone, but he'd arrived after Anneke passed away. Roelena barely knew this absent brother, but it was clear to everyone that he deeply regretted not coming home sooner. He also seemed to be missing his fiancée, Therese, but the train trip had only been affordable for one, although they wouldn't have been able to travel without a chaperone despite their April wedding plans. Neither his siblings nor his father seemed to know how to comfort this long-absent member of their family.

Roelena was in the kitchen when Marliese arrived. The warm, spring-like conditions had disappeared the day before Anneke died, and the cold-snap that followed kept everyone indoors. The house was crowded, the windows foggy with condensation. Roelena had been pleased her friend had made the effort to come. The two had even managed to sit in a quiet corner of the kitchen for ten minutes, and Roelena had shared her pregnancy news, bemoaning the fact that her *moeder* would never meet this child. Marliese hadn't stayed long, though, especially after Clarence sat next to Roelena at the kitchen table, taking his wife's hand in his as if making it obvious that it was his job to comfort Roelena, not Marliese's.

In the church basement amidst the mourners, Roelena saw Marliese had her coat and hat on. "You're not leaving already?" she exclaimed, not hiding her dismay.

"Every time I've tried to talk to you, there's ten others competing for your attention." Marliese commented.

"I know. Everyone wants to share a special memory of Moe. I appreciate it, but…" Roelena gave a tired sigh.

Marliese tucked her hand in Roelena's elbow. "That's because she *was* lovely. She certainly always made me feel like I belonged in your house as if I were a part of your family."

Roelena smiled. "And you are."

"Where's Karl?"

"He was fussing, so Clarence left. I wanted to go, too, but Clarence thought I should stay," Roelena looked around the basement and saw that half the mourners had already left. "Jakob will drive me home."

"Let me drive you home, Roelena. I've started the car, already. And Wilfred did something to the heater so it gets toasty warm. He's not a lot of things, my husband, but he is handy around cars."

"He's not here?"

Marliese was shaking her head. "He couldn't get away from the Research Station. Even with the cold snap, there's too much to do."

Marliese didn't share the fact that Wilfred hadn't bothered to ask his boss for time off to attend the funeral. When they'd argued about it, he'd informed Marliese in no uncertain tones that since he hardly knew Anneke de Haas he didn't see any reason why he had to attend what would be, for him, a boring funeral.

Roelena hid her relief that Wilfred wasn't with Marliese. She didn't like the man any more now that Marliese had married him than when they'd been courting. As girls, Roelena and Marliese pictured their future husbands being great friends, but Wilfred and Clarence had not forged anything close to a friendship. Both men were gregarious and outgoing, but Wilfred's humour came at the expense of others and he was vocal in his criticism whether of people or church practices, behaviours that set Clarence's teeth on edge. Plus, the few times Wilfred had been at their farm, he had the annoying habit of telling Clarence what work still had to be done and criticizing the renovations and repairs Clarence had made; yet, he never offered his expertise or volunteered his time to help them like their other friends did.

"Give me a minute to tell Jakob I don't need a ride," she said, resting her hand on Marliese's arm briefly before moving through the well-wishers to find her brother.

Soon after, the two young women were scurrying across the parking lot with heads ducked against the the cold wind. Roelena kept her gaze away from the recently dug grave in the cemetery on the south side of the church.

Marliese was right, Roelena thought once inside her friend's car. It was almost warmer in the car than it had been in the church basement.

Marliese placed her handbag on the bench seat between them, and Roelena noticed it for the first time. She pulled off her gloves and picked up the black patent leather purse. "This is new."

"Wilfred and I had a fight. This is the result."

"He bought this for you to say he was sorry?"

Marliese snorted derisively as she snapped open the clasp of the handbag. Roelena glimpsed lovely pink silk lining as Marliese retrieved her cigarettes and matches before her friend closed the clasp with a snap. "Ha! That man has a lot of words in his vocabulary, but 'sorry' isn't one of them."

Roelena hadn't smoked in months, but she didn't hesitate to set down the handbag and take one when Marliese offered.

Marliese's voice took on a familiar hard edge. "The handbag was my reward for not impaling him with the kitchen knife I had in my hand at the time. Although, if the knife had encountered his chest, it surely would have snapped in two. I'm convinced his heart is made of stone."

It always broke Roelena's heart to hear Marliese talk about her husband this way. She knew the two fought a lot. Even in public, they frequently exchanged snappy, hurtful insults. Roelena had never liked Wilfred, but since Marliese had made the choice to marry him, she felt her friend should try harder to be nice, to make things work. She was convinced as well that, if Marliese and Wilfred had a baby, things between them would improve. But Marliese had confided in Roelena the year before, telling her that she'd never once conceived in the three years her and Wilfred had been together. Marliese had confided that she would be happy to adopt a baby, but Wilfred refused on the grounds that he could never love another man's bastard.

"Please don't say things like that," Roelena insisted, shifting in her seat so that she faced Marliese in the stationery car. "It sounds so awful."

Marliese placed a cigarette between her lips then struck a match, holding the flame for Roelena before lighting her own. Both girls rolled their windows open a crack as they exhaled smoke.

But then Roelena was moaning, her free hand on her forehead,

Alarmed, Marliese leaned across the bench seat, trying to peer into her friend's face. "Roelena? What's the matter?"

Roelena moaned again, holding her cigarette out to Marliese "Take it! It's making me sick."

Marliese, with her own cigarette in her left hand, leaned in front of Roelena and rolled down the passenger window. She threw her cigarette out the open window, then did the same with Roelena's. "Is it the baby?" she demanded.

When Marliese made to roll up Roelena's window, Roelena put out a hand to stop her. "Leave it open a minute," she said, her eyes closed as she filled her lungs with the bitter cold air.

"My god, Roelena!" Marliese said. "You're pasty white. What should I do?"

Marliese was leaning across the seat, staring in concern into Roelena's face. "Damn it, Roelena, you're as pale as a ghost," Marliese said when Roelena didn't respond. "Shall I go and get one of your brothers? Or Greta?"

"No! They'll just tell Clarence about the cigarette and Clarence will blame you."

"I don't care. God damn it, Roelena, you're scaring me!"

"You're swearing has gotten worse," Roelena muttered, managing a chuckle as she rolled the window back up. She turned her head slowly, then gave her friend a weak, reassuring smile. "I'm okay. It's just, I haven't had a cigarette in so long. It's made my head spin. It's gone now, though." She sighed as she regarded the worried look on her friend's face.

"Didn't you promise Clarence you wouldn't smoke anymore?"

"Well...you're not going to tell him, are you?"

Feeling reassured that her friend was well, Marliese shifted back into her seat behind the large steering wheel. "I can promise you that the next time me and Clarence have a heart-to-heart, I'll try and remember not to say a damn thing."

The two women chuckled softly.

Roelena shook her head. "It's true though," she said.

"What's true? That your pregnancy has put you off cigarettes?" Marliese eyed Roelena.

"No. Well, that's seems to be true. But I meant your swearing. It's getting worse. Since when do you take the Lord's name in vain?"

"It's not as bad as the Catholics I work with. When Edna O'Neill spilled a pot of black ink on her cashmere scarf last week, she said 'Jesus Christ' followed by 'goddamn it all to hell'. And you know what? God didn't send a lightning bolt to smite her down. And good thing, too, considering there's two floors of books in that library. I couldn't abide getting burned up on account of a Catholic."

Roelena knew that her friend was deliberately exaggerating in an attempt to make Roelena laugh, which only showed how alike Marliese and Clarence were, not that either of them would ever admit it. Clarence had been cajoling her for days trying to lighten her heart. "You're a good friend, Marliese. Despite what Clarence says."

Roelena sighed at the anger that glinted in Marliese's eyes before her friend turned away to stare out the windshield. Roelena wished her words hadn't come out quite like that, but there was no way to undo her words now. The truth was, her husband didn't like Marliese, and Marliese didn't like her husband.

Not for the first time, and likely not the last, Roelena wondered how different her friend's life would have been had she married the only man who held the key to her friend's fissured heart.

18

TUESDAY, APRIL 8

One of the first things Clarence had done after he married his sweetheart was erect a swing in the stand of woods behind their house. She was living with a devoted husband rather than loud, obnoxious brothers, but he knew how much she enjoyed her little breaks away from the unending household chores. Because he wanted his handiwork to be a surprise for her, he'd covered Roelena's eyes as he led her out of the house, a playful grin on his face. It was impossible to keep her from guessing where he was taking her—obviously they were crossing their bit of yard in the back towards the trees that served as a windbreak to the big open field beyond, but he took great satisfaction and delight in the sound of her giggles. When he finally let her see where they were, he noted her flush of pleasure at sight of the wooden seat hanging from the tallest of the aspen trees.

Since then, he'd often catch a glimpse of her heading across the yard to the trees. He took immense satisfaction in making what improvements he could on their farm that pleased his wife. An enjoyable pastime for him while doing his tasks was thinking of things he could make or do on the farm that would please her.

Since Karl Benjamin's birth, he knew his wife spent much less time enjoying the swing, but on a hot afternoon when the sun was doing its best to prove spring was on its way, Clarence spotted her. He'd been going to the shed to get a handful of nails and a hammer to repair a sagging gate, but when he saw his wife in her dark red knitted cardigan ducking under the damp clothes she'd hung on the line that morning, he knew she was heading towards the swing. From the set of her shoulders and her listless stride, it was obvious she was feeling down. He changed direction and strode across the farmyard towards her.

Clarence was worried about his wife's despondency. He knew it wasn't just thoughts of Anneke that were making his wife sad. His mother-in-law had been dead for almost two months. They were all adjusting to life without her—well, maybe not his father-in-law, but that was different. No, Clarence knew Roelena wasn't feeling blue solely on account of her mother's passing. His wife's dejection was partly on account of the knowledge and heartbreak that this baby would never know its Oma, and partly due to worry about their son.

Clarence was worried, too, not that he'd ever admit it to Roelena. His job was to lift her spirits by being optimistic and positive. He couldn't let her know their son's mystifying discontent this past week had filled him with worry, too. The baby had always been happy and content, but these last few days he'd cried consistently. Roelena had taken him to the doctor, but he could find nothing wrong with the baby and blamed the baby's discontent on discomfort from his ever-present eczema. Clarence knew Roelena didn't believe the doctor's verdict, although like him, she would never challenge a medical expert. But the fact was, Karl had been living with eczema since birth. It hadn't bothered him in the past, so why blame his discontent on it now? Clarence also knew that worry for Karl made his wife want to consult her own mother for advice, which only added to Roelena's dejection.

As Clarence approached the line of thin leafless trees, his rubber boots leaving muddy prints in the sparse patches of snow, he reminded himself to assess Roelena's mood and determine what his still-grieving wife needed from her husband. If he had to, he could suppress his natural instinct to crack a joke or say something that might make his wife laugh. He knew—because Roelena had explicitly told him during a rather unpleasant argument two weeks before—that his cajoling wasn't always welcome, that sometimes she just wanted to be sad and she should be allowed that indulgence. He wasn't as certain of that. For some reason, he'd been born with a natural optimism. Although he knew Roelena appreciated and loved this aspect of him, he'd learned over these last weeks that his wife didn't necessarily welcome them every time she was sad. But he was nothing if not patient and was willing to give her the time and space she needed to grieve.

He could tell that Roelena didn't see him or hear his approach until he was practically upon her. His sudden appearance startled her, which was to be expected, but he was a little hurt to see that she didn't seem pleased to see him. Or perhaps he'd just imagined it. He could tell that she'd been crying, which was understandable given the circumstances. And besides, he told himself, just because he was eager to spend a few minutes with his wife didn't mean she had to feel the same. After all, it was her mother who'd died, and her father whose grief she witnessed almost daily. He needed to support her in this time of great need. He could do that, and gladly.

He bent and kissed her cheek, then stepped back and sat down a few feet away on a patch of brown grass, his back against the trunk of a tree and his face lifted towards the sun. Clarence eyed his wife in concern as silent tears coursed down her cheeks. It was difficult for him to do nothing in the face of her tears. He wanted to go to her and take her into his arms, but he sensed that she didn't want that. Unlike her sister-in-law Ingrid, Roelena wasn't prone to tears. Since Anneke's death, though, Clarence had learned that his wife did indeed cry. He wanted to fix things so that she wouldn't cry ever again but, of course, he couldn't fix anything about her mother's absence.

His patience paid off and Roelena finally began to speak. She pushed at the ground with the toe of her boot, making the swing sway slightly. "Karl seemed better this morning. He was playing on the kitchen floor. And then I happened to turn and look at him and saw he was standing. All by himself. He's not even nine months old and he was standing by himself, and I was so happy. And as soon as I saw it, my first thought was, *I can't wait to tell Moe.*" Roelena balled up the damp handkerchief in her hand as she wagged her head. "And he looked so proud of himself, his legs all wobbly and unsteady. And then he saw me looking at him and he gave me his special smile and got all happy and bouncy and lost his balance and fell. He bumped his head on a kitchen chair, and started to cry. When I was comforting him, all I wanted to do was tell him he could show Oma what a big boy he was." Roelena seemed oblivious to the tears on her cheeks and plucked at the handkerchief in agitation. "But then I remembered he won't ever get to see his Oma. He won't even remember her."

Roelena finally looked over at her husband. "I miss her so much, Clarence."

Clarence saw this as an invitation to help and immediately moved to crouch in front of her, resting his hands on her knees to stop the motion of the swing. He could feel the damp under the knees of his canvas work pants, but he ignored it. "Sweetheart, listen, okay? The first thing you're going to do is to stop fidgeting with your *zakdoek* and start using it on your face. That's step one."

He saw her unveiled exasperation and knew it was because he was being jokey, but he honestly didn't know what else to do. She made no motion to follow his advice, so he smiled and nodded at the scrunched up handkerchief. "I can't tell you what step two is until step one has been successfully completed."

He could tell Roelena didn't want cheering up. She wanted her mother back. She wanted her son to know his Oma. She wanted her son to be healthy. And her husband's silliness couldn't make any of that happen. But what else could he do?

"Wipe and blow. I know you know how. I've seen you do it before."

Roelena sighed and then smiled weakly. He knew it was more for his benefit than her own. "What's step two?" she asked after wiping her face and blowing her nose.

Clarence was pleased that his ploy at cheerfulness was proving successful, even if Roelena's efforts were only half-hearted. "Step two is allowing your adoring husband to comfort you. Come on, up you get," Clarence pulled Roelena up with him, then turned and sat on the swing with Roelena on his lap. He wrapped his arms around her and she leaned back against his chest, dropping her head into the hollow of his neck.

"I know what step three is," Roelena murmured in a husky voice.

Clarence grinned, pleased with himself. Step three was, of course, kissing. He was taken aback suddenly when she placed her hands on Clarence's and moved them to rest on her breasts.

Clarence tilted his head to meet her gaze. In her eyes he saw the same look as on those summer nights when they would make love, the last rays of the setting sun bathing their bedroom in soft light. Clarence's heart leapt in response to the desire reflected in her eyes. He cleared his throat before responding. "You think step three is a kiss?"

"Not just a kiss," Roelena said softly, turning her head so he could more easily meet her lips. "A kiss…and then..."

Clarence felt a wave of physical desire as they began to kiss. He'd always loved how responsive his wife was to lovemaking, and had initially been surprised at her willing passion. He loved knowing how much she enjoyed his caresses. Their lovemaking was always immensely satisfying for both of them, he'd always thought. But this time her urgency took him by surprise, not that he minded. He stood up, turning and stepping away from the moving swing until Roelena was backed against the nearest tree. He was enjoying their passionate kiss immensely until Roelena began fumbling with his clothes.

"Whoa!" Clarence broke the kiss and stopped her groping hands, nodding behind her shoulder towards the road. "That car could have seen us."

Roelena glanced towards the road, belatedly noticing the passing vehicle. At this time of year there was no dust to show the vehicle's passage. "No one will see us," she murmured. She began kissing him again, urgently, but when she pushed his lightweight jacket off his shoulders, he once again stopped her, staying her wandering hands.

He grinned at her, delighted with her passionate response. He loved making love to his wife, but they were outside. And Roelena was wrong. The occupants of that car, had they been looking their way, could easily have seen them. The line of leafless trees was thin and offered no protection from the gaze of a passing stranger. Or, worse, from the gaze of a member of their congregation!

"Roelena, we're outside." Clarence took half a step back from her, dropping her hands. He lifted his cap and ran a hand through his hair, re-setting the cap on his head as he regarded his wife. She was flushed and panting, and her gaze looked strangely dazed. "Phew. Sweetheart, you've got me... well, you know." He laughed sheepishly, glancing down before resting his hands on his hips. "I know you're not yourself, sweetheart, but this sort of thing is for later, at night. In the privacy of our bedroom."

"But Clarence." Roelena was looking at him, as hurt and confused as if he'd just told her he didn't love her anymore. "I want to do this now. Here," she added. She reached for him, but he engulfed her hands in his and held them still.

"Lena, sweetheart," he said in a tone that didn't hide his amusement. "Someone could see. And what if your Pa or one of the boys were to suddenly drive into the yard? It would be embarrassing for all of us."

Clarence couldn't imagine what had come over Roelena to be so physically ardent in the middle of the afternoon. And outside, too yet. It wasn't like her at all. If he was honest with himself, a big part of him wanted to follow through with what she was suggesting. But it wouldn't be right. And she would certainly feel foolish after, as would he. Roelena's passion had taken him by surprise, and he was more than willing to match it—but at the right time and place. But that didn't stop him from grinning with pleasure knowing he would be looking forward to bedtime for the rest of the day.

"Go on inside," he added with a nod of his chin. "Karl's likely to wake from his nap soon, won't he?" He stepped forward and gave Roelena a quick peck on the cheek, then quickly backed away as if concerned she might make a grab for him. "I'll see you at suppertime, sweetheart."

Clarence turned and moved towards the barnyard. He glanced over his shoulder at Roelena and saw that she was watching him, although he couldn't read the expression on her face. "I love you, sweetheart," he called, then turned and whistled tunelessly under his breath, feeling like a million bucks.

Roelena watched her husband stride away towards the barnyard. She could still feel the heat of her desire flushing her skin and knew her cheeks were glowing the way they always did when her and Clarence made love. She closed her eyes briefly, enjoying the heat that surged through her veins, welcoming it, willing it to drown out the sorrow that churned in her soul. But lacking Clarence as a willing participant, the feeling of desire soon morphed into frustration. She crossed her arms, feeling both dissatisfaction and pleasure as her forearms brushed against her hardened nipples. Why hadn't Clarence been willing to make love to her, now, when she desperately needed him? Now. Not tonight. She didn't care who drove by. Or what time of day it was. Or that they were outside. No one would have seen them.

She wanted to feel him burrow deep inside her and make her loose awareness of anything and everything but his touch. As they'd kissed, she'd been picturing the provocative image of Patricia Talbot leaning against the tree with her head thrown back, her arms loose at her sides and her mouth open in blissful response to the feel of the man's lips on her bare breasts. Roelena had pictured the same image the first time she'd seen their swing. She'd never dare tell Clarence that her crimson cheeks that day were on account of picturing the dark-haired man making love to Patricia Talbot in the woods rather than a flush of pleasure at sight of his surprise, as Clarence assumed.

She sighed heavily, reluctantly making her way back towards the house. It was pointless to remain by the swing. Today it didn't have the capacity to offer her the solace she was seeking.

Inside the house, Roelena stood in the doorway to the kitchen. There were all kinds of tasks she could do, but she couldn't bring herself to start any of them. Restless and strangely tired, she walked down the short hallway to the bedroom and fell onto their double bed, curling into a ball with her hands tucked between her knees.

When she closed her eyes she saw again the image of Patricia Talbot in the woods with her head thrown back and her eyes closed as she let her lover pleasure her body. That's what Roelena wanted. Why did Clarence have to be such a prude? She didn't want him to make love to her tonight. She wanted him now; now, when she was feeling overwhelmed by sadness and need, she wanted the oblivion his touch brought.

She lifted a hand to her full breast as she imagined herself leaning against the tree and Clarence's mouth on her exposed breasts. Keeping her eyes closed, she pulled up her skirt, her fingers shaking as they frantically searched for the place between her legs that ached to be touched.

It was over quickly. She lay on her back, stunned and breathless, feeling her heart hammering in her chest. She hadn't known she could do that to herself. She hadn't known it would be so intense.

But she did know it was wicked. The Bible didn't say it explicitly, but that kind of touching was wrong. It was a sin and, as such, it was shameful.

A wave of self-disgust rippled through her. Overcome with shame, she lifted a hand to her face and began to weep, then moaned in mortification when her nostrils filled with the scent clinging to her fingers. She drew her knees to her chest and wrapped her arms around her legs as she sobbed. *What had she done?*

Minutes later, her tears spent, she swung her legs over the side of the bed and rose. In the bathroom, she turned on both taps and began washing her hands, but then set down the bar of soap and picked up the small nail brush that Clarence used to get the grease off his hands after he'd tinkered under the engine of their old car. Roelena scrubbed and scrubbed, tears falling heedlessly down her cheeks. She knew she could wash away the treacherous smell, but she would never be able to wash away her wickedness.

At the sound of Karl's cry, her hands stilled. She took a few deep, calming breaths, then rinsed her hands and splashed water onto her face, relieved to smell only the sharp clean fragrance of soap.

She would have to pray for forgiveness. Pray and pray, and never stop praying. And never, ever be tempted in such a way again.

After drying her hands and face on the thin towel hanging from a nail beside the mirror, she paused and looked at her reflection. She didn't appear to be any different, but she felt different. She *was* different. She was a new kind of sinner now. *What had compelled her to commit such a sin?* A heavy blanket of humiliation settled onto her shoulders as she realized she was a changed person.

But she could no longer ignore Karl's cries. "I'm coming, *liefje,*" she murmured, hurrying from the room.

19

WEDNESDAY, APRIL 9

Roelena was standing by the kitchen sink, finishing the last of the dinner dishes. Clarence had just driven away, heading to the home farm to help Jakob and Sijmon repair the shingles on the barn roof. When she heard a car pull into the drive her immediate thought was dread that Clarence had suddenly returned, but then sighed in relief when she looked through the window and saw Marliese's car. She'd temporarily forgotten about the planned visit. All the shops in town, including the library, closed on Wednesday afternoons, and Marliese had arranged to come for tea.

Marliese's visit was a welcome diversion. Roelena had barely slept the night before. Karl Benjamin had taken ages to fall asleep and then, when she finally went to bed, Clarence was still awake and wanted to make love. But the desire she'd felt earlier that afternoon had not returned and, for the first time in their marriage—and contrary to the advice of her mother—Roelena refused her husband. He'd been hurt and puzzled, but that hadn't changed her mind.

But then, when he fell asleep and she lay awake beside him, she began to weep silently. She was a terrible wife, she told herself, and a horrible, disgusting person. Eventually she'd fallen asleep. She'd hoped to feel better come morning, but she hadn't. She'd awoken feeling even more weary than when she'd gone to bed and her head and throat ached. She blamed this weariness on her guilty conscious preventing her from sleeping soundly, and wished she could erase the memory of what she'd done, but it was lurking in the background, a constant reminder of her wickedness and shame. All she could do was to keep praying for forgiveness.

Roelena dried her hands on her apron and moved through the porch and out onto the stoop. "Hello," she called lifting a hand briefly in a wave when Marliese opened her car door, then hurried down the steps with an order for Blackie to come. He was a lovely pet, but tended to greet guests with uninhibited exuberance. "Blackie, down," she instructed again.

"Oh, you look lovely," Roelena crowed on seeing Marliese emerge from her car, suddenly aware she was smiling for the first time that day. Her husband had tried to make her smile at breakfast, and again when he'd come in for coffee and for dinner, but he'd only succeeded in irritating her. *Thank goodness for Marliese,* Roelena thought, feeling her mood lift.

Marliese paused and posed beside her car, smiling brightly. She was wearing a pale blue linen suit, the three-button jacket fitting snugly at her trim waist and the three-quarter-length sleeves ending just above her white gloves. Her hat had a matching blue ribbon, while her taupe pumps and bag matched the stripes in her high-necked navy blouse. She gave a stylish turn, making the pleated skirt twirl. "The new line came in at Kresgie's," she announced as she sauntered towards Roelena on the narrow, graveled walkway. "The saleslady assured me this was the latest fashion."

Roelena felt a wave of sadness as she watched her friend approach. Roelena's short-sleeved cotton shirt dress and rather ragged red cardigan made her look exactly what she was: A housewife on a farm. Marliese, meanwhile, looked like she'd just stepped off a page in the *Women's Home Journal*. But it wasn't jealousy that Marliese could afford lovely clothes, nor was it jealousy that Marliese's slim figure perfectly suited the stylish cut of the new outfit. Roelena was sad because the sight of Marliese with her stylish clothes and perfectly applied cosmetics made her worry that their differences—and the fact that Roelena was a mother and Marliese might possibly never become one—would create a gulf between the two women.

Marliese noticed her friend's sudden sadness and hurried forward, her stylish pumps clicking on the gravel. "Roelena," she said with a frown, stopping in front of her friend. "I didn't mean for my new clothes to make you sad. I know you can't afford the same things as me. I shouldn't have worn the outfit." She laid a hand on Roelena's arm. "I'm sorry."

"Stop," Roelena chuckled softly, turning and beckoning for Marliese to follow her inside. Almost immediately she realized she'd been foolish to feel sad. Regardless of how different their day-to-day lives were becoming their friendship was as strong as ever. "You're beautiful, Marliese, and you deserve to have stylish clothes to wear. I'm not jealous, honest. Well, maybe a little." Roelena smiled affectionately over her shoulder as her friend followed her through the newspaper-lined porch and into the house. "Here, let me take your jacket. I'll put it in the bedroom."

"Oh, don't bother. I'll just hang it on a spare chair. Is Karl asleep?" Marliese asked as she stepped into the quiet kitchen. But then she spotted the baby, sitting in his high chair, a plastic bowl of custard pudding on the tray in front of him. It looked like he hadn't eaten any of it, but had instead smeared it all over his face, matted it in his hair, and spread it everywhere he could reach. When he saw Marliese standing in the doorway grinning at him, he smiled widely, banging his spoon on the tray and jabbering loud nonsense.

Marliese immediately approached him, speaking in singsong, playful tone, an adoring grin on her face. "Oh! Look at you, *schatje!* Has your Mommy let you make a big mess?"

Roelena smiled indulgently at her son as she set tea things on the table. "He's been so happy, playing with his pudding. I just keep giving him more. Clarence will say I'm spoiling him, but I don't care."

"So you shouldn't," Marliese said, as always, happy to take Roelena's side.

"He'll need to go down for his nap soon. Have you had your dinner?"

"Yes, I had a sandwich. Can I take him out and hold him?"

"No, you cannot!" Roelena laughed when she saw Marliese's startled look. She gestured at Karl. "Look at him. He's a mess. And he'll ruin your clothes."

"I don't care about my clothes. Do I, *liefje?"* Despite her reckless claim, Marliese removed her jacket and draped it over the back of a chair, then took the wet cloth Roelena handed to her. She began wiping Karl's face and hands, cooing to him all the while. She made to pick him up, but he protested, reaching for his mostly empty pudding bowl. Marliese picked it up and handed it to him, saying, "You can have your pudding, see? *Tante* Marliese will let you play with it on her lap."

"Marliese, you'll get pudding all over your new clothes."

"There's barely a spoonful left in the bowl. Well, maybe give me a tea towel for my lap. And anyway, my clothes can easily be washed, can't they, *liefje?"* she added indulgently, sitting down and settling Karl on her lap. She took the bowl from him and set it on the table in front of them. He immediately swished his spoon into it, distracted when a small dollop of pudding spilled onto the pristine surface of the table. He slapped his free hand against the drop, then gurgled in delight as he smeared it on the table.

"You spoil him worse than me." Roelena chided in a gentle tone as she took the seat opposite Marliese.

"*Tante* is allowed to spoil her *kliene aap,* isn't she?" Marliese fawned, leaning forward to kiss Karl's temple. She'd been calling him 'little monkey' since he was a baby. "He's happy today, isn't he? Did the doctor know why he's been fussing lately? It's not teething anymore, is it?"

"He blames everything on Karl's eczema. I don't, though. I wish I knew why some days he's so unhappy."

"But he's happy today. Oh! I brought him a present," Marliese said, suddenly remembering. "Can you hand me my handbag?"

Roelena reached for the purse Marliese had slipped onto the back of Roelena's chair. "Marliese, his birthday isn't until August."

"Need I remind you of the prerogative of a *tante*?" Marliese smiled at Roelena as she took the bag. She removed a small bag from it but then frowned at Roelena as she set it down. "You don't look so good, Roelena."

Roelena was taken aback. "Well…thanks."

"No, I don't mean that in an insulting way. I mean, are you feeling all right? You look…flushed and tired. Is it the baby?" She glanced at Roelena's waistline, which had not yet discernably changed.

"No. Well, maybe." Roelena picked up the tea pot and poured the tea. She scooped half a teaspoon of sugar into the first mug and stirred it before placing it in front of Marliese, making sure it was out of reach of Karl's inquisitive hands. "Yesterday he was standing for the first time all by himself. The first thought that came to my mind when I saw him was to rush to tell Moe. Then I realized I couldn't. She's gone, and…I don't know. It just got me down. And Clarence, he doesn't really understand. He's always doing these silly things, trying to cheer me up. But I don't want him to cheer me up. I just want him to let me be sad. And then I feel bad because he's trying so hard to make me happy and I feel obligated to respond and be cheerful." The two friends eyed each other in silence. "I suppose it's selfish to want to be sad for a while?"

"It is not. You're allowed to be sad for as long as you need to be. The problem with Clarence—I'll be nice," Marliese protested with a smile, seeing the look in Roelena's eyes. "I know you think I can't say anything good about your husband—or mine—but I'm about to surprise you. Ah!"

Both women laughed as Marliese caught the bowl that Karl had lifted and flung. She replaced it in front of them, holding onto it so that Karl could play with it without sending it flying across the room.

"Clarence is one of those people who is naturally optimistic," Marliese declared. "He goes through life with his glass half-full, not half-empty. So it's no surprise that, when his wife is sad, he wants to make a joke to make her smile. Believe it or not, I think his intentions are good. It's his method that needs adjustment." Marliese smiled grimly. "That's not meant as an insult. It's good that he wants to fix things. And one of the things he wants to fix right now is you. What he doesn't know—and probably never will—is that we women don't always want a man to offer a solution to our problem. Maybe all we want is a hug and a cuddle… well, perhaps a bit more than a cuddle," she added, winking suggestively at Roelena.

You're as bad as him," Roelena said. As she felt a wave of embarrassed heat envelop her body when she remembered what she'd hoped to do with Clarence in the woods the day before, she shrugged out of her cardigan. She knew now that anyone driving by on the road could very well have seen them. And what had followed when she was alone in the bedroom had been so wrong. It embarrassed and humiliated her to think about it, which was why she was flushing. "You and Clarence are really so alike, although I don't suppose either of you would ever admit it."

"I most certainly will not. We're opposite ends of the pole. He doesn't like me because I'm—*Roelena!*" Marliese exclaimed, staring at her friend's arms. "What happened to your arms?"

Roelena looked down at her bare arms and frowned at the red spots covering the length of both arms. When she'd awoken that morning, she'd had an itchy rash at the base of her neck above her collarbone. She'd been distractedly scratching at it, as well as at her arms under her cardigan, all morning. It seemed her scratching had made the rash worse.

Marliese stood up and sat Karl on the linoleum floor, quickly placing the bowl between his legs when he protested at being separated from it. She went and stood beside Roelena, placing her hand on her friend's forehead. "Good god, Roelena! You're burning up."

"Marliese, I honestly don't care that you swear, but you have to not say such things in front of Karl. I don't want his first words to be...*good god.* Can you imagine what Clarence would say?"

"*Ja!* Clarence would think he finally had sufficient proof for you to stop spending time with me. But never mind about that. Roelena, I think you have the measles."

"I had the measles when I was little. You can't get them twice."

"Either way, you have to get to a doctor."

"No, no. It's just a rash. It will pass."

"Maybe, maybe not. But you have Karl to think about.

You have to stay healthy so you can care for him. *And* you're pregnant. And anyway, what if it is the measles? They're contagious, I'm sure of it. The doctor will need to examine Karl to make sure he doesn't get sick. Come on. I'm driving you both into town right now."

"I really don't think I'm that sick, Marliese," Roelena protested, even though her head ached and her throat felt swollen. And her skin suddenly itched mightily. "If I need to see a doctor, Clarence can drive me in when he gets back from the home farm."

Marliese ignored her. "Do you have any other symptoms? Have you been feeling off?"

"I've been feeling off since the day I got pregnant. You know that."

"But anything different recently?"

When Roelena didn't respond, Marliese frowned. "What are you not telling me?"

Roelena shrugged, then said reluctantly, "I had a headache pretty much all day yesterday. When I woke up this morning, it was worse." Roelena brought a hand up to stroke the base of her throat. "And my throat hurts."

Marliese pushed Roelena's fingers aside. "Here?" she asked, gently feeling Roelena's neck. "You've got red spots here, too," she said, pushing aside Roelena's collar. "And your neck feels swollen. Maybe you have the mumps."

"Isn't that a disease children get? Not adults."

"Inform me please, when did you go to medical school? I can't quite remember."

Roelena pulled a face. "When did *you?"*

Marliese ignored her. "You said Clarence is at the home farm?"

"Yes. He's helping Jakob and Sijmon repair the barn roof."

Marliese looked at her watch. "It's almost two o'clock. We

could be in town by two-thirty and back home again before Clarence even knows you were gone. That is, if the doctor could see you right away. One look at your arms, and he will."

Roelena rested her elbow on the table and propped her forehead against her palm. She couldn't decide what was best. She couldn't even think properly. She felt her throat close with suppressed tears. She really didn't feel good, but if she could just go to bed and have a good sleep she felt sure she'd be fine. "I just want to go to bed. Maybe you could stay while I have a nap?"

Marliese was shaking her head. "I don't think a nap will fix whatever it is you have. Look," she added at Roelena's doubtful look. "If I'm wrong and you're not ill, then what? You've taken a trip to town with me. When do we ever get to do that, just us? And if I'm right and you're more ill than you think, then you—and maybe even Clarence—will thank me for being here to drive you to the doctor. Come on. What do you say?"

Roelena heaved a sigh. "I say I don't have the energy to argue."

"Good. Then we're going."

"That's not what I meant, Marliese. I meant, I think I should just lay down."

Marliese shook her head. "Look at your arms, Roelena. No way. I'm taking you to the doctor."

Roelena looked down at her arms. Maybe Marliese was right.

Marliese saw her acquiescence and said, "Tell me what to bring for Karl." Marliese arched her perfect eyebrows as she looked at Roelena expectantly.

"You're a good friend, Marliese. Thank you."

Marliese grinned. "Yes. And don't you let that husband of yours tell you any different, you hear?" She started ticking her fingers, saying, “A change of clothes, a few diapers, his bottle, his blanket…am I missing anything?”

They both looked over at Karl who was still happily playing with the little bit of pudding in his bowl.

“His pudding bowl?” Roelena suggested with a weak smile.

20

MONDAY, APRIL 14

"Knock-knock. Maid service coming through," Marliese announced as she entered Roelena's bedroom carrying a breakfast tray. "Oh! You're up."

Roelena was sitting up and pulling a cardigan on over her nightgown. She gave Marliese a wan smile. "I'm tired of being in bed," Roelena said. "I think I'm well enough to get up."

It had been five days since Marliese had taken her into town. Doctor Oliver, nearing sixty, had taken one look at her and immediately diagnosed her with German measles. He hadn't prescribed anything, instead telling them it was a virus that had to run its course and giving them the bad news that Roelena would likely get worse before she got better, then advised if Roelena's fever got too high, she was to be brought to the hospital.

Doctor Oliver hadn't been able to hide his concern, though, that Roelena had contracted the German measles in the early stages of pregnancy. In response Marliese had asked if the illness could harm Roelena's unborn baby, but the doctor evaded her question, saying only that they would have to wait and see until the baby was born. That hadn't satisfied Marliese, and she'd pushed until the doctor reluctantly divulged that babies born to mothers who'd had the German measles in their first trimester often had issues with their eyes and could possibly even be born blind. Seeing their horror, he'd quickly added that, since Roelena was fourteen weeks along, it was very possible her illness wouldn't impact the fetus. Roelena knew, though, that she'd spend the remainder of her pregnancy worrying.

"Well, eat first and then decide." Marliese forced Roelena to stay in bed, placing the tray on Roelena's lap. "I've brought you a soft-boiled egg and toast, and a mug of tea." Worried that the tea might spill, she lifted the mug and set it on the narrow cupboard beside the bed, making room first beside the glass of water and the Bible, then she sat on the bed facing Roelena.

For the first time in days, Roelena was actually feeling hungry, but she eyed the tray without enthusiasm. She knew Marliese had been taking care of her every day, and she didn't want to sound ungrateful, but she hated the thought of runny egg yolks.

"I'm kidding," Marliese said with a laugh. "I wanted to know if your sense of humour survived your illness. It's a hard-boiled egg, just the way you like it."

Roelena chuckled in relief. "It's impolite to tease an invalid," she protested, repositioning the pillows against the headboard. She picked up the boiled egg from where it was balanced in an egg cup. "How's Karl?" she added as she began peeling the egg.

"You ask me that every time I come through the door. And every time I answer the same. He's fine." Marliese smiled brightly, glad Roelena was engrossed in her egg and thus less likely to detect her lie.

The baby wasn't fine. Ingrid told Marliese that morning

when Marliese had stopped in that he was fussing an extraordinary amount the last two days. The baby's eczema hadn't worsened, so Ingrid didn't think that was a problem, but he'd been crying rather a lot. Marliese could tell that Ingrid, as much as she loved Karl, would be happy to return him to his mother. She'd asked Ingrid if she thought Marliese should take him to the doctor, but Ingrid said to wait until Roelena was on the mend. Then Marliese could bring mother and son to the doctor.

"Clarence likes soft-boiled eggs, but they turn my stomach."

"I turn your stomach?"

Roelena looked up with a smile, setting down her egg. "Clarence!" she enthused.

Her husband was hovering in the doorway and seemed uncertain whether he was allowed in.

"Clarence was the one who insisted I boil your egg for seven minutes. *Exactly.*"

Roelena was taken aback by the friendly smiles her husband and Marliese shared. *They're being nice to each other?*

Clarence entered the room then, going to the opposite side of the bed and sitting down before leaning forward to kiss his wife on the cheek. He gripped one of her hands in both of his. "Are you feeling better, sweetheart?"

Roelena didn't have to think about her answer. She desperately wanted a bath and a toothbrush, but she felt miles better. "Yes. A lot better, actually."

Clarence lifted a hand to her forehead. "Any fever?"

Roelena smiled. "No, not at all."

"And the rash?" He pulled up the sleeve of her cardigan to reveal her forearm. "It's almost gone."

"And my skin doesn't itch at all anymore."

"After your bath, you should rub baby oil into your skin." Marliese suggested.

Roelena turned to her friend. "I can't believe you've been here all this time taking care of me," Roelena said. She'd been feverish, but she remembered Marliese always being there, and then saying goodbye each evening when Clarence came in. "You've been amazing," Roelena added. "Thank you."

Marliese smiled and shrugged. "I'm just relieved you're feeling better."

"Have you seen Karl?" she asked Clarence.

"Every day. Ingrid is taking good care of him," Clarence stated in a reassuring tone. He, too, knew that Ingrid was getting worn out from caring for his fractious baby on top of having three of her own underfoot. "It was better for you to have a quiet house to help you recover."

"And no one else got the measles? Not any of the children?" Roelena had been concerned she'd spread the contagious virus.

"No one we know of," Marliese answered. "You must've picked up the virus in town."

Roelena turned to Clarence. "Can you go get him? Please? I need to see him, and I'm feeling much better now."

"Sure, sweetheart. I'll go this morning. By the time you've had your breakfast and a bath, I'll have him home. All right?"

Roelena smiled at her husband, feeling suddenly overwhelmed with gratitude and love. Teary-eyed, she could only nod.

He kissed her again, then turned to leave, but stopped when Marliese addressed him.

"Clarence, when you're at Ingrid's, can you phone Dr. Oliver and book an appointment for Roelena for tomorrow?" The County of Bellecourt still hadn't provided telephone lines to Roelena and Clarence's road. "He should see her now that she's on the mend, just to make sure."

"Sure will," he said, before leaving the room.

Marliese looked at Roelena and smiled. "After you eat, I'll help you wash your hair. You'll feel like a new woman."

"Marliese..." Roelena picked up the egg again, but her hands stilled as she stared at her friend.

"What? Eat." Marliese insisted, gesturing at the food. "Your toast is already cold, and your egg soon will be."

"I'm astonished at how well you and Clarence are getting along."

Marliese grinned at Roelena. "It is a shocker, isn't it? He even laughed at one of my jokes yesterday. Can you believe it?"

Shaking her head, Roelena gave her attention to her breakfast tray, salting her egg. "If I had known I needed to get the German measles in order for the two of you to start getting along, I would've done so years ago." She took a bite of her egg, pleased to find it was perfectly cooked.

"It was a radical intercession on your part, I agree."

Radical intercession, Roelena thought. Marliese often used really clever words and phrases. Although Roelena knew what the phrase meant, she would never have been able to use the words in conversation. But Marliese had always been smart, and working in the library had changed how Marliese expressed herself. Roelena suddenly looked at Marliese with alarm. "The library! Shouldn't you be there?"

"Enough with the questions, Roelena. Have some tea," Marliese handed her the full mug.

Roelena obediently took a sip. "Really, though. Aren't you supposed to be at your job?"

Marliese leaned one arm behind her as she watched Roelena, pleased to see her friend's appetite. "I've been working at the library for almost two years now, ever since it opened, and I never asked for time off before. I'll phone them later and let them know that I'll be back on Wednesday."

"Wednesday? What day is it today?" Roelena finished her egg and took a bite of the jam-covered toast.

"Monday."

"Marliese, you can go back to work tomorrow. Even today. I'm feeling better now."

"Yes, you're *feeling* better, but feeling better isn't the same as being fully recuperated. You can't just get back into being a housewife and mother right away. No. I'm staying with you today, especially now that Clarence is bringing Karl back. And I'll come again tomorrow and bring you and Karl to the doctor."

Roelena had been about to take another bite of toast, but stopped, looking with alarm at Marliese. "Is Karl sick? Tell me truthfully, did I give him the measles?"

Marliese smiled brightly, wishing she had chosen her words more carefully. "No, he doesn't have the measles. He's just been fussing. I think his eczema must be getting worse, but perhaps he's just missing his *moeder*. Roelena, don't stop eating. Now that you're on the mend, you have a lot of missed meals to catch up on."

"What about you? And Clarence? What if either of you get the German measles?"

"Well, then it will be your turn to be nursemaid. But so far we haven't, so I wouldn't worry about it. The doctor said it's contagious before the rash even appears. So you would've encountered someone with the virus days or even weeks before the spots appeared. And anyway, I feel fine, and so does Clarence. Now it's just a matter of you getting your strength back."

Roelena rested her hand on her belly, looking worried. "I wish I knew if the baby is going to be okay." Even through her fever, Roelena had been worrying.

"We have to wait until the baby is born to know for sure, but the doctor said there's a very good chance you were already past the danger point, so focus on the good news. You're almost fifteen weeks along, right?" Marliese paused, waiting for Roelena's nod before continuing. "Clarence told me he asked the *dominee* to pray for you and pray that your baby is born healthy in church yesterday. So now everyone in the community is praying for you and your unborn baby. And you'll see. Everything will be fine."

Roelena suspiciously eyed Marliese above the rim of her mug. Her friend never, ever talked about God with any sort of respect. In fact, Roelena often wondered about her friend's faith, especially considering she now freely took the Lord's name in vain. True Christians didn't do that, did they? But it wasn't something she felt she could ask. Maybe this comment meant Marliese was right with God even though she rarely talked as if God had any meaning in her life. Regardless, Roelena felt comforted by Marliese's comments. And she would take a page from Clarence's book and choose optimism.

"You're a good friend, Marliese. I'm blessed to have you."

Marliese dipped her head. For the first time since entering the bedroom, she looked sad. "I've always been selfish. You and I both know that," she admitted, lifting her eyes to meet Roelena's gaze. "But you're the only one who's never made me feel bad about it."

Roelena chuckled. "You're not selfish, Marliese. Misunderstood, yes; but not selfish." She gave her friend a pensive look. "I don't know how I'll ever repay you for all you've done for me these last few days."

"Well, I'm eager to be promoted from nursemaid back to best friend," Marliese stated as she rose. "I'm going to go run a bath for you while you finish your breakfast."

Alone in her room, Roelena munched her toast, her thoughts swirling. The day the doctor pronounced she had the German measles, Roelena had drawn the conclusion that the illness had been God's way of punishing her for her unspeakable sin. And she did deserve to be punished, of that she was certain, but she couldn't bear that her illness might have in some way harmed her unborn child. But while she sipped her tea, it dawned on her that this conclusion didn't make sense. If what the doctor said was correct, then she'd picked up the virus days before the rash had appeared. And if that were true, then she'd been sick well before she'd done what she'd done. Regardless, she would pray every minute of every day that God would spare her baby.

21

LETTER TO ROELENA FROM HENDRIK

Dear Roelena,

Thank you for your letter dated 17 April. Gladys and I are both so thankful that you have recovered from the German measles. Your renewed health is an answer to our heartfelt prayers. You mention you haven't yet regained your former full energy and pep, but Roelena you must give yourself time to convalesce. Don't overdo things. I know how industrious you are when it comes to getting your chores done, but your good health must come first.

It is a concern, I know, about whether your episode with the German measles will cause damage to your unborn baby's sight. I can only say that worrying for the next four or five months will not change anything about that outcome. Didn't Oma de Haas have a saying about worry? Worrying is praying for what you don't want? *I believe she was right and I hope you take her wisdom to heart, although I understand, too, how difficult it must be. Regardless, Gladys and I are praying every day for the health of your next baby.*

In her last letter, Greta writes how low she feels sometimes from missing Moe and how it is a struggle then to find comfort in her faith. Pa's letters also read so solemn and grave. Greta has her four children (and I hear a fifth is on the way), so that keeps her busy, which is good I think at a time like this. I worry about how Pa will cope, though, without his helpmate by his side. But his faith is the strongest of anyone I know. And I need to take Oma de Haas's advice about worry, do I not? When I picture the farmhouse, though, I see Moe in it and sometimes for me it's a shock all over again to realize she's not there. I can only imagine how it must be for you and the others who go there daily or weekly. I pray for Pa, as I know how much he loved Moe, and I pray for Greta, who I know feels she lost her closest friend, and I pray for you and Ingrid and Jakob and all the others who loved Moe and who now must be there for Pa. We must also find a way to take comfort in knowing she's in her heavenly home where we will one day all reunite. And because we know that day will come, I truly believe we can find joy in the present again.

I know it was not a happy occasion for Gladys and I to be in Alberta in February for the funeral, but I'm grateful to have seen Moe before she died, and to have been with the family at such a time. I only wish Harri had already been married and been able to afford train fare for both himself and Therese as I feel he sorely missed his helpmate. He was far more shaken up about Moe's passing than I would have expected given his long absence from home, but we can never know the inner workings of another's heart, and I can only pray that he, too, finds solace in knowing our Heavenly Father's plan for us. I am so curious to meet Therese one day although it is strange to have a sister-in-law with whom I cannot speak unless, of course, between now and then, she learns English as I don't think anyone of us will be learning French.

It was also a special joy to see baby Alida and baby Karl again. They each changed so much from the babies Gladys and I met when we visited last fall, but babies do that, don't they? From a two-month old to a seven-month old they are unrecognizable. As Karl and Alida are so close in age, they will likely be good friends all their life long. We do so appreciate the photographs you tuck into your letters now and then as it's a delight to see the nieces and nephews growing and happy. Gladys and I pray we shall be as richly blessed one day with a herd of children of our own. I am sorry to hear Karl's teething troubles are still bothering him but am glad the teething powder seems to help. As Moe would say, this troubling stage will soon pass.

And now I must close as the evening draws to a close and my eyelids become heavy. I am always grateful for the rejuvenating power of sleep as there is much work to be done in the orchard this time of year. Our expansion plans keep us very busy, for which I am grateful. As always, there is satisfaction to be had when you see the good results of your hard work.

Stay well, Roelena, and put all your worries in the hands of our loving God and Jesus Christ His son.

Your loving brother,
Hendrik

22

MONDAY, JUNE 2

"*The hospital in Edmonton?"* Roelena stared at the doctor in shock. She absently jiggled Karl Benjamin on her lap, hoping it would diminish his fussing restlessness.

"Yes, Mrs. van Haarmelen. Karl's skin condition is troubling. The way his skin is peeling off the palms of his hands and the soles of his feet?" He shook his head in grave concern. "I think your only option now is to have the specialist in Edmonton examine him. He'll have far more training than I in these kinds of ailments."

They were in Dr. Oliver's office in Bellecourt, the third visit in as many weeks. Roelena was desperate for him to cure whatever ailed her baby, but it had never dawned on her that he wouldn't know what to do to cure Karl, nor that he would recommend they take their baby to see a specialist doctor in Edmonton. Did that mean Karl was far more sick than Dr. Oliver first thought?

She turned to regard Clarence where he sat in the chair beside her, wanting to know if he was as confused as she was but all his attention was on the doctor. Roelena realized

Clarence was still angry with her. They'd argued a few short hours before when she'd insisted he accompany her to the doctor's office. Clarence felt she was being overly anxious about Karl and repeatedly troubling the doctor wasn't helping. And maybe she was being overly anxious. She had indeed brought Karl to the doctor repeatedly, but that was because Karl wasn't getting any better. Roelena knew their argument had been a continuation of the argument they'd had the week before. Her motivation to do anything that would ease Karl's skin condition, which seemed to make him cry all the time these days, had prompted her to spontaneously purchase a yard of the finest silk from McMinn's Dry Goods store. She'd paid more for that one yard of fabric than she'd ever spent on groceries. At home, she'd cut the swath of fabric, using half to make diaper liners and the other half as a bottom sheet for Karl's crib, hoping that the material would soothe his irritated skin. But the only thing the silk had done was provoke an argument with Clarence when he found out how much it had cost. She didn't care though. It didn't matter to her. She would buy yards and yards of it and eat nothing but potatoes for weeks if it meant her son's suffering would be eased.

A wave of anger suddenly threatened to choke Roelena, but she didn't know if she was angry at Clarence or at Dr. Oliver. She was so confused. She didn't understand why the doctor had been saying for months that Karl's irritating eczema was causing his distress and that the skin condition would pass with time. Yet now he was urging them to take Karl to a specialist doctor in the city. If he didn't have the know-how to cure Karl's skin problem, why hadn't he sent them to this other doctor long ago?

Roelena wished she had the courage to challenge the doctor. Or perhaps she wished Clarence did. But who were they to challenge an educated medical professional? She hadn't even finished grade eight. And Clarence's education had been interrupted during the war and then he'd gone to a trades school for a year to learn carpentry. Dr. Oliver had years and years of education and training. He knew what was best. Didn't he? Roelena felt guilty for her anger, but that only increased her level of frustration.

She rocked Karl and shushed him under her breath, eyeing Clarence. Her husband was using his polite voice as he addressed the doctor, and that irritated her as well. She wished then that Marliese was with her instead of her husband.

"They'll be able to treat him there? They can make him better?"

Dr. Oliver waggled his head, offering neither a no or a yes. "They will have seen other children with this condition, which is why it's best to give Karl over to their care."

It sounded to Roelena like the doctor was evading the question. Was he? Or was her suspicion only a result of her anxiety? Regardless, she had to find the courage to ask if the city doctor would know how to cure Karl. She had to. "Doctor, will they be able to cure him?"

Clarence took Roelena's hand and gripped it hard. She knew he was telling her that her tone was marginally inappropriate, but she didn't care.

"I can only say again, if anyone can help him, they can."

The doctor's response was anything but reassuring. Roelena tore her hand from Clarence's grip, choking back her tears.

"When should we bring Karl to see this doctor?" Clarence asked in a courteous tone.

Roelena stood up before the doctor had a chance to respond to Clarence's question. "If we have to drive to Edmonton today, then we best leave now," she announced, jiggling the fussing baby in her arms. In six weeks, he would celebrate his first birthday, she told herself. Everything would be fine. He'd be one of those active toddlers causing five times more havoc than he did while crawling. And she would welcome it all, if only this unbearable thing that was making him sick would pass.

"Mrs. van Haarmelen, it's almost three o'clock," the doctor protested. "You can't go to Edmonton today. The specialist you need to consult with wouldn't be available." He must have seen her face crumple for he held up a hand in a gesture requesting patience as he, too, stood. "Stay here a moment, please. Let me go make a telephone call," he said, then left the room.

Karl fussed in Roelena's arms and she rocked him, murmuring soothingly in Dutch.

"Roelena, give him to me. You're upset and he feels it."

Clarence was right, she was upset, but she wasn't about to relinquish her baby to anyone, except maybe the doctor in Edmonton. She made no move to hand Karl to Clarence, but remained standing, walking in small circles behind the chair Clarence still occupied.

"Ask him, Clarence," she said instead, her voice low and demanding. She was on the brink of tears, she knew, but she was too stubborn to let them fall while still in the doctor's office. "Ask him why he didn't send us to Edmonton weeks ago—months ago—if he knew the doctors there had the knowledge to treat Karl. *Ask him that!*"

"I can't do that," Clarence argued, his voice low. "He's a doctor. He's educated. He knows what he's doing." Clarence made a visible effort to swallow his impatience. "Look, when we get to the University Hospital, the specialist there will know exactly what to do. You'll see, sweetheart. There's nothing to worry about."

"Stop telling me not to worry," Roelena hissed. "You're worried, too. Don't try telling me you're not. You know as well as I do that Karl must be really sick if Dr. Oliver is sending us to Edmonton."

"Roelena," Clarence rose to stand beside her. He lightly ran a hand up and down her back, but dropped it when she bristled in annoyance.

Clarence loved his wife and knew her to be a sweet and kind woman, but in the short time they'd been married he'd also learned she had a decidedly stubborn streak. He'd mentioned this once to his father-in-law. Kees had smiled, saying that Roelena inherited the trait from her equally sweet and equally obstinate mother.

"Arguing with me, or Dr. Oliver for that matter, isn't going to change anything," he said in as soothing a tone as he could muster. "Okay, maybe I am a little worried too. But I'm also glad Dr. Oliver is sending us to Edmonton. That means Karl will be well soon, doesn't it? You heard what he said. The doctors there are experts. This is an answer to our prayers, don't you see?"

Roelena closed her eyes and stood swaying gently, resting her lips on the top of Karl's warm head. She did believe that God listened when they prayed. She really did. Maybe Clarence was right. God was sending them to the specialist in Edmonton because the doctor there would know what to do. Just because Anneke had been sent to a hospital and died, didn't mean the same would happen Karl.

Dr. Oliver re-entered the room, closing the door behind him. "Have a seat, please," he said as he sat behind his desk. He had a piece of paper in his hand and waited until Roelena was seated before handing it to Clarence.

"I've arranged for Dr. Sullivan to examine your baby when you admit him to the University hospital tomorrow morning. He'll be there doing his rounds at eight o'clock. That will take a couple of hours, so make sure you're there no later than ten o'clock."

"Admit him? To the hospital in Edmonton?" When Roelena clutched Karl closer to her, he protested and she eased her grip. "You mean leave him there?"

"Yes, Mrs. van Haarmelen. I thought that was understood."

"No! I thought you wanted us to see a specialist at the University Hospital, but that he would give us something to treat Karl. I can't leave him in the hospital. It's too far away."

"He's just a baby, Mrs. van Haarmelen," the doctor assured. "He won't even know you're not there. If he were older, I would recommend you make arrangements to stay with relatives or friends in the city. But really, he'll be very well taken care of by the doctors and nurses at the University Hospital." Then he added with a benevolent, grandfatherly smile, "And before you know it, you'll be able to return to Edmonton to take him home. You'll see"

Roelena could no longer hold back her tears. Leave her baby in a hospital one hundred miles away? That was asking too much! She heard her husband politely thank the doctor and, through her blurred vision, saw Clarence tuck the piece of paper into his shirt pocket. When she felt Clarence's hand on her elbow, she rose and let him usher her out of the doctor's office.

When she was seated in the car with Karl on her lap, she broke down and wept. "I can't leave him there with strangers, Clarence. *I can't!"* She buried her face in Karl's hair, hugging the baby to her. His cries of protest mingled with hers.

Instead of starting the car, Clarence reached into the pocket of his trousers and pulled out a clean handkerchief. "Yes you can, sweetheart, because it means Karl will get better. Here." He tucked the handkerchief into her hand. "Stop crying. It's upsetting Karl."

Clarence was right. She was upsetting her baby. She had

to stay calm. Had to think of Karl and what was best for him. Roelena forced herself to breathe deeply.

"You're right," she admitted, nodding. She took the handkerchief from him and wiped her face and blew her nose, then wrapped her arms loosely around her fussing baby, gently rocking him. "Can we stop at Pa's on the way home?" she said to Clarence. "We'll need to use his car for the drive to Edmonton."

"Of course, sweetheart. I was going to anyway."

Clarence started the car and backed out of the angled parking spot, craning his head over his shoulder to ensure it was safe. In the first month of their marriage, he'd backed out of a spot just like this one thinking it was safe. He hadn't seen the other vehicle coming and had backed right into it. He'd been embarrassed and disgusted with himself, and hadn't told Roelena. Then, a month later, a notice came in the mail that he owed over one hundred dollars in damages to the owner of the car he'd hit. They'd had to borrow the money from Kees, and Roelena had good-naturedly teased Clarence about his secret indiscretion. Since then, not only was Clarence extremely cautious when backing out of angled parking spots, Roelena also usually grinned at him, a sparkle of humour brightening her eyes. Today, however, she didn't acknowledge his caution.

Clarence glanced at his wife and child, praying that the assurances he'd given her were true. It was times like these that faith in God was a comfort. God did love them, and God would never seek to harm an innocent child. But even as he tried to comfort himself with this thought, images of Holland during the German Occupation invaded his mind. He'd seen many sick and starving people deserving of well-being. Old people had died, but so had children. Innocent children. It was hard to reconcile the God of love they worshiped with the God who'd allowed such suffering to occur.

Clarence immediately banished this blasphemous thought. It wasn't God who'd let them die. It was the Germans, or rather, the Nazis. And there were no Nazis here, and no war. Karl Benjamin would be fine. And, in the end, hadn't God sent the Canadian soldiers to liberate Holland? The Hollanders had partied in the streets after that. God had saved them then, and God would save Karl now.

23

TUESDAY, JUNE 3

"I know it's frayed on the edges, but he's attached to his blanket. Please keep it with him at all times."

"Of course, Mrs. van Haarmelen. When I had my wee ones, they each had a blankie, too. I completely understand."

The diminutive nurse's accent reminded Roelena of Mrs. Dickson, the mailman's wife.

"Are you from Scotland?"

The nurse chuckled. "Well, close, but no. I'm from Ireland. And where's your accent from, then?"

"Holland," Roelena.

"Ach, yes. I should've guessed, what with your height and all," the nurse said. "I'm getting a crick in my neck just looking up at you."

Roelena could tell that the kindly nurse was trying to reassure her, but she would rather the nurse be serious than lighthearted. She looked at her baby instead of at the nurse. His face was flushed with fever, but he'd been strangely calm all morning as if he knew he'd come to this sterile place to get well.

"Rest easy, dearie," the kindly nurse insisted. "Doctor

Sullivan looks young, but he is a very well-respected pediatrician."

Before today, Roelena hadn't known what a pediatrician was, but now she knew it described a doctor who specialized in children's illnesses.

They'd left their farm before six o'clock that morning, eager and impatient to consult with the specialist. Sijmon had promised to come and milk their cows, but they'd departed even before he arrived. They'd shown up at the doctor's office in the children's unit hours before their appointment, surprising the nurses and the doctor. Instead of making them wait, though, he put off his round and ushered them into an examination room to assess little Karl.

Roelena wavered between feeling glad to see Dr. Sullivan and terrified that Karl needed someone with his expertise. But the doctor had almost immediately guessed what might be wrong with Karl. He'd called it acrodynia. She'd repeated the word in her head so she could remember it, not that it meant anything to her. But she didn't want to forget. She'd been concentrating so hard on remembering the word, she missed what the doctor had been saying. But he was telling them that the peeling skin on the baby's hands and feet supported this diagnosis and that Karl's condition was very advanced. It was a huge relief for Roelena to be given this immediate diagnosis after months of old Dr. Oliver's hemming and hawing about Karl's rash. Clarence had been right. This specialist doctor knew what Karl was really suffering from and thus knew how to cure him.

Roelena tore her gaze from Karl's flushed cheeks to look down at the nurse. "He knew right away that Karl's skin condition wasn't eczema. That's what Dr. Oliver in Bellecourt always said it was. But Dr. Sullivan called it..." Roelena hesitated, then repeated the word slowly and carefully. "Acrodynia."

The nurse's eyebrows raised. "Acrodynia?"

Roelena frowned at her. Was the nurse surprised? Concerned? Worried? "Do you know what that is? Have you had babies here before with the same condition? Do you know how to cure it?"

"Yes, yes. It's a blood problem that manifests in this kind of peeling." The nurse lifted one of Karl's hands and stroked the peeling skin on the palm. "Dr. Sullivan has successfully treated children with this condition in the past."

"He said he knew how to treat Karl." Roelena's voice wobbled then and she had to struggle to continue. "But he also said Karl was very, very sick."

The nurse responded in a reassuring tone. "Then wee Karl is in the right place, is he not? He needs the care only a hospital can provide. Oh, here's your handsome husband, come to fetch you. My, you're tall. Have you filled out the paperwork?" she asked when Clarence joined them. "We have your telephone number on file?"

"Yes," Clarence responded politely. "Well, we don't have a telephone yet, but I've put my father-in-law's telephone number on the form. He's only two miles away."

Roelena was eyeing the other occupants of the nursery ward. There were a dozen cribs in the room, and more than half were filled with babies of varying ages. Some were sleeping, a few were crying, and others were sitting listlessly in their cribs, looking dazed or sad. They all seemed forsaken and unloved.

Roelena met the nurse's gaze, wiping away the tears that kept leaking from her eyes. "What's your name?" she asked in a wobbly voice.

"You can call me Jennie," she said.

"Promise me you'll hold him when he cries? He needs to be held." Roelena looked at the other babies again. There was one other nurse in the room, but she was filling out a chart and seemed oblivious to sick children. "You can't just leave him crying in his crib. Promise me you'll hold him."

"We have nurses' aides who come—they're not here yet, but they will be soon—and they'll hold him. And we have candy stripers too. They especially love babies." When Roelena didn't look reassured, the kindly nurse added, "We'll all do our best to comfort him. We'll hold him as often as we can. I can see he's extra special," she added with a reassuring smile.

"He *is* special." Roelena wiped away her tears with the back of her hand. "And he likes to be held, like this," she demonstrated. "He wants to be able to see around him. He only tolerates laying cradled in your arms if you're giving him a bottle. Will you tell the others?" Her voice wobbled on her last words as she choked on a sob.

"Now, now, you're making it worse for yourself, and for the wee one. And in your condition, too." The nurse nodded at Roelena's pregnancy bump. She held out her hands to take Karl. "I know it's hard, but say goodbye now."

Roelena didn't loosen her grip, instead nodding at a baby who was crying. "But that baby is crying."

"I know. But the nurse's aides and candy stripers haven't started their shifts yet. I promise you, all the babies will be held and fed very soon. And visiting hours start in less than half an hour. Some of the mothers will be here then." The nurse gestured again. "Here now, let me take him."

Instead of handing Karl to her, Roelena turned to face Clarence and ducked her head, hugging Karl close. She rocked him, her tears soaking his little blue bonnet.

"Lena, honey," Clarence said softly, wrapping his arms around his weeping wife. He, too was fighting a thickness in his own throat. It seemed wrong somehow to leave Karl here. And strange, too, that Karl wasn't crying, but the baby remained quiet in his mother's arms as if he wasn't sick at all.

That or he was just too tired to cry. "Let the nurse have him. Dr. Sullivan will make him better. You'll see."

"I can't. I can't, I can't."

Clarence felt Roelena shudder, and he fought hard not to break down himself. He wished there was something he could do, anything, to make this less painful for his wife. "Yes you can, sweetheart," Clarence whispered into her hair. "It's for Karl's good. He'll get better here."

Roelena abruptly broke away from her husband's embrace and turned to face the nurse. She repeatedly kissed Karl flushed cheek, surprised he wasn't crying in protest at her smothering hugs and kisses. *Maybe he was already getting better,* she thought.

"You promise?" she demanded, blinking away her tears and making eye contact with the nurse. "You promise someone will hold him when he cries?"

"Of course, dearie," the nurse said, an edge of impatience creeping into her tone as she took Karl from her. She looked at Clarence and gave a definitive nod. "Best that you go now."

Through a blurred gaze, Roelena saw Clarence rest a hand on Karl's head then stoop to kiss his cheek. Then he turned and steered them both out of the ward.

Roelena walked blindly at her husband's side as they headed towards the bank of elevators. Inside, with no one sharing the space, she sank against Clarence's chest, clinging to the lapels of his Sunday suit jacket and grateful for the support of his strong arms. She wanted to go back to the ward and snatch her baby away from the nurse. But that wouldn't cure Karl. And Karl would be cured now. They just had to wait for a telephone call informing them when to return to collect him.

When the elevator doors opened, Roelena forced herself to take deep breaths as she strode at Clarence's side towards the exit. *Wait for the telephone call, that's all you have to do.*

Wait for the telephone call and then Karl will my back in my arms.

Outside the hospital, Clarence was surprised to see bright sunshine. With all the emotion he'd been feeling, Clarence would not have been surprised to step outside to see dark, threatening clouds. It felt odd, somehow, being greeted by sunshine and hearing the sounds of birds chirping in the trees and shrubs that lined the hospital parking lot.

Clarence kept an arm around Roelena's waist as they moved across the pavement towards their car. At the passenger side of the car, he opened the door, gently coaxing her inside. He hurried around to the driver's side, digging his keys out of his trouser pocket. Once seated behind the wheel, he looked across at Roelena. His wife's arms looked strangely empty. Their baby had rarely left them these last few weeks.

Clarence turned away and looked out the windshield. It seemed wrong somehow to drive away. He set his hat on the seat beside him and ran a hand through his hair, distractedly watching automobiles drive into the parking lot. Men and women, sometimes with children, parked and got out. Some walked leisurely; others scurried towards the entrance. Some carried flowers or small parcels; others were empty handed. Had any of them left their baby in the care of strangers? He wondered if he should've made arrangements for him and Roelena to stay with *Oom* Jan and *Tante* Stina on their farm. That didn't make sense, though. Roelena's uncle and aunt lived at least a 45-minute drive from the hospital. No, he thought, it was better to go home and have work to do on the farm. It would keep his mind occupied. In a few days they would get a telephone call from the hospital telling them to pick up their son. And then all would be well again.

Clarence realized he'd been so preoccupied with his thoughts as he stared out the windshield that he'd completely filtered out the sound of his wife's weeping. He turned to regard her again, worry etching lines into his broad forehead. She'd dropped her face into her hands and her strong shoulders were shaking with sobs. He'd been woolgathering, and done nothing to try to comfort her. What kind of terrible husband was he?

"Lena, sweetheart," he said, reaching into his pocket to dig out his handkerchief. He shifted across the seat and put his arm around her shoulders, forcing her to lean against his chest. "Here. Wipe and blow, that's what you say to Tomas." He held out his handkerchief. "Stop crying, sweetheart. We'll be back in a few days to collect him, and everything will be different then. Now, blow your face and honk your nose."

Roelena took the handkerchief, but didn't respond to his attempt at humour. She clearly wasn't interested in the kind of cheering up he had to offer. But it was all he had to give.

"Let's go home, Clarence," Roelena said in a neutral tone as she mopped her face.

Clarence waited for Roelena to raise her head. He was hoping she would offer him a smile in return, even a weak one, but she didn't. He sighed. *Good thing he had patience in spades,* he said to himself. That's what happened to boys growing up with a house full of sisters. He kissed Roelena's temple before shifting over to resume his seat behind the steering wheel. He felt a renewed sense of certainty that, soon, they'd be in this very same parking lot, overjoyed to be collecting their son whose health would be on the mend. Over the next few days, his sole job would be to convince Roelena of the same thing.

He started the car and began to back out of the parking

spot, then slammed on the brakes realizing he'd forgotten to shoulder check. No cars were in sight, so he continued to cautiously ease out.

Periodically during their return trip, Clarence tried cajoling Roelena into a positive outlook about having left their son in the hospital, that a week from now Karl would be much improved, but Roelena refused to be cheered. They didn't argue, but neither did they talk. Mostly, she kept her silent gaze out the window.

As soon as they returned home after exchanging Kees's car for their own at the home farm, Roelena busied herself in the kitchen making a pot of tea and slicing a loaf of bread. She set these on the table in front of Clarence with some butter and cheese. When she joined him, both still wearing their Sunday best, Clarence bowed his head and offered a heartfelt prayer to God pleading for Karl's wellbeing, expressing gratitude to God for the expertise of Dr. Sullivan, and thanks for the kindness of the nurse on the ward.

After the prayer, the couple ate their bread and drank their tea in silence, each lost in their own thoughts. Roelena suddenly pushed away from the table and her chair crashed loudly to the floor.

Clarence jumped, startled out of his own reverie.

"I'm going to Ingrid's. Do you want to come?"

He stared at her for a moment, not recognizing the hard, desperate edge that gleamed in her eye. "Do you want me to?" he asked.

"No. I mean," she dropped her head into her hands and rubbed at her face as if her cheeks were wet. They weren't. "It's up to you. I just don't want to be in this house without him. Don't." She quickly added, seeing him open his mouth.

"I was just going to say that I'll stay here," he stated, dropping his gaze to his mug. He was hurt that Roelena wasn't turning to him for comfort, but he knew when she was in a mood like this, no amount of cajoling on his part could lift her spirits. These unpleasant moods of hers had only started after her *moeder* died and Karl got sick. Once Karl was better, she would no longer have reason to be moody or angry.

"Do you want me to make you dinner before I go?"

Clarence shook his head, gesturing at the bread and cheese on the table. "No. This will tide me over until supper."

Roelena nodded. "All right." She stood a moment longer, as if trying to remember something, but then only added, "See you later, then," and left the kitchen.

Clarence sat, unmoving, as he listened to her departure. When the noise of the car faded, he rose slowly. His gaze fell on the overturned chair on the floor and he bent slowly to right it, pushing it gently, almost soundlessly, snug against the table. He couldn't believe that Roelena had left without giving him a goodbye kiss. She'd never done that before. Always, when the two went their separate ways, even if he only left to go to the barn or to do some other outside chore around the yard or in the fields, he always kissed her. Or if she left to go to town, to the doctor, or to visit Marliese or the home farm, she always kissed him before leaving. But today, she'd hesitated as if knowing she was supposed to do something before leaving. But then she'd left without kissing him. Was that intentional? If it was, he wondered if she blamed him for the foreign sound of silence in their little house, and hoped instead she was simply missing Karl so much that she'd simply forgotten.

They would have to talk about this, he decided. He would join her for supper at the home farm but instead of coming straight home after, they would go for a drive, maybe take the scenic route past Sandpiper Lake. She would have to talk to him then. And she would have to let him comfort her.

His optimism resurfaced as Clarence considered his wife's mood. It was temporary, this distance she'd created between them. They likely wouldn't have to take the long way home, he felt certain. When he arrived at his father-in-law's home later that afternoon, Roelena would kiss him, and he would know everything between them was fine again. An afternoon spent with Ingrid would put things in perspective for her. Women needed to talk to other women when they were sad or angry, didn't they? Then they went home to their husbands and were happy again. Isn't that how it worked?

And soon, very soon, Karl would be home and things would be back to normal.

24

THURSDAY, JUNE 5

The shrill, demanding sound of the telephone woke Kees from his sleep. He resisted, feeling sure that Anneke had been with him in his dream world, knowing he would lose the sensation of being with his beloved wife if he allowed himself to wake fully. But the telephone continued its insistent ringing, two short rings and one long, which meant it was a call for the de Haas farmhouse. His dream spiraled away and disintegrated in less than a second as Kees sat up in bed and opened his eyes. It was pitch dark, and he was suddenly disoriented. *What time was it?*

The phone rang again, two short and one long. Their house shared a party line with three neighbours, although strangely Jakob and Ingrid were connected to a different party line. The ringing of the phone was waking everyone who shared the line, though, that much he knew.

He automatically tucked his feet into his slippers as he rose, half stumbling in the dark towards the doorway of the bedroom. He flicked the switch on the wall beside the bedroom door the sudden electric lighting so bright he had to squint.

"Coming, coming," he muttered needlessly as the telephone resumed its shrill ringing, two short and one long. He entered the kitchen and switched on the overhead light, glancing at the clock on the wall, surprised to see it was ten minutes past three o'clock in the morning. For some reason, he'd assumed it was late in the evening, not yet midnight.

"*Ja,* hello?" His voice was croaky when he spoke. When he cleared his throat loudly he missed hearing the first words of the caller. "Again, please? Who is calling?"

He heard Sijmon enter the room and glanced over his shoulder to see his son slip through the door at the bottom of the staircase.

"*Ja,* this is Mrs. van Haarmelen's *vader,* father…I see…*Ach, nee!"*

Sijmon watched his father, a look of dread on his face. He'd known immediately upon waking that the telephone call had something to do with his sick nephew who'd been admitted to the hospital three days before. When he heard his father exclaim 'no' in Dutch, he had to swallow hard to quell the sudden lump clogging his throat.

"*...ja, Ik zal het hen vertellen.* I will tell them…*ja...dag*. Bye."

Kees hung up the receiver, but he didn't turn around and his hand remained on the telephone as if for support.

"Pa? Is Karl…?"

Kees blinked and straightened up. He'd forgotten about Sijmon. He turned to face his son, feeling suddenly like an old man, far older than his sixty-one years. He reached for a chair and slowly dragged it out from the table, sinking into it heavily before resting his elbows on the table and cradling his head in his hands.

How could God ask him to do this thing? Pass on this devastating news to his daughter? *How?* Anneke had been gone almost four months, but it felt more like four decades. He'd been taking what comfort he could in reminding himself that she was in her heavenly home. But this news had evaporated solace as if it had never been. Her absence felt suddenly sharp and excruciating. He felt his heart keening for her, and realized he'd made a terrible sound.

"Pa?" Sijmon asked.

Kees didn't lift his head. He hadn't heard his son approach but he felt his hand rest briefly on his shoulder.

"Pa. Has Karl died?" Sijmon asked when Kees didn't speak.

Kees shuddered at the awful sound of the words. He sucked in a deep breath and then dropped his hands from his face and lifted his head. The back of the wooden chair creaked as he leaned back to look up at the only child who still lived at home with him. Sijmon had such a quiet nature, not unlike Kees's own, that sometimes it felt like he lived alone. Kees nodded. "Twenty minutes ago."

Sijmon was expecting to hear his suspicion confirmed, yet it still shocked him. He pulled out a chair and sat down. As he stared at his father, he realized how much Kees had aged since Anneke's death. His parents had been true companions to one another, and although Kees only spoke about Anneke's passing with the comfort of knowing she was with God, Sijmon knew that his quiet, soft-spoken father had suffered considerably since his wife's death.

"The one thing," Kees said in Dutch, finally breaking the silence. He lifted a finger and wagged it briefly before allowing his hand to drop into his lap. "The one thing I have dared to expect of God is to spare my children the grief of losing a child. Anneke and I faced it. Three times."

Sijmon had only been two-and-a-half years old when his baby sister died and he didn't remember her, but he'd been a child of eight when Wiekje died. The easily recalled the unpleasant memories of seeing his otherwise cheerful mother crying, and the nightmares he'd had about others in his family dying. Wiekje had been healthy, like Roelena, robust and strong, and it had been a shock to the whole family when she hadn't survived her appendix surgery. His parents also lost the child whom Sijmon had been named after. That child died after having his tonsils removed at the age of seven. Anneke often told the story of how as a young child, that first Sijmon had loved to play on the banks of the canals. He would float sticks and leaves and little home-made boats. When he was four, he'd fallen in and Anneke, who couldn't swim, had jumped in after him. After they'd both been rescued, the precocious boy had the audacity to scold his mother that she, unlike him, had lost her *klompen* in the canal. Sijmon almost smiled as the image of his mother telling that story came back to him. A sparkle always appeared in her eyes every time she re-told that story.

Throughout the years, his parents and siblings often talked about these other children who'd died. They'd never been forgotten.

His father was speaking again, and Sijmon refocused on him.

"But in this age of modern medicine? Parents should be spared that." Kees paused and shook his head. When he spoke next, his voice broke. "My daughter should be spared that."

After several silent moments passed, Sijmon asked, "Pa? Should I get dressed and start the car?" He swallowed before speaking again. It took courage to say what came next. "Do you want me to tell Roelena and Clarence?"

Kees slowly shook his head. "No, son. I'll go. But I'll wait a while yet. In her condition, Roelena needs her sleep. Things will be hard enough for them, for the next little while, without suffering from lack of sleep."

Sijmon eyed his father's bent head. "Shall I make tea for you?" he finally asked.

"No," Kees stated. "Go back to bed. Try sleep for an hour or two yet before it's time to start the milking."

Sijmon could go back to bed, but he wouldn't sleep. "Shall I wake Jakob and tell him?"

"No, son. That, too, can wait. Go on to bed."

Sijmon rose reluctantly, feeling guilt that he knew of this tragedy yet his sister slept, oblivious to the heartbreak that was in store for her.

Sijmon paused at the bottom of the stairs. "Call me if you need anything, Pa." When no reply was forthcoming, he opened the door, its hinges creaking, and slowly climbed the stairs. When he got to the top he looked back the way he'd come. He hadn't closed the door at the bottom of the stairs and the light from the kitchen lit the bottom end of the stairwell.

It somehow didn't seem right to seek the comfort of his bed so he sat down on the top step, lost in thought.

Sijmon didn't know how long he'd been sitting there when he became aware of a strange, unidentifiable noise. He'd never before heard such a sound and it took a few seconds for him to place it. When he realized what it was, he rose abruptly and scurried as soundlessly as possible to his bedroom, closing the door and burrowing under the covers in an effort to drown out the sound. But his father's broken-hearted weeping had released his own flood of emotion, and Sijmon, for the first time in years, wept a river of tears into his pillow.

In the kitchen, Kees's hands covered his face as he sobbed, his shoulders shaking as spasms overtook him. He didn't seem aware of the wail of despair that came from deep within his chest, nor was he aware that he was muttering his wife's name over and over, crying out for her in his time of need. He'd thought the worst of his grief over Anneke's death had passed. He'd taken comfort in his faith, as he always did, knowing that his dear wife was with God in the place He reserved for her, and knowing also that someday Kees would join her in God's heavenly Kingdom. But to live in this quiet house without her was unbearable at times. He missed the little things, like the clicking of her knitting needles or the sound of her pen scratching on a page as she wrote her many letters to their loved ones. The absence of her slippers under the bed and the water glass on her night stand could take him unawares and a stab of pain would flatten him. Yet, in all those moments of grief and despair, he had been able to find comfort in his faith.

But he hadn't counted on this! He hadn't counted on his dearly loved grandson dying so prematurely. He hadn't considered having to tell his darling daughter that her first-born, her pride, her joy, had been taken home to live with their Heavenly Father. From his own experience, Kees knew that the only comfort he could give his daughter and son-in-law was the knowledge that little Karl was in a better place, in heaven with God. But he also knew from experience that these next few hours could provide nothing but excruciating confusion and pain.

Kees' sobs eventually quieted, and eventually he was able to pray again. He prayed for strength. He prayed for comfort. And today, for the first time in his adult life, alone and bereft, he prayed for faith, something he hadn't needed to pray for even after the death of three children and his beloved wife.

25
THURSDAY, JUNE 5

"Roelena." When his wife didn't respond, Clarence placed his hand on her shoulder and shook gently, calling her name again. "Roelena."

Her eyes opened.

"Your Pa just drove into the driveway."

Roelena sat up immediately. Their room was bathed in light. Had she overslept? A glance at the clock beside the bed showed it was half past five o'clock in the morning. Her Pa could only be visiting this early for one reason—the hospital in Edmonton had telephoned. Was Karl all right? Was he crying for his mother? Roelena's throat tightened as she envisioned her son's distress.

Throwing the blankets off, she scrambled for her slippers and knitted cardigan and hurried out of the bedroom behind Clarence. As she passed the kitchen, tucking her arms into the sleeves of her cardigan, she noticed the teapot on the table with the sugar pot and a mug, and realized that Clarence must have risen early and made his own tea. That meant that, despite his assurances, he was more worried than he let on.

But her concern for her husband was fleeting as she joined him on the outside stoop. "You're up already," Kees said needlessly as he approached them.

Roelena examined her father's face as he mounted the stairs. He looked tired, older, but then he had looked like that ever since Anneke's passing. As he made to move past her, he briefly rested his hand on her arm, but he avoided her gaze and said only, "Come inside, *kind.*"

Roelena shared an uneasy glance with Clarence as they followed Kees inside. Their dog, Blackie, looked up at them, wagging its tail, hoping its breakfast would be brought out soon. Roelena ignored the animal, letting the screen door bang closed behind her.

"Pa, did the hospital telephone?" Roelena demanded. She didn't wait for Kees to sit down at the kitchen table, didn't offer him tea, or take a seat herself. She stood with a hand to her throat, dreading the news her father brought, news that complications had arisen and her baby was more sick than they'd been led to believe.

Kees stood at the kitchen table, facing her, his hands resting on the back of a chair and his head sunk low into his shoulders.

"Ach, kind. Ik ben bedroefd." For the last three sorrowful hours, Kees had been praying for strength, praying for God to give him the right words to say to ease the pain he would inflict upon his daughter and her husband, but he was weighed down by a boulder of sadness. *I am filled with sorrow.*

He dragged a chair out from under the table and sat down heavily. *"Zitten,"* he said, gesturing for them to sit. When neither his daughter nor Clarence did as he asked, he wearily repeated his entreaty. *"Astublieft, kinderen...astublieft." Please, children, please.*

Clarence took his usual seat at the head of the small table. Roelena stood frozen as she stared at Kees, but now she moved forward abruptly and sat opposite her father. *"Pa.* What did they say?"

Kees reached across the table and took his daughter's hand is his, doing the same with Clarence's before turning to meet his daughter's gaze. *"Liefje,"* he said to Roelena, shaking his head.

Roelena gripped her father's hand. He was rarely physically demonstrative, and he hadn't called her *liefje* since she was a little girl.

"Pa?" she repeated in a small voice.

"Little Karl was called to God early this morning. I'm so sorry, *liefje*. So, so sorry."

Roelena stared at him, shaking her head, her eyes filling with moisture. "No, Pa. No, no, no! They're going to make him better. That's why we left him there." She turned to her husband. "Clarence, tell him," she demanded, as if all it needed to negate her father's words was for Clarence to agree. "They're going to make him better."

Roelena registered the dazed look in Clarence's face but continued to glare at him expectantly.

"Yes," Clarence finally said. "They were going to try and make him better." He nodded at Roelena as if pleased he'd given the correct answer, but then he jumped when her palm slammed against the tabletop, rattling the dishes.

"No!" she shouted, glaring at her husband. "They didn't say they would *try*. They said they would make him better. *You* said they would make him better." She jerked her hand out of her father's grasp and hugged both arms against the mound of her stomach, rocking herself as if the baby inside her were in her arms. "They said they would make him better," she repeated, staring accusingly at Clarence. "Don't you remember? Dr. Sullivan said so, didn't he, Clarence?"

Kees interrupted her. "Roelena, *kind*, stop. Let's pray

together, shall we? And ask God for the comfort only He can give."

"I don't want *comfort*," Roelena spat. *"I want Karl."* When Roelena said her son's name, something seemed to loosen something inside her and she began to weep.

Kees retrieved a clean, dry handkerchief from his pocket. Although Margaret Langelaar came every morning to do housework and some of the cooking, he'd ironed that square of linen himself. He liked ironing. There was something both soothing and satisfying about making the wrinkles evaporate. He reached across the table and tucked it into his daughter's hand.

"No. No, no, no, no." she moaned, her face in her hands. "Not my baby."

Kees looked over to Clarence, expecting her daughter's husband to comfort his overwrought wife, but Clarence seemed to be in a state of shock, unable to process his father-in-law's earth-shattering news. Kees rose then and walked around the table so he could kneel between them, resting a comforting hand on each of their shoulders.

What would Anneke say now if she were here? What would she do? Kees couldn't think, and wished only that his daughter would stop crying, but he also knew she had to let the tears run their course.

Maybe that's what Anneke would do, he thought. Wait patiently for the tears to come to an end, as they eventually must.

Clarence couldn't absorb the news his father-in-law delivered. He couldn't. His mind was stuck somehow, somewhere. Frozen. Rooted. Petrified.

He felt the presence of his father-in-law kneeling beside

him. He heard his wife sobbing and knew he was meant to be doing something—*comforting her?*—but he couldn't think.

And then he felt a kind of tug on his trouser leg. He glanced down, half expecting to see his feet stuck in sludge like the time he'd lost his rubber boot in the muddy bank of the abandoned beaver pond. What he saw instead was his baby son standing at his knee and smiling up at him. Clarence felt an immediate leap of joy in his heart. *Karl was alive!* And well. In fact, he was glowing with health. He was standing at Clarence's knee, steady and firm and confidant. But he was too young to stand on his own like that. Clarence saw then that Karl's eyes were different. No longer the eyes of a baby, but eyes full of knowledge and wisdom, and an indescribable kind of peace. Or perhaps well-being. When Karl saw he'd gained his father's attention, the look in his eyes seemed to bathe Clarence in rays of depthless love, enveloping the man in an unequivocal and inarguable state of utter wellbeing. In that insightful moment, Clarence knew Karl was dead, yes, but he was home; home in Heaven; home where all was well and would be eternally.

When Clarence felt a touch on his hand, he looked down fully expecting to see his son's perfect little hand on his; instead, he saw his father-in-law's hand resting on his, the skin spotted with age. Clarence looked to his other side, but Karl was gone.

He felt Kees put Roelena's hand in his and he held it loosely as he regarded his weeping wife. He felt suddenly bewildered. *Hadn't Karl just been right there, at his feet?*

But that wasn't possible. It had only been a vision.

Not *only*, Clarence corrected immediately. What he'd felt when he'd met his son's gaze? That had been undeniable. It was real. He could still see the all-knowing depths of his son's gaze encasing him in a powerful, all-encompassing state of love and well-being. He was overcome with a sense of certainty unlike any he'd ever held, more powerful than all his beliefs combined, that Karl was fine. Karl was *home*. The feeling lingered, euphoric and beautiful. And Clarence knew that, even though he would grieve desperately for the earthly loss of his first-born baby son, he would never forget Karl's visit—*from heaven?*—that brought clarity and certainty about Karl's well-being.

Clarence knew what he had to do then and his grip on his wife's hand tightened. He had to take care of his wife. He had to pass along the comfort, as best he could, of the certainty of knowing their son was in a place of love so grand and so vast that a lifetime of words could not hope to describe it.

"Sweetheart," Clarence said. His father-in-law was no longer there—*where had he gone?*—and Clarence sank to his knees on the floor beside his weeping wife, pulling Roelena into his embrace, feeling his own tears join hers. He was desolate his son would never walk this earth; and yet…and yet he still felt the power of knowing his son was at peace, he was at home, in Heaven. He knew what he'd seen hadn't been real. No one else had seen it. He'd never waste time trying to convince anyone, not even Roelena, that he'd seen Karl. But he knew, *he knew,* Karl was well, and happy, and so very, very loved. And he would wring every bit of comfort from that knowledge. And his sureness, his certainty of the eternity of love that enveloped Karl, would be the avenue he would take to bring comfort to his grieving wife.

He felt the euphoria again of Karl's presence; he could see his cherubic face shining with his own well-being. And when the grief of Karl's earthly absence became too much in the days to come, he would soothe himself by reaching for this feeling, this memory, this knowledge that love and only love surrounded his most dearly beloved, precious baby boy.

Clarence wasn't sure how much time had passed since Kees's arrival, but the three of them were still sitting at the table. He'd moved his chair so he was beside Roelena. She leaned against him, quiet now, her spasm of weeping spent.

"What time did he pass away?" Roelena suddenly asked, her tone listless.

Clarence looked expectantly at his father-in-law.

"They called in the middle of the night, shortly after three o'clock," Kees said. "They said he...he died at two-fifty." Kees saw the dull, silent accusation in his daughter's gaze before she closed her eyes. "I thought it best you should sleep, *liefje*. You have to think of the baby. The next few days will be difficult enough, without adding lack of sleep."

When Roelena's eyes opened again, he was surprised to see a kind of vacant look, as if her gaze had turned inward and she was no longer aware of her father or her husband's presence.

"What do we do now?" Clarence asked.

"I will help you. I'll visit Connors Funeral Home in town, then visit the *dominee*."

Kees had used the services of the funeral home in Bellecourt twice before, once fourteen years ago when his daughter Wiekje had died, and then again four months ago, for Anneke. They would remember him.

"Shouldn't Roelena and I do that?" Clarence asked, glancing down at his wife. She was sagged against him and seemed to have absented herself from their conversation.

Kees rested his gaze on Clarence, who was the stronger of the two in that moment. Kees knew from experience their roles would change. At times Clarence would be the stronger of the two, at other times, Roelena. But together they would make it through this, just as he and Anneke had done when they'd lost their darling children. *Oh, Anneke, I need you,* he wanted to say, but instead he looked at Clarence and said, "I'll make the arrangements because the two of you must go to Edmonton and collect Karl. Did I not tell you that? I'm sorry. They asked that you bring a blanket, to wrap him in. As soon as I get back to the farm, I'll send Sijmon to pick you up. At a time like this, and with a task such as this, it's best you don't drive."

Kees waited until Clarence gave him a dazed nod, then added, "I'll telephone Connors in town to make sure they're ready for you. We should have the funeral soon. It's best not to wait too long. It's...it's just better that way."

Roelena slowly pushed away from Clarence, sitting up on her own. "Funeral?" she asked, her tone puzzled.

"You don't have to worry about that, Roelena," Kees assured. Seeing his daughter struggle to process the worst possible news she'd ever have the misfortune to receive was breaking his heart. "I'll make the arrangements," Kees repeated, then addressed Clarence. "After, when what you must do today is accomplished, Sijmon will bring you to the house where we'll be together, the whole family."

Clarence nodded, knowing Roelena would find comfort in the presence of her loving family.

"What about telling everyone?" Clarence asked. "They should all be told." He thought of the shockwave that would ripple through their community upon hearing this terrible news. And their loved ones far away. Should they make telephone calls? Or send telegrams? What was best?

"I'll see to all that," Kees was saying. "For now, your only task is to get ready to travel to Edmonton. I'll send Sijmon to fetch you as soon as I get home."

"But I have to do the milking."

"No, Clarence. Jakob and I will come and do your milking."

Clarence felt himself nod again. His father-in-law's strength, he realized then, was unshakable, the foundation of his faith making him the stalwart pillar he and Roelena could lean on in this, their time of greatest need.

Clarence looked over at Roelena. She still appeared dazed and confused. "Sweetheart, do you understand? You need to get dressed, and then Sijmon will drive us to the hospital to pick up..." Clarence paused, swallowing the lump in his throat. "We need to collect Karl, and bring him to the funeral home in town."

"Yes." Roelena stood and moved slowly and carefully towards the hallway. "I'll get dressed."

Kees and Clarence shared a glance. "Will she be all right?" Kees asked.

Clarence nodded. "I'll take care of her."

"I have no doubt." Kees regarded his son-in-law, a man he'd always described as unstintingly optimistic and cheerful. That lighthearted countenance had evaporated, yet...yet he looked strangely composed. Perhaps he was in a state of shock. "And you, son? Will you be all right?"

Clarence nodded, unable to speak around the lump in his throat. He hadn't forgotten the feeling of that beautiful vision, yet the reality of what lay ahead for him and his wife —especially his wife—was weighing on him.

Kees removed a piece of paper from his pocket and handed it to Clarence. "This is the building you must go to, to retrieve...Karl. I...they said to bring a blanket. Did I tell you that?"

"Yes."

Kees sighed. "I should go."

"Will you pray with me first?"

"Of course." Kees looked towards the doorway. "Should we wait for Roelena?"

Clarence shook his head, leaning forward and folding his

hands on the tabletop. "Leave her be for now. Pray for her though, and me. I don't know how..." Clarence's chin trembled as he looked towards the doorway through which Roelena had left. Although the feeling of Karl's wellbeing in his Heavenly Home lingered, he too felt hopelessly inadequate when he thought of the depth of his wife's grief. "I don't know how to get Roelena through this."

Kees rested his hand on Clarence's. "With God's help, son. With God's help. That's the only way."

Then Kees bowed his head and began to pray.

26
THURSDAY, JUNE 5

Roelena rode in the car between her brother, who was behind the wheel, and her husband. She stared sightlessly out the windshield, her thoughts, as they had been in the hour since her father's visit, consumed by her baby. Her Karl.

She'd accepted the reality of his death. She had. She understood what it meant. He was gone. He would never grow older, never be a toddler or go to school or be a teenager. She understood that, even accepted it in a strange, powerless way.

What she couldn't reconcile was that she'd slept on, oblivious, for hours after he'd died. That seemed so wrong. That wasn't something a mother would do, was it? Why hadn't she woken the instant he'd passed? After all, she was his only mother. She should have known, But she'd slept. And not fitfully, but deeply. What kind of mother was she that she didn't even know her baby was dead; a baby who relied on her for his food, his warmth, his comfort. *His life!*

But he hadn't relied on her for his life, had he? Because

she'd given him away to a distant hospital, to strangers. And now he was dead.

She'd only half-listened to the dialogue between Clarence and her father, yet she somehow was able to recall every word. Her Pa would telephone the others. He would make arrangements for the funeral. He would visit the *dominee*. Her Pa knew what to do and she would let him.

When Sijmon turned into the parking lot of the hospital, it felt as if only minutes had pass, as if time had folded in upon itself. How long ago was it that she and Clarence had driven into this parking lot? How long ago had Clarence reassured her that everything would be fine, that the next time they went to the hospital they'd collect their son. Only they were collecting their son, but not in the way Roelena had envisioned. It had never entered her head they would soon return to collect her son's…body. Even in the silent tomb of her mind, Roelena tripped on the word. *Body. Her baby son's tiny body.*

Roelena didn't look over but she knew Sjmon had stopped beside the parking attendant's tiny building and was rolling down his window. She heard him say, "We need to go to the Lincoln Wing. Where is it and where should I park?"

Roelena frowned. Why did they need to go the Lincoln Wing? That wasn't where they'd left Karl. They'd brought him to the Children's Wing. She was sure of it. But it was far too difficult to form words and speak them, so she remained silent. After all, what difference did it make. Karl was dead.

Karl was dead! She wanted to wail. She wanted to gnash her teeth and tear her clothes like the grieving women in the Bible; yet, at the same time, she knew that would take a reserve of energy that she simply didn't have.

She saw Sijmon put a ticket on the dash of the car, felt them moving again.

Roelena only half listened as Clarence spoke her name,

told her they had an appointment to see Dr. Sullivan. He'd already told her that, but it made no sense. Roelena didn't want to see that confident young doctor again. He couldn't make Karl better. He hadn't made Karl better.

A thought tickled on the edges of her mind. Did she blame him for Karl's death? Should she? She didn't know.

When Sijmon parked the car and turned off the ignition, Roelena could feel her husband's hand on her arm, urging her to look at him. She didn't want to. Then he was out of the car, holding open the passenger door and leaning in, calling to her.

"Roelena, come inside, sweetheart. Sijmon will stay in the car."

I am a statue, she thought, but then Clarence reached in and gently tugged on her arm and she found herself stepping out of the car.

A picture of the friendly nurse suddenly appeared in her head, the one who sounded like Mrs. Dickson. What was her name? *Jennie.* The nurse had promised to have someone hold Karl when he cried. Had she kept her promise? What if no one had been holding him when he drew his final breath? What if he'd died all alone in his crib on the starched white hospital sheet, strangers with white hats and jackets as oblivious to his passing as she had been? But that couldn't be. They'd said he died at two-fifty in the morning. Or was that the time when they'd noticed he died?

Roelena heard the sound of a breathless sob and knew it was her own. She felt Clarence support her with an arm at her waist and realized he was ushering her across the parking lot. They entered the double doors of the hospital and walked down corridors that looked strangely familiar to her. For a brief moment, Roelena felt the weight of Karl in her arms. She'd been carrying him the last time she'd walked this way. But she looked down and saw her empty arms and the sensation vanished. She no longer had a baby to carry!

But she'd been thinking something important. What was it? *Had someone been holding Karl when he died?* That was important; it was the only thing she needed to know, the only thing that mattered.

And then the young doctor was standing in front of them. What was his name? Dr. Sullivan. He was talking, but she couldn't process his words. She studied him, noticing how his eyes were darting, never meeting hers and never landing anywhere for longer than a second or two. *Why wouldn't he look at her?* His eyebrows, she noticed, were thick and heavy, like side-ways exclamation marks. Funny she hadn't noticed that before. Beneath his hospital jacket, she saw he wore a white shirt and a navy tie with red flecks. The spots looked like blood splatters. She supposed if he did get blood on the tie, it would blend in, which made the tie a practical choice. But that was silly. If he wanted to wear clothes that would blend in with splattered blood, why chose a white shirt and a white hospital jacket?

She noticed his feet below the hem of his perfectly creased trousers. His shoes were shiny, expensive-looking. He was rocking back on his heels, then forward, then back. Why was he rocking? He wasn't holding a baby. He was still talking, she saw. She felt she had to make her own mouth move as well. Why had she wanted to do that? She remembered then, and spoke, the sound of conversation suddenly loud in her ears where before there had been a vacuum of silence.

"Was someone holding him when he died?"

The doctor stopped talking and very briefly met Roelena's gaze before his eyes skittered away.

"The nurse, Jennie, she promised someone would hold him if he cried," she stated, her tone matter-of-fact.

The doctor hesitated, then said, "Yes, Mrs. van Haarmelen, I believe someone was holding him when he died."

Roelena nodded, then abruptly turned and began walking back the way they'd come. She heard Clarence's footsteps running behind her, catching up with her, felt his arm at her waist. She saw that he was holding a manila envelope in his other hand. She felt certain she should ask about the contents, but doing so would take too much effort.

When they exited the building, she heard Clarence say, "The Lincoln Wing is on the other side of the hospital complex. We'll drive there, and park close to the entrance."

She understood his words, but said nothing, instead walking at his side in silence across the parking lot to her Pa's car. She ignored the door he opened to the front seat of the car and instead wordlessly climbed into the back seat, barely registering when Clarence gave her a concerned glance before climbing into the front seat.

It seemed only moments later that he was standing at her open door again.

"Are you coming in?" Clarence asked.

"No." Her response was immediate. She hadn't known she could think and speak so quickly. But her tongue and mouth had known what to say. She would not enter that hospital ever again.

She was aware that Clarence stood in silence beside her, knew her brother had turned to glance at her, but that changed nothing. She wouldn't enter the Lincoln Wing. She knew what was in there and she couldn't bear it.

"It's okay, sweetheart. I'll go," Clarence finally said.

As soon as the car door closed, Roelena turned to watch Clarence stride away, the white afghan her *moeder* knit bundled against his chest. In her peripheral vision she was aware Sijmon was watching him as well. She was glad it was

Sijmon who was with them and not her Pa. Sijmon didn't need to speak either.

Clarence entered through a set of double doors above which was a sign, *Lincoln Wing*. She wondered who Lincoln was, then wondered if there were other dead babies in that wing. Did parents like her and Clarence come here on a regular basis with an empty blanket, only to re-emerge from the building with…with what? Roelena stared, not taking her eyes off the spot where Clarence had disappeared. She could not have said how much time had passed before he reappeared with a middle-aged nurse. Not the kindly nurse named Jennie, but a tall, skinny woman carrying a blanket-wrapped bundle.

Roelena wanted to look away but was riveted by the sight. She knew her baby was inside that blanket; her Karl, her perfect baby boy. She wondered if, in death, his skin was still red and irritated. She hoped it wasn't.

And then Clarence was getting into the back seat through the door behind Sijmon and that woman was carefully transferring the bundle she carried to Clarence's waiting arms.

Roelena said nothing, only held out her arms. She closed her eyes once she held the precious, blanketed bundle, hugging her baby against her chest. There was no warmth in the bundle. She knew her baby was dead, but she was so grateful to hold him. She moaned then and felt her husband slide beside her and pull her into his arms as she began to sob, her arms hugging the still, cold form, her face buried in the soft wool.

She wasn't aware of time passing. As if from a far distance she heard Clarence and Sijmon's voices, but she didn't assign any meaning to their words. Clarence was still beside her in the back seat. She was still holding the bundle. Her cold, still baby. But he would never again feel any pain, never again cry. Was there comfort in that thought?

He'd been such a happy baby before he'd gotten sick. Roelena let herself be pulled into soothing memories, smiling in her mind as her thoughts drifted to the baby shower the church women had hosted. She'd received so many lovely presents for Karl. Her favourite gift had been the *Baby's First Year* book. That wasn't from any of the church ladies, but from Hendrik's wife Gladys. It had come in the mail. Roelena had enjoyed recording notable things about Karl in that book. On the page labelled Identification Marks, she'd written *blue* beside "colour of eyes" and *black* beside "colour of hair". Beside "colour of eyebrows and eyelashes" she'd written *none*. At the time, she'd thought that category odd. Didn't the people who printed the book know that babies weren't born with eyebrows and eyelashes? At least not the babies she'd seen. Beside "complexion" she'd written *rosy red*, little knowing at the time that he would suffer so excruciatingly from eczema. Except it hadn't been eczema, had it? It had been...what was the word? Acrodynia. *No, don't think about that,* she scolded herself. Think about the book. There had been another category on the page marked "Identification Marks". What was it? Oh, yes. Under "remarks" she'd written, *very lovable*. And he was. He was so very, very loveable. Even when he fussed, he'd been easy to love because she knew he only fussed on account of his discomfort. He'd always been a lovely baby, a beautiful baby.

Roelena stared unseeing out the window. An image of the cold, still baby within the bundle in her arms flashed across her mind. No! She wouldn't think about that either. She would think about Karl's baby book. She liked thinking about that. There was a page titled "Measurements at Birth". She'd written his weight—*seven pounds, fourteen ounces*—but the other headings—length, circumference of head, chest measurements, birth certificate number—she'd left blank thinking them rather silly. But on another page she'd listed all the gifts and pasted in the congratulatory cards, carefully spacing them so they could be read again later.

She recalled the day Karl had been playing with his pudding. He'd been so sweet and funny that day. He'd made her and Marliese laugh.

Laugh. As if she would ever laugh again. There was no place for laughter inside her, nor would there ever be.

She pictured her Moe then. She'd laughed frequently and easily. That suddenly puzzled Roelena. Her Moe had buried three children. Yet laughter had found her again. How was that even possible? Roelena would ask her Moe just as soon as they got home. But then she realized she couldn't, could she? Moe was dead, just like Karl.

Roelena felt something release in her mind then as if a thread tethered to the tapestry of her life snapped and the shuttle on the giant loom of her life shuddered to a halt.

27

SATURDAY, JUNE 7

She almost lost her footing, and had to clutch Clarence's arm as they slowly made their way across the cemetery following the pallbearers. Four of her brothers—Jakob, Sijmon, Willem, and Pieter—carried the coffin from the church to the graveyard.

It seemed wrong to her that four large men carried such a small box. They dwarfed it. They should have asked Greta's boys to carry it. They were easily strong enough. But no, that wouldn't have been right. They were only eleven and nine. Besides, children couldn't be pallbearers. Could they? But it was wrong, somehow, her brothers almost tripping on each other as they balanced the miniature coffin on their shoulders. Why hadn't someone insisted on a larger coffin?

She watched, strangely detached, as her brothers gently deposited the coffin on the platform next to the open grave. The scene felt strangely familiar. Was she dreaming this? No. This was real. Then she understood why it was familiar. Before, in the other scene, the coffin had been larger. It had held her mother, not her son. It had been bitterly cold that day. She shivered, remembering how cold her mother must have been wearing only her Sunday dress inside that thin box. Would Karl be cold? Roelena looked up. The sun was shining. There wasn't a single cloud to mar the blue. How could that be? Why weren't there any clouds? There should be fury in the sky, shouldn't there? Wasn't God sad? Why wasn't God grieving? But wait, it was good that it wasn't cold, wasn't it? The hot sun warmed the box, warmed the baby inside. Warm was much better than cold.

Roelena could feel the warmth of the sun on her skin. She wished the warmth would penetrate beneath her skin, wished it could evaporate the cold, dark, black cavity that pushed so painfully against her ribs. But the sun had lost its power to warm her.

Those standing at the graveside began to move away, and Roelena frowned. Why was the *dominee* looking at her? He was holding his Bible, but it was closed. Shouldn't he be reading from it? Or praying? She thought of her Pa's prayer from the night before. He'd asked God to give his daughter strength in her time of need. He'd asked for strength for all of them, but especially for her and Clarence. She remembered that. She had meant to tell her Pa that it wasn't strength she needed, but warmth. Warmth to banish that cold black creature taking up all the space inside of her. But God would know it was there. He would hear the words of the prayer, but He would know that what she truly needed was simply warmth.

Upon returning to their own farm after the funeral, Roelena had gone straight to bed even though it wasn't nighttime. She'd lain there, her mind touching on her mother, her sister Wiekje, her baby Karl, touching and then fleeing, wanting to believe they were together in heaven, then overcome with sorrow at knowing in her lifetime she would never see any of them again.

Clarence brought her a tray of food, but she ignored him, ignored the food.

But now Ingrid was there. She wouldn't let herself be ignored and made Roelena dress and then steered her into the kitchen. Roelena sat at the table with Jakob and Clarence while Ingrid busied herself at the stove, setting out buns, and rustling about in the pantry for cheese, butter, and jam. Roelena had slipped on her winter cardigan even though she knew it was summer, and sat huddled and listless at their kitchen table.

Clarence and Jakob were opening cards and reading them out loud before setting them in front of Roelena. She couldn't hear properly, though; they were speaking too fast for her to absorb their words. She felt Clarence put a piece of paper in her hand. She looked down and saw it was a sympathy card. She stared at it. She couldn't hear what the others were saying but she could focus her eyes and read the words.

Be comforted knowing your son is with the Savior now, for though yours is an earthly loss, it is a heavenly gain for little Karl.

She saw that Popke and Geertruida de Koekkoek had sent the card. Geert's parents. She seemed to recall that they'd lost a baby in infancy, although it was difficult to remember.

Another card appeared in her hand. *Nothing happens by chance, but all for the good of those who love the Lord.*

Nothing happens by chance? What did that even mean? Had God predestined Karl to die at such a tender age? What was the good in that? And how did her loving the Lord make it good that Karl had died? She looked at the bottom of the card and saw the signature of Mr. and Mrs. Hans Fenema. *Mijneer* Fenema had been the choir director a lifetime ago when Roelena had been young and carefree and dreaming of her future.

Another card. *Although we cannot always see it, the Lord's ways are best. Find comfort in prayer and in knowing that your little one is with Him now.*

That was from the Langelaar's. But what does Cornelia Langelaar know? Who was she to offer comfort when all her children were alive? She'd never lost a child! *Or had she?*

Roelena understood that she was supposed to appreciate the sentiments expressed in the cards, but that simply wasn't possible. She dropped the card and let her hand drift to her lap. In her head, she heard fragmented echoes of what had been said at the funeral; everyone—the *dominee*, the mourners, her family—they'd urged her to seek comfort in prayer.

But she hadn't prayed. Not once. She couldn't. Did it make sense to pray to the God who'd taken Karl? And why had God taken him? Why had she been given Karl if God had a plan to take him away so soon? Would a loving God really do that? Each question churned in her head, and then fell away unanswered as if chopped off like a scythe in a field of oats. Would it have been better not to have had her baby to love for ten months and eleven days? But there was no scythe making that question fall away. She knew the answer. Never; she would never regret the joy Karl's presence brought.

Roelena was distracted from her thoughts when Tomas and *kleine* Kees came running into the kitchen, hollering and complaining. She knew they were shouting; yet, their noise was strangely muted. She observed Ingrid shushing them, observed their sudden and silent stares as they turned to regard their aunt. She eyed them curiously as if she'd never seen them before. Strangers familiar enough to name. She could see them asking questions, but their words held no meaning for her. The others understood, though, so it didn't matter that she didn't.

She felt a touch on her arm and turned, slowly, as if balancing a fragile china urn on her head. Jakob was talking to her. She strained to hear him, but it was all so difficult. She watched his mouth move, but she understood nothing. Why was it so hard to hear? She hadn't ever had hearing problems before. Even when she'd been feverish with the German measles, she could still hear. Maybe it was a complication left over from having had the German measles. But no, that was loss of sight. And it was a complication that might affect the unborn baby, not the mother. Roelena looked down at her pregnant belly, saw her hands resting in a natural protective pose on the mound of her stomach. *Her baby.* But Karl had been her baby. And now he was gone.

She felt the hand on her arm again and the letters of her name appeared in her mind instead of being heard by her ears. She looked to the side and saw Jakob still there. What did he want? He was holding out a church bulletin for her to take. That's right. It was Sunday today. She hadn't gone to church. She hadn't even gotten out of bed until Ingrid made her.

She took the page from him and focused on where he was pointing.

We express our sincere sympathy to Mr. and Mrs. C. van Haarmelen upon the sudden death of their son, Karl Benjamin, at the tender age of only ten months and eleven days. The funeral was held in the church at two o'clock yesterday afternoon. May the Lord comfort them in their loss, and let us all seek to learn the lessons the Lord would teach us by this reminder of our frailty.

Frailty. That was a good word. Very apt. She hadn't realized Karl Benjamin had been so frail, but he had been. She re-read the paragraph. Had the *dominee* written this? She'd never thought about who wrote the words on the church bulletin. She knew that Gertie van Laar typed the words on a typewriter, but who actually thought what words should be on the page?

She watched as Ingrid plucked the bulletin from her hand and placed a bowl of soup in front of her. Roelena looked down at it, perplexed. She hadn't asked for soup. Had she? She felt Ingrid's touch on her arm and watched as Ingrid's lips moved. Her voice was so distant and slow, a little like that long-distance phone call they'd made to Clarence's parents after Karl was born, but yet too far away for her to hear properly. It was all so strange.

She felt someone touch her other arm and watched, baffled, as Jakob placed a spoon in her hand. Why was he doing that? She looked over and noticed for the first time that Alida was on his lap. Had Alida always been there? Alida was only a few days older than Karl. She was chubbier though, and had fat, rolly-polly legs.

When Jakob nudged her hand again, Roelena looked down. She'd forgotten about the bowl Ingrid had placed in front of her, the spoon in her hand. The soup was hot. She could see the steam. Would it be hot enough to warm that cold, black thing inside her?

Roelena scooped up a spoonful, put it in her mouth, swallowed. How strange. The liquid had no taste, no heat. Should she say something to Ingrid? She eyed the others. They didn't seem to notice that the soup was as tasteless and tepid as wet sawdust. And if they were willing to be polite and eat it, then she supposed she must as well. She took another mouthful, but it didn't taste any better than the first.

She was tired suddenly, too tired to lift the spoon. Too tired to move her mouth and say she was tired. With the last of her strength, she pushed her chair away from the table and stood.

That was all right, wasn't it, to leave the table if she needed to lie down? It was the middle of the day, she knew, but she was so tired. And so cold. And it was Sunday, wasn't it? There was no work to be done on a Sunday, so it must be all right.

She would lie down. She would bury herself with blankets, and then maybe, just maybe, she'd finally be warm.

28

CARD FROM HARRI TO ROELENA AND CLARENCE

Dear Roelena and Clarence,

My wife and I want to convey our deep sadness at the news of the death of your sweet baby boy Karl. We chose this sympathy card as it commends Karl to God's care, which is the only true solace at this difficult time. That this sorrowful time comes so soon following Moe's death must feel like too great a burden for you to carry. Please know you are not alone, and draw comfort in the words of Matthew 11—Come unto me, all ye that labour and are heavy laden, and I will give you rest.

Therese asked me to translate a Catholic prayer that she hopes you will find meaningful. In English, it would say, "Lord God, you are attentive to the voice of our pleading. Let us find in your Son comfort in our sadness, certainty in our doubt, and courage to live through this hour. May our faith remain strong through Christ our Lord."

May peace find its way into your hearts. Our fervent prayers are with you at this difficult time.

Your loving brother and future sister-in-law,

Harri and Therese.

29

THURSDAY, AUGUST 21

Roelena pushed the door of their old car closed with her hip, holding the half-empty crate of groceries with both arms. "Blackie, down!" she ordered, nudging the excited dog away.

She hadn't needed to go into town, but she also hadn't been able to abide the quiet of the house. So she'd driven to town and wandered into the grocery store with no sense of purpose, eventually buying a few dry goods. Then she'd crossed the street into Kresgie's and stumbled on the perfect gift for Ingrid.

She stepped with care along their graveled path, encumbered by the ever-increasing size of her belly. One more month and the baby would arrive; one more month and she would know if her baby was healthy; one more month and the void of silence that filled the little house since Karl's death would be dispelled.

In the kitchen, Roelena put away the groceries, and then set the crate out on the stoop for Clarence to stash later in the empty granary they used for storage. Back in the kitchen, she sat at the table and clicked opened her handbag, eagerly retrieving the flat brown paper bag from within. She tilted the bag, letting the silky-smooth rayon scarf slide into her hands. When she'd spotted the sky blue and dandelion yellow scarf on the sale rack in Kresgie's, she immediately pictured it on Ingrid. It would complement Ingrid's blond hair and blue eyes perfectly.

Roelena didn't usually buy anything on impulse, as they certainly didn't have extra money to spend on non-essentials. If Clarence had been with her, he would have said the gift was unnecessary, and he would have been right. Ingrid wasn't expecting a gift, which made it all the more pleasurable to buy.

Ingrid had been helping Roelena in so many ways. She popped in with her children—sometimes just the baby, other times all three *kinderen*—bearing freshly baked pies, cakes, or cookies, then stayed to chat with Roelena about inconsequential things. Her presence and that of her children temporarily lifted the shroud that swathed the little home in a pall of unnatural silence. Best of all, Ingrid never demanded chatter in return. Roelena appreciated that Ingrid was allowing Roelena to grieve in her own way, in her own time, something Roelena's husband seemed incapable of doing.

Roelena glanced at the clock on the wall. Ten minutes before two o'clock. She pictured Ingrid in the new house on the home farm. Jakob would have finished his dinner and was likely out doing some chore. Ingrid would be alone in the house with the children. Roelena had intended to give Ingrid the scarf on Sunday but she suddenly felt compelled to visit Ingrid immediately. She stood and went to the counter, rummaging through the smallest of her kitchen drawers for a suitable ribbon to wrap around the gift.

When Clarence drove the tractor into the barnyard he was surprised to see their old car in the drive. At mid-day, he'd gone into the house for dinner as usual, but Roelena had simply set his bowl of soup on the table alongside some sliced bread and cheese and announced she was going into town for groceries. He'd barely had time to say good-bye before she vanished. He hadn't expected her back until much later in the afternoon. Did he dare hope that she'd missed him? His heart lifted a little at the thought.

He parked the tractor and headed towards the house, eager to see his wife. Maybe this afternoon he would finally succeed in lifting her spirits, even if just a little. He'd been trying so hard to get through to her, but most days he felt stymied. He understood her pain, he really did. And he knew she needed time to heal. But he desperately longed for her to lean on him to help her through this. Instead, she'd become closed. Not unkind, not angry, not hostile, but not loving. Nothing he tried seemed to get through to her. He'd offered so many words, but she seemed unaffected by them. So he'd offered silence instead, paired with gentle, kind gestures, hoping his actions spoke louder than his words. But nothing he did penetrated the aloof shell she'd wrapped around herself. He sometimes felt at his wit's end, yet he knew it was simply a matter of time. And he had patience in spades, and determination, as his mother had always claimed. No matter what, Roelena must know he was here for her, always.

As he opened the screen door at the top of the stoop he startled Roelena, who'd just entered the porch.

Roelena held her handbag in one hand and a small ribbon-wrapped package in the other. "Oh! I didn't hear you," she exclaimed.

"I didn't think you'd be home so soon. This is a pleasant surprise," Clarence enthused with a genuine smile. He made to wrap his arms around her, but she stepped back, avoiding his embrace.

"Your clothes," she stated.

Clarence's smile faded as he regarded his wife. He suspected she was using her town dress and his soiled work clothes as an excuse to avoid his touch. She had once loved his tactile nature, but since Karl's death more than two months before, Roelena had not wanted, or even seemed to need, his affection. Clarence missed her touch; he craved it, needing it like a man dying of thirst needs water. It wasn't that he was demanding sex—the touch of her hand on his would have been enough, at least for now. That didn't mean he wasn't keen, very keen, to resume their bedtime physical intimacy. They hadn't made love since before Karl's death. Roelena claimed her pregnancy would makc lovemaking uncomfortable, an assertion he didn't understand given they'd enjoyed sex until very close to Karl's birth. But sex or no sex, he simply wanted her to touch him. He ached for the warmth of a shared hug; ached too, for the warmth of shared conversation, shared laughter, even shared tears.

Clarence stood aside. He didn't insist she hug him. He knew she had not come to terms with the reality of Karl's death. Clarence had difficult moments, too, yet he could always bring himself back to that sense of well-being he'd experienced during that strange, life-altering vision. And with his innate and natural tendency to look to the future with hope and anticipation, knowing God had many blessings in store for them, Clarence was willing to put the tragedies of the past behind him and move on. He believed his wife would eventually do the same and simply needed more time to reach this conclusion. Patient and determined, that's who he was.

"Were you coming to look for me?" Clarence asked, his tone hopeful.

"No, sorry." Her eyes skittered away from the warmth in his gaze. She stepped forward, forcing him to move out of the way. The screen door banged closed behind her. "I only came home to put away the groceries. I've got a gift for Ingrid."

"A gift? What for?" Clarence winced inwardly at the sharpness of his tone, but he'd been so certain she'd come home early to be with him. This idea had been so pleasing, that it was now impossible to hide his disappointment.

Roelena gestured with the package in her gloved hands. "To thank her for all she's done."

Clarence felt a wave of resentment ripple under the surface of his skin. He didn't try to hide his frown or his irritation. "All *she's* done?" he challenged.

Roelena frowned and spoke in the same impatient tone she used back in the day when Willem had done something exasperating. "Yes, Clarence. I want to thank her for all she's done. Without her, I don't know how I could've gotten through these last two months."

"What about me?"

"What about you?" she snapped.

Clarence closed his eyes and told himself to remain calm. He was thankful Ingrid—all their family and friends, but especially Ingrid—was so patient and understanding with Roelena, helping her in every way possible to navigate the emotional minefield that followed Karl's death. He was thankful they understood Clarence and Roelena were also worrying about the health of their unborn child. But he was inordinately hurt that his wife not only avoided being intimate with him—and he didn't just mean physically—but that Roelena would credit Ingrid with helping her through the last two months. Clarence had been bending over backwards to be supportive, trying any means possible to prove to her that she could rely on him in this difficult time. In fact, he'd taken consideration, thoughtfulness, patience, and understanding to a whole new level. Yet Roelena wanted to thank *Ingrid* for all *Ingrid* had done. *Ingrid,* not Clarence.

Clarence opened his eyes and regarded his wife, slowly releasing his breath. When he spoke, he deliberately used his most gentle tone. "Stay with me," he pleaded, briefly touching her arm. "We can go for a walk. Well, maybe not a walk," he teased with a pointed look at her belly. "We can find a comfortable place to sit in the shade, or go for a drive, or—"

Roelena interrupted him, turning away and addressing him over her shoulder. "No. I'm going to Ingrid's."

Clarence reached out, placing a hand on her forearm, stopping her. "Please, sweetheart?" he pleaded softly. "I'm asking you to spend the afternoon with me. It's important to me."

"Let me go," Roelena demanded, jerking out of his grasp.

She stopped abruptly, and lifted her gaze to him. He could see the guilt in her eyes, saw the all-too-brief apologetic smile she offered. But then she was scooting down the steps, her free hand on the wooden banister for support.

"I'll be back in time to cook your supper," she stated in a neutral tone as if nothing was amiss.

All the hurt and irritation that had been brewing within Clarence for the months she'd been rejecting him suddenly erupted. "Why are you treating me as if I'm repulsive?" Clarence demanded.

Roelena was on the gravel at the bottom of the stoop. She stopped at his words and turned to look up at him, then visibly flinched when she saw the fury in his gaze. "What… what do you mean?" she stammered.

"You know damn well what I mean," he growled, his eyes flashing as he glowered down at her. He had never before sworn at his wife. He wouldn't feel guilty about it. Nor would he apologize. "You've been giving me the cold shoulder for months. Is it too much to ask that you show a little warmth to your own husband? Why don't you want me touching you? I used to be married to a warm, loving wife. But now I find myself married to a cold, aloof woman who recoils every time I touch her."

"Don't be ridiculous," Roelena snapped. She turned toward the car and then almost tripped over the dog. "Blackie! Get away!" she yelled in fury, striding angrily down the graveled path.

"Don't you damn well call me ridiculous," he yelled at her retreating back. "You're the one being ridiculous. You used to *beg* me to touch you."

Roelena turned sharply to glare at him, the size of her belly making her movements graceless. "Is that what this is about?" she accused. "You're being ridiculous. I'm pregnant, remember?"

"We made love all the time when you were pregnant with Karl. You begged for it," he accused. He knew he had crossed a line, that he was now seeking to embarrass her deliberately, even wound her. She hated being teased about her very healthy sexual appetite. But he couldn't seem to stop his anger; it spewed from him like a geyser. "You wanted it right up until Karl was born. You've always wanted it. Don't deny it, Roelena."

"You're being ridiculous!" she spat. "You're behaving like a child, only worse."

"I am not behaving like a child," he roared. "But I am tired of you flinching every time I try and touch you."

Roelena scoffed. "I don't!"

Her outright denial infuriated Clarence. *"You do!"* He shouted, slamming his fist against the flat edge of the railing. "You should be seeking comfort in *my* arms, not tripping over yourself to thank *Ingrid*." He momentarily hung his head, then lifted it and stared at Roelena. When he spoke next, his anger was still evident but the volume of his voice had, at least, diminished. "Roelena, we should be comforting each other," he stated.

When he made to move down the steps towards her, Roelena seemed to panic. "No. I'm leaving," she flung over her shoulder. She snatched open the car door and clumsily tossed her purse and package inside as if she couldn't get away from him fast enough.

His wife, Clarence realized, was repelled by him. After all his gentleness and understanding and his tiptoeing around her, what did she do? She fled. A wave of rage and frustration ignited deep within him. With a wild-sounding yell, he turned and gave the railing that lined the four steps of the stoop a vicious kick, heard the satisfying sound of splintering wood.

He stood panting as if from a long run, staring at the result of his footwork. Two of the grey, weathered spindles were splintered right in half, their edges raw and ragged. A third sagged. *As broken as their relationship*, he thought to himself.

He rested his hands on his hips, aware of the rapid beat of his heart and his panting breaths. He couldn't remember the last time he'd lost his temper.

He noticed the dog eyeing him from a few feet away as if with caution. He lifted his gaze from the damaged railing and turned to regard Roelena. She was staring at the broken railing from behind the open door of the car, her eyes wide and her mouth open.

"How can you not want me touching you, Roelena?" Clarence asked quietly. His anger had spent itself. He knew there was nothing left of it now except hurt and disappointment. "I need my wife. It's not fair that you're punishing me for Karl's death."

He saw Roelena close her eyes and swallow. When she opened her eyes, she seemed to struggle to meet his gaze.

"I'm not punishing you."

"But you blame me for some reason."

Roelena looked sightlessly into the distance, shaking her head. "I don't," she finally said, her tone weary. "I don't blame anybody. Not even the doctor. I don't know why he had to die, but he did." She shrugged. "It happened. We have to move on."

Clarence wanted to approach her, but he was scared if he did move, she would slip into the car and drive away. And she was talking to him more now than she had in the two months since Karl had died. He remained standing on the stoop. "But you're not moving on, Roelena," he argued. "That's the problem, *you* are not moving on." He gestured emphatically at his chest. "*I* want to move on. *I* want us to be happy again. I *know* we can be happy again. I'm looking forward to the future, to *our* future. But I can't do that without you. You're my wife, Roelena. I'm tired of walking on eggshells around you. No, that's not true. I'm not tired. I'm bloody exhausted." His voice rose when she dropped her gaze. "What about my needs, Roelena? Have you given me a single thought? We both know the answer to that. A resounding *no*. Listen, I understand that you're full to overflowing with your own hurt and your pain. Believe me, I know. But what about my hurt? My pain? Must I remind you? *Karl was my son, too."* Clarence's voice broke and he began to weep in silence, staring towards his wife in misery, the gulf between them as big as an ocean.

When he heard Roelena slam the car door, hope flared within him. But then he heard the sound of the starter coaxing the engine to life, and he slumped heavily down onto the stoop, lifting his elbows to his knees and dropping his head into his hands. *She was leaving him. In this terrible state, with all this pain, she was leaving him.* Sobs shook his shoulders.

Usually it took a number of tries to start the temperamental automobile, but the engine was still warm from Roelena's drive to town. Moments later, Clarence heard the sound of the car moving down the driveway. He lifted his head and screamed his wife's name. He knew she couldn't hear him over the sound of the car's engine. But even if she had, he knew she wouldn't have stopped.

30
THURSDAY, AUGUST 21

Marliese noticed the distant cloud of dust on the road ahead of her and felt sure it came from a car turning out of Roelena and Clarence's driveway. Perhaps Clarence had left on some farm errand, a circumstance that would previously have filled her with relief; however, since Roelena's episode with the measles, she and Clarence had been, if not friendly, at least comfortable with each other. That didn't mean his conservative outlook still didn't irk her at times. Just last Sunday the four couples had sat together—Jakob and Ingrid, Frank and Greta, Wilfred and Marliese, and Clarence and Roelena—and the contentious subject of the new Psalter Hymnal had arisen, again. Clarence was adamantly opposed to it and Marliese was abundantly bored by the topic so she'd dragged Roelena away. She'd heard Clarence repeatedly argue his side of the disagreement, stating they should honour tradition and that the songs of praise taken from the Bible's book of Psalms—which made up the current hymnal—were sufficient. Marliese thought it was ridiculous any of them were still even talking about it because really, it was just a song book.

When Marliese turned into Roelena and Clarence's drive a minute later, she didn't at first notice Clarence sitting on the top step of the stoop, but when she did she stopped the car and stared out the window. It was barely two o'clock in the afternoon and he would normally have been out in the fields or in the barnyard doing some chore or another. But he was here. And their car wasn't. Which could only mean that the cloud of dust she'd seen had been made by Roelena's departure. Not for the first time, Marliese wished Clarence and Roelena had a telephone, but the lines still hadn't been installed along this country lane. Marliese didn't bother to turn off the ignition; instead, she rolled down her window and poked her head out to address Clarence.

"Hello, Clarence," she called cheerfully. She was about to ask where Roelena had gone, but bit back the words, speechless suddenly upon seeing the tracks of tears on his smudged and dirty face. Her first thought was panic that something had happened to Roelena and the baby, but that didn't make sense. Clarence wouldn't be sitting there doing nothing. Then it dawned on her that Clarence and Roelena had argued. *What the hell?* That was unlike them.

She sat for a moment, undecided, as she watched Clarence self-consciously scrub his face with his shirt sleeves. She expected him to rise and stride away in embarrassment, but he remained on the stoop. Could she leave now without somehow acknowledging his dejection? She thought not. Well, there was nothing for it. She took a deep, fortifying breath then shut off the engine and stepped gracefully out of the car, half-heartedly patting the over excited dog on the head as she made her way down the short graveled path.

Clarence's head hung between his hunched shoulders as she approached and Marliese could see nothing of his face. "Clarence?" she asked in a soft tone, stopping at the bottom of the steps. When he didn't acknowledge her, she bent forward slightly to rest a gloved hand on his knee. "Clarence, what happened? Where's Roelena?"

Clarence looked up, his eyes red and puffy. When he responded, his tone was hoarse. "She's gone."

Marliese stepped back, startled. *Gone?* There wasn't a day that went by where she didn't think at least once about leaving Wilfred, *but Roelena leaving Clarence?* That she couldn't have anticipated. She looked to where the dust cloud had long since disappeared then realized how foolish she was being, that is was only her wish to be gone from her own marriage that made her incorrectly interpret Clarence's response.

Marliese turned back to Clarence, finally noticing the splintered railing. Her eyebrows arched in surprise. She knew first-hand what the wreckage of a spousal argument looked like, and this one had been a doozy. She lifted her eyes to regard Clarence with new insight. When she addressed him, her tone was deliberately, albeit gently, mocking. "I didn't realize you two were in the same league as me and Wilfred."

Clarence scoffed. "Well beyond it now, I think."

Marliese couldn't imagine Roelena doing anything that would make this good-natured man—and yes, she was willing to admit he was nice even if he had conservative viewpoints she didn't agree with—lose his temper.

"But…what happened?"

"She'd rather spend time with Ingrid than with her own damn husband," Clarence spat.

Marliese's eyebrows raised. First the broken railing. Now the swearing. She hadn't known Clarence had it in him.

But his obvious distress tugged on her heart-strings. She couldn't leave him like this, so she brushed away some dirt from the second step, two below Clarence, and sat down. She was glad she'd worn her mauve and navy gingham dress, which would easily conceal a few specks of dirt. She shifted sideways so she could look up at Clarence. She was rarely at a loss for words, but this situation was so unexpected she had to think hard about what to say.

Her tone was mildly chastising. "So, if she's gone to Ingrid's, then she's not really gone."

Clarence narrowed his red, puffy eyes as he regarded Marliese. "What did you think I meant when I said *gone*?"

"Oh…" Marliese waved a hand nonchalantly. "Gone…to town. I mean, that would have been a wasted journey for me then, wouldn't it?" She changed her tone, feigning outrage. "The County of Bellecourt has got to bring telephone lines to this lane."

Clarence eyed Marliese, then shook his head. "Bullshit, Marliese."

"Oh, my! Two swear words in less than…" Marliese made a show of looking at her slim wristwatch. "Ninety seconds. Goodness gracious, Clarence. Who are you and what have you done with my best friend's husband?"

Marliese immediately regretted mocking Clarence. She was sharp with Wilfred all the time, but she didn't need to be snippy with this man, and certainly not while he was in such a state. "Sorry," she said, holding up a hand. "If you have to cuss, then cuss. Who am I to judge?"

When silence enveloped them, Marliese tried to imagine Roelena sitting with Wilfred after one of their glass-shattering fights. A part of her wanted to make her excuses and flee, yet she knew Clarence deserved her compassion and respect given his and Roelena's wretchedly awful situation.

She nodded at the broken railing. "Your handiwork I assume? You need to get Wilfred to give you some tips."

Marliese waited for Clarence to ask what she meant, but when he remained silent, she continued. "He tends to avoid breaking anything that he might have to repair later. He'd say, grab for the dishes, or an ashtray." Marliese added with a sardonic smile, "I tend to grab for a kitchen knife, the longer and shaper the better."

"Why did a smart woman like you marry such an idiot?"

Marliese was startled by Clarence's question. They'd become friendly, yes, but not confidantes. She'd never have guessed he'd be so direct, or even admit that she was clever.

But it seemed Clarence didn't expect her to answer instead following his question with a more important one; at least to him, she guessed.

"Why does she blame me for Karl's death?"

Marliese stared at him, momentarily speechless. "For heaven's sake, Clarence. She doesn't blame you."

"Yeah. She does." Clarence looked down, dangling his wrists between his bent knees. He sighed heavily before lifting his gaze to meet Marliese's. "It's been ten weeks since he died, and she still doesn't..." He looked away. "I think she wishes I wasn't here. I think if she never saw me again, she wouldn't miss me."

Marliese was taken aback by Clarence's statement. That he was sharing his innermost feelings with her was shocking enough, but that he'd drawn such a flawed conclusion? Their fight must really have been a doozy if Clarence was concluding Roelena didn't love him to pieces. Marliese knew Roelena adored Clarence. He was everything her friend had always wanted in a husband. Marliese shook her head emphatically. "That's nonsense, Clarence. Why would you think such a thing?"

Clarence shrugged. "She can't stand the sight of me. She can't bear for me to touch her. She seems to forget that..." Clarence dashed away the fresh tears that welled up, darkening his watered-down blue of his eyes.

She noticed he didn't seem embarrassed by his tears but

held her gaze. She couldn't imagine her own husband shedding tears, let alone in front of Roelena.

"She forgets that he was my son, too." He choked on a sob, then added with a strangled wail, *"Karl was my son, too."*

Marliese bit down hard on her lip as she witnessed Clarence's pain. She wished he was angry instead of sad. When a man was in a rage, she knew hiss and spit and claw, but she didn't know what to do with a man who cried. She looked away, blinking back her own tears, silently cursing when she realized she'd left her handbag in the car. She slipped off one of her gloves and dabbed at the corner of her eye, then evaluated the black smudges of mascara on the curled edge of her finger.

"I miss him so much." Clarence continued to speak through his tears as if now that he'd started he couldn't stop. "I miss him every minute of every day. But she doesn't see that. She doesn't know that I want him back just as much as she does. He was my son, too, and I miss him so much." Clarence crossed his arms on his knees and dropped his head, resting his forehead on his arms.

His muffled sobs were too much for Marliese. She rose abruptly, blinking hard to stop her tears and tugging off her other glove as she walked briskly back to her car. She reached into the open window and tossed her gloves on the seat before retrieving her handbag. She popped it open and slipped out her handkerchief. Keeping her back to Clarence, she carefully dabbed at her eyes.

An image of Conrad appeared in her mind. She usually didn't let herself think about him, but somehow Clarence's unashamed tears reminded her of Conrad, despite never have seen her old flame cry. But she knew Conrad was like Clarence in this aspect. He wouldn't be ashamed to cry if he was hurting, especially after something as devastating as losing a baby. She wanted to sob then, too. Instead, she banished the image of Conrad with a well-practiced mental gesture and took a deep, steadying breath, then turned and walked back to Clarence.

She stood at the bottom of the steps, eyeing him, relieved to see his tears had stopped.

When Clarence met her gaze and frowned, Marliese lifted a brow. "What?"

"You look desolate, Marliese. Did I say something to make you sad?"

Marliese was instantly defensive in the face of Clarence's painfully accurate intuition. But she wouldn't be vulnerable in front of this man. Or any other, for that matter. "Don't be ridiculous," she snapped.

Clarence instantly bristled. "Bloody women," he muttered, wiping the last of the wet from his face with a crumpled blue hanky. Clarence looked up and met Marliese's defiant gaze. "It must be exhausting being married to you."

"Excuse me?" Marliese was utterly shocked Clarence would say such a thing. But he was right, that she had to admit, at least to herself. It was exhausting being married, that she knew for sure. But she wasn't about to have that conversation with Clarence. "I should go," she said in a soft tone.

Clarence nodded his head. "Sure. Are you going to Ingrid's?"

She nodded. As she turned to leave her eyes fell again on the splintered railing. She paused, uncharacteristically and briefly indecisive. Then she nodded at his recent handiwork. "Are you intending to fix that?"

Clarence eyed the damage. He felt he should bristle at her question, but his anger was spent. He felt utterly drained suddenly. He nodded. "I don't suppose Roelena needs a reminder of my childish temper tantrum."

"Actually ..." Marliese hesitated. She had a wealth of experience fighting with her spouse, a little less experience making up, and almost no experience forgiving each other; yet, she felt inclined to give advice despite not having been asked. "Why don't you leave it, just for a day or two."

Clarence eyed her suspiciously. "Why?"

Marliese shrugged. She wasn't sure herself. She was tempted to share something of her own emotional fragility and spoke quickly, before she lost her courage. "Sometimes I think Wilfred and I will not survive another fight. I mean that literally. If you knew how satisfying it is for me to imagine stabbing the man with a kitchen knife, well..." she shrugged and sighed. "But Clarence, you and Roelena are different. Right now, it might seem like you can't get past this." She waved a hand, indicating their argument. "But surely if anyone can, the two of you can. So..." Marliese hesitated, not sure if she could continue, but she'd already meddled more than she should. A little more interference wouldn't make much difference at this point. She tapped the railing decisively as she met Clarence's gaze. "This is evidence of something that needs fixing in your relationship. I think it speaks to your broken heart—both your broken hearts."

Marliese shrugged again, feeling a little foolish. *Who was she to give marital advice to her best friend's husband?* "Maybe you need to..." Marliese's eyes went back to the damaged railing.

"Be more patient?"

Marliese chuckled. "No. But maybe Roelena needs to see this tangible reminder that *your* heart is broken too." She gave an embarrassed laugh. "Maybe I should keep my mouth shut and just go back home."

"No, don't. I mean, don't go home. Go visit with Roelena and Ingrid. She's always happier after seeing you."

"She is?" Marliese looked pleased.

He nodded.

"And you?"

Clarence gave her a sardonic smile. "I'm always happier seeing you leave."

Marliese chuckled briefly, but then grew serious. "Will you be okay?" she asked with absolute sincerity.

"Yeah," he nodded, smiling self-consciously as they stared at each other. "You should go see Roelena. Make sure she's okay."

Marliese nodded, then lifted her hand briefly in a wave. "Bye," she said before turning and walking to her car. She opened the driver's door and gave a half-hearted smile to Clarence before getting behind the wheel. She reversed, then waved as she put the car in gear and headed down the driveway.

31

THURSDAY, AUGUST 21

Clarence stayed on the step and watched Marliese turn onto the road. A cloud of dust billowed behind her car as she accelerated.

When he'd lifted his gaze and seen the pearl-grey gloved hand resting on his knee, he'd considered blaming her for Roelena's changed behaviour, yet he knew that was unfair. He'd looked up at the stylish woman who was his wife's best friend, acknowledging to himself that Marliese was a strikingly beautiful woman. He'd always thought so. She belonged on the pages of those women's magazines Roelena loved. But he wasn't attracted to that kind of beauty. He'd always believed surface beauty was barely less artificial than the cosmetics some women applied so artfully.

Clarence used to think Wilfred and Marliese deserved each other. He hadn't believed Roelena when she'd insisted that Marliese married Wilfred because he showed up at a time when her friend was vulnerable—and thus reckless. Clarence had always scoffed at that notion, thinking Marliese didn't have a vulnerable bone in her body, but he was beginning to realize he'd been wrong about his wife's best friend, that Marliese's outer beauty hid a complicated, deeply emotional woman. He'd seen the warmth of concern shimmering in her brown eyes just now, and her vulnerability too, although clearly that only made her defensive. But then again, Marliese's eyes were always brewing something. Or throwing throw daggers. More than a few had been directed at him over the years, but mostly they were volleyed at Wilfred. He wondered what she would have been like had she married a kind man instead of the one-dimensional irritant that was Wilfred.

Regardless, what she'd said was astute. He turned to look at the broken railing, hearing her words echo in his head. *This is evidence of something that needs fixing in your relationship. It speaks to your broken heart, both your broken hearts.* Maybe Marliese was right. Maybe he should postpone fixing it until tomorrow, or even the day after that.

He rose slowly, then looked towards the barn. There were any number of chores that needed doing. He hesitated, but then turned and opened the screen door. He walked slowly into the house, pausing in the doorway of the kitchen, then moving on until he was in the bedroom. He sank onto the bed, laying on his back and staring up at the ceiling as he reviewed the vicious argument he'd had with his wife. He needed fresh wisdom about how to go forward, together, as a husband and wife.

Hoping to soothe himself, he closed his eyes, reaching for that feeling he'd received when he'd had the vision of Karl. It always made him feel better when he recalled that beautiful, indescribable moment with his beloved son. But for the first time, Clarence couldn't revive it, or summon it, or whatever it was he did to feel soothed by it. It was well and truly out of his reach. Was it gone for good? Or was the mountain of pain that now burdened him blocking his access to it? He didn't know, but the loss of it filled him with despair and he began to weep silent tears.

Within only a few minutes, though, the blessed relief of sleep overtook him.

Roelena dashed away her tears as she turned out of their drive and onto their road. She and Clarence had argued in the past, but never as bad as that. She pictured again the splintered banister. She would never have dreamed that her calm, good-natured husband had the kind of fury inside him that would cause him to do that kind of damage. In the five years she'd known him, she'd seen him angry, more than once, but it was usually frustration on account of an uncooperative cow or their car breaking down for the umpteenth time. Never anger at her, though, and never uncontrolled.

She knew her tone had been undeniably sharp. She'd seen the hurt in his eyes, but she truly had not wanted to spend the afternoon with him. He would've done what he always did—tried to cajole her into feeling better. His habit of always trying to lighten the mood annoyed and irritated her beyond measure. She knew this was unreasonable given it had once been something she admired about him. But the reality was, she didn't want to be in a happier mood. So she'd glared up at him, furious at being reminded of having rejected his overtures. She was pregnant, for goodness sake. She thought he understood that she was just too uncomfortable right now to be intimate. And she'd been utterly mortified when he'd made that awful comment about her enjoyment of their amorous activities. He made her sound sinful, as if she were wanton. His accusation made her recall that horrible time when he'd rejected her advances at the swing and she'd done that wicked deed. She hated being reminded of that.

And then he'd made that awful accusation, saying she blamed him for Karl's death. Awful because it had an element of truth. They both knew it. But she didn't blame him for Karl's death. She blamed him for giving her hope; she blamed him for letting her believe that bringing Karl to the University Hospital would make him better; and she especially blamed him for being willing to get past Karl's death, to move on and look with optimism to the future. She begrudged him this ability. And her resentment boiled and churned beneath the surface of her skin like bubbling lava threatening to spew. How could her husband have the audacity to move on? *How could he?* And how could he expect her to do the same?

Roelena kept one hand on the wheel and dug into her handbag for her *zakdoek,* wiping her wet face as best she could. A part of her hated herself for getting in the car and driving away from him, yet at the same time she was relieved to be away from his ragged emotion.

He didn't understand her struggle. If she told him about that cold, black creature inside her who fed off her pain, he'd laugh at her. Well, maybe not laugh. But he'd dismiss it as something not real. But it was real. It was there every moment of the day gnawing, gnawing.

The problem, Roelena realized in a sudden moment of clarity, was that Clarence was under the mistaken impression she still had a well of understanding and warmth inside of her. But she didn't. Whatever flame had been inside her had been extinguished, leaving her as cold as the ashes of a long dead fire. She'd been so unprepared for Karl's death. She was barely managing to contain her pain.

Which begged the question, what were they meant to say to each other when she got home? She certainly didn't want to revive the argument, or relive it. She didn't want to talk about it at all. But Clarence always, *always* wanted to talk.

And hold her. He was always reaching for her. It was exhausting evading him. The only touch she wanted was Karl's, and that she could never have again. She chose instead to focus on the day when she would hold her new baby in her arms. Whether it was blind or not seemed irrelevant now. She simply knew that nothing would start to right itself until her arms were filled with the new baby.

32

THURSDAY, AUGUST 21

Ingrid had just changed baby Alida's diaper when she saw Roelena's car turn into their drive. She walked out onto the stoop of her and Jakob's house, her plump, fourteen-month-old baby on her rounded hip, lifting Alida's hand to wave as Roelena stepped out of the car.

Ingrid was worried about Roelena, but she did her best not to let it show while in Roelena's presence. Ingrid wouldn't let herself imagine what it might be like if Alida were to die; it was too unspeakable to even contemplate. Nevertheless, Ingrid's heart wept every time she saw Roelena's shuttered features. It was obvious to anyone that her sister-in-law was barely coping with the death of her baby, a horrific event by any account but made worse by having occurred only four months after the passing of her dear mother. Even though Roelena hadn't confided in her, it was obvious to Ingrid that Roelena resented Clarence's ability to regain his positive outlook after Karl's death, and that she didn't welcome his well-intentioned hovering. Ingrid loved Clarence, but she'd come to realize that her easy-going and kind-hearted brother-in-law was at a loss when it came to handling his wife's grief. So Ingrid followed her intuition and allowed Roelena to dwell in whatever emotional state she chose during this trying time, offering her sister-in-law unwavering friendship and unstinting, silent understanding.

The baby jiggled her whole body in excitement when she saw her beloved aunt approach them. *"Moe-moe-moe-moe,"* she burbled.

Ingrid didn't think Roelena's smile was forced when she bent to greet Alida, catching one of her little hands and planting a kiss on it. Ingrid's daughter had been born only a few days before Karl, and Ingrid knew without having to be told that Roelena sometimes felt pain slice through her heart knowing that every new accomplishment Alida did was now something Karl would never do. Ingrid admired Roelena for not harbouring any bitterness or resentment that this lively, determined little girl was alive when her own baby was not; she wasn't convinced she would've had such an open heart towards Karl if their roles had been reversed.

Roelena gave Ingrid a wan smile. "She still calls everyone Moe?"

Ingrid appreciated that Roelena asked in Dutch, mildly ashamed that she still couldn't claim fluency in English.

"She does. And no one seems to mind, except me," Ingrid stated with a cheerful smile. "How are you today?" she added, her smile fading and her eyes troubled as she assessed Roelena's troubled countenance.

"Fine," Roelena responded. Her gaze skittered away, but Ingrid didn't push for a truthful answer.

With her free hand, she pulled open the screen door, then pointed with her chin, "Go on in," she said.

Once in the kitchen, she could tell that Roelena was distracted when she didn't immediately ask about the absence of her nephews. "Do you want to hold Alida?" Ingrid asked as Roelena sank into her usual kitchen chair facing the kitchen counter.

"Sorry, what did you say?" Roelena asked.

"Just asking if you wanted to hold her," Ingrid said.

"Of course I do," Roelena enthused, setting her handbag on the table and holding out her arms and taking Alida from Roelena.

But the baby squirmed in Roelena's arms, no longer interested in being held. She'd learned to walk recently, and seemed only willing to sit on someone's lap if they were reading her a book or feeding her. Roelena reluctantly put Alida down, making sure she was balanced on her chubby little legs before releasing her.

"Where are the boys?" Roelena asked.

Ingrid smiled, pleased she'd finally focused enough on their present surroundings to notice the unusual quiet of Ingrid's house. "Jakob loaded the weaned pigs, the ones for Hendrika and Harm. They're getting married next week, remember?"

Harm Kikstra, one of the three immigrant young men who'd joined their community at the same time as Clarence, was three years younger than his fiancée, but that had never seemed to bother either the self-assured young man or Hendrika.

"You heard they're going to live on de Berg's old farm, east of Bellecourt?" Ingrid added. "They have only two milk cows, so Hendrika's father purchased some of our pigs to start them out."

"I did know, yes. It's pretty countryside there."

Ingrid tilted her head. "Not as pretty as here," she observed, then asked, "Do you want tea or coffee?"

"Tea, please," Roelena said. "Does Jakob have Tomas and *kleine* Kees with him?"

As she went to fill the kettle, Ingrid was forced to step

around her toddler, who had opened the pantry cupboard and removed one of the small items from the lowest shelf.

"Oh, *dankje,* Alida," Roelena said, smiling and taking the tin of baking powder the toddler held out for her.

"Yes, and thank goodness," Ingrid stated in an emphatic tone. It was a blessed relief when Jakob took charge of their two rambunctious boys. "Those two just don't know when to quit. They're either the best of friends making as much noise as possible, or else they're mortal enemies making even more noise."

As she spoke, Ingrid set the table with tea things; two cups and saucers, a small jar of *theelepeltjes,* and the milk and sugar. She continued talking as she transferred homemade cookies from a tin onto a plate before taking a seat across from Roelena. "When Tomas goes back to school next month, *kleine* Kees won't know what to do with himself. But at least it will be quieter in here."

"He won't, will he?" Roelena agreed, then reached to rescue the tin of peaches the toddler was struggling to deliver.

Ingrid grinned in amusement as she watched her daughter toddle purposefully back to the pantry. "You know, Jakob bought her a toy telephone from the five-and-dime last week and she completely ignores it. Instead, she does that," Ingrid nodded her head. "Over and over, bringing the items to me whether I'm in the bedroom making the beds or out on the stoop hanging the wash. I moved those small items out of her reach to prevent her from doing it again, but she howled her frustration and wouldn't be distracted. I finally had to move them all back to the bottom shelf just to keep her quiet. That girl is far more determined and focused than Tomas and *kleine* Kees combined."

Ingrid was glad to see that her comment made Roelena smile, but she wished her sister-in-law's eyes weren't so dull.

"That might be frustrating for you now, but it will likely serve her well as an adult."

"Maybe. Her next favourite pastime is taking out the lids from the pots and pans," Ingrid gestured at the cupboard doors next to the sink. "She bangs them together, making more noise than the boys."

Ingrid saw the cloud in Roelena's eyes, and knew her words had reminded her sister-in-law of the baby she'd lost. Likely Roelena was thinking that Karl alive and getting underfoot in the kitchen banging pot lids together was preferable to the strange quiet in her and Clarence's home. Ingrid wished she could say something that would help her sister-in-law, but instead lifted the plate of cookies. "Here," she said, offering it to Roelena. "Have an oatmeal cookie. And no need to feel guilty, either. We're eating for two, right?" she added, placing a hand on her pregnant tummy.

This was her fifth pregnancy, although it would be her fourth child as she'd miscarried her third pregnancy at only two months. That had been hard for her and Jakob. They'd been so eager to enlarge their growing family. But then she'd conceived again and they'd welcomed their first daughter. Now another baby would arrive in time for Christmas.

For Ingrid, the joys of the present helped soothe the hurts of her past. She felt certain that when Roelena's baby was born next month—*and please, God, let it be healthy*—the hurt over losing Karl would be soothed. And even if the new baby was born blind on account of Roelena's having had German measles, Ingrid knew Roelena and Clarence would shower their baby with love. And then perhaps the emptiness Roelena felt without a baby to hold would finally begin to recede.

Roelena politely took a cookie, taking a small bite.

Ingrid took a cookie for herself, taking a large bite before setting the plate back on the table.

"Huppie, huppie," Alida chimed in her baby voice, eyeing Roelena's cookie. The childish word was her version of the Dutch *een hapje*, which meant 'a bite'. Roelena first accepted a tin of mustard powder from Alida, then held out her cookie to the child, waiting until Alida took a bite before setting it down on the saucer of her tea cup.

"I'd be scared she might drop one of the heavy cans on her toes," Roelena said.

"Oh, she already has, more than once. She howls in righteous anger for two minutes, and then starts all over again."

Roelena smiled as her niece toddled back towards the pantry, returning with a tin of vanilla custard powder that Roelena added to the array of dry goods accumulating on the table in front of her. The little girl paused long enough to take another bite from Roelena's cookie, then headed with single-mindedness back to the pantry.

The kettle whistled and Ingrid rose to make the tea. "Once the cupboard is empty of all she can reach, I'll put her down for her nap. She should go down now, but she'll put up such a fuss, it's just not worth the battle."

"Moe would say you're spoiling her," Roelena teased.

"*Ja,* she would," Ingrid agreed with a chuckle. "But she wouldn't mean it in a bad way." Ingrid set the teapot on the table then resumed her seat across from Roelena. "I miss her."

Roelena accepted the cake of yeast from Alida and put it on the table. "Me, too."

Ingrid didn't protest when Roelena changed the subject, but she did believe that talk about loved ones who'd died was healthy, although she acknowledged it was too soon for Roelena.

"I brought you a present," Roelena announced in an overly bright voice. She clicked her handbag open and retrieved the small brown bag from inside.

"What?" Ingrid was completely surprised. They only exchanged presents on special occasions. "Why did you buy me a present?"

"You've been so helpful these last few months, and I just wanted to say thanks. Here," she said, handing the parcel to Ingrid. "I hope you like it."

Roelena distractedly took a tin of sardines from the child and put it on the table with the other items.

"Moe-moe-moe-moe." Alida was looking up at Roelena, one small hand patting her *tante's* leg for attention, the other pointing at the pantry shelf she'd just emptied.

Ingrid set down the small package and stood, adroitly sweeping up her daughter. "Time for your nap, *schatje*. Say 'night-night' to *Tante* Roelie."

Alida wailed in protest and wouldn't hold still long enough for a 'night-night' kiss from her aunt, pushing against her mother and reaching with both arms outstretched towards the pantry, but Ingrid ignored the baby's tired protests and disappeared down the hallway. While she was gone, Roelena replaced all the items.

"Oh, you didn't need to do that," Ingrid scolded when she re-entered the kitchen.

"I don't mind. Will she cry for long?"

"She'll stop in about two minutes," Ingrid announced with confidence as she resumed her seat and helped herself to another cookie. "She cries every time I put her in her crib, night or day, but she almost always falls asleep within minutes."

Roelena picked up the teapot and strainer and poured tea for both of them. By the time they'd each stirred sugar into their cups, Alida's muffled cries had stopped. "That wasn't even two minutes," Roelena observed.

Ingrid's response was wry. "She likes her sleep; she just doesn't like being put in her crib."

"Open your present," Roelena urged, pushing the brown paper parcel closer to Ingrid's elbow.

"You really didn't have to buy me anything." Despite her protest, Ingrid was delighted with the surprise. She picked up the package and carefully untied the bow, setting the ribbon aside for reuse. She peaked inside the small bag, but her avid expression turned to dismay when she drew out the vivid blue and yellow scarf.

She glanced at Roelena, and saw her sister-in-law's face fall.

"You don't like it?"

Ingrid didn't immediately respond, but instead let the scarf pool onto the table at her elbow as her vision blurred. She felt foolish as tears trickled down her cheeks, knowing Roelena would never understand. And it wasn't just the pregnancy, which truly did make her cry at the drop of a hat, but sight of that scarf brought with it a forgotten memory. Roelena, she saw, was horrified and utterly confused about what caused this fresh rain of tears.

"Ingrid? What's wrong?"

"Nothing's wrong," she sniffed. "It's not that I don't like it. It's..."

Ingrid kept her eyes on Roelena as she retrieved her *zakdoek* from her apron pocket and wiped her nose. "I do like the scarf. I do!" she insisted, her tears passed. "But...can I ask? What made you choose it?" Ingrid nodded at the pool of blue and yellow at her elbow.

Roelena shook her head, dumbfounded. "I just thought, with your blue eyes and blond hair and lovely complexion, it would look so good on you. But Ingrid, I don't understand. Why would a pretty scarf make you cry? What did I do wrong?"

"Ach! Don't you know by now?" Ingrid picked up the scarf and began carefully refolding it. "*You* didn't do anything wrong. You don't do things to make me cry. That brother of yours, maybe, but not you." She smiled, hoping her teasing comment would erase the stricken expression on Roelena's face, but when it didn't, Ingrid's own smile faded and she sighed heavily. "It's those rotten Germans, not you."

"The Germans?" Roelena looked bewildered. "What did a blue and yellow scarf have to do with the Germans? The ugly Nazi flag had been red and black."

Ingrid put an elbow on the table and rested her chin in the palm of her hand. She eyed Roelena, then sighed heavily.

"You don't have to talk about it, Ingrid. It's okay."

Ingrid dropped her hands into her lap as she shook her head. "No, no, you're being so kind buying me a gift for no reason. The least I can do is tell you why I'm being so silly. I'm all right now, honestly." Ingrid proved it by tucking her handkerchief back into her apron pocket. "No more tears, I promise. It's just that some images come back into my mind so vividly, you know? Suddenly I see something that triggers a memory and then it's all so fresh again." Ingrid picked up her cup of tea and took a sip, then placed it carefully on the table in front of her, wrapping her hands around it.

"You can't imagine what it was like, Roelena. And I'm so glad you can't. But that day when the Germans were fleeing because the Canadians were coming? That was quite the day. I was sick, I remember. I'd eaten something bad and had been vomiting for most of the night. That morning, I was feeling better and was laying on the couch in my aunt's front room. Her farmhouse is right on the edge of town, right up against the lane. The window sashes are low so I could occupy myself looking out at the passersby. They were mostly Germans that day, in trucks, on motorbikes, and others on foot. They had a long journey to get to the German border. Those on foot had to flee from the village children who were delighting, or so it seemed to me, in chasing them. They were even throwing stones just like they'd do if foxes came near their chicken coops."

Ingrid was looking out the kitchen window, her gaze unfocused. She wasn't seeing the row of spruce trees that lined the far side of the property but was reliving the images from that long ago day.

"You would expect, wouldn't you, that their faces would show fear, knowing their enemy was chasing them, knowing they had lost? The young ones *were* fearful, but they were boys, really. Not men." Ingrid turned to regard Roelena, pausing to take a sip of her lukewarm tea before continuing. She shook her head. "They should never have been soldiers in the first place. They were far too young. But some of the older German men?" Ingrid sneered. "They were so arrogant and superior, their faces contorted with anger and resentment. They probably believed they would soon return and subjugate us once again. I felt hatred for *those* men. It was men like that who'd killed my *vader* and stolen my home. If you never knew how to hate before, well, you can bet a war like that will teach you."

Ingrid paused, staring down at her mug as she absently turned it in small half-circles.

Roelena filled the silence. "But, Ingrid, what does that have to do with the scarf I gave you?"

Ingrid looked up at Roelena, almost surprised to see her sister-in-law across the table from her. She'd been so immersed in her memories she'd forgotten Roelena's presence. She shook her head. "It doesn't, Roelena. It's what came after the retreat." She sighed, shoving the cup and saucer away and absently picking up the scarf, shaking it out and letting the silken fabric slide against her hands. "It really is a lovely scarf, Roelena. But I'll never be able to wear it. Nor do I want to see anyone else wearing it."

"That's fine, Ingrid. I'll donate it to the Salvation Army

next time I'm in the city. But I'm so sorry I bought it. It didn't dawn on me it would make you recall painful memories."

Ingrid's eyes grew misty, but when she lifted her head to gaze at Roelena, her voice was steady. "You must know, don't you, about the Dutch girls who were girlfriends to the German soldiers? Well, some called them girlfriends, many others called them by worse names."

Roelena nodded.

"I knew hunger. So did a lot of people. And cold, fear, all of it. Those girls overcame their fear and their hunger by... associating with the German soldiers. You know what I mean. But those poor girls," she swallowed as her eyes shimmered with tears. "The day after I'd witnessed the Germans filing past our house—this was a week or two before I met Jakob—I was on the street with the others, happy, filled with joy, all of the emotions that came with liberation. No one could stop smiling. Then, suddenly, there was this awful ruckus. I thought at first the Germans had returned, but no. A group of villagers—some I later learned had been in the Underground—were dragging two of these girls down the street by their hair." Ingrid began to weep silently as she lifted a hand to her scalp. "How it must have hurt, being pulled by the hair across the cobblestones like that. The girls were shrieking for mercy. I wish now I had left right then and there, but I didn't, and now I'll be forever haunted by what came next."

Ingrid was staring out the window again, oblivious to her surroundings, oblivious to the tears on her sister-in-law's cheeks on seeing Ingrid weep.

"Two kitchen chairs appeared in the square; I don't know where they came from. The villagers tied those poor girls to the chairs. They'd been pleading for mercy, but once they were tied up, they shouted curses instead. You should have heard them. And the villagers? Oh, the hatred on their faces. It was awful to see."

Roelena had her handkerchief in her hand and wiped her face as she said, "Ingrid, you don't have to say any more. Not if it's making you so unhappy."

Ingrid gave Roelena a weak smile as she removed the handkerchief from her apron pocket and wiped her face. "You know, I can't decide if it's better to talk about these things and get them out—release the terrible memories like setting a caged bird free. Or keep them buried inside. I just don't know."

"If you want to talk, I'll listen. But you decide."

Ingrid looked contemplative for a moment. "I want to tell you. You bought me that beautiful scarf and you deserve to know why I won't wear it. Besides, talking with you always makes me feel better."

The two women shared an affectionate smile before Ingrid continued her disturbing tale.

"It didn't dawn on me that the Dutch, who were now liberated, could be as hateful and horrid as the Germans. But I was wrong. And it wasn't just the ringleaders who'd tied up the girls. Most of the people in the crowd were equally as cruel. Every face around me was a face of hate. They were screaming insults. Some even threw stones, but their aim was poor and they hit the captors, so that soon stopped. Lots of people got close enough to spit on them, though. They called them terrible names and kicked them with their wooden shoes. I was so confused. Would the villagers expect me to do the same? Because I just wanted the villagers to stop.

"And then one of the village women strutted up to the first girl with a pair of scissors in her hands. I thought she was going to stab her, but she grabbed a chunk of her hair and cut it off. And not carefully, either. She tugged real hard, jerking that girl's head back. It must have hurt. I've always had a tender scalp. I hate anyone brushing my hair. I could feel that girl's pain. And that village woman who had the scissors? Her face was filled with this horrible kind of joy and triumph. It was so awful, Roelena.

"Then more women were there, with more scissors, and they kept cutting and cutting. I remember seeing big swatches of blond hair floating away. It was like the hair was eager to be free of the heads of these wicked girls. Then, as if that wasn't enough," Ingrid wiped at her tears with the back of her hand. "Some village men appeared with razors. They shaved those poor girls' heads bare." Ingrid had to stop for a moment as she choked on her tear. She gestured uselessly at her head as she resumed talking. "They were silent by then, those girls. Weeping instead of cursing, helpless to stop the cruelty being done to them. And with their arms tied, they couldn't wipe the snot and tears from their own faces. They'd been so pretty before. Now they were ugly, deformed.

"They were cut loose then, and the chairs kicked out from under them so they fell. I can still see their faces. They looked like a caged tiger I once saw in a circus in Amsterdam. They got to their feet and held each other. Their own villagers had done this to them. I don't know if their own families were there that day. And then they had to scurry away because now a throng of children were throwing stones and chasing them. Children, Roelena! Children filled with so much hate. It was so awful."

Ingrid took a few deep breaths as she wiped at her wet face. Her blue eyes shimmered with unshed tears as she refocused on Roelena. "A few days later I saw those girls. They'd wrapped their bald heads with brightly patterned scarves tied on top, here, on the forehead." Ingrid gestured to where the knot would have been. "Even if you hadn't known what had been done to them, it was obvious they had no hair.

That's why I can't wear that scarf, Roelena. The one had these exact colours, bright yellow flowers on a blue background." Ingrid nodded at the scarf that now lay pooled at her elbow. "I remember it because it was so beautiful and bright. I hadn't seen nice clothes for so many years. I actually envied that girl her colourful scarf. Can you believe that? Her German boyfriend would have given it to her, but I envied her for it."

Ingrid seemed to notice for the first time that Roelena had also been crying. "And I've made you cry. I didn't mean to do that. Don't tell Clarence. He'll be so annoyed with me."

Roelena smiled as she wiped away the last of her tears. "Only if you promise not to tell Jakob that I made you cry."

The two women smiled wanly at each other. They both startled when a loud knock sounded on the door. They'd been so engrossed in their conversation they hadn't heard anyone arrive.

Ingrid got up, patting her damp face with her palms. "Do I look like I've been crying?"

"ja."

"Potverdrie," Ingrid swore the Dutch equivalent of *good gracious,* but her intonation made it sound far worse.

"It's Marliese," Ingrid called from the porch in a tone of immense relief.

When Marliese entered the kitchen on Ingrid's heels and saw Roelena, she placed her hands on her slim hips and feigned annoyance as she eyed first one women and then the other. "You had a crying session without me? How dare you."

Ingrid pulled out a chair. "We've had enough of tears haven't we, Roelena? You, Marliese, are going to sit down and cheer us both up in the way only you can."

33

THURSDAY, AUGUST 21

Marliese had failed abysmally at cheering them up, Roelena thought as she drove the two miles to her home later that afternoon. Instead, she'd told them about the state in which she'd found Clarence, relaying the gist of her conversation with him.

Roelena had cried again, feeling wretched about how she'd behaved with the man she'd professed to love above all others. For the first time since Karl died, she confided in her two closest friends that she'd been deliberately aloof with her husband, confessing her resentment about how he'd cultivated her belief that Karl would be cured by the doctors in Edmonton; a resentment that only seemed to grow given his ability and willingness to move on and re-calibrate his natural optimism for their future. She confessed how this bitterness had not lessened despite the passage of time. She even admitted that whatever grief Clarence carried, no matter the size, it was still too large for her to acknowledge. Her own anguish was already more than she could bear.

What she didn't dare admit was how she felt as if she was

hanging on by a thread—to what, she couldn't say—and that if she lost her tenuous grip on that thread, then…

Well, she didn't know what then, but she did know it made her afraid. She also didn't share that she couldn't see her way into the future with Clarence, not with Karl dead and buried. And she certainly didn't share anything about the cold darkness inhabiting her ribcage; the overwhelming burden of this strange, foreign emptiness was impossible to describe.

An hour after Marliese's arrival Alida woke from her nap. By then, everyone's tears were spent. Roelena felt a little less burdened. Sharing some of her deepest hurts hadn't made anything better; Karl was still gone, and always would be. But it had dulled the sharpness of her pain.

Ingrid made more tea and the three women continued chatting while Alida once again emptied the pantry of all she could reach. Marliese and Ingrid urged Roelena to talk openly and honestly with the man who adored her, enticing her with their belief that sharing her feelings with him would ease her distress rather than add to it. They even made Roelena promise to talk to Clarence. And not just talk, Ingrid gently scolded, but listen as well, reminding Roelena that he deserved nothing less from his wife.

Roelena didn't know what she would say given how she'd practically run away from Clarence, but the more she chatted with her closest friends, the more she felt it wouldn't be as hard as she'd once thought and she promised to make the effort to share some of what she'd been feeling. She'd been thoroughly astonished that Marliese could offer any sort of wisdom about nurturing a loving relationship. When Ingrid disappeared for five minutes to change Alida's diaper, she'd asked Marliese why someone so unhappily married could offer seemingly astute wisdom on relationships. Marliese had simply shrugged and said she only had to imagine herself being married to Conrad.

When Ingrid returned, the ladies' conversation shifted to reminiscing about the strong, loving presence Anneke had been in their lives. Ingrid recalled the winter when the sleigh Anneke was driving her and Cornelia Langelaar home from a Ladies Aid Society meeting had tipped as she made the turn out of the church yard. Although the sleigh had righted itself, all three women had toppled into the soft snow in the ditch. Ingrid described how Cornelia Langelaar had been stuck upside-down in a snow bank, her chubby, stocking-clad legs wiggling helplessly in the frigid winter air. Ingrid and Anneke had tried to help the poor woman, but their task became increasingly difficult on account of their inability to stop laughing. By the time Ingrid finished relaying the tale, the three women were clutching their sides and sputtering, tears of laughter on their cheeks as they imagined the scene.

That's how Jakob found them when he returned with four year-old Kees half asleep in his arms. The women had been so absorbed in their hilarity, they hadn't heard him return, or noticed that Tomas had stayed in the yard to play with the dog. Jakob was dismayed to enter his kitchen to see three women in tears, but his alarm quickly changed to relief when he realized theirs were tears of laughter. Handing *kleine* Kees to Ingrid, he pulled out a chair and demanded to know what was so funny.

Ingrid recounted her story, which Jakob remembered, and then he shared an amusing story about seeing Cornelia Langelaar emerge from the outhouse at the lake with the hem of her dress caught on her garter and showing far too much of the backs of her not insubstantial legs. When *kleine* Kees joined in their laughter, they laughed all the more at his innocent delight.

Marliese and Roelena left in their respective cars shortly after that, and now Roelena was almost home.

Half a mile from her house, Roelena suddenly slammed on the brakes, bringing the car to a sudden halt. No other vehicle was on the road, nor had Roelena hit anything or run over anything. A cloud of dust enveloped the car for a moment as if undecided where it was meant to go now that the car had so abruptly stopped.

A thought had come to Roelena; a notion so huge it was like a thunderclap going off in her head. She'd instinctively stopped the car; unconsciously keeping her foot pressed on the brake pedal.

There was no room in Roelena's mind except for this all-consuming thought. When Karl died, she'd known without a shadow of a doubt that there would never be an occasion for her to ever laugh again. She'd conceded that eventually she would smile, perhaps even go as far as a half-hearted chuckle. But nothing on this earth would ever again cause her to be overcome by laughter. With Karl dead, it simply wasn't possible.

Except she had. And not just once, but repeatedly over the course of that afternoon. How had that been possible?

Quiet tears trickled down Roelena's cheeks as she stared out the windshield. *What kind of mother was she that she could find joy in life, however brief, when her baby son was dead and buried in the cold, dank earth? How could she have betrayed the memory of her beautiful little boy by daring to laugh?* She felt a deep shame about her capacity to laugh, knowing she'd been able to do so because for that hour she'd forgotten about Karl.

What kind of mother was she that she could forget, even for a minute, that her baby was dead?

With a broken wail, Roelena dropped her forehead onto the steering wheel and sobbed.

But her reserve of tears was low. Moments later she sat up, reaching for her handbag to retrieve her damp handkerchief.

As she mopped her face and blew her nose, she realized Clarence would take one look at her and know she'd been crying. Despite their terrible fight, he'd take her into his arms and likely try to coax her into a better mood. Instead of rebuffing him as she'd done for the last six weeks, she'd do what she'd promised; she'd share some of how she'd been feeling. They'd talk and she would listen, or try to, at least. And maybe Ingrid and Marliese would be proved right and Roelena would feel lighter for having shared her crushing emotional burden.

Roelena put her handkerchief back in her purse, then took her foot off the brake pedal and resumed driving. A minute later, she turned the car into their driveway and parked, turning off the ignition, listening distractedly to the engine cough a few times before it died.

The dog bounded up to the car, its tail wagging, but Roelena stayed behind the wheel for a time. She looked at the house, feeling both apprehensive and scared at the thought of facing Clarence.

When she finally pushed the door open, the hinges creaking, she greeted the dog before lifting herself from the car. Her advancing pregnancy was making it more and more difficult to move comfortably.

As she approached the steps, her eyes fell on the broken railing, and she paused. That damage could be fixed with relative ease. She knew the damage done to their relationship would take significantly more time and effort.

Taking a deep breath, she climbed the steps and quietly entered the silent house.

34

LETTER TO ROELENA FROM HENDRIK

Dear Roelena,

It fills me with joy to send this letter of congratulations on the birth of your healthy baby girl. Clarence telephoned just before supper and he sounded overjoyed. Both Gladys and I have full and thankful hearts knowing you have been delivered a precious child in glowing health, and thankful too that you are also doing well.

I know this must be a dreadfully confusing time for you, Roelena, feeling the joy that comes from the gift of welcoming a perfect child into the world, yet also feeling the absence of dear little Karl. I hope your sweet daughter will help mend the breaks in your heart. I imagine, too, that at this time you must be especially feeling Moe's absence. You have suffered greater hardship this year than any of the rest of us, what with losing mother, and then the worry of whether your German measles harmed your unborn child, and then the hardship of Karl's passing. Take to heart the words of the Apostle Paul when he asked in Romans 8, who shall separate us from the love of Christ? The Apostle's answer is that no tribulation or depth of pain shall ever be able to separate you from the love of our God, which is in Christ Jesus our Lord. Remember this, dear sister, when you are feeling the absence of your darling son and our own loving mother. Gladys and I are both looking forward to meeting this new addition to the family and regret that we were not able to manage a trip to Alberta this fall. But perhaps next summer, Lord willing.

Our small congregation continues to grow and we can now boast fifteen families and five single men. We're saving to buy some land and build a proper church, but for now we continue to meet in the building we rent from a United Church. The news we hear is that the flow of immigrants will continue for a number of years. With increasing numbers, our Christian Reformed community here can do nothing other than thrive. One day, hopefully within a time frame that would benefit my own children if we are ever to be so blessed, we also hope to build a Christian school.

Gladys is loving her new Singer sewing machine. Right now she has it set up in the second bedroom, but she loves that one day when we have children, she could pack it away in its portable case as then she'd have to sew at the kitchen table. She is very industrious, as you know, and can sew anything she sets her mind to. She had a windfall of fabric last week. She does house-cleaning as you know for a handful of ladies, most of them elderly. One of those women's daughters had an aunt who died who was an avid sewer. Apparently the aunt had a room full of material and Gladys was given it all. She spent an afternoon sorting it all by colour and now has it organized in stacked empty crates for easy access. It's a wonderfully generous gift, but if that happens again, we won't have room in our two-bedroom house for all the material.

There is much to do in the orchard at this time of year and we generally take advantage of the evening's light, which is why this letter is so short as my eyelids quickly become heavy once I'm in the house after the evening's work is done. But I wanted to write to you upon hearing your good news so that I could convey my deep happiness and thankfulness on the joyous occasion of the arrival of your healthy baby.

Your loving brother,

Hendrik.

35
THANKSGIVING MONDAY - OCTOBER 13

The date for Thanksgiving was initially set by federal proclamation and generally fell on the second Monday in October, and has become a tradition that celebrates both the harvest and multiple other blessings throughout the year. Since its inception, the Pine Glade Christian Reformed Church held a morning service every Thanksgiving Monday, in addition to the two Sunday services the day before. The *dominee's* wife always decorated the table beside the pulpit with harvest bounty, including wheat sheaves, corn, gourds, nuts, and flowers. The theme of thankfulness was also reflected in the liturgy, prayers, sermon, and the hymns performed by the Young People's Society choir.

Roelena was in their small kitchen dressed in her Sunday clothes, her best gloves clutched in one hand, all set to go to the *kerk*. She was in two minds about attending the Thanksgiving Monday service, disliking the thought of leaving her baby for the first time. But she'd missed both Sunday services the day before. It wasn't as if Clarence wasn't capable of taking care of the baby for the two short hours Roelena would be absent. She hadn't been able to nurse at all this time, so Clarence could give little Brenda her bottle if she awoke while Roelena was away.

Roelena absently clicked open her handbag, the garnet bracelet on her wrist glittering darkly in the morning sunshine streaming through the window. She automatically checked to make sure she had a clean handkerchief, money for the collection plate, and a few peppermints. Snapping her handbag closed, she looked over at Clarence where he stood hovering in the doorway to the hall.

"I'll manage just fine, sweetheart," Clarence assured, moving into the room and pulling Roelena into his arms. "You know she only cries when she's hungry, and I can remedy that easy enough." Clarence nodded at the sterilized bottles Roelena had left on the countertop. "And anyway, she might not even wake up while you're away."

Roelena gave her husband as reassuring a smile as she could muster, feeling no need to correct Clarence's assumption that her lack of enthusiasm was on account of leaving Brenda for the first time. Her despondency was more on account of the residual discomfort she still harboured about their rather strange argument the previous night.

Unlike Roelena, Clarence was his usual cheerful self that morning. He was good at that, Roelena thought; good at moving on and leaving the past in the past. Perhaps Clarence was right. An hour in *kerk* giving thanks for their blessings would make her feel better.

Over these last two months they'd made great strides at renewing their marital harmony, especially since Brenda's birth. But they hadn't regained that enviable state of wedded bliss they'd once known, despite their best efforts. She wasn't sure they ever would. It wasn't that she'd stopped loving Clarence; of course she still loved him. But her love was less intense, less all encompassing. She was no longer that naïve innocent who'd once believed the man she married was above reproach. She sometimes felt guilty that identifying what she perceived as his shortcomings had diminished the depth of her love for him, but she didn't know what to do about it besides simply living with it.

It changed a woman, burying her baby. In those weeks between losing Karl and Brenda's birth, she'd felt in limbo. An untethered childless mother. Children without parents were orphans; men and women without spouses were widowers and widows. Why wasn't there a word to describe parents whose child had died? She'd concluded it was too unspeakable to be assigned a word; yet, that didn't stop it from happening. She was living proof, as were countless others. But she was a mother again, tethered to her new baby.

Brenda was a welcome distraction from that which still wasn't quite right between her and Clarence, but it had been talk of Brenda that started the argument the previous evening. She'd put the baby down at half-past seven o'clock and then taken her usual seat in the front room next to her knitting basket. Not long after, Clarence finished the Dutch novel he'd borrowed from a recent immigrant who'd joined their community earlier that year. He gave Roelena a summary of the heartwarming story about a Christian family in Indonesia whose faith had been challenged by many hardships, one of which was the loss of their nine-year old daughter during a severe typhoon.

"You should read it," he said. "It would do you good."

Although she did her best to hide her annoyance, Roelena bristled at his words. *Do her good?* Despite what he might think, in her own way and in her own time she was doing just fine. The arrival of their perfectly healthy baby had shrunk the cold, black thing residing within her; it was no larger than a pin prick nestled against the underside of her ribcage. She knew her fear kept it alive, and accepted that she might never be free of it. How could she not live in a constant state of fear when any capricious illness could take little Brenda just as it had claimed Karl? Her *ouders* had been forced to stand at the graveside of a child not once, but three times. Roelena would not survive that. Although she'd once longed for a big family of her own, she would be satisfied with little Brenda, and would focus all her love and energy on ensuring the health and wellbeing of their one precious child. She knew she was over-protective of the baby, knew also that it bothered Clarence to see this, although she was thankful he wisely refrained from explicitly criticizing her for it.

"With each new baby," Clarence said, "you'll be more and more able to put the tragedy of Karl's death behind you."

Roelena had to struggle to keep her expression and tone neutral and kept her eyes on the sock she was knitting. "Brenda is only a month old. I can't even think about having another baby," she responded.

"Well, not now," Clarence quickly amended. "But as Psalm 127 states, children are a gift from God. And it's not up to us to determine when and how often God bestows these precious gifts."

Roelena gritted her teeth. She didn't want another of God's gifts if God was going to take it away a few months later. She couldn't bear that. Not again.

"I don't want to be pregnant again," she stated as calmly as she could manage, then added with feigned sincerity so as to avoid an argument, "At least, not for a very long time."

In her peripheral vision, she'd seen Clarence toss his book onto the table beside his chair and adjust his posture, sitting up straighter and re-crossing his legs. She knew he wholeheartedly disagreed with her. She also knew he was struggling to squelch his indignation.

"I thought you loved being pregnant?"

He was right. She had loved it, especially with Karl. She'd always been strong and healthy, but while she was pregnant with Karl, she'd glowed. Everyone had commented on it. Even her hair had been extra shiny. While pregnant with Brenda, she'd suffered bouts of nausea every day for the first three months, and then only mild nausea after that, yet she'd still loved being pregnant.

She wanted to say she had no intention of ever falling pregnant again, but instead said, "I did love being pregnant. But there's no rush. Brenda is only a month old," she repeated.

"Of course," Clarence stated, quick to agree. "But we shouldn't wait too long. We don't want Brenda to be years older than her next sibling. Having a brother or sister close in age is better."

Roelena lifted her gaze, no longer able to hide her scowl as she absently nudged the loops of yarn along the needles so she wouldn't accidentally drop a stitch. "Don't use *we* when you mean *you*. *You* may not want to wait before having more children, but *I* do."

"No, you don't. You've always wanted a big family. Besides, you'll be more yourself again once you have more children."

Roelena dropped her hands into her lap and clenched her jaw. "Oh really?" She flung the sarcastic phrase at him like a dart.

"Yes, really," he insisted.

Hearing the note of stubborn obstinacy creep into his voice, she dropped her gaze and resumed her knitting. She didn't want to fight with Clarence. They had been getting along so well since that day he'd kicked in the railing. They weren't as close as they'd once been, but they were living in a fragile kind of harmony. But she was not backing down. She needed his agreement about avoiding another pregnancy. And if that meant having it out now as opposed to later, so be it.

Clarence sighed heavily. When he next spoke, his tone was deliberately light-hearted. "I was under the impression that *we*…" Clarence let his words hang in the air.

Roelena knew he was waiting for her to look at him, but she kept her gaze on her knitting.

"That *we* wanted a big family," he continued. "Yes, Karl died. And granted, that makes it hard to think about having more children who also might get sickly and die. But Roelena, it doesn't make sense to be afraid that our future children will also die."

Roelena spoke in a low, accusing tone, addressing her clicking needles. "You know as well as I do that when Karl was Brenda's age, he was *fine*."

"Sweetheart," Clarence said gently as he leaned forward and rested his elbows on his knees. "We will never have a guarantee that Brenda will always be healthy. Those kinds of things don't come with a guarantee. Not from God, or from any doctor on this Earth. But we can trust that God cares for and protects us all, children and old alike. We'll always be safe and secure so long as we look to Him for guidance."

"But God didn't keep Karl safe," Roelena retorted, regretting her words as soon as she spoke them. She didn't want him to know just how much she was struggling with her faith. She couldn't bear being preached at about what she should and shouldn't believe, or should and shouldn't feel; not from her husband, and not from the *dominee*.

"Roelena," Clarence entreated. He reached across the narrow coffee table that separated their chairs and rested a hand on his wife's rigid knee. "Karl truly is in his heavenly home. I *know* this. I wish you would believe it, too, and take comfort in the knowledge."

Clarence often spoke of Karl now residing in his heavenly home, of being happy there in a place of bottomless, eternal love. Roelena knew her parents had also taken comfort in knowing their darling children were in the heavenly home God prepared for them. She'd once believed it herself. But that was before Karl died. She wanted to scream at Clarence that their baby should have been allowed to remain in his earthly home, that it had been far too soon for him to go to his heavenly home. She knew it was dreadfully wrong to be so angry with God, but who else was to blame?

She wouldn't dream of confessing this grave sinful thought to anyone, not Clarence, not her Pa, not Greta, not Ingrid, not their *dominee*, not even Marliese. She might have been able to confide in her *moeder*, she *needed* to confide in Anneke now more than ever. She needed to ask her own *moeder* how she'd lived through the loss of not one, but three children's deaths. How had Anneke come to terms with God taking those children to their heavenly home? But God had seen fit to take her *moeder* as well. And although Roelena sometimes caught a glimpse of the comfort she could eke from imagining little Karl in the arms of his *oma* in heaven, the image mostly made her angry. Karl should be in Roelena's arms. Here, on Earth!

Roelena's vision suddenly blurred, but she'd knitted so many socks, she could do it with her eyes closed. She blinked rapidly, forcing the tears away before they could fall. Roelena re-crossed her legs, forcing Clarence's hand to fall away. "Can we wait until Brenda is older to have this conversation?"

Clarence leaned back in his chair with a disgruntled sigh. After a few minutes of silence, Roelena dared to believe the conversation was over, but then her husband spoke again, his tone light and teasing. "Roelena, sweetheart, unless you plan on sleeping on the sofa, we can't ensure you won't get pregnant."

Although they hadn't yet made love since Brenda's birth, in the last month before she'd been born, and despite Roelena's ballooning belly, Roelena's sexual appetite had returned in full force, easily matched by her husband who'd been suffering from weeks of neglect. Their renewed physical intimacy had gone a long way towards revitalizing their emotional bond.

Roelena flushed under his intense gaze, but kept her eyes on her knitting. Her husband's banter meant that he wasn't taking her perspective seriously. "There are ways," she asserted.

Clarence sighed. "Yes, there are ways. I can…withdraw at the end."

"Yes. And the rhythm method. I can track my cycle. That's apparently effective." Her sentences were abrupt and clipped. Sex had always been a taboo subject and it was an embarrassing and uncomfortable subject for her to talk about, even with her husband. "When we resume…making love again, I want you to agree that we will take measures. Maybe even…"

Clarence knew exactly what she meant, but he wanted her to say it. "Even what, Roelena?" he spat.

"You know what I mean."

"Ja, I know what you mean." Clarence crossed his arms against his chest and stared moodily at his wife. "But I'm a married man who wants a family. I should not have to buy condoms." Clarence sighed again, but when he next spoke his tone was conciliatory. "Look, why don't we talk about this, later, when you're more…"

Roelena dropped her hands into her lap again and glowered at him. "More what? More inclined to see things from *your* point of view?"

"No. I wasn't going to say that. I just meant more...reasonable."

"Reasonable? Are you accusing me of being unreasonable?"

Clarence heaved a sigh and rose. "No, sweetheart, you're not being unreasonable. We'll do it your way. For now. I'm going to go make tea," he added as he left the room.

Roelena looked down at her hands. She knew his departure signaled the end of the conversation. She also knew when he came back into the room, he would either find something to read or he'd initiate a different topic of conversation as if they'd never argued. Which should've filled her with relief. After all, Clarence had agreed, albeit reluctantly, to forego having children, at least for the foreseeable future. The question she was asking herself now was, *if taking measures to halt further pregnancies were truly what she wanted, why did she feel so miserably bereft?*

36

THANKSGIVING MONDAY - OCTOBER 13

The church was full, but there was just enough room for Roelena to squeeze into the middle of the pew beside Ingrid. As usual, the service began when the *dominee* and the members of the Consistory filed into the church, the *dominee* walking to the pulpit at the front while the elders and deacons on the Consistory went to sit with their wives and families in the pews.

Roelena's thoughts kept drifting to the previous evening's argument with Clarence, but she feigned attention as the *dominee* took the congregation through the familiar liturgy, automatically bowing her head for the prayers and mechanically singing the hymns when the organist pumped out accompaniment on the wheezy old pump organ. Her eyes followed the members of the Young People's Society choir as they filed to the front of the *kerk* and took their positions for the choir performance. That had been her once. A lifetime ago.

Later, after the *dominee* concluded his sermon, Roelena realized she hadn't heard a single word. When he invited the congregation to bow their heads for the final prayer, she folded her gloved hands and bowed her head and made a special effort to listen.

"Lord, we ask that you hear our prayer today," the *dominee* said, *"on this special day, this day of thanksgiving, for we know that without your love, we are as nothing. We offer our humble thanks for the blessings that you so richly bestowed on us throughout the year. Our lives are ones of plenty, and we owe this blessing of abundance to your love and care. May we be grateful each morning for the gift of a new day, and grateful each evening for the good we received and the good we were able to do for others. We thank you, too, for the steadfast love you bestow upon us and for your continued devotion to our health and happiness. We ask that you guide us towards hearts filled with thanksgiving and praise for all that has happened in days past and days still to come. Teach us to be joyful always, to pray continually, and to give thanks in all circumstances, knowing your will is being done in all things, which is our greatest comfort. Our dearest Heavenly Father, we offer our thanks to you for our families, for the blessing of our parents, our sisters and brothers, our children and grandchildren. Thank you..."*

Roelena stood abruptly and pressed in front of Ingrid's knees, startling her sister-in-law out of her meditative state of prayer, past *kleine* Kees who was half asleep leaning against his mother's shoulder, and past Tomas who looked up at his aunt in wide-eyed amazement, gawking at this unprecedented behavior; no one ever walked out of church in the middle of the service, and certainly never during prayer. She pushed past Jakob. He abruptly straightened up, turning his long legs sideways to make room for Roelena to escape into the aisle.

Tomas and *kleine* Kees both turned their heads to stare after their aunt as she hurried towards the exit. When Jakob ordered them in a whisper to face front and close their eyes in prayer, Tomas did as he was told, but not before he'd noticed adult members of the congregation with their eyes open and watching the hurried departure of his aunt.

Roelena burst outside, stopping on the outside landing and gulping air, shuddering with each breath. Despite the sunshine, a cold wind whipped around her warning of winter. She relished the sharp feel of it against her hot cheeks that were now awash with tears.

Thankful? How could she thank God for her health and her home when she would trade all of it to have Karl back? How dare the *dominee* expect her to thank God? How dare *God* expect her thanks?

She felt the familiar wave of guilt about her blasphemous thoughts. She rested her hands on the flat wooden railing, gulping in air as she tried to calm the racing of her heart. When her gaze fell on the cemetery, she thought of her sister Wiekje who'd been residing there for over fifteen years. Her mother had been buried there for only eight months, and her baby for half that. Roelena banged her fist on the railing, a wail of frustration and anger erupting from deep within her. *Was she truly meant to sit inside that sanctuary and thank God for His so-called blessings when her baby lay cold and lifeless in a dirt-covered box? Was that what God wanted from her?*

"Roelena? *Gaat het wel goed?*" Ingrid demanded from beside Roelena.

Roelena felt Ingrid's arm go around her waist, saw her face peering up at her in deep concern. Roelena wanted to scream, *No, I'm not alright!* But instead she wiped her wet cheeks with her gloved hand and said. "I'm fine. I just needed some fresh air."

Ingrid rubbed a sympathetic hand on Roelena's back. Her look of concern didn't fade, but she lightened her tone. *"Brr.* If fresh air is what you wanted, you certainly got it. Too bad Marliese isn't here today; she'd offer you a cigarette."

Roelena nodded, knowing Marliese and Wilfred were away for the weekend.

"Should I drive you home? Jakob can take the boys and come get me later."

Roelena shook her head, then took a deep breath and finally spoke. "No thanks, Ingrid. I'll be fine now. Honest."

When they heard the organ begin to play, they both glanced towards the closed doors of the church. The congregation would be standing now to sing the closing hymn.

"I can drive myself home. I should go now, before the service ends," she added when she heard the muffled sound of the combined voices beak into the hymn taken from Psalm 92, *How good it is to thank the Lord*. "People will ask questions, and I don't..."

"I understand." Ingrid put her hands on each of Roelena's arms and spoke in a gentle tone. "You don't have to explain, Roelena. Go on home, and hold that beautiful baby close to your heart."

Roelena had to close her eyes and swallow hard to force away the tears. Ingrid had a way of getting to the heart of things, without judgement and without any expectation that Roelena needed to behave differently. They weren't a demonstrative family, but Roelena gave Ingrid an affectionate hug. When she pulled back, she said, "I'm so glad Jakob married you."

Ingrid got teary then, too. "Stop," she said, stepping back. "Or you'll have me in tears. Will you still be coming over later this afternoon for Thanksgiving supper?"

It would be the first time since Anneke's funeral that the family—except for Hendrik and Harri—would be together for a formal meal.

"Of course. We'll come early so I can help you and Greta with the cooking."

"No you won't. Greta and I are quite capable of cooking dinner, and your Pa and Sijmon are a big help in the kitchen."

"All right." Roelena didn't bother arguing, especially since the congregation was on the last verse of the hymn and would be exiting the church soon. "I'll see you about four o'clock then?"

"Yes. And Roelena?" Ingrid briefly patted Roelena's forearm. "With time, it will get easier. I promise."

Roelena nodded, then turned and hurried down the steps eager to be on her way.

What she really wanted to know, she thought as she walked towards her car, her footsteps crunching on the gravel, was how much time had to pass before it got easier?

PART III

1953

37
LETTER TO ROELENA FROM HENDRIK

Dear Roelena and Clarence,

Thank you for your letter dated April 3. As always, I so appreciate hearing all the news of home. I am sorry to hear about this spring's mouse plague. What a trouble to contend with, and how awful it must be to have your fields over-run with the detestable creatures. I hope the population decreases as the summer unfolds and certainly before the fall so that the combine harvest doesn't include chopped mice with the crops. Unfortunately, I read your letter aloud and when poor Gladys heard your description of driving over a moving stream of mice on your country lane, she had to dash away to be sick. Which brings me to the wonderful news I'm delighted to share.

Gladys is expecting our first child! We have been waiting for over three years for this welcome news, and my heart is filled with joy and anticipation as I write these words. As you know, she had two previous pregnancies that failed early, but we are now well past the danger point and the doctor assures us we will meet our little bundle of joy in early September, right about the same time that Greta is due to have their fifth. I wish I could tell Moe this news as she was always so pleased when the others announced she would be an Oma again, but I'm certain she is rejoicing in Heaven, just as we are here on Earth. Gladys is doing well, although she continues to suffer from an over-sensitive stomach. She does not complain but remains intent on the end result, which makes all her present discomfort worthwhile.

I hear that Ingrid's great-aunt in the Netherlands died last month. How sad for her. I know that without their great-aunt, Ingrid and Klaas would've had nowhere to go during Holland's terrible hongerwinter *in the last year of the war. As expected, her brother Klaas inherited the farm, which is slowly beginning to recover, according to Ingrid. I think in every letter she talks of a future visit by her brother to Canada, which I pray for her sake comes to fruition before too long. But at least she need not worry about his future as he seems well set up to succeed.*

The orchard is thriving. I believe I mentioned a few years ago that we had the chance to purchase more land. This coming harvest, the fruit from that orchard will provide its first full crop, God willing. Like all farming, everything is dependent on the weather and God's grace, but we remain hopeful and eager to reap the benefits of having tended and nurtured the saplings into mature, healthy trees that will provide plentiful harvests for years to come. No matter the small problems that always seem to arise, I can honestly say how satisfying it is for me to be an orchard farmer. I thank God daily that this opportunity arose when it did. I feel blessed to do honest work that I enjoy, work that provides for my family, and maybe someday provides a legacy for my children.

Did you know Peter is thinking of coming here for six weeks in the summer to work for me? He wants to see if the climate I boast of here is to his liking, although really he must spend a winter here before he can make an informed conclusion on that score. As we all know, he wants to be a veterinarian, but the years of study and the expense may be too much for Pa. Regardless, Gladys and I would be happy to have him here. Seeing as he still has two more years of high school, he doesn't have to decide about university for some time to come yet.

I've had another letter from Harri. He's writing more frequently now than he ever did before marrying Therese. He has really settled into family life, which is a good thing given they have twins on the way. Once they're born next month, he'll likely have less time to write, which would be a shame as I'm thoroughly enjoying this growing friendship with my rather enigmatic older brother. It seems Moe's death changed his appreciation of family, or perhaps his more open heart is due to Therese. Or maybe it's simply due to the many variables of life that shape each of us. But now I'm bordering on philosophising and we can't have that, at least not from me. We'll leave that type of intellectual pursuits to the family members attending university.

I'm pleased that Willem has agreed to come back to the farm for the summer once his exams are done. He sure sounded disappointed he didn't get the job as a laboratory assistant for the summer, but as he stated in his letter, these jobs usually go to the students who are in third or fourth year, so he remains hopeful for the next year or the one after that. Jakob and Sijmon will be glad of his help on the farm as he's always been a hard worker, despite his many other challenges, which all seem to have gone by the wayside. He also mentions a girl (unnamed) in his letters. Do you know anything about that? I'm guessing it's not serious (or she's not Dutch), which is why she remains unnamed.

Gladys and her niece Joyce—do you remember her? She is more like a sister to Gladys as they are so close in age. They have been re-painting the interior of our house. Gladys had intended to only paint the nursery, but in typical Gladys fashion—she never does anything halfway—we will be living with paint fumes for the next few weeks as she's doing every room in the house. But at least the work will be done long before the baby arrives. Gladys is also loving her new Singer sewing machine. She is sewing up a storm, new curtains in the house, and all kinds of things for the baby, in neutral colours of course. Whether we have a girl or a boy matters not at all, but Gladys will be very happy when she can purchase either blue or pink fabrics. She doesn't complain, but she is often, and rather randomly, overcome with nausea, although she never actually vomits anymore. I must admit when I see her suddenly gagging, with nothing happening and thirty seconds later she is fine, I almost want to laugh. I have enough sense not to, but it is rather comical. And when there are no pickles in the refrigerator, she can be rather fractious, another trait that inwardly amuses me. If the baby is a boy, we've agreed to name him Cornelius after her father. We have yet to agree on a girl's name. Is it the same for you and Clarence, struggling to agree on a name that will last the lifetime of your child? I had no idea Gladys and I would have such differing views. I like simple, uncomplicated names, but Gladys is inclined to like girls' names that I deem silly. Cassandra is one she particularly likes and one I particularly dislike. I do hope to have a say but in the end I will be happy to let her decide.

I continue to enjoy my visits with old Mr. Hunt down the road. Gladys is less enamoured with him on account of his rather unpleasant body odour—she has a far more sensitive nose than me. But I still find him fascinating and generally make my way down the road to his house once a week for what he calls a chat-and-chew, although he does most of the chatting and all of the chewing. I've taken to smoking a pipe and no longer touch cigarettes, but nothing would make me try chewing tobacco.

I'm guessing you won't receive this letter until you are back from your vacation. I hope you and Clarence had an enjoyable break and that all went well on the long drive. I look forward to hearing the news from our Iowa relatives.

And now my day is done and I'm ready for bed, so I will bid you goodnight. May God continue to bless you all. Give baby Brenda a kiss from me and a second from Gladys.

Your loving brother,

Hendrik.

38

THURSDAY, MAY 7

By the 1830s in the Netherlands, mandatory allegiance to the state church splintered the Dutch protestants, resulting in large groups of people seceding from the state church and forming their own Calvinist congregations. By the late 1840s, whole families—and sometimes even entire neighborhoods—of Dutch Calvinists desiring increased religious freedom and new opportunities left their homeland for America. These agrarian Dutch immigrants, eager to settle on uncrowded lands where they and their families were free to lead honest, godly lives, risked most of their wealth on the chance of economic improvement and religious freedom in the New World. The combined cost of passage, expenses, and land purchase—approximately $1.25 an acre—was substantial.

Their ocean voyage across the Atlantic, which took up to eight weeks, subjected the passengers to terrible storms and hardships. Young mothers gave birth to new life. Those travelers who died, adult and child alike, were committed to graves in the Atlantic.

Upon reaching America, most of these Dutch Calvinist immigrants settled in either the forests of western Michigan or on frontier farms in central Iowa, founding towns and villages with Dutch names such as Holland in Michigan State or Orange City in Iowa, named for the Dutch royal colour. These early farming families, accustomed to rural life in Holland where they lived in close quarters in small houses on tidy farms whose fields had been cultivated for more than sixty generations, had to adjust to a life of solitude and isolation that was, at least at first, primitive. On the widely spaced farms in Iowa, the Dutch built temporary homes dug into the earth with walls and chimneys made from layers of prairie sod, roofs made of branches covered with prairie grass or straw, and doors of sackcloth and woven twigs, and brought with them their Calvinist religion, establishing the first of what came to be scores of closely-knit Christian Reformed Church communities.

That first wave of Dutch Americans, after a decade or two on the frontier, reaped the rewards of their sacrifice and hard work and were beginning to enjoy increased prosperity and well-being, as well as religious freedom in their Christian Reformed Churches. Letters carried across the Atlantic to friends and relatives in the Netherlands relayed first-hand evidence that this New World was a land of great opportunity that boasted higher wages, fertile soil, and the abundance of cheap land. The stream of Dutch immigration continued into the twentieth century, with families and single men settling into established communities of third- and fourth-generation Dutch Calvinists or founding new communities. In the aftermath of World War II, tens of thousands of Dutch immigrants joined those already in America, making Dutch Americans in several counties in Michigan and Iowa one of the largest ethnic groups.

The Alberta de Haas family had relatives among the populous Dutch in Iowa. Harry de Haas, Kees's youngest brother, had left the Netherlands in 1923 with his bride to farm near a Dutch settlement called Pella. Fifteen years later, Harry moved his young family to Cedar Rapids where Harry and his wife's brother took over the operation of a general merchandise retail store, an enterprise that by the late 1940s made them more than moderately prosperous. Together with a handful of Dutch Calvinist families, they also established the first Christian Reformed Church in the growing city.

Earlier that year, Roelena's worried father had taken Clarence aside and asked what he thought of the idea of taking Roelena on a road-trip to visit her cousins in Iowa. It was obvious to anyone who knew Roelena that she hadn't recovered from the previous year's heartbreaks, and Kees was troubled, a concern Clarence shared. Although Roelena had stopped writing Conrad for a time after he'd broken Marliese's heart, Roelena and her pen-pal cousin corresponded frequently and enjoyed a close friendship.

Clarence, welcomed Kees's suggestion. To him, it seemed as if his wife had a veil over her heart. He'd witnessed a thinning of this shroud since Brenda's arrival, but it hadn't lifted. It wasn't that he expected Roelena to be unchanged by their son's death; he'd changed too. How could losing one's dearly loved firstborn son not alter a person? But Clarence could draw comfort from knowing he'd been visited by his dead son; a visit from Heaven. He could still reignite that feeling of utter peace and wellbeing he knew flowed to him from Karl's Heavenly home, a place where love was so boundless and eternal it could only be felt, not described. Which was why he'd never shared anything about that ethereal visit to Roelena. There had never been a time when he thought Roelena would be open to hearing what he'd seen and the peace and love he'd felt in those first devastating moments. Perhaps one day. But first, he'd wait for time—with the help of Brenda—to heal the rawness of his wife's wounded and grieving heart. He worried sometimes that Roelena would never truly heal. He still wasn't sure how he felt about that possibility.

Kees thought a change of scenery might help his daughter, and offered both his car, which was more reliable than the one Clarence and Roelena owned, and enough cash to cover the cost of gas. Kees had also retained Sijmon's agreement to take over Clarence's farm chores during their absence, as well as Ingrid and Jakob's agreement to care for baby Brenda.

Clarence had been enthusiastic about his father-in-law's plan. He'd been living in Canada for six years but had taken little time to see the country. In the spring before Karl was born, he and Roelena had driven through the Rocky Mountains to visit Hendrik in British Columbia's Fraser Valley. They'd stayed one night in Banff—one of the most beautiful places he'd ever seen, a fact he enthusiastically reported to his family in the stunning postcards he'd mailed to The Netherlands. They'd returned with as many crates of peaches, apples, pears, and cherries that would fit in the car. But Clarence had never been east of Edmonton or south of the border and had jumped at the opportunity when Kees had presented it to him.

Clarence was inordinately grateful for the kindness and generosity of his father-in-law, who was still suffering from the loss of his own dear wife. To Clarence, the man seemed diminished. Never quick to laugh—that had always been Anneke—Kees had become particularly solemn and grave over the past year.

When Clarence broached the topic of this vacation to his wife, Roelena had been enthusiastic, although she immediately vetoed leaving Brenda behind. She'd promptly written to Conrad, asking if a visit in May after seeding was completed would fit with his and Louise's schedule. Since then, and for the first time in months, Clarence had basked in his wife's renewed anticipation and excitement.

Sitting behind the wheel of his father-in-law's 1941 Ford, Clarence gave thanks again for both his kind-hearted father-in-law and his wife's cousin in Iowa he'd yet to meet who had so generously opened his home for the duration of their ten-day visit. They'd been driving for four days. For the first and third night on the road trip, they'd stayed in modest motels, but the second night they'd parked on the side of the road and slept. It had been only moderately restful, but it saved them money. They'd agreed that, once they arrived at their destination—Conrad and Louise's home in Cedar Rapids—they could catch up on any missing sleep.

Roelena's excitement about her and Clarence's road trip to Iowa surprised even herself. Four-and-a-half years before, when Conrad's heart-wrenching letter to Marliese had broken her best friend's heart, Roelena stopped what had been fairly regular correspondence with her cousin. She'd simply been too angry with him to write. But Conrad continued to send her Christmas cards despite the fact that she didn't respond in kind. It wasn't until after Marliese married Wilfred in the summer of 1950 that Roelena finally wrote a short note to Conrad, including a reference to Marliese's recent nuptials. Since then, she and Conrad had exchanged long and regular letters, although Roelena deliberately left out any mention of Marliese despite Conrad's casual questions about his old flame. Conrad and Louise had married in the fall of 1949, eight months after

Conrad's devastating letter to Marliese. In their renewed exchange of letters, Conrad shared the news of their son Harold and daughter, Christina Mae.

Immediately upon receiving Roelena's letter asking if she and Clarence, along with their baby, could visit in May, Conrad had telephoned Roelena—the lines had finally been installed earlier that year on Clarence and Roelena's stretch of road. Roelena felt excitement bubbling in her veins while she'd chatted with Conrad, glancing at Clarence and sharing his grin of unabashed pleasure. After she and Conrad agreed on suitable dates for their visit which would be finalized after seeding began, Conrad announced that Louise was pregnant with their third child due in late July. Conrad followed this short telephone conversation with a long letter that included advice on the best roads to take and places to stay on the long drive from Alberta.

"Forty-eight more miles," Clarence announced happily as they drove past a sign showing the mileage to various cities along Highway 150 in northeastern Iowa. He looked at the large face of his wrist-watch. "It's half-past seven o'clock now. We'll be there well before dark."

"Won't it be nice to be in a proper home again?" Roelena enthused.

"I just want a decent cup of tea," stated Clarence. The tea they'd purchased at various truck stops along the way had been disappointingly tepid.

"And this little tyke needs a proper bath," Roelena added, smiling down at the happy baby on her lap. The baby was gnawing alternately on a rattle gripped in one chubby hand and a soggy digestive biscuit in the other. Roelena was proud of how well Brenda had adapted to sleeping in the buggy bassinet on the back seat of her father's car.

"Conrad said that, once we reach the city limits, it will

take about fifteen minutes or so to get to his house, right?" Clarence asked.

Keeping one hand resting on Brenda's chubby legs, Roelena retrieved an envelope from her handbag that had her name and address written in her cousin's messy scrawl. Roelena removed the letter, then had to keep it out of reach of her baby's grasping hand. She picked up the dropped rattle and gave it back to Brenda, then read aloud the specific directions Conrad had provided.

"It sounds complicated," she said, laying the open letter on the seat between them so it would be easily accessible once they reached the city.

"I'm sure it will make sense once we get there. It won't be any different than finding an address in Edmonton," Clarence assured.

Cedar Rapids was equivalent in size to the city in Alberta the couple frequented once or twice a year, but Roelena wasn't feeling confident about her ability to navigate in the strange city.

"Look at those lilac bushes. Another week and they'll be blooming," Roelena gushed as they passed a farm yard.

The further south they drove the more signs of spring they saw. Although the weather had warmed in Alberta and they'd made good headway towards finishing seeding—Sijmon and Jakob probably had it finished by now—theeir Alberta trees had only the barest hint of leaves when they'd left. The spring flowers and fully blossoming fruit trees they spotted during their long journey were welcome signs of a spring that was still days if not weeks away in the Bellecourt area.

"It's a treat to see all this colour early in the year, that's for sure," Clarence agreed.

"I wonder what Conrad's wife is like." Roelena was apprehensive about meeting Louise. On the one hand, she was the girl who—in Roelena's mind—had stolen Conrad from her best friend. Out of loyalty to Marliese, Roelena felt she had to refrain from being overly friendly with Conrad's wife so she wouldn't feel like a traitor to her best friend. On the other hand, the disappointment about Marliese and Conrad was well and truly in the past. Marliese had been married for three years, albeit unhappily. Marliese had been genuinely happy for Roelena about her well-deserved vacation and hadn't expressed any anxiety about Roelena's potential friendship with Conrad's wife. Regardless, Roelena felt conflicted about what she should feel regarding Louise.

"Sweetheart," Clarence said in a cheerful tone. He reached across the seat between them to take her left hand in his, briefly taking his eyes from the road to smile at her. "I don't know anyone who doesn't like you. Why wouldn't Louise like you?"

Roelena shrugged, pulling her hand from Clarence's to pick up the sticky rattle Brenda dropped again. "Well, you know," she said, absently wiping the rattle on the baby's flannel cloth before letting Brenda reclaim it.

"Is it because of Marliese?" he asked, putting both hands back on the big steering wheel.

"Don't mention Marliese when we're there, okay? I'm not sure if Louise even knows about all that. A part of me still thinks that Conrad was a total rat for leading Marliese on, but it's in the past. Let's leave it there."

"Sure thing, sweetheart," he said. "I've got to say, I've heard so much about Conrad and Louise, I feel like I've already met them."

"Cedar Rapids, fifteen miles," Roelena crowed when she spotted the next mileage sign. "We're almost there, *liefje,*" she added, tickling the baby just for the delight of hearing her contagious giggle.

Brenda was an adorable baby, good-natured, plump, and

glowing with health. She was so different than how Karl had been in those last two months of his short life when he'd fussed almost incessantly. But Brenda was content and happy, glowing with health. Roelena took nothing for granted, and prayed every day that this blessing of health continue.

When they entered the city limits, Roelena held Conrad's letter in one hand, reading out each step of his meticulously detailed instructions. Despite her earlier misgivings, they didn't encounter any complications as they navigated through the unfamiliar city. Once on the correct street, she read out house numbers, then crowed, "Five-eight-one-four! That's it. Oh, look at the flowers," Roelena added as Clarence pulled up in front of a charming bungalow.

Low-lying shrubs adorned with pink blossoms edged a well-manicured lawn. The perimeter of the house itself was just as colourful with its beds of brightly coloured tulips, daffodils, and purple and pink hyacinth that Roelena swore she could smell despite still being in the car.

"There's Conrad," Roelena cried out. She opened the door and stepped out of the car, the stiffness in her limbs forgotten. "Conrad!" She waved excitedly as she shifted Brenda onto her hip.

Conrad leapt across the lawn as if he were still a teenager, then enveloped Roelena and Brenda in an exuberant hug. "Roelena! My *favourite* cousin. Welcome to Iowa."

Roelena felt her throat constrict unexpectedly at Conrad's affectionate greeting. She hugged him back with her free arm, blinking rapidly when she stepped out of the all too brief hug. She was embarrassed that she felt so emotional upon reuniting with her cousin and was glad he didn't appear to notice. He'd already turned to Clarence with a welcoming grin as he held out his hand. The two men, both tall and blond and so obviously Dutch in their looks, shook each other's hands in a hearty grip.

Roelena noticed the women descending the three shallow steps from the front door, smiling a welcome. She looked nothing like Roelena had imagined. Where Marliese was slim, stylish, and striking in her dark good looks, Louise was short, blond, flushed, and plump—although the later might be due to the fact that she was almost seven months pregnant. Roelena had expected...she wasn't sure what she'd been expecting, but certainly not someone so different in looks to Marliese.

"Welcome to our home," Louise gushed in a warm tone as she crossed the yard towards Roelena.

As she met the shorter woman's gaze and felt Louise engulf her free hand in both of hers, Roelena felt enveloped in an almost tangible wave of genuine warmth and guileless pleasure reminding Roelena of her mother's cousin in Andijk. Anneke had always described Hiltje as someone who'd never had a bad thought about anyone or anything, although Anneke had accompanied that statement with a perplexing shake of her head as if the state of perpetual niceness was somehow suspect. Roelena thought Louise might be a lot like her mother's cousin.

"It's lovely to finally meet you," Roelena stated with a smile of her own that was equally heartfelt. "Thank you for your generous hospitality. I hope having three houseguests descend on you isn't putting you out too much."

"Nonsense." Louise released Roelena's hand and waved away Roelena's concern. "I was so pleased to hear you were coming. Conrad talks with great fondness about his Canadian cousins and his trip to Alberta all those years ago. We intend to repeat it one day. You may very well find *us* imposing on *your* hospitality," she stated with a playful grin.

"We would love that." Roelena turned to share her pleasure at this news with Clarence, but the men were standing at the open trunk of the car unloading their traveling cases and hadn't heard Louise's comment. Chatting up a storm already, Roelena thought to herself as she regarded the two men with an amused smile. It was already clear she wouldn't have to worry about those two getting along.

"And this is little Brenda?" Louise was asking, lightly brushing a finger against the back of the baby's hand.

Roelena regarded Brenda with a proud smile. Just before entering the city, she'd taken away Brenda's half-gnawed digestive biscuit. Ignoring the baby's cries of protest at this unfair treatment, she'd cleaned Brenda's hands and face as best she could with a cloth and some water from their drinking canteen.

"Yes, this is Brenda. And she's been so good this whole trip," she announced proudly, jiggling the contented baby against her hip. "Weren't you, *schatje?"* she added, briefly nuzzling her cheek against the fine hair on her daughter's scalp. "But she's in need of a proper bath, and will be very happy to crawl around once she gets used to her new surroundings."

"Our two are already asleep in bed, but they will love entertaining her, of that I'm certain. Will she come to me?" Louise held out her hands in invitation.

"Oh, yes, she's not at all shy," Roelena handed the baby to Louise. "Be forewarned, though. She's a shameless flirt," Roelena added.

As predicted, Brenda smiled brightly at Louise, showing off two teeth that had recently appeared on her bottom gum, then got distracted by Louise's gold wristwatch.

"I know. It's pretty, isn't it?" Louise gushed. "Oh? You want to have it? Okay, here you go." Louise flicked the fastener and pulled the watch off, handing it to to the baby who immediately put it in her mouth and started gnawing on it.

"No!" Roelena reached to take the wristwatch away, but Louise waved away Roelena's concern.

"It's fine. It's only a watch. Babies love shiny things. *Don't they?"* she added in an indulgent tone, obviously delighted with Brenda.

They were interrupted by the approach of the men.

"You must be Louise. I'm Clarence. I'm very pleased to meet you." Clarence stepped forward and gave Louise a quick kiss on the cheek.

Louise beamed up at the big man who now stood with an arm casually draped over his wife's shoulders.

"Hey! You're not here five minutes and you're already flirting with my wife?" Conrad accused in a playful tone.

Despite the flush that darkened Louise's cheeks at Clarence's unexpected and chaste kiss, Roelena could see that Louise wasn't at all self-conscious or embarrassed, and instead chuckled along with her husband.

"I'm so glad you've made it here safely. Welcome to Iowa, Clarence."

"Thank you. But I think it's my daughter who can be accused of flirting. It looks like she already has Louise wrapped around her little finger," Clarence stated with a pleased grin, nodding at the confiscated watch in Brenda's fist.

"Your precious daughter has indeed charmed me. And I don't mind one bit. Isn't she lovely, Conrad?"

Conrad bent to address the baby. "Hello, Brenda," he said, tickling her neck with his fingertip. Brenda tucked her head into Louise's neck, chortling in delight at Conrad's attention.

"Oh my, what a darling," Louise enthused, hugging the baby close.

As Roelena watched Louise with her baby, she felt her

throat constrict as a wave of thankfulness for her Pa almost overwhelmed her. What nervous apprehension she'd felt had entirely evaporated. It was good, *so good,* to be here, she thought.

Their hosts didn't notice her tear-filled eyes and were instead herding their guests, with Conrad and Clarence carrying their luggage, into their lovely home.

39

SATURDAY, MAY 16

By definition, a cocktail is a beverage with at least three flavors, one of which is alcohol, and often garnished with fruit or olives. The first recorded use of the word as an alcoholic beverage was in the early nineteenth century, one hundred and fifty years before Roelena de Haas tried her first cocktail at her cousin's home in Iowa.

Ensconced in a comfortable wing chair in Conrad and Louise's living room, Roelena sipped a cocktail from a tall, slim tumbler. The drink had a name—Singapore Sling—although when she'd asked Conrad what the drink had to do with Singapore, he couldn't say. Like all the fruity cocktails her cousin had been plying her with during their visit—many of them served in delicate crystal glasses that Louise called stemware—this one was delicious.

"I can't believe you're leaving in less than two days," Louise wailed as she rose from the davenport, retrieving her cup and saucer from the coffee table. "Honestly, it feels like you just got here. Ten days seemed like a nice long visit when you first proposed it, but it's just flown by, hasn't it? No, sit down, Roelena," she admonished with a wave of her hand.

"Finish your drink. If no one minds, I'm going to plead pregnancy exhaustion and go to bed."

"Oh course we don't mind, Louise," Roelena assured. *"Welterusten,"* she added in Dutch, inviting her hostess to sleep well.

Louise and Conrad only had a handful of the most common Dutch words in their vocabulary.

Louise responded in kind. "And thanks to both of you for treating us to a film," she added from where she stood beside Conrad's chair. "It wasn't at all necessary, was it, dear?"

"No, it wasn't," agreed Conrad, reaching up to hold his wife's hand where it rested on his shoulder.

Earlier that evening, Conrad's youngest sister Susan, who was now sixteen years old, had babysat their three children so that Clarence and Roelena could treat their hosts to a film as a way of extending their thanks for Conrad and Louise's hospitality. They'd seen *The Greatest Show on Earth,* a film about a circus and the people who made their living as performers. Clarence and Roelena, who hadn't been to a film in well over a year, both felt a little overwhelmed by the colour and activity in the film, but Louise and Conrad had been enthusiastic.

"I don't want to contemplate leaving," Roelena stated, pulling a face. "Let's not mention it again until this time tomorrow evening, okay?" The next day was Sunday, and early Monday morning the Canadian couple would begin their return journey.

"Good idea. I'm happy to live in denial with you," Louise joked, then stooped to kiss her husband. "Good night, dear." Louise made to leave the room, but then stopped and addressed Roelena. "Don't wash the glasses," she instructed in a firm tone, then added with a chuckle. "By now you'll have discovered that, despite my Dutch forebears, I'm not one of those Dutch housewives particular about having a spotless kitchen before going to bed."

Roelena smiled at Louise. "I won't. Thanks, Louise," she added as Louise left the room.

Clarence, who'd been sitting next to Louise on the long davenport, slouched more comfortably against the pillows now that he had the sofa to himself. He stretched his long legs out in front of him, loosely balancing a balloon shaped glass of brandy against his chest. When he yawned widely, the glass tipped dangerously, but the swallow of amber liquid in the glass didn't spill. "Man, I'm sleepy, too. Are you, sweetheart?" he asked, looking over at Roelena.

"I'm not, strangely," Roelena responded. "That film has left my mind all abuzz." She took another sip of her drink, settling more comfortably against the padded, high-backed wing chair. She lifted her feet—clad in a pair of elegant, store-bought slippers Louise had gifted her upon their arrival and which were the nicest Roelena had ever owned—to rest on the ottoman that matched the wing chairs. Her cousin's house and furniture were far nicer than anything Roelena and Clarence had seen; yet, they'd both felt at ease in the modern home thanks to Louise and Conrad's warm hospitality.

Roelena lifted her glass, her garnet bracelet catching the light as it shifted on her wrist, and took another sip of her delicious cocktail. At home, she and Clarence were more or less teetotalers, in part out of habit and in part due to a lack of money for luxuries like alcohol. On those occasions when they visited in town with Greta and Frank, Clarence often had a glass of whiskey with their brother-in-law. Greta didn't like alcohol of any kind, and while Roelena didn't like the taste of whisky—the only alcohol Frank and Greta ever offered—she did enjoy the occasional glass of wine now and then when her and Clarence visited Marliese and Wilfred.

But things were different in Iowa. *Everything was different in Iowa,* Roelena thought.

Although Conrad and Louise were Dutch Calvinists just like Roelena and Clarence, their lives were very different. The four of them had talked about the distinctions on more than one occasion, and concluded the differences were due to a handful of reasons. Conrad and Louise lived an affluent life in a city rather than a modest life in a small rural community; Conrad and Louise were second- and third-generation Dutch respectively, whereas Roelena and Clarence had both been born in their homeland; the American couple earned their livelihood from a retail business, whereas Roelena and Clarence didn't have anyone in their circle who owned a retail operation; and Conrad and Louise had an extensive range of Canadian friends in addition to those in their Dutch Christian Reformed circle. Neither Roelena nor Clarence could boast any friendships outside of their Dutch community, unless Roelena counted the postman and his wife, Mr. and Mrs. Dickson. The differences in the cousins' lifestyles meant that Conrad and Louise regularly engaged in the kinds of secular activities that Roelena's conservative community would have considered inappropriate, including going to films and indulging frequently in alcoholic beverages—although Conrad insisted they were only serving drinks daily on account of the visitors.

Almost every evening after all three children had been put to bed, the four adults visited in the cozy living room of Conrad and Louise's modern home, with Clarence sipping brandy or port and Roelena sipping whatever concoction Conrad chose to create. Over the course of their visit, she'd developed a taste for the fruity cocktails served in Louise's elegant array of crystal glasses. Roelena couldn't imagine owning such items, but if her kitchen ever boasted such beautiful crystal in a far distant future, she likely wouldn't dare use any of it.

Clarence yawned again. "I'm off to bed," he announced, sitting up, his eyes heavy with sleep. He drank the last swallow of brandy, then placed his empty glass on a coaster on the coffee table. "What about you, sweetheart?" he asked as he came to his feet.

Before Roelena could answer, Conrad spoke. "I'm not sleepy. Stay up and chat with me for a while if you like, Roelena."

"Okay," she said, nodding at Conrad, then looked over at her husband. "You go on to bed," she said. "I'll join you soon."

She watched Clarence detour around the coffee table intent on giving her a goodnight kiss before retiring. She found she liked the taste of Clarence's kisses after he'd had a glass of brandy, but couldn't decide if that was simply due to her having had a cocktail or two herself. Regardless, she lifted her face towards her husband.

After giving Roelena an affectionate kiss, Clarence bid them goodnight and left the room.

"Another cocktail?" Conrad asked when Roelena's straw made an inelegant gurgle as she drained her glass.

"No, no, don't go to the trouble."

"Well, I'm having another," he said, rising. "It's no trouble." He took her empty glass, then added, "I'll be right back."

Roelena settled more comfortably into her chair, tucking a leg under her buttocks and smoothing out her pleated skirt. She supposed she was tipsy, and had been tipsy on more than one occasion since their arrival. She also supposed that most of the people in her community—well, not Marliese—would be horrified not only about Roelena getting tipsy, but also for sitting so inelegantly on Conrad and Louise's lovely furniture. But since they would never know, Roelena decided not to care.

Conrad returned and handed Roelena a fresh glass with a slice of orange draped on its lip. As he walked over to the cabinet where the hard liquor was stored, he grinned over his shoulder at her. "If only your Pa could see you now," he teased, splashing an inch of brandy into his snifter.

Roelena smiled to herself as she took a sip of her Singapore Sling. Her family would not be able to reconcile the Roelena they knew on the farm with the Roelena curled up in the elegant burgundy wing chair sipping a cocktail from a tall crystal tumbler. What struck Roelena as even more strange was that she didn't feel at all guilty. She'd initially felt like she was doing something naughty in those first few days, but she didn't now. In fact, she felt more contented and, strangely, at peace than she had in a long while as if she'd been granted a license to enjoy the indulgences available while visiting her American cousin.

"You look like a contented cat who's just licked the cream bowl empty."

Roelena laughed. "That's kind of amazing. I was thinking along those same lines."

"That you feel like a contented cat?" Conrad asked as he resumed his seat in the matching chair.

"Not the cat part. Contented, though." She took another sip of the delicious beverage and then allowed her head to loll against the back of the chair, shifting slightly to meet Conrad's amused gaze. "I was thinking about home—Pa and all the others—and how horrified they'd be if they knew I'd been slightly tipsy practically every night since arriving."

"Am I out of focus?"

Roelena squinted in exaggeration. "Not anymore."

Conrad chuckled, but then his smile faded. He steadily eyed his cousin above the rim of his glass. When he spoke, it was in a serious tone. "Is it deliberate on your part, not ever mentioning her?"

Roelena looked down at her cocktail and took another sip. Not mentioning Marliese had been deliberate, but she hadn't considered that maybe Conrad would blatantly introduce the subject. "Oh, silly me," she stated as she lifted her gaze to regard Conrad. "I can't believe we've been here all this time and I haven't told you about Ingrid. She's lovely, you know, and a very good match for Jakob although he, of course, is tiresome enough to turn that equation around and say he's the one who's a very good match for her. But seriously, they're so well suited. Ingrid puts up with his silliness and he adores her. And it's lovely to see him as a father. And three kids already. Isn't that just so hard to believe?"

"Roelena," Conrad chided solemnly. He didn't smile as he held his cousin's gaze.

Roelena sighed, rolled her eyes, then took a fortifying sip of her cocktail. In the back of her mind throughout their visit, Roelena had been evaluating what Marliese's life would've been like had she married Conrad and moved to Iowa. It took no effort at all to picture her stylish and accomplished friend in this beautiful home with its elegant furniture.

But instead of launching into the topic of Marliese, she stated in a solemn tone, "I'm still mad at you, you know. Don't misunderstand, I love Louise. She's sweet and kind and giving. And smart. And so cheerful and funny. But what you did back then, Conrad?" Roelena looked away and shook her head. "It wasn't nice. Or respectful. I think I'll always be a little bit mad at you for letting her down." She'd earlier thought it was important not to mention Marliese, yet here she was speaking far more frankly than she'd ever imagined she could about that long ago betrayal. She supposed it was the alcohol that loosened her tongue.

"How mad was *she?*"

When Roelena answered, she didn't respond to his question, instead stating, "You know, the more I get to know men, I mean grown men—my husband, the husbands of my friends, my brothers—the more I realize you don't know women, do you? You marry us. You live side-by-side with us. You have children with us. But you still haven't figured it out, have you?"

"Figured what out, Roelena?" Conrad asked, his tone becoming testy.

Roelena untucked her feet and sat up, feeling slightly dizzy. Careful not to spill her beverage, she used her feet to push aside the ottoman, then crossed her legs before reclining once again into the tall-backed chair and looking over at her cousin. "Conrad, what I'm trying to say is, *I* was the one mad at you. She's never once said anything nasty about you." Roelena saw she'd surprised her cousin. "She was never mad at you. Disappointed, yes. Devastated, absolutely. Hurt. Stunned. Bewildered. But angry?" she shook her head. "Never. To be honest, that surprised me. And annoyed me, truth be told. She comforted herself with the knowledge that you loved her, despite your decision to marry Louise. I suppose it speaks to the depth of her feelings for you." In response to Conrad's abashed look, Roelena added rather impatiently. "Oh, for goodness sake, Conrad. This speaks to my point about you not understanding women. How could you not know she would be utterly crushed?"

Conrad looked away. He took a sip of brandy, and another, then said, "I'd always envisioned Marliese in a fit of temper upon receipt of my letter. She was so passionate and vibrant."

"You pictured her all these years angry, throwing things, cursing you, right?" At Conrad's nod, Roelena continued. "And I'm guessing that made you feel a little less like a rat, right? Because you deserved her anger, deserved her curses.

You behaved despicably and therefore you deserved to be hated."

Conrad frowned at his cousin. "Well, shoot, Roelena. Don't hold back."

"I'm not meaning to be harsh, just honest." Roelena shifted, sitting up a little straighter, ignoring the way her vision wobbled when she moved her head too quickly. She was surprised at her own candour, surprised as well about how good it felt to express her former resentment without a flood of emotion overtaking her. She was free to be honest and forthright because she and her cousin had a solid friendship based on a foundation of love and family connection. So she continued in the same vein, ignoring the tiny voice that suggested maybe her candour was actually the result of her third cocktail.

"You broke her heart, Conrad," she accused. "At the time, I was appalled. I think I felt more betrayed by you than she ever did. That's why I stopped writing. But Marliese never spoke ill of you. Not once."

"Why ever not?" Conrad finally asked.

"Why didn't she hate you, you mean?" Roelena leaned back in her chair as she looked down at her glass, surprised to see the tumbler almost empty. She leaned her head against the wing of the chair and rolled her head slowly to face Conrad. She had to take a moment to focus. "Because you idiot," she insisted, a smile of affection diffusing the insult. "She loved you. Simple as that. Turning that love into hate would go against who she is, against what makes her tick." Roelena sighed heavily as she eyed her cousin. She really did love Conrad, although she would always be a little angry he'd hurt Marliese. "Clearly, you didn't know her as well as you thought. People assume, because she's bold and outspoken, that she doesn't have deep feelings. Almost everyone thinks she's thick-skinned and tough, but they've got it wrong. On the inside, she's…" Roelena felt a dawning realization. "You know I'm just realizing she *is* just like Louise. Except Marliese only lets a handful of people see her sweetness while Louise lets everyone see hers."

"I agree," Conrad exclaimed. "I've always thought they would be the best of friends. They each radiate a special kind of warmth. It's expressed differently because of their personalities, yet it's the exact same quality."

"Anyway, all that was years ago. Does it even matter now?" Roelena swirled the remainder of the drink with her straw, enjoying the tinkling sound made by the shrinking ice cubes.

"What's her husband like?" Conrad asked, breaking the silence.

"Wilfred?"

"That's his name, Wilfred? What's his last name?"

"Kampenaar."

"What's he like?"

Roelena sighed, thought about refusing to answer, then decided against it. She and Conrad would have this conversation once and then the subject would never be raised again. "He's very handsome. Exceptionally, actually. They make a gorgeous couple. They live in town in a nice house. He the on-site tradesman at an agricultural research station."

"Are they…"

Conrad didn't finish his question, but raised his eyebrows as he held Roelena's gaze.

Roelena knew what he was asking. *Are they happy?* She was a little disappointed Conrad wasn't courageous enough to say the words himself, but then he did say them.

"Are they in love? Is she happy?"

A disturbing thought suddenly occurred to Roelena and she sat up. "Conrad?" Roelena asked, working once again to focus on his face. "You don't still have feelings for her?"

Conrad looked away, shaking his head in dismissal before turning back to Roelena. "Of course not. Not like that. I love Louise. I love the life we've made together, the kids, our home. I'm happy." He paused, taking a sip of his brandy. "But I think about her now and then. She was special, you know? And with you being here, I've been thinking about her more than usual. But not in a way that is disloyal to Louise. Does that make sense?"

Roelena sighed, slumping back into the chair. "I suppose." She smiled a drunken happy smile. "She is special, isn't she? Do you know that Clarence didn't like her at first? They've only become friends recently."

"That surprises me. Clarence loves to have fun, and she is nothing if not fun."

"Yes, well, according to the old Clarence, Marliese isn't a good influence. He blamed her for the fact that I used to sneak cigarettes behind Pa and Moe's back—I quit smoking since marrying Clarence. And he blames Marliese if I swear. But I have my own mind and I make my own decisions. Marliese can't be blamed for leading me astray. If I want to swear, I'll...bloody swear."

"My rebellious cousin at her worst," Conrad teased.

"You know," Roelena said, suddenly serious again. "It's just dawned on me that Clarence has changed since I first met him. I'm just realizing that. He's really quite conservative, you know." She frowned. "Or, at least, he used to be."

"The same Clarence who's snoring in my guest room due to ingesting copious amounts of brandy?"

In response to Conrad's look of disbelief, Roelena laughed. "Yup. The very same one." Roelena grew thoughtful. "He's not so adamant about certain things, anymore. Last Sunday in your church, we sang from the new psalter hymnal." She stabbed a finger at him a couple times for emphasis, before dropping her hand heavily onto the arm of the chair. "I didn't realize until just now, but Clarence used to be adamantly opposed to our churches adopting that hymnal. *Adamantly.* But he didn't say a thing, did he?" Her tone was tinged with wonder. "You know, he has changed. Ever since..." Roelena paused, then glanced sideways at Conrad. "Well, ever since Karl died, I guess."

"I can only imagine how awful that's all been, Roelena. And I'm so sorry. He talked to me about how hard it's been for you."

"He did?" Roelena was surprised. Clarence and Roelena mentioned Karl frequently, but she resisted talking about his actual death. She met Conrad's gaze, smiling fondly at her cousin. "I'm glad he talked to you. You like him, don't you?"

"I do, yes." Conrad said, then paused melodramatically. "Do you like him, too?"

Roelena grinned. "You're such an idiot," she accused fondly, then sucked on her straw draining her glass noisily.

"Shall I make another?" Conrad asked.

"Thou shalt not." Roelena's response was immediate. She'd been tipsy more than once, but now she was worse than tipsy. "I've had enough. More than enough." She sat staring at the remains of ice in her glass, then said, "I can't believe I didn't realize how much Clarence has changed. I mean, in a good way. Oh!" she exclaimed breathlessly, sitting up. She turned her head carefully, then stared wide-eyed at Conrad. "Do you think this means I can start smoking again? Do you have any? Cigarettes I mean, not those stinky cigars."

"My cigars are *not* stinky. And no, I don't have any cigarettes. And no, I don't think you should start smoking again. It doesn't suit you."

"Because I'm a woman? That is so old-fashioned," Roelena complained, placing her empty glass on the coffee table. "That's something my *ouders* would say. I'm surprised at you, Conrad. I thought you were a modern man."

"I'm serious. Smoking doesn't suit you. Or Louise."

Roelena stifled her hoot of laughter. "Louise? Smoking? I can't picture it."

"My point exactly."

"But I'm not Louise. And Marliese would be thrilled to have me share cigarettes with her again."

The cousins' grins faded as they stared at each other soberly. Their conversation had come full circle.

"She still smokes?"

"Yes. And looks good, doing it, too." Loyalty ran deep in Roelena.

"Of course, she does. There's nothing she could do that she wouldn't look good doing." Conrad frowned. "Did that make sense?"

"I understood it perfectly."

"Well." Conrad's frown cleared. "I'm better at this than I thought."

"Better at what?"

"Talking about Marliese. You've no idea how often I've wanted to write to you and ask about her. In my letters, I tried putting in subtle questions hoping you would understand their hidden meaning."

"And you thought I didn't get it? And that was why I didn't respond with news of Marliese? Conrad, what do you take me for? Your so-called between-the-lines questions were obvious. I was even tempted to show them to Marliese."

"And did you?" Conrad looked alarmed.

"Of course not. She's got her own life now, and you're not in it. And same goes for you."

"You're right." Conrad took another sip of brandy. "You didn't answer my earlier question, though. Is she happy?"

Roelena had been jiggling her foot, but at his question, her motion stopped. She realized she didn't want to be truthful with Conrad about Marliese's unhappy marriage.

"Do you really think Marliese would marry without being in love?" Roelena hoped Conrad wouldn't notice she'd dodged his question.

"Of course not. Do they have children?"

"None yet, but you know Marliese. All in her own good time." She couldn't possibly tell him that the doctor now thought it unlikely Marliese would ever conceive. Nor could she tell him that Wilfred refused to adopt *another man's bastard*, as he so succinctly put it. Conrad wouldn't hesitate to adopt, that much Roelena knew.

Conrad nodded, seemingly satisfied with her response. "They live in Bellecourt?"

"Yes. She works at the library." Conrad looked suitably impressed, so Roelena continued. "You should hear her. She comes out with words I never even knew existed, although that's not much of a surprise. I only had three years of schooling here. I mean in Canada. There was this fancy word she used the other day that I'd never heard before." Roelena frowned, trying to remember. "What was it? Anthro something."

"Anthropology?"

"No. She said it was a word that meant giving animals human emotions."

Conrad nodded. "Anthropomorphism."

"And I thought you only played sports?" Roelena teased, thinking once again how well suited Conrad and Marliese would have been. Not that Roelena hadn't grown to love Louise. It was a shame Marliese had so quickly and foolishly married Wilfred rather than wait to meet someone equally as suitable as Conrad.

Roelena yawned suddenly. "Goodness me. If I don't go to bed soon, I'll fall asleep in this chair." Roelena squinted at the clock on the mantle. "Quarter to one?" she exclaimed. "That can't be right."

Conrad glanced at his wristwatch, then nodded his head. "It's right."

"I don't even stay up this late on New Year's Eve," Roelena said, pushing herself up to stand. When the room wobbled, she grabbed the back of the tall chair and gave herself a moment to regain her balance.

Conrad stood, picking up the glass from the coffee table. "If you're cranky tomorrow, just blame me. It's my fault for keeping you up so late."

"It won't be your fault, Conrad. But thanks anyway. *Welterusten.*"

She turned to leave the room ahead of him, but paused when Conrad spoke her name.

"Thanks for telling me about Marliese," he said in a soft tone. "I'm happy to have the chance to talk about her after all these years. I appreciate it, Roelena."

Roelena nodded slowly, but said nothing as she turned and left the room. She had to keep one hand on the wall as she made her way down the hallway to the guestroom. Once in the bedroom she shared with Clarence, a playpen in the corner for Brenda, she had only sufficient energy to undress and none to find her nightgown, crawling into bed wearing only her panties.

Hours later, when the first hint of approaching dawn filtered into the guest bedroom, Clarence awoke, observed it was too early to rise, and luxuriated in the knowledge that there were no chores to do and he could go back to sleep. He rolled over, slipping an arm around his wife's waist, then came fully awake when he realized Roelena was as good as naked. She never slept without her night-gown, even in the summer when it was too hot for blankets.

He knew he shouldn't wake her, but he couldn't resist; he couldn't *not* caress all that bare skin.

A short time later, Roelena smiled dreamily as she drifted back to sleep, feeling deliciously satiated from their spontaneous lovemaking. Clarence was definitely loosening up, she thought. He used to believe making love was a bedtime activity, but they'd made love in the soft light of dawn. In another man's house, and on the Sabbath day, no less. Roelena sighed contentedly, absently hoping that Brenda would sleep for at least a few hours yet. Her eyes suddenly opened wide as a thought crossed her mind.

They'd taken no precautions to ensure she wouldn't conceive. Roelena was wide awake now, calculating when her next monthly cycle was due to begin. She squeezed her eyes shut when she realized they could very well have made a baby during their early morning lovemaking.

A strange thing happened then as she let her mind imagine the possibility of another child. Warmth enveloped her from the inside out. Goosebumps rippled across her flesh. And in that precise moment, she felt the departure of the cold, dark creature who'd been crouching inside her ribcage since Karl's death.

It felt to her as if a weight had suddenly been lifted; yet, it was more than that. Something wonderful now inhabited her chest cavity. Something that pulsed with light and warmth and love. The underside of her skin felt fizzy and alive. She felt weightless, as free as a bird fluttering from its cage, as joy bubbled inside her as tangible as the pillow beneath her head.

She turned to check if Clarence was awake, but he was sound asleep. As she drank in the sight of his beloved face so close to hers, she began to weep tears of joy, feeling how deeply and desperately she loved this man. She lifted her hand and gently, lighter than a feather's touch, traced the outline of his brow, then burrowed into his chest, closing her eyes and breathing in his intoxicating scent. She felt utterly and blissfully happy. She thought of her *moeder's* death, expecting her joy to recede, but she remained happy. And then she dared herself to remember Karl's death. The ache to hold him again, to breathe in his scent, to nourish him with love and watch him grow was still there; yet, it didn't extinguish her joy. The love pulsing inside of her was strong and steady, unwavering.

When her mind entertained the possibility of having created another baby, a thrill surged through her veins. For long minutes, she let herself bask in that blissful feeling, a smile lifting the corners of her mouth. As her breathing grew soft and quiet, one last, fleeting thought drifted along the landscape of her drowsy mind; if indeed she was pregnant, and if the child was a boy, she would name him after his dearly loved brother, Karl Benjamin.

40

THURSDAY, MAY 21

"Are you looking forward to being home?" Clarence asked.

The setting sun was behind the highest peaks of the range of magnificent snow-covered mountains that framed the horizon west of Calgary. The wispy clouds above were tinted with orange and red. In little more than two hours, they would return to their farm.

Roelena looked over at her husband, her eyes bright with thoughts of their modest little home. "Yes," she answered.

"Even though there's no shower in the bathroom, no matching wing chairs in the *living* room, no liquor cabinet, and no *stemware* for fancy cocktails?"

"Yes." Her simple response seemed to reassure Clarence about the modest home he provided for his wife and child.

When the couple shared a warm smile, Clarence patted the cushioned bench seat between them. "Come closer. Sit next to me."

Roelena looked over her shoulder at Brenda. The baby had finally fallen asleep in her bassinet wedged between an empty wooden crate that had been filled with food from Louise for their journey and a second crate overflowing with sports equipment that Conrad had gifted them. Roelena moved her handbag and then shifted across the seat until she was snuggled against Clarence's shoulder, her forearm and hand resting on his thigh. "It's not seemly, you know, for a married couple to sit as if they're still courting," she teased.

Clarence grinned happily, letting his right hand fall to her knee and keeping his left on the steering wheel. "They? Seemly is for *us* to say," he refuted.

Roelena smiled, hugging his arm to her chest. The two sat in comfortable silence, enjoying the panorama of oranges, yellows, and golds unfolding in a breathtaking display above the Rocky Mountains.

For the four days they'd been journeying since leaving Iowa, they'd talked almost constantly, but not about people they knew, ideas they had for renovating their home, or what was going on in the church community—all topics they'd covered on their drive to Iowa. On the return journey, they'd shared their deepest thoughts and beliefs, revealing their innermost feelings on a more profound level than they ever had before. Roelena revealed more of herself to Clarence in the four days of travel than she had in the three years they'd been married.

For the first time, she divulged the reality of that cold, dark thing that had made its home inside her after Karl died, and then did her best to describe how it felt in that unexpected moment of departure. Clarence, in turn, summoned the courage to tell Roelena about the vision he'd had of Karl standing at his knee. He tripped over his words at first, feeling foolish, knowing it hadn't been real. But he was adamant about the feeling bequeathed to him by that vision, revealing that, in quiet moments, he could summon it and savor the feeling of having his heavenly child at peace at his knee. Roelena finally understood then why Clarence had seemed to be coping so well with the death of their son. She confessed how she'd resented both his willingness to accept Karl's death and his ability to invite happiness back into their life.

The couple shared tears and laughter as they talked. They made new promises to each other, more meaningful than even their wedding vows, pledging to make a greater effort to sense the other's needs, to really listen, and to share both the good and the not-so-good; they promised to learn from each other and lean on each other. Roelena also promised, if and when hardship came their way again, she would not draw away from Clarence like she'd done after Karl died. She would share her emotional burden with him and, in doing so, benefit from the succour that comes as a result of sharing her burden.

"That's really something, isn't it?" Clarence commented after they'd been silent for a time. He'd been glancing back and forth from the road to the sunset above the mountain peaks. "You sure don't see that view in the Netherlands."

Roelena chuckled. "Before coming here, I thought the dike beside my village was a mountain."

It was too dark for Roelena to clearly see Clarence's face, but she could hear the smile in his voice when he asked, "Are you happy?" She was a little startled by his question, but she was also pleased to know that, unlike before when that cold, black creature had pressed against the undersides of her ribcage, she would have been annoyed by the question and unable to respond. "I am," she murmured, then added. "You know what's strange?"

"What's strange, sweetheart?"

Roelena smiled. She didn't think she would ever tire of

the way her husband called her 'sweetheart'. "On our wedding day I was so in love with you."

"And that's strange?" he asked, feigning shock.

"No, silly. You didn't let me finish. What's strange is that, on our wedding day, I didn't think I could get any happier. I didn't think I could love you more than I did then. But now I do. Way more."

Clarence only had to turn his head slightly to plant a quick kiss on Roelena's temple. "You know how happy it makes me to hear you say that?"

"How happy?"

Clarence wagged his head, as if daring himself to respond honestly, then stated in a fast, clipped tone. "Happy enough to want to pull over onto a side-road and show you."

"Clarence!" Roelena felt her body immediately respond to his risqué suggestion, but that didn't mean she wasn't shocked. Clarence generally kept bedroom talk for the bedroom.

"Clarence?" she squeaked when he signalled to turn and began braking. "You're not really going to...?"

"You don't want to?" he asked, unable to hide his disappointment.

Roelena chuckled headily. "Oh, yes. I want to. Definitely. But...in the car?"

"It's almost dark." Clarence turned off the highway onto a narrow graveled road. Trees boasting new spring leaves lined the sides of the unfamiliar lane, but they weren't dense enough for what the amorous couple had in mind.

"What if someone sees?" Roelena asked after they'd driven half a mile.

"Well..." Clarence hesitated, then added in a tone laced with bravado. "If they do, we're far enough away from home we won't be recognized."

Roelena sputtered, imagining her and Clarence parked on the side of the road somewhere in their community and having someone like Widow Roorda or the *dominee* discover them.

After driving for another mile, Clarence pulled onto a narrow turn-off into a field, the sides choked with Saskatoon bushes. The car bounced a little on ground rutted by tractor wheels. He turned again onto the edge of the field, bringing the car to a stop under a dense canopy of willow and birch trees. He shifted into park, shut off the ignition, and then turned to take his wife into his arms.

"What if Brenda wakes up?"

"We can be quiet. And quick. Can't we?"

Twenty minutes later, a lopsided grin plastered on his face, Clarence backed out from under the shelter of the trees and turned west onto the graveled road, heading back to the highway. The baby remained soundly asleep behind them.

Roelena snuggled against her husband's side. Warmth enveloped her in the afterglow of their lovemaking. She was still trying to get over the shock of having sat on Clarence's lap on the front seat of her Pa's car with her skirt bunched at her waist as they made love while parked in a farmer's field. She wasn't sure she could ever get in her father's car again without envisioning what they'd just done.

Clarence was certainly full of surprises lately, she thought. He laughed at her when she got tipsy and made love to her in places other than their own bedroom at hours other than bedtime. The image of her old neighbour Patricia Talbot and her beau flashed through her mind. She'd been such an innocent back then, Roelena thought. She hadn't understood the emotion that transformed Patricia's face, that had made her look so...boneless. Roelena understood now. She pictured herself and Clarence in those woods, her back against a tree, her head thrown back and her arms loose at her sides. She envisioned Clarence's hands fumbling with the buttons of her blouse, Clarence's hands lifting her breasts from the stark white of her brassiere, Clarence's lips and hot breath on her skin, warming her, heating her to the boiling point.

"You're awfully quiet," Clarence observed after he turned north onto the paved highway and accelerated.

Pinpoints of headlights snaked towards them on the two-lane road, a line of red taillights stretched ahead of them.

"What are you thinking about?" he added.

Roelena grimaced, thankful Clarence couldn't see her blush. "I'm not sure you'd want to know."

"Well, then you're mistaken. I want to know everything you're thinking. I thought we'd already established that."

Roelena took a deep breath. She'd never told anyone what she'd seen Patricia Talbot doing in the woods that long ago day. She hadn't thought she ever would. But Clarence was no longer the straight-laced man she'd married who'd had a rather black and white view of right and wrong, appropriate and inappropriate. Karl's death had altered him. It had changed them both. Something inside each of them had been irrevocably altered. What amazed Roelena was discovering that this altered state had an element of more-ness. She had a heightened appreciation for everyday things like a shared smile, a kind word, the brush of a hand; all moments to cherish. The ache of Karl's absence would always be with her, and with Clarence despite his cheerful nature, but because of it, they regarded life differently. It was all so very odd to reconcile, she thought.

"Well?" Clarence asked, interrupting her complicated thoughts. "Are you going to tell me?"

Roelena had almost forgotten what they'd been talking

about, and now felt a renewed sense of trepidation. She wasn't really contemplating telling Clarence what she'd seen Patricia Talbot do, was she? But she and Clarence's altered relationship seemed to expect it. And at least it was pitch dark now. He wouldn't see her blush.

She took a deep breath, then spoke. "Once I saw…this was ages ago—before I met you. I was at the swing in the woods at the home farm and I saw something that…well, I never could have imagined. Ever. Even now that I'm married." She felt the heat in her cheeks as she went on to describe what she'd seen. She hadn't been expecting, though, that recounting it out loud would revive her hunger for Clarence's touch. And by the way Clarence's hand was exploring the inside of her thigh, she knew he was as eager as she to return home and make love again.

"That's…wow," Clarence finally said after exhaling deeply. "That was the couple who stopped to help us fix the flat that day we went to Edmonton?"

"No. I mean, yes, that was the woman. But the man she was with that day—her fiancée—wasn't the man she was with in the woods. I've never seen that man again."

Roelena was looking towards Clarence's profile, trying to assess his reaction. In the light from the dashboard, she saw his Adam's apple bob up and down.

"Do you remember," Clarence said, then had to pause to clear his throat. "This must have been a year ago at least. You came outside one afternoon and I met you by the swing. I think it was shortly after your *moeder* died. We started kissing and you wanted to…you know? There. In our woods."

Roelena had forgotten about that day, but remembered it vividly now, especially what she'd done after. She used to believe that what she'd done was wicked, but she didn't believe that anymore. What she'd done wasn't right. And she'd never done it since. But it didn't make her wicked. She'd gained a new perspective on account of the previous year's heartaches. Her beliefs about what was good and bad had permanently shifted. Roelena touching herself wasn't a sign of her wickedness or sinfulness, it was simply evidence of her weakness during a difficult time. "That was a month or two after Moe died, and just before I got the German measles," she said.

Clarence paused, cleared his throat again, then asked, "In that moment, were you thinking of Patricia Talbot and what she and her beau had done?"

Roelena hesitated, feeling the blush heat her cheeks, thankful for the camouflage of darkness. "Yes. I…it comes to me now and then and…I suppose I shouldn't think about it, but I do sometimes."

"Uh, you don't have to be apologetic," he wagged his head insistently.

Roelena was distracted by Clarence's hand caressing her leg and adjusted her posture so that his drifting fingers could reach the bare skin above her stockings.

"You mean…you don't mind that I think about that scene sometimes?" she asked a little breathlessly as Clarence's finger slipped under the stocking's top edge.

"Actually…I think I like it that you think about it."

"You do?" Roelena felt her heart beating rapidly. Should she tell him the other part? How that episode had ended for her? "Clarence?"

"Yes, sweetheart?"

Roelena hesitated, closing her eyes. She wanted to tell him. She wanted to be open and honest about everything the way they'd promised each other. But would Clarence understand? After all the talking they'd done and the promises they'd made, could she trust that he wouldn't judge her harshly? "I did something after that. I'm not proud of it, but..."

"Did what?"

She could tell Clarence wasn't really listening to her. His thoughts were focused on only two things; staying in the lane on the darkened highway and the bare skin of her legs above the top edge of her stockings.

Roelena spoke in a rush of words. "I went into the house and laid on our bed, kind of mad at you still. My head was full of these images of Patricia and my body just wanted what you hadn't been willing to give, so I..."

Clarence's hand stopped. She watched his profile in the dim light and saw again his Adam's apple bob up and down.

"What did you do?" Clarence's voice was hoarse.

"I...touched myself," she whispered, staring wide-eyed at Clarence.

"Here?" he asked, moving his hand to rest on the cotton fabric of her underwear.

She sucked in a breath and closed her eyes as a wave of pleasure radiated through her entire body. "Yes," she whispered.

"Until...?"

"Mmhmm."

Clarence withdrew his hand and gripped the steering wheel with both hands. Roelena opened her eyes as silence filled the car. Had telling him been a mistake? Had she now ruined all they'd gained in the last few days?

Clarence braked suddenly and once again signaled to turn off the highway.

"What are you doing?" she asked, her eyes wide.

The car skidded slightly when Clarence took the turn onto the gravel road too fast. "Do you see those woods up ahead?"

The line of trees was just visible against the eastern horizon. Roelena sat in stunned silence for a brief moment, then began to shake with quiet laughter. "At this rate, we'll never get home," she sputtered when Clarence drove into a field and parked under the trees.

Clarence turned off the ignition and reached for her, saying, "Home is here, sweetheart, in each other's arms."

41

TUESDAY, MAY 26

Marliese walked into Roelena's kitchen, but then stopped in her tracks as Roelena turned to greet her. "Good lord, what happened to you?"

Roelena brushed the back of her hand lightly across her face as if dusting off flour. "What do you mean? Is there something on my face?"

Marliese usually made a bee-line for the baby, but today she ignored the high chair where Brenda sat and instead approached Roelena.

Roelena smiled quizzically at her friend's unusual behaviour. "Marliese, I haven't seen you for a month. Are you going to stand there staring at me or are you going to give me a hug?"

Clarence and Roelena had arrived home the Thursday before. Roelena had talked briefly on the telephone to Marliese the day after, but Marliese hadn't been in church on Sunday and this was the first time the friends were seeing each other since Roelena's trip.

"You," Marliese said dramatically, pointing a finger at her friend, "look absolutely *amazing.*"

Roelena glanced down at her clothes. She was wearing an old housedress that wasn't remotely flattering, no stockings, house slippers, and her apron. She'd pinned her hair in place that morning, but had otherwise made no effort with her appearance. She was more than a little confused. "What on earth are you talking about, Marliese?"

Marliese flapped her hand up and down in front of Roelena. "You've changed. You're *glowing,* Roelena."

Comprehension dawned in Roelena's eyes. Of course, her friend, who knew her so well, would notice the subtle changes in her countenance. So had Ingrid, although Ingrid had been far less blatant than Marliese.

Marliese continued. "If this is what a trip to America does for a person, then I should have made one long ago. You look radiant." Marliese finally leaned forward to hug Roelena.

"Oh, Marliese, you're being silly, but thank you."

The two women separated and Marliese finally turned her attention to Brenda.

"I need to feed her and then she'll go down for her afternoon nap," Roelena warned.

Marliese stooped to kiss the little girl's fat cheek, nuzzling her neck and making the baby giggle and squirm. "Let me feed her," she said as she took the chair beside the baby. "What's on the menu today?"

"Pureed carrots with ground beef. But she won't eat unless she's allowed to feed herself. I've got some sliced banana here to distract her. Sneak in a spoonful of carrots and beef every chance you can."

Marliese laughed.as she took the bowl of warmed food from Roelena." Is Clarence coming in for his dinner?"

"No, he's seeding at the home farm all afternoon. But you knew that, didn't you?"

Marliese grinned at Roelena, shrugging.

Roelena dropped the sliced banana onto Brenda's

wooden tray, then pulled out the chair across from Marliese, watching as her friend fed her baby. Not for the first time she thought about how great Marliese would be with kids of her own. It would have softened her, smoothed the sharp edges that so often showed. "It's Tuesday today. Aren't you supposed to be at work?"

Marliese shrugged. "I took a day off." Looking up, she eyed Roelena between spooning food into Brenda's mouth. "You do look amazing, you know. Different. If I'd have taken those painting lessons I always wanted, I would want to paint you now, although I doubt I'd be good enough to capture it. Whatever *it* is." Marliese paused to stare at Roelena. "You look happy, Roelena. And peaceful," she added.

Roelena brought her hands to her flushed cheeks. "Marliese, you're embarrassing me."

"I don't mean to."

"Well...okay then," Roelena said, dropping her hands into her lap.

"Are you saying nothing's different?"

Roelena smiled and looked away. "No." She looked back at Marliese. "Everything is different."

"In what way?"

Roelena hesitated, her first thought veering to her and Clarence's seemingly insatiable physical desire for each other. But their lovemaking, she knew, was only the outcome of what had truly changed. How could she attribute words to that something within her that was now different?

"Oh? Like that, huh?" Marliese winked and nodded towards the bedroom, then hooted as Roelena flushed scarlet.

"Marliese! You're incorrigible," Roelena accused, using a word she'd learned from one of Willem's teachers. "You're the only person I know who...makes those kinds of innuendoes. Hasn't anyone ever told you it's not decent?"

"All the time," Marliese said with a long-suffering sigh. She turned back to Brenda and slipped in another spoonful of meat and carrots. "But when have you ever known me to be concerned about what's decent? Besides, half the stuff I say is for shock value. It entertains me. You must know that by now."

"I do, yes. Have you eaten dinner? Do you want anything?"

"No, maybe tea later. I came over so I could hear all about your trip."

Roelena sighed and leaned back in her chair as she gazed sightlessly out of the window above the sink. Where to start? "It's been…" Roelena shook her head as she returned her gaze to her friend. "It was so hard coping after Karl's death. Especially so soon after Moe died. And on top of that the worry about whether she would be born healthy." Roelena nodded at Brenda. "I…we lost our connection, Clarence and me. And most of that was my fault. What's different now is that I'm finally able to let Karl's death—and Moe's—be a tragedy in our past rather than one that ruins our present. Or discolours our future, I suppose. Does that make sense?"

Marliese nodded. "Perfect sense."

"Not that I don't think about Karl every day, every hour," Roelena added. "Of course I do. But the difference is when I think of him now, my first…emotion, I guess, is a kind of quiet joy. Being his mother was a privilege and a blessing. Thoughts of Karl no longer equate solely to the pain of his death." She shook her head in frustration, wishing she were more articulate. "I don't think I'm explaining it well."

"I think you are," Marliese insisted as she scrapped up the last of Brenda's pureed food. Still occupied by the few remaining slices of banana on her wooden tray, the baby obediently opened her mouth as Marliese addressed Roelena. "Something happened, perhaps enough time passed, that let you release the pain of Karl's death. It's no longer infecting you. It was like a thorn in an open wound. Now the thorn's been removed, the wound can heal. That's the difference I see in you. You were hurting before. Now you're healing."

"You're so…oh, I don't know the word in English. *Welsprekend.*"

Marliese smiled. "Eloquent? Thank you."

Marliese set the empty bowl aside then reached behind Brenda's neck to expertly untie her bib. She used the bib to wipe the baby's face, with Brenda wiggling against the unwelcome attention. Once she was done, Marliese lifted Brenda out of her high chair and settled the baby on her lap. "Can I hold her for a while before she goes down for her nap?"

"She usually drinks her bottle in her crib. Do you want to give it to her instead?"

"I'd love to."

Roelena was at the counter preparing a bottle for Brenda. At night, before the baby's bedtime, she heated the milk, but during the day Brenda drank it cold. On catching sight of the bottle, the baby grew impatient, reaching for it and crying, but then was immediately silenced when Marliese popped the nipple into Brenda's mouth. Marliese adjusted the baby more comfortably in the cradle of her arm, keeping the bottle propped up even though Brenda's little hands rested on each side of it.

"Tell me everything," Marliese urged.

"Let me put the kettle on for tea," Roelena responded, then added with a mischievous grin over her shoulder, "seeing as it's too early for a cocktail."

Marliese stared at her friend. "Did I hear correctly? Since when do you drink *cocktails?*"

Roelena filled the kettle and brought it to the stove. "Since Conrad has a very well-stocked liquor cabinet. And since discovering that fruity cocktails are rather delicious." She struck a match to light the gas stove, then deposited the kettle above the flame before resuming her seat. "Delicious enough to get me slightly tipsy pretty much every evening we were there." Roelena bit her bottom lip and shrugged in delight at her confession.

Marliese's eyes sparkled. "Conrad got you hooked on cocktails?"

Roelena chuckled. "I'm not hooked, but I can honestly say I thoroughly enjoyed learning the difference between a Singapore Sling and a classic Champagne cocktail."

"Good lord. And Clarence *let* Conrad ply you with cocktails?"

"Well, since Conrad was also plying Clarence with brandy…" Roelena gave a mischievous shrug.

"Tell me how this miracle came about," Marliese demanded, rocking Brenda gently as the baby drank.

Roelena shook her head at Marliese's blasphemy. Clarence might have become less conservative over this past year, but he would definitely take exception to Marliese causally referring to anyone but Jesus performing miracles. She sighed, sobering as she reflected on the past year. "I've been dreading the anniversary of Karl's death. It's next month, you know. June eleventh."

"I know." Marliese said quietly. Then, when Roelena didn't resume speaking, she added. "But I don't understand. You're sad, of course, but you seem okay talking about it now. What changed?"

"Everything," Roelena stated. "You know how hard Karl's death was for me? Well, what I hadn't shared with you or anyone, not even Clarence, was that I felt this…The only way to describe it is that it felt like a cold, dark, empty creature was inhabiting me." Roelena briefly lifted a hand to her side as she added, "Pressing against my ribcage. Whatever it was, it fed off my heartache and my fear. I'm certain my sorrow gave it life. Sounds utterly ridiculous, doesn't it?" Roelena met Marliese's eyes and was surprised to see an intense sadness in their dark brown depths.

"No, Roelena," Marliese assured softly. "Not to me. Go on."

"Well, that…creature remained within me. It got a little smaller that day I talked with you and Ingrid. Remember? The day you found Clarence weeping? And it got a lot smaller the day Brenda was born, especially finding out she was healthy after worrying so long. And with each day Brenda stayed healthy, it got a little smaller. You would think that eventually it would disappear altogether, but it never did. I could still feel its presence, even though it was the size of a pin prick. And if something terrible happened, I knew it would overtake me again. There's so much I realize now, looking back. But at the time, I didn't understand what was happening, you know? I just lived with it. And I never went back to being the woman Clarence married. How could I?" She wagged her head. "I've been forever changed."

"Of course you have. What mother wouldn't be? But I still don't understand. What's changed exactly? Why are you so obviously different?"

When the kettle started spitting water, Roelena rose and turned off the flame. "I wish I could put my finger on it and say, *this,*" she explained as she prepared the tea things. "*This* explains the change. *This* is what made me look at everything in a different way. But there's not one thing, unless that one thing is the trip to Iowa. I mean, it was so freeing to be completely removed from the family here, away from our rather limited community and from everything familiar. It was…liberating. That's a big word for me, isn't it?"

Roelena set the teapot on the table, along with mugs, the

tea strainer, spoons, and milk and sugar, then resumed her seat.

"Don't be ridiculous," Marliese responded with a frown. "You make it sound like you're an uneducated illiterate."

"But it's a really important word. And it describes perfectly how I feel. To completely get away from your usual surroundings—no habits, no routines, no chores, no expectations. In that new, unfamiliar space a person can't help but think about who they are and what makes them tick and what they dream of and how they want to get there."

Marliese smiled. "That's called introspection."

"Introspection. Huh. Another new word for me." Roelena put her elbows on the table and leaned forward as an idea came to her. "Marliese, you and Wilfred should go on a holiday. It might do you a world of good."

"A holiday in Iowa to visit Conrad?" Marliese teased.

Roelena sighed, knowing Marliese was making a joke to avoid talking about herself. She picked up the teapot and filled each of their mugs, then nodded at Brenda. "She's falling asleep. Shall I put her in her crib?"

Marliese gently tugged the nipple out of the baby's mouth and set it on the table. She stared down at the drowsy baby, rocking her gently. "Let her sleep in my arms for a while, okay?"

Roelena heard a tone in her friend's voice that alarmed her. "Marliese? Are you okay?"

Marliese nodded without looking up. "Of course. Tell me more about your trip," she added.

Holding the sleeping baby, Marliese looked vulnerable and defenseless, at least to Roelena. "Marliese, tell me what's the matter. Did something happen between you and Wilfred?"

Marliese looked up, her eyes sparkling playfully as she

smiled at Roelena. "When is there something *not* happening between me and Wilfred?"

That was the truth, Roelena thought. The two were always at each other's throats.

"Tell me more about your trip, Roelena," Marliese insisted.

"Well." Roelena took a sip of her tea, absently watching Marliese put sugar into her tea, careful not to disturb the now sleeping baby. "Conrad and Louise were...." Roelena eyed Marliese. "Are you sure you want to hear about Louise?"

Marliese nodded emphatically. "I do, yes. Definitely."

"Well...they were perfect hosts." Roelena gauged Marliese's reaction to her statement, but saw nothing to dissuade her from continuing. "They have this gorgeous house with beautiful furniture that should feel uncomfortable to someone like me. I mean, I've never been in a house like that before. But instead, because Conrad is so nice and Louise is so...sweet and giving and kind, it felt so homey. Clarence and I were both so relaxed. We had picnics in the park by the river, and toured the countryside, and visited with my other relatives. We even learned to play tennis. Well, attempted to play," she amended.

"That sounds lovely. I've always wanted to learn to play tennis."

"Well, I'm sure you would've been better than me. I was terrible." Roelena chuckled at the memory. "We dined out at two different restaurants in one week, can you imagine? One was a delicious Chinese buffet. And we saw a film. And every evening before going to bed, Conrad made me a different cocktail, and Clarence drank brandy or port. And it all just seemed so natural because of their house and, I don't know, their being American and city people and kind of rich, I suppose."

"So, the cocktails caused the deep introspection?"

Roelena chuckled. "Hardly. But being in a completely different setting doing completely different activities and not being responsible for getting chores done, is that what causes that introspection? I don't know. But all that, on top of the warmth and hospitality of Conrad and Louise, well…it allowed me to release the pain I'd been holding onto for so long. Near the end of our visit, I felt that cold, dark thing leave. It was so real when I felt it. And I realize now its presence was preventing me from being happy again. And now…" Roelena lifted her hands and shook her head, at a loss for the words that might better explain her altered state of being.

"I think I understand. You're finally on a path of healing from the pain of Karl's death *and* you've fallen head over heels in love with your husband. For the second time."

Roelena chuckled. "Yes, I suppose I have. But he's not the same man I married. He's less black and white. More lighthearted. And I don't mean more jokey. He's always joked around. I mean, he knows to value the small things, like oh… I don't know, it's so hard to explain."

"Like a special look shared across a crowded room that has so much meaning it would take pages of words just to describe it."

"Yes, exactly." Roelena paused, frowning. "It's like that for you and Wilfred?" That was a surprise to her.

"No." Marliese shook her head. "No, it's never been like that for me and Wilfred."

"Oh. You mean…Conrad?"

Marliese nodded sadly. The two women stared at each other until Roelena reached across the table to grip Marliese's free hand. "I didn't mean to make you sad by talking about him."

"Talking about Conrad isn't what's making me sad. Tell me about him, though. Is he happy?"

Roelena smiled, releasing Marliese's hand and leaning back in her chair. "You know, he asked the very same thing about you."

"He did?" A distant light shimmered in Marliese's eyes.

It dawned on Roelena then that Marliese still loved Conrad. Her tone when she addressed her friend was soft with new understanding. "Yes, Marliese. He did."

"What did you tell him?"

"That you and Wilfred made a very handsome couple. I also implied that you and Wilfred were happy." Roelena eyed Marliese's profile as her friend gazed down at the sleeping baby in her arms. "But it's not true, is it, Marliese?" she added.

Marliese sighed and looked up, meeting Roelena's eyes. Grief, melancholy, regret, and loss radiated in waves from the depths of her dark eyes, yet there was no hint of tears.

"No, it's not. Conrad was 'it' for me, you see. But I wasn't for him, was I? And I've learned to live with that. So it didn't seem to matter who I married. Love, the real kind, the deep kind, the kind that makes you appreciate having experienced it? That kind of love will never come to me again."

"Oh, Marliese, don't say that."

Marliese shrugged again. "I know I didn't tell you when we talked on the phone on Friday, but Wilfred and I drove to Banff on Saturday morning and spent the weekend there."

"You did? A weekend away is bound to make things better." Roelena stared at her friend, puzzled. Why did Marliese still look so sad?

"Things *are* better, but not the way you mean." Marliese sighed heavily. "Roelena don't be angry with me, okay? I hate to think I'm a disappointment to you."

"What are you talking about? You could never be a disappointment to me. Why would you even think such a thing?"

"Wilfred and I got along better in these past three days

than in our three years of marriage. We talked finally, really talked, about our marriage and our dreams, what we wanted from life. And at no point in our conversation did either of our dreams coincide."

"But, it's a start, isn't it? To share your feelings, to talk about them?"

"A start to a new life, yes. We agreed—for the first time in years, we actually agreed—that we would...well, there's no easy way to say this so I'll just say it. I'll be filing for divorce."

Roelena felt like a giant clock had suddenly stopped ticking as she tried to process the implications of Marliese's shocking announcement. *Divorce?* Divorce was unheard of. No one in their community divorced. People worked things out. Or they went to the *dominee* for advice. Or maybe they simply realized they had to put up with how things were, like Mrs. ter Horst with her lazy, good-for-nothing husband. *But divorce?*

"You *are* disappointed," Marliese accused.

"No." Roelena shook her head, but was at a loss for words. "No, not disappointed," she finally said.

"What then?"

"Marliese, you have to give me a minute to absorb this. I can't simply..." She brought her hands up and put her fingers on her temples as if that would help her process the news. "Just give me a minute, would you?" Roelena abruptly rose, then stood motionless as if trying to decide what she'd meant to do. *Divorce?* What would people say? How would the family and the community cope with such an unheard of event in their insulated little congregation?

When she finally lifted her head and looked across the table at her friend, she was astounded to see Marliese's face awash with tears.

"Marliese." Roelena rushed around the table and sank into a crouch next to her friend. What a selfish fool she was,

thinking about everything and everyone except Marliese. “Please don’t cry,” Roelena wrapped her arms around Marliese’s neck and pulled her head against her shoulder, taking care not to wake the sleeping baby.

Marliese wrapped her free arm around Roelena’s waist and began sobbing in earnest, talking as she did. “I’m sorry! Everyone will hate me now. It’s my fault. I know that. I told Wilfred that, too. It’s all my fault. I should never have married him. I’ve made us both so desperately unhappy.”

“Shush, Marliese, shush. It’s okay, hush now, don’t cry.” Roelena murmured, rocking her friend as if she was a child. “It’s not all your fault. And no one’s going to hate you. Hush now, hush.” Roelena pulled away to examine Marliese’s face. “Oh, Marliese. How can you think people will hate you? Everyone loves you, me more than anyone.”

“But you’re disappointed in me.” Marliese dabbed at her eyes, frowning at the black line of mascara at her fingertips.

Roelena retrieved the fresh handkerchief from her apron pocket and gave it to Marliese, marveling again at how undeniably beautiful Marliese was despite her eyes being puffy and red-rimmed. “Never. Not in a million years. Now, give me Brenda. I’m putting her in her crib.” Roelena stood and gently disengaged the sleeping baby from Marliese’s arms.

As she hurried out of the room, Roelena couldn’t help but think how strange it was that at the very moment when her life had begun to shine with the promise of blessings to come, Marliese’s life was unraveling at the seams. She gently deposited the sleeping baby in her crib, then hurried back to the kitchen. She moved a chair so she could sit right beside Marliese, concern filling her eyes as she peered into her friend’s face.

“Are you going to be okay?” she asked, gently stroking her shoulder.

Marliese nodded. “I’m sorry.”

"Don't be ridiculous? How many times have I cried on your shoulder lately?"

"That's different."

"Why? Because you act tough? Marliese, you don't fool me. You never have. I've always known you're about as soft as they come. Softer."

Marliese began to cry again, quietly this time. "I don't like being analyzed," she protested. She delicately mopped her face, then grimaced when she saw the smudges of mascara on the handkerchief. "Damn! I told myself I wasn't going to cry," she wailed. "I came here to tell you I'm happy. I am. Really."

"You don't look particularly happy," Roelena chided. "I'm just sorry I made it worse. I shouldn't have responded so poorly to your news. I'm a terrible friend."

"No, you're not. You're a better friend to me than I am to you."

"Oh really? And how are we measuring that?"

"Because everything I do is for selfish motivations."

Roelena hooted softly. "You mean taking care of me when I had the German measles? And buying me that gorgeous fabric so I could make a new dress for the Iowa trip? That was you being selfish?"

"Yes," Marliese said, wiping her eyes carefully now that her tears had stopped. "It gave me pleasure to do that. Which makes me selfish."

"You're talking nonsense," Roelena argued, standing. She picked up their mugs of lukewarm tea and dumped the contents into the sink, then resumed her seat across from Marliese and poured them each a fresh cup of tea. "Never mind trying to figure out who's a better friend to whom. How is Wilfred taking this?"

"That's the surprising part." Marliese sighed heavily as she folded the handkerchief and settled back into her chair.

"You'd think we'd have a rip-roaring, vase-throwing fight when I bring up divorce. Instead, we end up having the calmest, sanest, most mature discussion we've ever had. The truth is, he's not any happier than I am. And we can't go on like this. If we do, one of us will kill the other."

"I don't like it when you talk like that. You're not being serious."

"But I am serious about the divorce. And you *are* disappointed. Don't deny it."

"What kind of friend would I be if I didn't support you?"

"The kind who doesn't believe in divorce? Our whole community will judge us for it. Well, they'll judge me. Our church is against it, which is why I offered to file for divorce. Then if anyone needs to be excommunicated, it will be me."

"The church wouldn't do that, surely?"

Marliese shrugged. "They might. Regardless, I'm fine being the one to initiate the divorce. Wilfred will certainly capitalize on being the injured party, but I can hardly blame him for that."

Now that the initial shock had worn off, Roelena felt a growing compassion for her friend. The community could believe whatever they chose and do whatever they had to, but it wouldn't change anything in Roelena's heart. "Our lives are nothing like we imagined they would be, are they?" she reflected. "I mean, yes, I have a husband and a child like I always wanted. But it never entered my mind that my baby would die. It never entered my head that it was possible to stop loving my husband, even for a short time. Nothing has turned out the way we expected, has it?"

Marliese scoffed. "I was a silly, foolish dreamer."

"Never, Marliese. And there's nothing wrong with dreaming. Dreams give us hope."

"I do know that, actually. That's why I had to ask Wilfred for a divorce. Living with him is living without hope."

Marliese shook her head. “And that’s not living, so I’m choosing to get out of a miserable marriage and see what I can make of my life on my own.”

“Good for you.”

“Do you really mean that?”

“Yes. Absolutely.” And it was true. Fifteen minutes before, Roelena had thought Marliese’s life was falling apart at the seams, unraveling uncontrollably. But now she realized how wrong she’d been. “Do you know what’s strange? A month ago, before I’d worked out all this other stuff, I don’t think I could have truly supported you. I think I would have encouraged you and Wilfred to work it out, to stick together. I mean the church teaches divorce is not an option, and I’ve always believed that. I think I even believed it thirty minutes ago. But now, I realize that’s not true. At least, not for you.” Roelena met Marliese’s gaze. “The truth is, you’re not happy. You’re miserable. So is Wilfred. Why should you be sentenced to life with one another as if you’re criminals and marriage is a prison? You haven’t done anything wrong.”

Startled by Roelena’s vehemence, Marliese gave a hiccoughing kind of laugh. “I agree. The only wrong thing I did was fall in love with a man who didn’t love me.”

“I don’t think that’s true. He did love you.”

“Did he say that?”

“He didn’t have to, but I’ve no doubts that he did. It’s just that the obstacles were too big, at least for him. I’ll always believe Conrad was a fool for not rebelling against his parents, for not coming to Alberta and marrying you on the spot. He should have worked harder to invite you into his life. But he didn’t, and that’s his loss. Regardless of all that, *you* deserve to be happy.”

Marliese smiled shakily. “I think I’m finally coming to realize that myself.”

"I have to say, I'm wishing I had the ingredients to make one of Conrad's cocktails right now."

Marliese giggled, a little of the sadness lifting from her eyes. "Oh Roelena, I'm going to miss you."

Roelena stared at Marliese in consternation. "Miss me. Why? Where are you going?"

"Wilfred is staying in Bellecourt, in the house. It makes sense. It's close to his job. Since everyone in church is going to blame me—after all, I'm the one with the sharp tongue and the contrary nature—I have to leave."

"But you don't need to leave the community just because it suits Wilfred to look like the victim."

"I know. But I've always felt stifled here. You know that. I'm moving to Calgary."

"Calgary?" Roelena was shocked. "But…is there even a Christian Reformed Church there? I can't remember. There wasn't when we were in Young People's."

Marliese spoke gently. "I want to live where I'm Canadian first, not Dutch. I want to be far enough away from everyone —except you, of course—to really feel free to be who I am. whoever that is. And there's no way I can do that in a Dutch community. So I'm not looking to join a congregation."

"But why Calgary?"

"One of the girls I work with at the library, she has a sister who takes in lodgers. I'm hoping she has room for me. Once I land a job, I can get my own place."

"You mean you would live alone?"

"I think I'd like it. And it's not all that uncommon these days."

"It is for Dutch Calvinist women."

Marliese laughed. "That's the point, though, isn't it? I don't want to be a Dutch Calvinist. It doesn't suit me."

Roelena couldn't imagine her life without the church and the community of fellow believers. Yet, at the same time, she understood that Marliese, who'd always felt caged by their conservative community, would be attracted to moving away. Well, no matter where Marliese went, Roelena had no intention of losing contact with her friend.

The two women suddenly sighed in perfect unity, which made them laugh.

"Oh, Marliese," Roelena said once she'd caught her breath again. "Are you going to be okay?"

Marliese nodded. "I am now. For the first time in years, I truly believe I'm finally going to be okay."

42

FRIDAY, MAY 29

As Clarence pulled into the home farm driveway and parked behind Frank and Greta's car, Roelena saw her oldest nieces and nephews playing in the abandoned car where her mother used to sit and knit. Greta's four—Bradley, Norman, Josephine, and Lambert—and Tomas's younger brother, *kleine* Kees. Ingrid's daughters—two-year-old Alida and baby Rosalie—must be in the house, thought Roelena.

Upon seeing the car arrive, Tomas abandoned his playmates and came tearing across the yard of the home farm to greet them. It was his seventh birthday, and the family was getting together for a meal to celebrate.

Roelena got out of the car, balancing Brenda on her hip. "Happy Birthday, Tomas." She stooped to give her nephew a one-armed hug. "Seven years old, already. You're not a little boy anymore, are you?"

"I'm in grade one," he insisted as if that refuted her reference to his no longer being a little boy.

Clarence came around the front of the car. "Hey, kiddo. Happy Birthday," he said, tousling the lad's hair as he handed him a wrapped present.

The gift held miniature cowboys and Indian figurines, a close match to the set belonging to his older cousin Bradley that Tomas had always coveted. Roelena knew that Greta had purchased a cowboy dress-up set for Tomas that included a sheriff's badge and a toy pistol, while Tomas's Opa had carved a set of miniature wooden horses.

"Thank you, *Oom* Clarence! Can I open it now?"

"Ask your Moe," Clarence wisely responded.

Tomas ran ahead of them into his *Opa's* house.

Roelena and Clarence, entering the kitchen behind Tomas, both laughed when they heard Tomas arguing with his mother.

Ingrid was at the counter, scooping steaming boiled potatoes from a pot into a serving dish while Greta, who'd recently started wearing maternity clothes even though she was almost six months pregnant, was setting the table.

Tomas was holding up his most recent gift. "But Oom Clarence said I could open it now," he insisted.

"Whoa. Is that what I said, kiddo?" Clarence asked.

Tomas looked only slightly chagrined as he eyed his uncle, reminding Roelena of Willem. "Not *exactly*," he quibbled.

"Tomas?" Ingrid spoke in a tone that didn't bode well for Tomas if he didn't answer the next question honestly. "What did Oom Clarence say? *Exactly.*"

Tomas hung his head, looking down forlornly at the gift in his hands. "He said, *ask your Moe.*"

Greta laughed, then chimed. "Well, ask her then."

Tomas looked at his mother in unveiled hope. "Can I open it now?"

"No, you cannot. You know that. Put it with the others."

Tomas reluctantly turned and placed the present on the sewing table in the corner beside three other parcels. One was from his grandfather, one from his *Tante* Greta and *Oom* Frank, and the other was from his parents. He set his arms on the table, leaning his chin on his crossed arms and staring at the gifts longingly.

Roelena poked her head in the front room behind Clarence to say hello to her father, Frank, and Jakob, seeing Alida on the floor at his feet playing with the coloured blocks. Back in the kitchen, she went to the counter to help Ingrid dish up the last of the food, slicing the meatloaf while Ingrid scooped the green beans into a serving dish.

"Where's Rosalie?" Roelena asked. Rosalie was Ingrid and Jakob's fourth child, born on New Year's Eve.

"Sleeping on Pa's bed."

"Pieter," Roelena exclaimed in surprise as her youngest brother entered the kitchen from upstairs.

Pieter lived with Greta and Frank during the week and came home to stay with Kees and Sijmon on weekends when it didn't interfere with his sports, social activities, or other school commitments. He had one more year of high school and then he was planning to study biology in university with the aim of eventually becoming a veterinarian.

"I didn't know you were going to be here. I thought you would be madly studying for exams."

"Don't you know your kid brother is so smart, he doesn't have to study?" Pieter joked. His tone changed as he addressed the baby in Roelena's arms. "Hi Brenda. Come to Uncle Pieter?" he asked, taking his niece from Roelena.

Pieter got a lot of practice with young children, although Greta's youngest, Lambert Frank, was already almost four years old.

Roelena frowned as she stood beside Pieter and assessed his height. "Are you taller than last time I saw you?" she accused.

"I've grown almost an inch in the last two months" Pieter announced proudly.

Roelena turned to Greta. "What are you feeding him?"

"Let's just say thank goodness he comes over on Sunday night with a crate full of food from the cellar, else we'd run out," Greta responded with a laugh.

Through the kitchen window she saw Willem and Sijmon returning from completing the chores.

"Was Jakob as tall as Pieter at seventeen?" Roelena asked.

Before Greta could respond, Willem, the shortest of all the siblings except Greta, entered the kitchen and responded.

"We're not talking about baby brother's growth spurt again, are we? He might have grown taller than me, but don't think he's better," Willem warned, heading to the sink to wash his hands with Sijmon on his heels.

"Ha," Pieter challenged, playfully adopting a boxing stance. "Better than you in a lot of things. Especially now that you're officially the runt of the litter," he added, punching Willem on the shoulder.

Willem had returned home a few weeks before and would work on the farm for the summer. He was the first of their family to not only graduate high school, but attend university. It sometimes boggled Roelena's mind that her most troublesome younger brother had become such a scholar and, at least most of the time, a nice young man—although she'd pull out her fingernails before admitting that in front of Willem.

"Boys, get out of the way," Roelena instructed, shooing them away from the kitchen sink. "Go wash up in the bathroom. You're in the way here."

"Is that my birthday cake?" Tomas interrupted, suddenly distracted by the cake his mother brought from the pantry and set on the counter. He scurried across the kitchen to get a closer look.

"I don't know. What does it say?" Greta placed her hands under his armpits and lifted him so he could look down at the cake.

"Happy...Birthday...Tomas!" He grinned up at his mother, then his aunt, the thrill of this special day evident on his face.

"Pieter," Ingrid said. "Round up the kids from outside, would you? Supper's ready."

Twenty minutes later, after eating their supper, Tomas blew out the seven candles on his birthday cake and then everyone watched and clapped as Tomas opened his presents. After the final prayer, the ten adults remained at the table, sitting back in their chairs and sipping their tea while they chatted. Nine children played on the floor at their feet, with eight-month old Brenda crawling amongst her cousins and causing havoc when she scattered the carefully arranged armies of cowboys and Indians.

At the outcry that followed, Ingrid ordered the older children outside, reassuring Tomas that she would guard his new treasures with her life. As soon as the children vacated the kitchen—excepting Brenda and baby Rosalie who now sat on their respective mothers' laps—the room quieted, and the adults resumed their conversation.

"I still can't believe Harri and Therese had triplets. It's one thing to know you're having twins, but then to have three?" Roelena refolded the letter she'd just read, handing it back to Kees.

"At least they're not identical. I can't imagine not being able to tell my kids apart," Frank said.

"And they've chosen lovely names, haven't they, Pa? Moe would be pleased."

"She would, *ja,*" Kees answered, nodding gravely.

"And thankfully they're not too strange," Jakob quipped. "We'll be able to pronounce them when we get the chance to meet them."

"Antoinette, Angeline, and Agathe," Greta said. "I like them all."

"I think it's Aga-TEY," Willem corrected, taking the letter from where Kees had lain it beside his plate on the table. "Not Agatha. Yes, see? It's spelled with an 'e' at the end, not an 'a'."

"And that makes 'tey'?" Frank asked.

"Wait. What makes you the expert?" Jakob challenged. "Are you studying French in university, or chemistry?"

"I didn't say I was an expert, but I know a whole lot more than you," Willem scoffed

Jakob snorted. "If you think one year of university—"

"Have you written them back yet, Pa?" Roelena interrupted with a glare at Jakob that indicated her desire to introduce maturity back into the family's conversation.

"*Ja,* of course. And I reminded Harri I'm too old to learn French, so he must make sure his daughters learn to speak either English or Dutch so I can converse with them when I meet them."

"Are you planning to visit them?" Frank asked.

"Why not? I can take the train. But not this year. Maybe next year."

"I'd go with you, Pa," Pieter said. "We could go after I graduate, before I start a summer job."

"Perhaps," Kees said, nodding.

Roelena saw her Pa looked pleased at this idea. She was glad he had something to look forward to, and Pieter's company would be ideal on such a long journey.

"But none of us will be able to talk to Therese," Greta said. "Harri writes that she doesn't know a word of English. And where they live, there's no real reason for her to learn."

"I picked up some French when I worked for Pierre Boutilier," Clarence said. "I might be the only one of all of you who can have a conversation with her."

"I finally understand," Jakob exclaimed with exaggeration. "I knew there was a good reason why Roelena married you."

"She married me because she wanted a change from her ill-mannered, odious brothers," Clarence jibbed.

"Hey," Pieter protested. "I'm not ill-mannered."

"Admittedly, you are the best of the lot," Clarence conceded with a grin.

"Boys, enough with your teasing," Roelena protested, mostly out of habit.

"Pa," Greta interjected. "It was one thing for Harri to marry a Catholic, but are you okay with their children being raised Catholic?"

Roelena added, "What would Moe say? Remember how she reacted when she thought Jakob had married a Catholic?"

"What?" Ingrid said, startled. "You didn't tell me that," she accused her husband.

"That's because Roelena remembers it wrong," Jakob insisted. "Moe was upset that we got married in the *Hervormde kerk* instead of the *Gereformeerde kerk*."

Kees spoke up on his late wife's behalf, directing his comments to Ingrid. "Moeder was only concerned that you would find it difficult to settle in our community if you weren't of our religion. But you settled in fine and became one of the family. She was more than pleased with Jakob's choice of marriage partner, you know that. And she felt the same for Harri even though Therese is Catholic. It's an answer to our prayers, although not the answer we were expecting. We can be thankful Harri has found God again... even if it is the Catholic God."

It came as a surprise to Roelena that her father was so easily able to accept Harri raising his kids in the Catholic faith. But she'd experienced a lot of surprises over the last few weeks. In that moment, it struck her as strange that, for years, she'd been under the impression that life went on rather predictably when, in fact, the one constant in life was the unexpected and the unforeseen. Her mother dying abruptly, despite her long illness; Roelena contracting German measles; then sweet, precious Karl dying, and her husband becoming a friendly stranger; then a new baby, filling the silence of her empty home and melting some of the ice that had encased her heart; then their spontaneous trip to Iowa and rediscovering her love for her husband; and then, shockingly, Marliese's revelation. And now the surprising news of Harri becoming the father of triplets with his French Catholic wife. Even more surprising, her father's acceptance of having Catholic grandchildren. After all these unanticipated outcomes, Roelena was certain nothing could ever truly surprise her again.

"Speaking of weddings…"

Everyone turned and stared at Sijmon. He so rarely contributed to group conversation that his interruption rendered them all speechless for a moment.

"Margaret Langelaar and I are engaged."

The only noise in the room was Brenda and Rosalie's happy burbling baby chatter. The adults had all been rendered speechless. Roelena tore her gaze from Sijmon to look over at her father and saw he was as astonished as the rest of them.

"Did you know?" she whispered to Clarence. But he shook his head, seemingly more astounded by Sijmon's news than she was.

"Well." Kees was the first to recover from the shock, although he appeared rather dazed. "Congratulations, son. She's a fine girl, and from a good family too."

"Wait a minute, Pa," Jakob protested, holding up a hand as if to stop traffic. He sat across the table from Sijmon and eyed his younger brother with suspicion. "Margaret Langelaar?"

"Yes. Margaret Langelaar."

Roelena could see that Sijmon was enjoying having disconcerted his self-assured older brother.

Jakob frowned at the brother who worked side by side with him on the farm on a daily basis. "Since when have you been courting Margaret Langelaar?"

Sijmon shrugged. "Since always." Like usual, Sijmon's answers were short and simple. "Ingrid, is there more cake?" he asked.

Ingrid, who'd been staring at her brother-in-law, finally closed her mouth and hurriedly dished up the last piece of cake, handing it to Sijmon quickly as if the sooner he got his cake the sooner he would provide a satisfactory answer to explain his astonishing news.

"Always? When, always?" Jakob persisted.

"Yes, since when?" Greta demanded, finally finding her voice. She appeared as affronted as Jakob by Sijmon's surprising news.

"We've always been courting."

"You haven't," Willem insisted. "You're pulling our leg."

"I'm not. We agreed years ago we'd wait until she was eighteen before we got engaged." Sijmon shoveled a forkful of cake into his mouth, looking around the table at his family, unperturbed at the unusual amount of attention he was receiving. "She turned eighteen, last week," he added as if that explained everything.

Roelena had been staring at Sijmon as if he'd grown a horn, and finally demanded, "You agreed years ago? Like when she used to come and help out in the house?"

"Uh-huh," Sijmon said, his mouth full of cake.

"I still don't understand how long this courtship has been going on?" Jakob demanded. "Or why I didn't know about it."

"It had nothing to do with you," Sijmon stated.

"Leave him be," Kees interrupted when he saw Jakob

about to protest. He turned to Sijmon. "Margaret Langelaar is a nice girl. This is good news, Sijmon. Worth celebrating. Your mother would be pleased."

Sijmon looked at his father and smiled. "I know. But that's not why I'm marrying her."

"Oh?" Jakob interjected, annoyed his questions weren't getting answered. "Why are you marrying her then?"

"Because I love her." Sijmon shrugged as if the answer was obvious. "Always have. Always will." He shoved the last bite of cake into his mouth and, as he chewed, nonchalantly met the gazes of his stunned siblings and in-laws.

Roelena stared at her quiet, predictable brother, the one who she secretly thought was a little boring and who she'd assumed would end up a bachelor because he never showed any interest in girls. He'd taken them all completely by surprise. All along, he'd been biding his time, waiting patiently for the girl he loved to grow up. Sijmon, the quiet one, Roelena thought, was now Sijmon, the secretive, subtle one. And here Roelena had just convinced herself nothing much could surprise her anymore.

Sijmon put down his fork and sighed wearily as he looked around the table. "What?" he said. "You mean you really didn't know?"

At his statement, everyone but Jakob choked with laughter. Even Kees chuckled heartily.

"Didn't know?" Jakob pointed an accusing finger at his brother. "How could we know? You are a sly, deceitful worm." He rose and went around the table to approach Sijmon. "I suppose I have no choice but to congratulate you." He held out a hand as Sijmon rose, but at the last minute he grabbed his brother's head and pulled him into a football hold, giving his crown a painful knuckle rub as he stated loudly above Sijmon's struggling protests, "Never withhold important information from your older brother again, do you understand?"

Sijmon wiggled free and stood back, grinning in playful amusement. "You thought you were the slyest, marrying Ingrid without telling us. You're peeved because I've stolen your crown. Well, I can't help it you're not clever enough to keep it."

That was practically a speech for the usually reticent Sijmon.

"Not clever enough?" Jakob affectionately shoved at Sijmon's shoulder, then pulled him close and gave him a bear hug. When Jakob stepped back, he pointed a threatening finger first at Pieter and then at Willem. "You. And you."

"Me?" Pieter protested.

"What did I do?" Willem demanded.

"If either of you think you can get away with pulling a stunt like this, you better think twice."

"But I'm only seventeen," Pieter croaked.

"I don't care if you're twenty-seven. You fancy a girl, you tell big brother," Jakob thumbed at his chest. "You hear?"

"Huh," Willem challenged. "Why should I?"

"Because." Jakob leaned across the table and grabbed a handful of Willem's shirtfront. "You don't want to make an old man of me before my own kids are grown."

Roelena leaned against Clarence's shoulder and laughed at Jakob's playful antics, knowing they held an element of seriousness. He didn't like being out of the loop. But they'd all been out of the loop. Not one of them could have predicted Sijmon's startling announcement.

It was pointless, Roelena thought, to ever try and predict what would come next in this precious adventure called life.

She finally realized she was okay with not knowing what would come. Her life was mounted on a firm foundation of love, in her own family with Clarence and Brenda, in her friendships, and in her extended family where the corner-stones had been laid long before her birth. Her future, she knew, likely held the promise of hardships, but it also held a wealth of blessings still to come.

AUTHOR'S NOTES

Although all the characters in *An Ordinary Immigrant* are entirely fictional, many of the events and circumstances are derived from my mother's experience as an immigrant to a Dutch Christian Reformed community in central Alberta. The character of Roelena is certainly not my mother, but below is a list of the events/anecdotes that my mother and Roelena share.

First Nations couple lived in a tent on their yard during my mother's first summer in Canada. My grandfather had purchased a quarter section of land (164 acres), but only 40 acres had been cleared. With the help of this Native American man, my mother's father and older brothers used horses to clear their quarter section. The Native American wife did come to the house one day and asked to borrow my grandmother's iron, although this word was mistaken for the Dutch word for eggs. And, like Anneke, my grandmother who was a typical neat and clean Dutch housewife, was immeasurably impressed.

Like Willem, my mother's brothers collected arrowheads they found in their fields.

Like Roelena, my mother would take a horse from the farm and ride bareback to go berry picking.

In the same way that Kees bought a nearby farm for Clarence and Roelena after they were married, my grandfather bought a farm two miles east of their homestead for my mother and father, who married in 1951. My parents first house had no running water, electricity, or telephone. Once a month, my father would give my grandfather a cheque to slowly repay the cost of the farm. When this debt was halfway paid, my grandfather said they no longer had to make further payments.

Like Roelena's husband, my dad immigrated to Alberta (in 1948) at the age of nineteen after completing a trades course in Arnhem. My father also left behind a large family in Holland (two younger brothers and four sisters), and (I believe) felt welcomed by my mother's parents and siblings in the same way Clarence did.

The events that Ingrid recounted about being in the Netherlands during Liberation following the Nazi Occupation are based on fact. I had the honour of interviewing John and Maria Kruit, both of whom had been children in the Netherlands during WWII. It was from Maria Kruit that I learned of the heart-wrenching story of the Dutch girls who'd been girlfriends to the German soldiers and how they were humiliated by their own villagers who shaved their heads as punishment. Maria remembered those girls proudly wearing their brightly coloured scarves to cover their bald heads. Re-living that terrible time with me was highly emotional for Maria, and I hope I have done some of her memories justice.

Although my parents never took a road trip to visit my mother's relatives in Iowa, my mother did drive to Iowa with her own parents on two occasions when her mother's health allowed it. She remained pen-pals with some of these cousins all her life.

Like Anneke's medical issues, on 27 February 1953 my grandmother died from a heart attack after years of heart trouble. At that time, my parents' first baby was seven months old and my mother was ten or eleven weeks pregnant with her second.

Shortly after my grandmother died, my mother contracted the German measles, and then had to contend with the worry for the remaining months of her pregnancy that her second baby's eyesight would be impaired (it wasn't).

My parent's first baby died on 4 June 1953 at the age of ten months and eleven days a few days after being admitted to the University Hospital in Edmonton. At the time of his death, my parents had been married less than twenty months. Here are a list of parallels that I imposed on the fictional characters:

- Even as a child, I was fascinated by this older brother who'd died at such a tender age. I remember asking my mother how it felt to have her baby die, and she would always say, "it felt like

I would never laugh again, but then the rest of you came along and I found I did laugh again."

- Like Roelena and Clarence, my parents were asked to collect his body and bring him to their local funeral home. Nowadays, that seems atrocious (and it's illegal). My mother remembers bringing a blanket to wrap him in. A memory that always stood out for her was when the doctor came to talk with them and how his eyes wouldn't meet theirs and he was rocking back and forth on his heels.
- While researching for this book, I purchased a copy of this baby's autopsy report. I don't believe my parents even knew an autopsy had been performed.
- Unlike Roelena and Clarence, my parents were never told why their baby died. My mother only ever said that he got sickly and cried a lot, and then he died. As immigrants, and with little education, my parents never thought to challenge doctors or demand answers. It wasn't until 1981 when my sister's doctor wanted to investigate some of our family medical history, that we learned he died of pneumonia, a complication from his having infantile acrodynia, also known as Pink Disease, a reaction to the exposure of mercury, an ingredient in teething powders and diaper rinses. I've since learned that Pink Disease was prevalent in children in the early 20th Century. There is a fascinating article called The Rise and Fall of Pink Disease (by Ann Dally, 1997, The Society for the Social History of Medicine) that details the specific social setting in which the disease developed and how the medical profession dealt with it within the limitation of contemporary knowledge and

practice. In the autopsy report, the doctor uses the word "idiopathic", which Ann Dally says was a term that was "freely used and regarded as sufficient explanation." (p301). She also states that "mercury was withdrawn from most teething powders after 1954, initially through voluntary action by the manufacturers because of adverse publicity and probably in the hope of avoiding statutory prohibition." (p302) At about this same time, Pink Disease all but disappeared.

- I can understand why my poorly educated immigrant parents didn't demand answers about their baby's death, but the question I cannot answer is why the doctors never told my parents about Pink Disease. I can only surmise that the medical professionals were either protecting medical product suppliers from liability, or protecting parents like my mother from blaming herself for having used a teething powder or a diaper rinse that ultimately killed her baby. My research claims that many children were diagnosed with Pink Disease but only one in 500 died. Was the reason for the deaths of these other babies also withheld from those other parents? I'll never know.
- Roelena's character has a baby book where she recorded things about Karl Benjamin, words taken directly from the only baby book my mother ever compiled (even though, or perhaps because, she had seven more children). As well, the sympathy cards Roelena read in the book are word-for-word from the sympathy cards my mother pasted into that book.

ACKNOWLEDGMENTS

My biggest thanks are owed to my mother. As a child, I often asked her to tell me a story about the olden days. She never failed to deliver a new anecdote and thus inspired this novel long before I ever thought to write it.

I initially wrote this book for an audience of one—my mother. She loved to read, and always had overflowing bookcases and stacks of library books around her. My goal in interviewing her and doing research for this book was to write what she would consider a 'good story'. I'm so thankful she was able to read an early draft of this novel before she passed away, but I'm even more pleased she loved it.

I want to thank my sisters, Anita Moes, Grace Berkenbosch, and Gwen Bosch for reading multiple iterations of this story and offering feedback, (Gwen, your dedication and editing skills are epic!); and thanks to my brother Richard for letting me pick his brain about rather inconsequential farming practices.

Heartfelt thanks are owed to my friend Angie Neal who read multiple (and not very good) early drafts—thanks for catching all those stubborn typos. I am grateful to my Uncle George for sharing his stories about being a soldier in the Prinses Irene Brigade, and to his wife, Aunt Edyth, who shared what it was like for a "Canadian" girl from Ontario to become a farmer's wife in a small Dutch CRC community in rural Alberta. I am grateful to my oldest cousin, Ruth Krabbe for reading and editing an early version of this manuscript. I owe a deep debt of gratitude to John and Maria Kruit in Calgary who allowed me to interview them about their experiences in the Netherlands during the war.

For her invaluable editing and wordsmithing, my heartfelt thanks go to Anne Correia. I owe sincere thanks to my fellow story-teller friend Jeannette Bedard for paving the way to indie-publishing. I'm delighted with the cover of this novel, which utilized my family's old photographs. Thanks to my friend and talented graphic designer, Jina Mousseau, for creating a cover that is just right for this story.

I'm especially grateful to Anka Tunnissen in Amsterdam for advising me on the correct Dutch words to use. Whatever errors might be in the novel are utterly and emphatically mine. I need to stress that any historical errors or inappropriate translations of the Dutch language in this novel are entirely the fault of the author.

ALSO BY

The Ordinary Immigrant series:

The Ordinary Immigrant – New Beginnings

The Ordinary Immigrant – Ties That Bind

The Travelers' Chronicles series:

The Reluctant Traveler

The Traveler's Stone

The Reluctant Thief (forthcoming)

AFTERWORD

Thank you for reading *An Ordinary Immigrant – Ties That Bind*. And a special thanks, too, for your reviews and for telling your friends about the book.

I hope you also enjoyed Book One of this two-book series, *An Ordinary Immigrant – New Beginnings*.

If you want to contact me, you can email me through my website, CorinneAarsenBooks.com.

Thanks for reading!

46398391R00241

Made in the USA
Middletown, DE
27 May 2019